EUTOPIA

A NOVEL OF TERRIBLE OPTIMISM

DAVID NICKLE

CZP

ChiZine Publications

LIBRARY AND ARCHIVES CANADA CATALOGUING IN PUBLICATION

Nickle, David, 1964-
          Eutopia : a novel of terrible optimism / David Nickle.

ISBN 978-1-926851-11-2

          I. Title.

PS8577.I33E98 2011   C813'.54   C2010-907884-5

CHIZINE PUBLICATIONS
Toronto, Canada
www.chizinepub.com
info@chizinepub.com

Edited and copyedited by Sandra Kasturi
Proofread by Chris Edwards

**Canada Council   Conseil des Arts
for the Arts   du Canada**

We acknowledge the support of the Canada Council for the Arts which last year invested $20.1 million in writing and publishing throughout Canada.

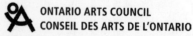

**ONTARIO ARTS COUNCIL
CONSEIL DES ARTS DE L'ONTARIO**

Published with the generous assistance of the Ontario Arts Council.

To Tobin, in hope and love

EUTOPIA

A NOVEL OF TERRIBLE OPTIMISM

Dr. Charles Davenport
c/o The Eugenics Records Office
Cold Spring Harbor, NY

August 15, 1910

Dear Charles,

The infant is safe.

I want to set that down before anything else. I shall write it again, and swear to it, and underscore it, so there can be no doubt:

The infant is safe.

I trust this will set your mind at ease. After the communiqué that you will have doubtless received from Garrison Harper by now, I can only imagine you must be gravely concerned. We have had words here in my library, Harper and I.

I believe that I have answered his accusations, primarily concerning my methodology in dealing with the Trout Lake investigation. But I am under no illusion that he went off satisfied. No doubt he is sitting at his desk in that vulgar mansion of his on the hill, composing his libel as I write this. He will send his letter off with a rider this evening. I must wait until morning. Thus will you receive Harper's account before mine.

I might predict what it will tell you: that the doctor, in a fit of depravity, abandoned his scientific observation of the mountain people, against the express orders of Harper, and invaded their community—plied them with drink, beat a young mother with a walking stick, snatched her baby from its cradle, and ran, like a madman, into the deep mountain night.

The doctor (Harper will have written), in so doing, violated the very principles of Compassion, Community and Hygiene, upon which the fair Eliada rests.

Harper will beg you to agree to the doctor's dismissal. He will insist that you send a physician who will content himself seeing to those principles—a physician who does not preoccupy himself with matters of science—who understands the practicalities of administering society take precedence over all. He will question the doctor's—my—fitness. He will tell you that I have harmed an infant.

These are lies, Charles. I did not feed liquor to mountain men. I did not strike a woman with my stick.

The infant is safe.

If all goes well, shortly I will provide you with the testimony of the men who had accompanied me: Mr. Bury and Mr. Wilkens. They will attest as true, that when we found the infant, it was abandoned—left in a bed of dried needles and sap at the base of a pine tree.

Really, can one be surprised? The people of these hills are degenerate. They are the flotsam of the wagon trains of the last century, left here to fester in their immorality, for generations.

Bury found it. He was scouting the edge of our camp at dusk. Bury came running back as Wilkens and I were heating tins of stew on the kerosene cook stove and admiring the view of the Kootenai River Valley in the vanishing light.

He was in a state of near hysteria, which was unusual—for Mr. Bury is as hard a man as Eliada sustains. At first, he was unable to explain what it was he found. It was a fire that produced no heat; a great bird, that cried out in song, with a voice like a woman's; a beast; and some other things also, which he could not clearly describe.

I did feed Bury a small jigger of whiskey then, but only to calm his nerves such that he could lead us back to the spot, where I might observe this thing he'd found firsthand.

It was some distance from the camp—further than Bury ought to have ventured in a simple patrol. He intimated that he may have been following the song, which caused him to stray, and he became quite apologetic.

The pine tree where the infant rested was part of a small copse of them, growing from a flat ledge near a stream. Facing the east, it was in growing shadow. The infant lay on its back there, staring up into the pines. It cried out, pitiably, as we approached. Bury pointed, his hand shaking, and I confess that I scolded him.

"It's a baby," I said. I crouched beneath the branches and finally approached the infant on hands and knees, met its eye for the first time. "Nothing more."

And so I ordered Wilkens to give me his coat. Folding it into a makeshift blanket around the infant, I lifted it to my chest and made my way back to my men. Then we returned to the camp, and I took the infant inside the tent.

This, Charles, is what transpired. The infant was abandoned. I saw to it that it came to no harm.

When we returned to Eliada, I brought the infant straight to the hospital. It sits here at my side now, in a cradle brought up from the nursery. I do not even entrust its care to the nurses here. I will not so much as permit them to see this child—and I shall not let it out of my sight—because here is the truth of the matter:

This infant that we found in the woods—on the side of mountain . . . it is magnificent. Where the indigenous folk here are bent and degenerate, subject to *the gigantism and the harelip and criminality which is a consequence of their breeding . . . this child is, how shall I say? It is perfection. It is the height of nature. It is a Mystery, or—dare I say it—a Miracle.*

Rest assured—no matter what Harper suspects, now or later . . . this child will come to no harm. I will not allow it. The infant is safe and I shall ensure that safety with my life—with all the life I have.

Were I so equipped, Charles, I swear that I would suckle this child myself.

Yours in Service,

Dr. Nils Bergstrom
Chief Physician-in-Residence
Eliada Hospital
Eliada, Idaho

PART I

NURTURE

1

Mister Juke

Not ghosts.

Although their owners might have pretended otherwise, Dr. Andrew Waggoner knew it. The sheets that loitered and whistled and kicked at the mud on this dark hillside in northern Idaho tonight were not ghosts; nor were they devils, nor duppies, nor spectral things of any kind.

When Andrew was a good deal younger, his Uncle Elmer had told him: ghosts were what the Ku Klux Klan originally intended with those sheets they wore. They wanted to make the poor Negroes think they were beset by the implacable spirits of the dead, Devils straight up from Hell—and not merely small-souled white men with lynching on their minds.

Maybe on some other Negro, the evil light of the kerosene flame in the twilight would make a mix with all those flapping sheets, that eerie un-musical whistling noise they were making, and that would be enough. But Andrew Waggoner was not that kind of Negro and he knew.

These were not ghosts.

They'd got Andrew just outside the hospital—done the deed as the last of the sun fell toward the pine-toothed edge of the Selkirk Mountains, west of Eliada. If he'd been paying better heed, not been smoking and brooding and keeping to himself, Andrew might have seen who they were. He didn't think anyone would be caught wearing their mama's bedsheets that close to town.

It didn't really matter much, of course. The truth of his predicament was awful in its simplicity: five men in sheets. One Negro, tied and on his knees. How does something like that end well?

Andrew did not think of himself as a religious man, but as one of those sheets bent down in front of him, he thought about praying.

As matters resolved, however, he didn't have to pray or even make up his mind on the matter. If God was paying any attention at all, He spared Andrew the indignity of supplication by tossing down a bone.

"You are going to watch this, Dr. Nigger."

The man in the sheet spoke in a voice Andrew thought he might recognize.

"It is Waggoner," said Andrew. "Dr. Waggoner."

He said "doctor" slowly, because he wanted to make that part of his name especially clear right now. Andrew Waggoner was a doctor, trained by some of the finest surgeons at Paris Medical School, graduated with honours, Class of 1908; he had been a resident here at Eliada's hospital for nearly a year. He was not some hog-tied vagabond nigger that these men could feel right about killing.

"This isn't right, Robert," he said. "You got to know that."

The sheet rustled like it was in the wind. The two eyes peering out through holes in it narrowed. "You don't know names," said the sheet. "You don't know nothing."

Andrew let himself smile. He was right. Robert Vernon was the man behind that sheet and that gave him something to grasp.

"Robert," Andrew said, "you sweep floors at the hospital. You got a sister in Lewiston with a wedding coming up—it's Harriet, am I right? Harriet Ver—"

Andrew didn't get the last name of "Vernon" out, because at that moment the sheet drove its fist into his gut. He wished he could have stood up to it, but it was a vicious punch and it sent the air whooping out of his lungs and made him bend and fall hard on his behind.

For an instant, looking up at the sheet, he hated himself as much as the rest of them hated him. Getting on a first-name basis with white men in whiter sheets wasn't going to get him anything. He was going to die, die twitching at the end of a rope, and there was nothing he could do about it—and he had it coming, stupid weak nigger that he was.

It was only for an instant. As soon as he heard the whimpering, wheedling sounds coming from behind that sheet, he remembered how Vernon slouched and limped behind his broom and wouldn't meet a man's eye in the light of day.

Andrew had a fine idea who the weak idiot was in this conversation. And it sure as hell was not the one with the medical degree from Paris.

"You don't know nothing! You don't know my family name you dirty God-damn nigger!" Vernon hollered.

A foot came out from beneath the sheet and caught him in the side. That hurt worse than the gut punch—it might have cracked a rib—but Andrew held on. He still had a chance. A slim one, but things were not as bad—not yet—as they were for poor little Maryanne Leonard.

§

It had been an awful day for the poor thing, started bad enough and ended up as bad as it could get. She was pregnant, with a child that no man in Eliada owned up to.

There was talk that she'd been raped by one of the bachelors who worked the mill, or maybe by one of the hill folk passing through. Maybe someone nearer.

Her brothers said they'd found her that morning in the privy, bent over herself as she squatted on the hole, just weeping and crying and cursing Jesus who she said had come one night and done this to her. There was blood coming out of her middle parts and they reported an awful smell coming up from the pit. So they brought her to the hospital on Sunday morning, hoping to find Dr. Bergstrom maybe. But when they got there, Dr. Andrew Waggoner was the only doctor in the house.

He should have been more wary of the sick girl. Even in New York, a Negro doctor touching a white woman's privates would cause a problem. But in New York, it would never get that far because the doctors wouldn't be so scarce that there was any need for a Negro doctor in the hospital. That was what sent ambitious young Dr. Andrew Waggoner here to this little Idaho mill town of Eliada, improbably blessed with a decently equipped hospital where he might learn and develop his craft.

He should have stopped. But listening to the story they told him, and looking at the girl, he couldn't turn her away.

Doing so would mean leaving Maryanne Leonard in the care of her brothers, one of whom likely as not was complicit in giving the poor girl what Andrew was pretty sure was an outhouse abortion.

So Andrew smiled deferentially, told them: *Bring her in*. And he got ready to do what he could, which as it turned out was nothing much.

§

"Leave him," said another sheet. "He's got to be awake to see how he's going to die."

This sheet was taller, and wider too. Andrew did not know who this one was by his voice, and as he looked up at it he realized: he had been gone a spell. The boot had come again and again, in the ribs and in the back and the chest, and there had been a forest of pain, and it had hit in his head, and he must have fallen unconscious. Now he was back.

Through swollen lips, Andrew asked the new sheet: "Who are you? You the Grand Dragon or something?"

"Quiet," said the new sheet. He leaned in very close—so close that Andrew could smell his breath (not liquored, but ugly, soured as it was with coffee and seasoned with tobacco) and see the flesh around his eye (it was lined, used to squinting at sun, and tufted with a thick black eyebrow whose hairs poked out through the torn-out eye hole in the sheet) and feel the heat off him.

The stranger in the sheet stood up.

"You are one unlucky nigger," he said, aloud. "Yesterday, we might have just put the scare in you—run you from town. But after what you done to pretty little Maryanne . . ."

Andrew started to protest:

He hadn't done that thing to her abdomen. He hadn't done anything but try and give her some comfort with a shot of morphine; try and find the source of the bleeding and make it stop; look at that opening like a caesarean cut (if the blade that had made it were blunt, and handed to her baby who used it to cut itself out from the inside) and tried to clean it, cover it, stitch it. "Jesus done it to me!" she'd screamed, thrashing on the table in the hospital's operating theatre. "Jeee-Susss!" She said that again and again, even as the morphine took hold, even as the life went out of her.

Andrew had wanted to go out to the brothers after that, and ask: *Any of you boys named Jesus?*

"It wasn't me. She was gone," Andrew said. "She'd lost too much blood. Her womb was *ripped*. Somebody did it . . . but nobody could have—"

He stopped before the sheet's raised hand could come down in his face.

16

"You know," said the sheet, his voice low now, "that's the first true thing that came out of your nigger mouth since we brought you here. It wasn't you that did this to her. We do know that. We ain't fools."

"Then why—?"

The sheet looked over his shoulder, wagged his head. "Get him up. And bring out the freak."

Andrew almost screamed in pain as two of them hoisted him up to his knees. Two others walked around behind him, to the wagon. He tried to look but his head wouldn't quite turn the way it should, so he had to listen to the rustling of the tarpaulin, some grunting, and a sliding sound.

As he listened, he realized:

They're not taking out a picture book here. They've got someone else in there.

The person had been quiet when they'd hauled Andrew along, thrown him in the back—but Andrew didn't have a sense about how he'd have missed him even so.

Andrew turned his head just a little, and watched as he came into his view.

The sheets were hauling a tall man, thin as sticks. White or Negro, Andrew couldn't tell because he was not only tied like Andrew, but had a sack pulled down over his head. His legs moved strangely, like they'd been broken at the calf and had a joint added there. The high whistling noise that Andrew had thought was coming from the Klansmen got louder, and Andrew worked it out—it was not, had never been, coming from one of them. It was coming from under the sack.

"So what," said the sheet, "can you tell us about this fellow here?"

"Will it make a difference?"

"May it might."

The two others pushed the second captive to the ground in front of Andrew, while another brought the kerosene lamp closer. One of the men pulled the hood from him, while another held the lamp up.

Andrew squinted. There was something wrong with the light, or maybe his vision had been fouled by the blow to his head, or maybe he was just losing his sanity in the course of staring down his own death. The man's face didn't seem right. It had an odd bend to it at the forehead, and the mouth seemed too wide, and the eyes . . .

The eyes couldn't have been that black. They seemed like they were all pupil, no iris. Eyes didn't work that way.

That wasn't the end of the strangeness, though. The hair sprang like winter-dead branches from his scalp and he was true, boneyard white. If the Klansmen were looking for their ghost to frighten even an educated Negro, they'd hit near the mark with this one. Andrew had seen queer things in Paris—pictures of hunchbacks and feeble men and women; dwarfs and giants—even photographs of old John Merrick, the Elephant Man of London.

But there had been nothing quite like this face.

Andrew blinked, and looked again, and swallowed hard and painful as he looked.

It must have been the scrambling of his brains, because when he looked again, the face seemed to have changed.

It was suddenly very beautiful, fine-featured; the face of a pale-skinned girl, black hair floating above her head like she was underwater. Her lips were not wide, but puckered into a rosebud aperture, from which the lovely whistling music came. And he blinked again, and when his eyes opened, they pulled the captive away.

"Recognize him?" said Robert Vernon, who by now had pulled his own sheet aside. "You recognize him, nigger. You do. You brung him here. And he did that thing to Maryanne. Fuckin' rapist, and you brung him."

"I—I'm not seeing right," said Andrew. He felt as though he was spilling out of himself; he heard his voice hitch, in that weak, begging way. "You hit me on the head and I can't see right." And he added, hating himself: "I'm sorry."

"You're sorry," said Robert. "That's right, you're sorry."

"Tell us," said the tall man. "No point playing stupid. We know you been keeping this freak under guard. Robert found him a week ago."

Robert nodded. "In the quarantine," he said. "Livin' like a king. The cause of all our woes an' livin' like a king."

"In quarantine," said Andrew.

The quarantine was a barn-board outbuilding almost as big as the hospital itself, that he had only visited once—the day he'd arrived and Dr. Bergstrom was showing him around the whole compound. He'd never been inside, because there'd never been any need.

"Nobody," Andrew said, "is in quarantine."

"Callin' me a liar, nigger?" said Robert.

Andrew swallowed and took a breath. If he kept himself just so, the pain wasn't too bad. He kept his breathing right, the fear could be pushed away. So he did and he did.

"Look," he said. "I'm telling you what I know. That quarantine's been empty since autumn."

"Before you were here," said Robert.

"Before I was here." Andrew said. "I'm sorry. I've never seen anybody in there. And I've surely never seen—that. You think he raped Maryanne? Or—cut her?"

The tall sheet made a throat-cutting motion to one of the others. "That's enough," he said. "He doesn't recognize him either. Let's get on."

With that, the hood fell back over the head of the poor fellow and they hauled him back to the tree.

It was a maple, and over one thick branch that extended out and swooped down to nearly touch the ground, someone had slung two lengths of noose-tied rope.

The sheets went to work. Robert wrapped his arms around the man's legs and with a cracking sound from his own bad knees, lifted as another took the poor victim by his shoulders, and a third helped guide his neck to the noose while the last two held the other end of the rope where it crossed the tree branch. Andrew thought there would be more of a fight, but the fellow had an odd calm to him as the rope went over his head, and pushed down over the sack and around his neck. There was a stillness, a terrible quiet, as the men stood there, holding their captive aloft, delicate, like they might be thinking about the right and wrong of what they were doing.

It didn't last long, that moment.

Robert Vernon let go of the legs and the others let go of the arms, and the maple branch bent somewhat as the rope went tight. The two on the rope's other end hauled the rope over the branch, and the lynched man rose in the night.

Andrew didn't know when he'd started work on the rope around his wrists. But he knew as the poor man's legs twitched and shook and bent, and the keening whistling started up again—far louder this time, almost like a tiny scream—he'd managed to loosen a knot. Nothing dramatic—it was just looser, not untied, and there were other knots after this one before he'd be free. But although his fingers were numb and fat with his own blood, they were still a surgeon's, and they knew what to do. They would get those knots, because if they didn't—well, their doctor would end up on that rope. That was not how Dr. Andrew Waggoner was meant to leave this world. Even if he was slow to realize it, his fingers knew.

Luckily, the sheets seemed to have no idea.

Their victim raised high enough—maybe three feet off the ground—they tied off the rope, and came back to watch him die. Behind him, the cart-horse whinnied.

Andrew slipped the knot free. The second was not so tight, and he got that one going much more quickly. What was he going to do when he got them free? None of the men seemed to have guns, at least none outside their sheets. So he might just be able to run for it. Except he was cramped and sore and his rib felt like it could be broken. He could probably still outrun Robert Vernon with his bad knee. But the rest?

Andrew set his teeth. It was hard to think, with that whistling getting as loud as it was, so he just kept at work. How could that whistling be getting louder? The hanged man's airway should be about shut. The noises he could make should have changed, become more strangled and quieter.

The sheets were thinking the same thing. One of them had his hands over his ears, while their leader was shouting something else, something like an instruction. Two of them moved to obey—if, that is, they'd been told to grab the dying man's belt-loops and pull him down to break his neck. They grabbed tight, threw their own knees from under themselves and dangled.

The final knot slid undone and Andrew slid out of the ropes. He closed his eyes tight and gritted his teeth, blinked and pushed himself up. On hands and knees, he turned around, and with the fire in his rib making him want to weep, made for the wagon.

He didn't get far.

Andrew gasped, and his arms slipped from under him, and he thought: *I've been shot.* Then he found himself rolled over. He was looking into the face of Robert Vernon. The sheet was off him now, and he held a stick—no, a handle for an axe. Instinctively Andrew raised his hand to ward him off. The axe-handle hit him in the elbow with a sickening *crack!*, and he clutched it, as Robert Vernon raised his club again.

There was another *crack!*, and Robert stood there for what seemed like a long time, weapon raised. Then Robert fell backwards into the dirt. The axe-handle fell against Andrew's hip. The sky was empty but for early evening stars and a fat yellow moon rising on the horizon.

The high whistling continued, but Andrew thought it might have been joined by another sound: the barking of dogs, and the *crack! crack!* of gunfire.

That would be good, he thought, if it were true. Then his eyelids slid shut and he let himself rest a moment.

§

Andrew's eyelids flickered as someone bent close. Not a sheet. Not a ghost. It had dark little eyes, though, a face bent the wrong way. It puckered its wide mouth, and leaned forward. It breathed out an awful smell, like formaldehyde, and looked up, started, and moved fast off to the right. Andrew felt the scant weight of it on his chest only then, by its sudden absence.

Someone screamed not far off, and Andrew blinked twice before he just gave up and closed his eyes.

§

"Dr. Waggoner."

Andrew felt a sharp slap on his cheek, and another.

He coughed and blinked and opened his eyes.

This time the light of a kerosene lamp was nearer him, and there was someone else leaning in. Someone he recognized.

"Doctor," said Sam Green. "You hear me?"

"I hear you," said Andrew.

"Good. You know who I am?"

"Sure."

Sam Green was the boss of the Pinkerton crew. He and Andrew went back— to October, when they'd met at the train station in Bonner's Ferry some forty miles to the south of here.

Sam was wearing his bowler hat and what looked like his Sunday best. His normally ruddy face was crimson over the starched collar and tight-wound tie. Normally when he was on duty, Sam would wear something a bit more comfortable. But today was Sunday and unlike Andrew, he was a church-going man.

"That is good," said Sam. "You haven't been entirely addled by those bastards."

"Those—" Andrew tried to sit up but the pain in his back and ribs was too much. "Those bastards," he said slowly, "are Klansmen. They hanged a man."

21

Sam might have smiled under his thick moustache, or he might have grimaced. "They are piss-poor Klansmen if that is what they even are. Anyone can pull a sheet over their head."

Andrew coughed again, and winced. God, it hurt.

Green stood up. In his right hand, Andrew saw, he was casually dangling his still-smoking Smith and Wesson Russian revolver by the trigger guard.

"They hanged a man, Sam. They were going to do the same to me."

"And we shot and killed three of them," said Sam. "You stay put here a moment. Rest a spell."

As he turned and stepped away, Andrew chanced to lift his head to see what he could see.

Andrew counted three lanterns casting beams here and there among maybe a dozen men and who knew how many dogs working the base of the hanging tree.

Nearer by, Andrew saw the bodies. The nearest belonged to Robert Vernon. There were another two further upslope toward the hanging tree, collapsed on one another, their sheets flowered bloody. Sam stepped over them like they were fallen branches and joined the others.

"He ready to move?" Sam called.

Someone in the crowd answered, "He'll move. None too pleased about it though."

"Would you be?" asked Sam.

And with that, the crowd broke and two men hauled a stretcher out. On the stretcher was a figure bundled in dark cloth, and (Andrew thought) tied down. The stretcher tipped and twisted as the two men carrying it tried to manhandle it away. Andrew leaned his head back and shut his eyes.

They'd hanged a sick man and tried to hang a doctor, and earlier on they'd murdered a young girl and her baby.

Christ in Heaven, there was going to be hell to pay.

§

"Couple of things," said Andrew when Sam came back to him.

"You have gathered your thoughts?"

"Yes," said Andrew. "First. There's been a murder. Not that poor fellow just now hung, either. Another. Maryanne Leonard."

Sam Green raised his eyebrows. "The girl with child? I had been given to understand she died of . . . womanly troubles."

"She did," said Andrew. "But I examined her. I believe her troubles were brought on by an abortionist. An inexpert one."

Sam looked away at that, and Andrew let him be a moment. This was nothing for a good Catholic fellow to hear on a Sunday evening.

"You think," said Sam finally, "that these fellows were hanging you in part to keep you quiet on the subject?"

"The thought had crossed my mind. Yes."

Sam snorted, lowered his head to look at his feet, and said in a low voice: "Fucking animals." Then he looked up, met Andrew's eye. "Pardon my French."

"It is important that they not be allowed to take the body away. It will need to be examined for proof," said Andrew.

"I wouldn't worry about that," said Sam. "Dr. Bergstrom is back at the hospital now. He has not released anything to anyone."

"Bergstrom's back? When—"

"After supper," said Green. "We saw him at the hospital. These bastards left the place in a mess."

"So he sent you after us?"

Sam's moustache twitched. "So we found you," he said. "That's what's important. And now you've told me about the murder you suspect. Anything else?"

"I think," said Andrew, "I'm going to need some help out of here."

"That so? Can't imagine why. You feel all your fingers and toes, Doc?"

"Yes, I feel them just fine. But I think my back is hurt and I can't get up right now. I think you'd better bring over that stretcher you used to carry off the body."

"Body?"

"Yes," said Andrew. "The hanged man. That other murder. I've got respect for the dead—but I'm going to need that stretcher more than him right now."

Now Sam was grinning. He knelt down and patted Andrew on his shoulder. "Nobody died here tonight," he said, "but some cowardly bastards. Old Mister Juke is fine as ever he was."

"Mister—Juke?"

So the hanged man had a name.

"You, now . . ." Sam sat down on the ground, propping his gun on his knee and looking off over Andrew's head. "You do look like you could use some help. But we got to get Mister Juke back to our own wagon. They'll come back with the stretcher when that's done."

"Sam," said Andrew, "don't go changing the subject. He was hanged. He can't be fine. He—"

"Hush," Sam said. "You are a smart Negro, Dr. Waggoner. I don't believe I have said so before, but I have a great respect for you in that regard. You managed to get yourself into doctoring school in Paris, France, and back out again with a medical degree. And now, you can set a bone and you can cut out a swelled-up appendix with your eyes closed I expect. But even you can't expect to know everything on Heaven and earth."

Andrew frowned and thought about that.

"Tell me something," he finally said. "Did you come up here looking for me, or were you here to get that Mister Juke back?"

"Oh, we're bringing you back," said Sam. "But like I said, boy: 'There are more things in Heaven and earth, than are dreamt of in your philosophy.' See now?" he said, winking again. "You ain't the only one read a book."

"How long," said Andrew, "has Mister Juke been in the quarantine? Why did nobody tell me? And just precisely what—who—is he?"

"No, no," said Sam. "You won't get that from me, old friend. Not more from me. You can ask Dr. Bergstrom when you get back. Not," he added, "that I am recommending it."

Sam Green leaned back. To show the conversation was done for now, he started to whistle.

2

A Damn Germ

FEBRUARY, 1911

Jason Thistledown's mama was tall and beautiful and strong; stronger of arm than many a man and more powerful of spirit than any two. Yet in the end it was not a man nor two nor even a gang of them, but a damn germ that killed her.

The night it happened it was just the two of them alone in the cabin as a terrible howl of a blizzard ran outside. The blizzard was bad for the pigs, and as it turned out one of them died because Jason would not go outside and see to them. He knew the risk in leaving the pigs out like that, but sometimes a man's got to decide, and if there's no man about, the decision falls to a boy. To Jason's way of thinking, when the choice is between standing by your mama and a seeing to a sty of swine, there's no choice at all.

He sat there and gave her water until she stopped taking it. He tried singing to her like she used to sing to him, but that felt foolish, so he said he was sorry but he was going to have to stop. He thought she might like to hear a story so he told her the one about Odysseus and Polyphemus, until he realized it became too terrifying in the middle part where Odysseus' men were one by one devoured by the terrible Cyclops. His mama (lying on her bed, unable to move or speak, with blood welling at the base of her fingernails; brown, putrid fever-sweat accumulating in her bedclothes) didn't need more terrifying. So he said he was sorry and tried to think of a less frightening tale. At length, Jason had to admit he didn't know many stories that weren't upsetting in some way or another, so he said he was sorry.

"I guess sayin' sorry's one thing I can do fine," he said and tried to laugh at his little joke but wound up crying.

He cried a long time, but managed to get his wits about him before the germ delivered its *coup de grâce*.

Later on, Jason was glad for that. He was sure his mama wouldn't have liked to have had the last sight of her son being him blubbering like a baby.

At that hour, however, Jason had not yet seriously entertained the notion that his mama was going to be having a last anything of anything. She was just poorly. She was quite poorly, sure, but she hadn't been that way for so very long. The coughing started up on the way back from the store at Cracked Wheel, and that was just a day ago. It was probably a flu germ, she'd said, but she'd had flu before and always just walked it off. She was more worried about Jason coming down with it, and so ordered him to the far end of the cabin for all the good that would do.

Jason hadn't come down with a thing—not so much as a sniffle. That, to his way of thinking, meant that whatever it was, it wasn't much of a flu at all.

Still believing this, Jason dried his nose and got up from his chair and went to see to the wood stove, which was starting to cool. He dug around in the wood box and came up with a stick of birch that looked about right, and opened the stove's front and shoved it in. It raised a little flurry of sparks in the bed of coals inside. Jason blew on it a bit, and fanned it with his hand, poked it with his fingertips until it was just right. Then he closed the door and wiggled the flue to make sure it was properly open so the fire would take.

When he got up, that was it.

Later, Jason would think that it was better his mama saw him tending the fire as she died. His mama valued that sort of thing, that *self-sufficiency* as she called it. Self-sufficiency had seen her raise Jason alone here in the wilds of northwest Montana—laugh at all the folks who'd said she, born and raised in the east and come out here only late in life, wouldn't last a year now that her husband was gone.

Yes, he would think, she probably took a deal of comfort in watching him see to his needs; more comfort than having him right there beside her as the life fled her flesh.

Yet there at the deathbed, Jason didn't even cry. He just stood, hands hanging dead weight at his side. He shuffled over to her bed, and fell to his knees, and died himself or so it seemed to him.

His mama was gone; taken from him by a God-damned germ.

§

It was on February 12, 1911 that she died.

Jason did not look at the clock when it happened, but sometime afterward he remarked to himself that it struck eleven in the night; so he surmised she'd died prior to eleven but past what might normally be the supper hour, although they had not had a proper supper, and he finally hazarded a guess and wrote this down in the front of their Bible:

8 OCLOCK (OR THERE-ABOUT) IN EVENING
FEB 12 1911
ELLEN THISTLEDOWN
LOVING MOTHER OF JASON
DIED OF FEVER
IN HER OWN BED

He wrote those words the morning of February 13, before he ventured outside to check on the pigs and found that one of them had died too—a young boar that Jason's mama was fattening for slaughter. The freeze had taken care of the slaughter, and by the time Jason had come out, the remaining four pigs were taking care of the carcass.

The whole homestead was snowbound—one side of the cabin was covered in a drift of white that went from the roof shingles to the ground in a smooth curve, like the snow that ran down the distant western mountain peaks, and the blizzard had left no path between cabin and pigsty. Jason started through the white anyway but it was tough going.

He was finally reduced to hollering, "Stop! You're eatin' your own! Damn cannibal hogs!" The swine paid him no heed.

Jason swore a storm, and waved his arms, and finally, in frozen exhaustion, turned back to the cabin.

With that picture in his head, he knew there was no question.

No matter how he loved her, Jason Thistledown could no longer live under the same roof as his mama—reduced as she was to nothing but soured meat.

When he composed himself, he found a shovel and began digging a path from the cabin. The sun was as high as it would get, casting a shortening shadow to the north by the time he'd made it to the side where the woodshed stood. There was a good half-cord of wood stacked within. But Jason looked to the braces. They were six feet from the ground, and spaced adequately for the task.

Against the wall in the shed was a stack of pine planks, bought by him and his mama that autumn past in hopes of setting down a proper floor in the cabin. He lifted two of those planks into the rafters, making a high platform that he reckoned would keep her safe from predation and wolves until the thaw.

"I am sorry, Mama," he said as he hefted her sheet-wrapped body over his shoulder and put a foot on the ladder. She was wearing the same sheet she'd died in, and he had not washed her, and even in the sharp February cold she gave a stink like a shallow privy.

"I guess," he said as he rolled her onto the makeshift platform and settled her on her back, "sayin' sorry's one thing I can do fine."

§

The winter finished hard, one storm after another hitting the Thistledown homestead in a succession of punishing smacks that blanketed the snow in thick layers. Jason fought back dully—each day clearing a path between the door of the house and the woodshed, and halfway along cutting off another path to the sty. He waited a few days but finally succumbed and became diligent in throwing feed to the cannibal swine, creatures he was coming to hate but could not bring himself to kill.

He told himself that when the thaw came, he would trade the sty of them for the finest of coffins, and the churchyard plot nearest to Jesus, a tombstone carved with his mama's saintly visage and words from the most eloquent preacher in Montana to send her Heaven-ward.

Toward such an end, the pigs would have to be fed daily, lest they ate one another to extinction before winter's finish.

Aside from the daily feedings, however, Jason did not spend much time tending the pigs.

Most times, he sat bundled in the woodshed, the Winchester in his lap. As the days grew longer, Jason grew more certain that his mama's frozen resting place was not so secure. Three years ago, during a winter not so harsh as this one, his mama had bent down and showed him tracks in the snow.

Dogs? Jason guessed, and his mama had corrected him: *Not dogs, Jason. Wolves. A pack of them. That's what the gun's for.*

Jason had not seen wolf tracks around the homestead this winter, but he was on the lookout for them all the same—particularly as the snow climbed higher, nearer the height of the braces, and his mama's frozen body.

He only felt truly safe for his mama when another blizzard blew, and the cold came so strong that nothing—he hoped—could live outside shelter.

Otherwise, he guarded and he patrolled, to make sure no strange tracks came near. He thought of how he would kill a wolf if it came. He counted his ammunition and thought how he would kill five of them. He began to think how he might kill a man if it came to that.

He grew thinner. He felt a hardness come over his face, and when he looked at it in the glass, he thought he looked like someone else. It was worse when he tried to smile, so he didn't.

Instead, he guarded. And he waited—for the weather to break, so he could get moving, begin the business of trading the lives of his swine for a funeral for his mama.

§

The sun grew brighter and the smell of old leaves and pine needles came up from the ground. The crackling sound of icicles breaking could be heard, and when in the early morning he stepped onto the stoop, Jason felt a near thing to joy.

Soon, he could be off to town. Soon, he could finish things right: trade the cannibal pigs for the best coffin, an eloquent preacher and the plot nearest Jesus.

He pulled up his coat and set off for the woodshed through the now-slushy path he'd dug for himself. He felt like he should tell his mama something—that everything would be fine, her soul would be soon on the way to Heaven. But having spent the days watching over her, he was fairly certain she was not there to hear it.

All the same. Jason wanted to see her. Maybe whisper it.

But he stopped before he got far, and cursed himself. This was, of course, the first time in weeks he had headed there without the rifle. And this morning was also the first that he had seen tracks, other than his own.

Jason stepped back into the cabin, took hold of the Winchester, and with considerably greater care, crept around the cabin's side to the woodshed.

§

How do I shoot a man?

The question suddenly became relevant, because the tracks he saw were not wolf tracks. They were boots, and by the look of them they were heading up from the direction of Cracked Wheel before they stepped down onto the path and disappeared.

Jason stood against the wall of the cabin, rifle held to his chest, heart hammering, and peered around. He blinked, and thought:

How do I shoot a woman?

She wore a black overcoat with a fur collar and a fur-lined hat; she was stout but not overly so, and carried in one hand a carpet bag. In her other hand—her right hand—she held a revolver. She was looking up into the rafters, faced away from Jason.

Well, he thought, stepping out and lowering the rifle, *one thing's sure. I do not shoot her in the back.*

"Drop the gun, please ma'am." He was surprised at how calm his voice sounded, even as the thought occurred to him: should she turn too fast, or jump away, or do anything dangerous, he would have to shoot her. Somehow, he would have to shoot her. "I have you covered."

"Oh!" The gun fell from her hand, as did the carpet bag. She raised two small gloved hands. "Please don't shoot. May I turn?"

Her voice made Jason think of easterners. Which made him think of his mama.

"You may," he said. "What are you doing here?"

The woman turned, her feet making a sucking sound in the dirt. Jason judged her to be older than his mama had been, but not much. She wore eyeglasses, and he thought them to be very thick, because her eyes seemed very large.

"Is that Ellen?" she asked, motioning to the rafters.

Jason took a breath and lowered the rifle. He didn't expect this strange woman would be trading gunfire with him. But that wasn't to say he was ready to trust her yet.

"You didn't answer my question," he said. "What're you doin' here, if you please?"

"I'm—" she looked back up "—oh my. That is Ellen, isn't it? Oh, poor dear Ellen. Did she succumb too?"

"She's dead, if that's what you mean," said Jason. He stepped toward the woman—keeping an eye on the revolver all the while. He felt a piece of him break off in his chest as he said the words. "My mama's been dead—some time now."

The woman looked down, and brought a gloved hand to her eye. "Oh. Your mama."

"Ma'am," said Jason, collecting himself, "who are you, please?"

She looked at him again, with those great big eyes. They seemed less sure of themselves this time.

"I am Germaine Frost," she said. "I am, well . . . I suppose I am your aunt. Ellen Thornton was my baby sister."

§

It was hard to credit it at first. Jason's mama had been tall and blonde-haired, with a firm jawline and a lean, strong figure. Germaine Frost was in many respects the opposite. She was not as tall as Jason, and the line of her jaw was obscured by thick jowls, and her hair was black as an Injun's.

And leaving aside the glasses, there was the fact that Jason could recall no point at which his mother had talked of any aunts or uncles.

Jason wished she might have. But he supposed this was as good a time as any to meet one of them—he was in need of relations now as never before.

He gathered Germaine Frost's revolver, her bag, and carried both to the cabin. Germaine—Aunt Germaine—followed at a respectful distance. As they came to the stoop, she asked him to stop a moment.

"Have you washed inside?" she asked.

"Washed—"

"Inside," she said. "The house. It is a plague house, after all. It may still be infected."

"Infected?"

"With the disease that took my dear sister. Although not you, young master—Jason, is it?"

"Yes ma'am. Jason Thistledown's my name. And no ma'am. I did not wash. Not especially, inside I mean." He shuffled his feet. "It's pretty ripe in there I guess."

"Well, Jason," she said, and put out her hand, "let's have a look. Please hand me my bag."

Aunt Germaine set the bag down in a drift. She took a little handful of snow, and scrubbed the handles of the bag where Jason had held it. Then she took more snow and rubbed it in her gloved hands before opening the bag. She rooted through some neatly folded cloth until she pulled out a small handkerchief, with strings coming out of each corner. Jason watched as she placed the cloth over her mouth, then reached up and tied it behind her head like she was doing her hair. In the end, the little handkerchief covered her mouth and her nose. Finally, she pulled off her hat and took off her coat, and set them down atop the carpet bag.

"Very good," she said, her voice muffled by the cloth. "Now let us see how you have been getting by, Jason."

Jason stepped aside to let Aunt Germaine through. She did not get far inside.

"Oh my," she said. "Where does one start?"

Jason looked past her to see what she meant. The cabin was a simple enough place to his eye. One long pine table with a couple of chairs, the wood stove in the middle of it, a tiny windowsill and the beds at one end of it. All in one room.

"This," she said, "is a breeding place for germs. The ground itself is your floor! Had you been staying outside all the time, Jason?"

"No ma'am."

"Did you isolate your dear mother as she was ill?"

"No ma'am."

She turned to him. Her eyes seemed very large behind the glasses. "And after she passed. You've remained here for how long after that?"

"Don't know."

"Weeks?"

"Months."

"Oh my."

She stepped back outside, and leaned close to him. "It is all right, my dear," she said. "I am well-trained. Open your mouth. And turn to the sun, please, so I can better see."

§

Two hours later, Jason Thistledown was naked as the day he was born, up to his breast-bone in a tub of scalding hot water that Aunt Germaine had made him boil up on the wood stove and haul to a level spot in the lee of the house, and rubbing himself down with a black, stinging bar of soap from the carpet bag.

Jason tried to argue. "I'm not sick," he said. "If I was carrying this germ, wouldn't it make sense for me to be sick? It's got to be gone now!"

"No," said Germaine, "it does not. You clearly have an immunity."

"How can you know that?" he demanded. "And how would it be on my clothes?"

She pointed back at the house. "Fetch the water, Jason. And get in it. This is not a discussion." She clapped her hands. "Hop to it."

Now, sitting in the water, Jason wondered how in the course of less than an hour he could have moved from contemplating shooting a woman to hopping to it when she hollered.

Part of it, he suspected, was that she did seem to know what she was doing. She examined him like she was a doctor, and when he asked about that she said that back in Philadelphia she had worked as a nurse. She seemed to know a lot about germs, and when he asked about that she made a joke about them being her namesake. "The girls used to call me Germy behind my back," she said and laughed.

It wasn't all that funny, but Jason laughed too. He hadn't done that in some time, laughing aloud, and it felt good to finally clear the pipes.

"What girls?" he asked.

Aunt Germaine's smile faded a bit. "Oh you know," she said. "The other nurses."

Jason hadn't a chance to ask many more questions the next couple of hours, as he followed Aunt Germaine's very precise instructions about how to heat the water, where to do the bath and most importantly how to wash his clothes and himself.

Finally, as he finished the last spot at the very back of his head, he started up again.

"Aunt Germaine," he said, "how is it that I never heard of you? You and mama have a fallin' out?"

"Not precisely that," said Germaine. "Let us say that we married into different circles."

"That's how come you're called Frost, and not Thornton?"

"Yes. That is how come."

Jason set down the soap in the snow. It bled little spider legs through the white. "How come you're here now?" he asked.

Germaine turned around, glancing at Jason then away. "I was—nearby, when I learned what had happened here."

Jason gave her a look. "How nearby? Nobody's been here all winter to see what happened."

His aunt pulled off her gloves, and wrung them together. "Nobody has," she said. "And you have not left the homestead, and no one has come."

"Too much snow," said Jason.

His aunt didn't say anything to that. She kept her eyes down, while Jason worked it out: news had come from here that was not about his mama, but still bad enough to draw relations nonetheless.

His hand fell back into the tub, and although the water was still quite warm, he shivered.

"What happened in Cracked Wheel? More people get sick?"

Aunt Germaine looked up. Her eyes might have been big and wet again, but the sun reflected off the glass so Jason could only surmise it by the tone in her voice.

"The whole town," she said quietly. "It is gone."

§

Jason would never set foot in the cabin again, of that he was sure.

As the sun set below the mountains, the flames were already reaching higher than treetops. He felt himself hitching to cry all over again as he watched the flames take it, and the woodshed, and his mama—who was going onward with no coffin, no tombstone, no sweet-voiced eulogy from the best preacher in Montana: a quiet recitation of the Twenty-third Psalm by Aunt Germaine, a lick of flame to kerosene, and then . . .

Fire.

Aunt Germaine stood beside him, her arm around his shoulder as the flames went higher. "Jason, this is something no young man should have to do, but so many do. You are very brave."

Jason coughed, to hide that he was crying. "Not my idea," he said, quiet enough that he'd figure his aunt couldn't hear. But her ears were better than her eyes and she answered him:

"You wouldn't know," she said. "You haven't seen the town yet. You haven't seen what this germ does."

"I know well enough," he said. "Mama should be buried."

"Why's that?" Germaine raised her voice as the flames hit the woodpile. "She Catholic? A Jewess?"

"You know she ain't," said Jason.

"Then cremation is still good enough for my sister. It was good enough for Mr. Frost, it's good enough for Ellen."

Jason swallowed hard. They had had a falling out, Aunt Germaine and his mama—that was a sure thing.

"If we do not do this," said his aunt, "then what happens when some trapper comes by in the melt, starts rooting through the house and picks up that germ? What happens, I will tell you, is this: it is an epidemic. Like the cholera."

"Is that what this is?"

Aunt Germaine put up her hand. "The flames are taking," she said. "Let us pray for your mother's immortal soul."

"All right," he said. "I will."

And Jason bowed his head, and after a moment of sad quiet, he imagined a great celestial light descending over this infernal pyre. And imagining that, he thought up a prayer.

Oh Lord, he prayed, *please see my mama to Heaven where she belongs. And Lord, see to it, please, that should my pa ever wish to speak with her from where he writhes and burns in that Other Place*—

Jason opened his eyes and stared into the flames that consumed the cabin old John Thistledown had built the year Jason was born.

—please, Lord: see to it he stays where he is and keeps his damn peace.

§

A month ago, shooting the pigs might have brought Jason some measure of satisfaction. Now—somehow, the act seemed capricious; low-down cruel. But Aunt Germaine insisted.

"They are probably fine," she said. "But who knows if whatever it was that took poor Ellen is not also somehow attached to the swine?"

"It don't seem likely," said Jason. "And anyhow—those pigs have value at market."

Aunt Germaine shook her head. "There is no market," she said. "Not close by. Go on, young man. Take your shot."

"Well," he said doubtfully, "they *are* cannibals."

In the end, Jason was down six bullets from the Winchester, having missed with one and but wounded with another.

He made sure to gather up the casings for reuse before he and his new aunt started off, in the dawn light, toward the snow-choked pass to Cracked Wheel. Jason wondered how they were going to do it. But as they crossed a rise that had been beaten down by Aunt Germaine's footsteps, and rounded a tree, he saw it. There, sticking out of the snow, were two pair of snowshoes.

"Have you ever walked in snowshoes?" she asked.

"'Course," he said. "There was a couple pair that burned up on the back of the woodshed. Didn't think of them until now."

"Well, it is a good thing I thought ahead," said Aunt Germaine. "See? I brought an extra pair."

"In case of survivors," he said.

"That is right."

"That was good thinking, Aunt Germaine."

Aunt Germaine reached out, tossed one pair of shoes onto the snow, and stepped onto them. She motioned for Jason to do the same, and then looked at him very intently.

"I will look after you, Jason—from now on. I'll see to you. We are, after all, family."

"Family," said Jason as he stomped his feet into place on the snowshoes. He hadn't thought he'd be using that word again, but it felt good coming off his tongue.

"Let me carry your bag, Aunt," he said as they headed off south.

3

The Horror at Cracked Wheel

Cracked Wheel, Montana, was the biggest place that Jason Thistledown had ever visited, but he was wise enough to know that didn't mean much. From talking to others when they came to town from time to time, he understood that Cracked Wheel was but a flyspeck next to the great towns of Helena, of Butte, of Billings. He knew that all combined, they weren't any of them a thing to compare to Philadelphia where Aunt Germaine came from, or New York, where the scale of things dwarfed whole mountain ranges.

Still . . . there were more than a hundred people who made their homes here around a main street of log-and-board buildings. There was the Dempsey store, which handled dry goods and hardware and coffee and spices and the mail. When the season was right, they'd even get apples and such in, and when it was wrong, it would be applesauce, or anything else you might imagine sealed inside a tin can. There was a saloon, which Jason had not entered since he was very small, where you could get a room as well as a meal and a whiskey. Across the road was Johnston Brothers, a little storefront that offered doctoring and barbering and undertaking depending on your needs. And next to it was the town office, a low clapboard building where the records were kept of births, deaths and land titles.

That was where Aunt Germaine led him. "It is the one building that I dared enter before I came to you. I am not dead. So I believe it is safe."

"Safe."

Jason kicked off his snowshoes at the edge of the sidewalk and looked around uneasily. Huge drifts licked up the sides of buildings and swelled over the eaves of rooftops, from which icicles the size of men dangled and dribbled into icy pits in the snow. The wide street was nearly trackless—but for the oval scratches of their own snowshoes, and some older ones that maybe Aunt Germaine had made when she'd headed out.

"This ain't safe," he said. He pointed at a hole in the glass of the front window, big as a thumbprint. The panel had been covered with a little wooden board, but no one had cleared the glass. "Look. Someone's been shooting."

Germaine didn't hear him. She pushed open the front door to the town office. "Come inside," she said. "Help me start a fire in the stove."

Jason had to wait a moment for his eyes to adjust to the scant light. He had been inside very few times. He knew there was a long, dark wood counter in the front and a few desks behind it, with some wooden cabinets and a big wall of tiny little shelves for notes. It was all shadows now, musty smells of paper and dust, an uneasy chill left from colder days.

"Come on in," said Aunt Germaine. "I've told you, it is safe. There are no dead in here."

Germaine struck a match and set it to lamp wick. It illuminated her face for an instant before she moved away, scraped a chair across the floor and set down.

"Start a fire in the stove," she said, "and I shall make some tea."

Jason stepped around the counter. "Are we staying here?"

"Until there is more of a melt on the road," said Germaine, "yes, I believe so. It's all right. The clerk here went to his own bed before he passed. And there's a fine store of tinned food I found last time I tarried. Come. Bring my bag. I will busy myself with my own work."

Jason hefted her bag onto a clear space on the desk, which was otherwise covered in a stack of leather-bound ledgers.

"Thank you, Jason," she said, and dug into the bag until she found a long wooden box. She set it in front of her, turned a latch and pulled from it a neat drawer, with white paper cards lined up. Then she opened a ledger, and, noticing that Jason was still watching her, repeated: "Thank you. Now start the fire. When it is going, we shall find some tea—and perhaps something to eat."

§

A meal of tinned ham and pears in his belly, teacup only half-drunk beside him, Jason slept for he didn't know how long next to the roaring fire he'd stoked in the wood stove. When he woke, it was darker than before—the lamp was doused and somewhere in the Cracked Wheel Town Office, he could hear Aunt Germaine's rhythmic snores.

God, he must have been tired. Thinking through how the last day had gone, Jason could see how he'd get that way. It was amazing that he hadn't burned the whole town down, starting the stove fire, like he'd burned down his mama's homestead.

He got up and stretched. His eyes were accustomed to the dark, and he could see Germaine stretched out on a wooden bench on the customer side of the counter. It was hard to tell for sure, but he thought she had the Winchester cradled in her arms.

Jason looked over to the last place she'd been—the desk, next to the ledger. That had been something else he'd wanted to ask her about—exactly what it was she was doing there.

But every time he tried, she'd tell him to go do something else for her until he got so tired he fell asleep. Aunt Germaine was no fool, that was true.

Well, he thought, *now the tables are turned, Aunty. Can't fib when you're asleep. Let's see what you been up to.*

He didn't want to wake her, so Jason took some care. He lifted the ledgers off the table, and set them on the floor behind the counter. Then he did the same thing with her box of cards—which was still unlatched and open. And finally, when all that was in place, he took the lamp, and a box of matches, and with them crouched down behind the counter, next to the book and the box, and started checking through it.

He looked at the ledgers first. They were pretty easy. Stamped on the front were the words "Births & Deaths," and inside were lists of names, set down by the year and the month and finally the day. They listed parents in some cases. Further along the page, there was sometimes another date—sometimes not. It wasn't hard to figure it out: the first date was a birthday; the second, the date of dying. The earliest date for either, Jason saw, was 1844, which was, he suspected, the year that some fool settler had broken his wagon wheel and given the town its name. Subsequent years took up more pages, and as it moved on through boom and back to bust, far fewer. 1892 through '95 all fit onto one page, with two or three lines to spare.

Jason couldn't resist what came next: he flipped through to 1897, and the month of January. Sure enough, there was his name: *Jason John Thistledown.*

Next to it: *John & Ellen Thistledown*. He thought seeing that would make him smile, but it turned out looking at his mama's name written like that in some stranger's hand had the opposite effect, so he closed the book.

He turned to Aunt Germaine's box and those cards. On the front of it there was a simple gilded engraving:

ERO

And underneath that:

Cold Spring Harbor

Jason pulled out a card and squinted at the tiny handwritten notes on it. The card was harder to figure than the ledger.

It had a name on it too—FLANNIGAN, Anne—and there was a number (1892) that might have been a birth date. There was a place name too: *Indianapolis, Indiana*. But the top of it was a line of nothing but numbers. Then there was a space, and a percentage:

43 %

Underneath that, there was a word that Jason had never seen before. He sounded it out in a whisper:

"E-pie-lep-see."

Jason shrugged, and slipped the card back into the box.

A bundle of them after that came from Indianapolis. More names, more numbers. He saw that *Epilepsy* word after only a few of them. On other cards, new words replaced it: *Consanguineous*; *Degenerate*; *Feebleminded*. Then he was past the Indianapolis cards, and onto a new locale:

Ossining, New York—Sing Sing.

The numbers were the same length, but the names seemed to be all of men. And the words that came after were more recognizable:

Thief. Rapist. And *Habitual Criminal.*

"Murderer."

Jason nearly knocked over the lamp, catching it and steadying it as he turned.

Aunt Germaine leaned on the counter, rifle laid across it. She was not wearing her glasses, and the lamplight made her eyes tiny pits of fury; her mouth worked like an air-drowned trout as she stammered, and finally, shouted:

"*Murderer*! You would kill me! Me!"

Jason swallowed and stood, and Aunt Germaine recoiled from him, as though he were some bandit. "Away!" she cried. "Away!" She pushed herself back against the bench where she'd been sleeping, and cowered like a child just woke from a nightmare.

And why shouldn't she have nightmares? Jason's mama would wake from them often enough, and she hadn't seen half the horror that her sister had, here in this town. . . .

Jason stepped up to his side of the counter.

"I'm sorry, Aunt Germaine," he said softly. "Calm yourself. I was lookin' in your bag. Just started—having a look at those cards you got. I'm not aimin' to kill you. Hush."

Germaine drew a breath at that, and squinted at Jason. "You were looking at . . . the cards. From the top of the bag?"

"That's right," said Jason. "I'm sure sorry. I should have asked—"

"Yes, you should have."

"I'm sorry, Aunt Germaine," he said. "I guess—"

"You were curious," finished Germaine. She reached down and found her eyeglasses, and set them on her nose. She drew a deep breath. "That is only natural for a boy awake in the night in a place such as this. *Curiosity*. Better, I suppose, that you satisfy it going through *my private things* than rooting through the charnel house over in the saloon. Well, Jason, tell me: is everything clear to you now?"

Jason had to admit that nothing was any clearer now that he'd snooped through Aunt Germaine's things, and said he was sorry once more.

"Perhaps," she continued, "you have a question then? Something that you might have asked me earlier, as we ate the dinner I prepared for you? Drank the tea I brewed for you?" Jason felt his face flush with shame. Any questions he had, and there were more than a few, got buried in that shame. Aunt Germaine's lips pursed, and she nodded as though he had confirmed something.

"Let me hazard a question for myself then. 'What, oh dear Aunt Germaine, ever are you doing for the Eugenics Records Office?'"

Aunt Germaine didn't say any more that night. She was clearly upset at her nephew for invading her things like that, so ordered Jason back to sleep while she carefully replaced the box into her bag, and moved it next to her.

But they were there for days after, and she soon forgot her anger—her strange night terror—and set about answering her own question.

§

When Aunt Germaine was quite a bit younger and Mr. Frost was still of this world, she took a hungry interest in the foundling science of biology—"Like medicine," she said, "but with an interest in all living things."

"I thought you were a doctor, or a nurse or some such thing, all you know about germs," said Jason. "Didn't you say you were a nurse?"

"We are getting ahead of ourselves," said Germaine.

Mr. Frost was a doting husband and so indulged his wife's passion as much as his pocketbook would permit. He purchased her a microscope and kit for making slides—allowing her to view the most minute specks of life—and a small library of volumes which included: Herbert Spencer's *Social Statistics*; Charles Darwin's *The Origin of Species*; and of course, Charles Galton's seminal tome *Inquiries into Human Faculty and Development*.

"What about *Bulfinch's Mythology*?"

"That is not a biology book," said Aunt Germaine.

In addition to her reading and her microscopy, Mr. Frost's fortune enabled Aunt Germaine to attend summer lectures at the Brooklyn Institute of Arts and Sciences in New York. That was where she first heard Dr. Charles Davenport speak.

"Looking at him, one could see the divinely inspired brilliance," said Aunt Germaine. A native New Yorker who had completed his studies at Harvard University, Charles Davenport was engaged with the Institute at their biological research station at Cold Spring Harbor in Long Island. He was a tall man, stooped, in his early middle years then but with a goatee going to white on a chin and an expression of sheer intellectual vigour in his eye.

"Sheer intellectual vigour," repeated Jason. "Now what's that look like?"

"Studious. Serious," said Aunt Germaine.

Charles Davenport was a zoologist—which is to say that he studied the ins and outs of the animal kingdom. The first lectures that Aunt Germaine encountered were discussions of studies he had made of lower life forms such as he might dredge from the harbour: pill bugs and molluscs and primitive fish.

It was clear to Aunt Germaine, however, that he was most interested in the study and improvement of the kingdom's greatest achievement.

"What was that?" asked Jason.

"Man," said Aunt Germaine.

Dr. Davenport even then had very clear ideas about the way that man might be bettered. In the course of his lecture, Aunt Germaine recalled, he stopped and asked the room:

"Why do we study these lowly, wet creatures? These things that cling to the bottom of rocks and suck up algae? Is it because we have a direct application for them in our lives? Surely not. Then why?"

Aunt Germaine's hand shot up, and when he called upon her, she answered: "Toward the betterment of all mankind?"

"Excellent, Madame," said the doctor. "Precisely. For we are all made from the same protoplasm. And in understanding these creatures—how they live and eat and, forgive me Madame, how they breed—we can better understand how we might live, might eat, might breed. To our race's betterment, of course."

This occasioned, said Aunt Germaine, some controversy in the lecture hall, as some wondered whether the doctor was comparing humanity to common garden slugs by some blasphemous design. But Dr. Davenport was not deterred.

"Our ignorance," he said, "is appalling, when it comes to the understanding of the effect of interbreeding on the races and the children they beget. And the consequences might be severe, should we not move swiftly to eradicate that ignorance."

Jason wasn't sure that he would have been any less put off than the others who were there. "I know I ain't a garden slug," he said. "Or descended from one either."

"Do not be so certain, Jason."

"And what did he mean about interbreeding?" asked Jason. "What consequences are those?"

Aunt Germaine sat back.

"You and your mother raised swine," she said. "Perhaps I can explain it that way. How is it that you get a prize pig? Do you pray for one? Do you purchase two inferior pigs and mate them? No. You feed and keep a good sow. And from time to time you bring in a prize boar."

"If there's one around," said Jason.

"All right," said Aunt Germaine. "If there's one around. If there is not—and you mate your beautiful sow with some—oh, some stringy, undersized, sickly little pig . . . what sort of offspring would you expect?"

"Not so fine," he said. "I expect."

"There is a saying that Dr. Davenport coined some time after that. Breed a white woman with a Negro—the baby's a Negro. A German with an Italian: Italian. A white fellow with an Indian squaw?"

Jason guessed: "A baby squaw?"

Aunt Germaine clapped.

"You mean to tell me Dr. Davenport was talking about breeding people the way farmers breed pigs."

Aunt Germaine beamed. "It is a science," she said. "A new science."

"A new science." Jason shook his head. "That's something."

"Do you know what it's called?"

He shrugged. "Breeding, I guess."

"It is called that. But there is a better word."

Aunt Germaine leaned forward, her hand on Jason's arm.

"Eugenics," she said. Her eyebrows sprang up over the top of her glasses for an instant, and she smiled. "Eugenics, Nephew."

"And now there's a Eugenics Records Office," said Jason. "I guess it caught on."

The ERO as Aunt Germaine called it had started up officially in the last year. But it had been a dream of Dr. Davenport's for more than ten years.

"Dr. Davenport contacted me *personally*," said Aunt Germaine, "to join his crusade."

"Crusade?"

"A figure of speech. Call it a mission. The mission, then, of the ERO was to compile an immense list—of every man, woman and child in America. Divided, of course, into segments."

"Segments."

"Of the population. Am I speaking too scientifically for you to follow, Jason?"

"I'm following." Jason took a sip of coffee. "Dr. Davenport contacted you to help him make this list with segments and all."

"Very good. Last year, he engaged a number of very proficient researchers— nurses, biologists, breeders, and so on—to travel out to the far corners of this nation, and compile this list. We all gathered at Cold Spring Harbor. We learned how to gather the information so as to be most useful to the enterprise. And then, one by one, we set out."

"To Sing Sing?"

"Among other places, but yes. Sing Sing and prisons and hospitals are places that we have visited. It is particularly important to understand the scope of the criminal and the infirm, after all. For those—illness and stupidity and criminality—are among the things we hope to one day eradicate."

"I thought you were eradicating ignorance."

"Do not be disrespectful, Nephew."

"I'm sorry, Aunt."

That box of cards contained Aunt Germaine's contribution to Dr. Davenport's bold enterprise. The numbers—fully eleven digits long—were each one of them different from the next, and matched up with particular folks. The descriptions underneath (*Habitual Criminal*, *Rapist* and so on) were indications of what was wrong with them.

The percentage numbers said how good that person was overall. One of the things that the ERO was on the lookout for, said Germaine, was all the people that fell into the very lowest percentage. Jason couldn't figure that.

"Why not look for the highest percentage?" he asked, and Aunt Germaine nodded and smiled at that.

"Why not indeed?" she said, and went back to work, entering the names and ages of the poor people of Cracked Wheel. They weren't exactly murderers or habitual criminals or sufferers of epilepsy, but they weren't the top of the percent either. They couldn't have been that special. The germ had killed them all.

§

Jason only ever saw one of them before he and Aunt Germaine finally left Cracked Wheel. Several times he had nearly summoned the will to enter the saloon, and see what Aunt Germaine meant when she called it a charnel house. But each time he turned away—hands stuffed in his pockets or in fists at his hips—fear inhabiting his gut like a ball of raw dough—and stomped, defeated, through the ever-muddier street back to the town office.

It was finally in the Dempsey store that he confronted the dead of Cracked Wheel. It was only one of them, but one was enough.

Jason went into the store as prepared as he could be. He wore one of Aunt Germaine's handkerchiefs over his face, and he'd dipped it in the juice from a jar of pickled onion (which she had said would help kill the smell). To make sure he didn't stumble over anything in the dark, he carried the kerosene lamp in one hand. And so he wouldn't have to make more trips than one, he carried a big sack in the other. He was on an errand for a few items that, as Aunt Germaine put it, they could not do without.

First, they needed more food and ammunition. It was going to be a week's journey anyhow to Helena and the rail station and they couldn't make it on what supplies they'd found in the town office.

And second, Jason needed a decent suit of clothes. If he were going to get on a train with Aunt Germaine, he could not be wearing his mama's home-sewn duds. Jason, having proved his own immunity to the germ, was the one who would have to go inside.

"It is possible that the store is as safe as the town office. I simply cannot say for certain because I have not been inside," his aunt said.

So under a crisp blue sky, hands full and shaking, Jason made his way across the muddy road and to the store. The shades were open, but the awning cast a shadow to make it entirely black within. So Jason stopped to light the lamp and then pulled open the door. He wondered as he entered if this would be enough to put "Thief" next to his name on the card that Aunt Germaine wrote for him. The sign on the door said "Open"—and that, he thought, should count for something.

Jason glanced back to where Germaine stood at the stoop of the town office, wringing her gloves nervously. *"Courage,"* she mouthed at him. Then Jason stepped into the dark.

The pickle juice helped mask it, but the minute he crossed the threshold Jason could tell he was not alone in the store. The smell reminded him of his mama at the end, only sweeter, if sweet could make a fellow upchuck his breakfast.

Jason's inclination was to stop breathing it, so he stood there still for a moment, breath caught in his throat. He held the lantern high and surveyed the room.

The Dempsey store was pretty big, with a ceiling maybe a dozen feet up and shelves running all the way up every wall. Free-standing shelves held blankets and clothing and made a dark little alcove in the back. And there was a long counter with a box for money and a little balance scale on it for folks that still

46

liked to pay with metals. Jason could see everywhere but behind the counter and in that little cubbyhole in the back—and there were no bodies he could see. He worried about those other spots, though: behind the counter, behind the shelves. Anything could be in there, and he didn't think it would be anything he wanted to see.

His lungs were burning, so he took a big gulping breath and that set him coughing—the air from the pickle juice stung fierce, and the smell was only worse for gulping it in. *All right*, Jason thought, *no point dawdling*. He set to work.

He got to the clothes and food cans first. Both were in the open, although he had to use the stepladder to get at a shirt and an overcoat that would fit him properly, they were so high up. He found himself a pair of new boots too—they were rawhide, but stained dark and etched with a swirling design, and were marked to cost three dollars. He also took a couple of blankets, because who knew what they'd need on the trail, and a folded sheet of canvas that he figured he could make into a tent if they needed it. He spent some time checking out the different cans of food and ended up taking a lot more than they needed.

Finally, there was nothing for it. He had to get ammunition: a box of cartridges for the Winchester, another box of bullets for Aunt Germaine's revolver. And all of that was behind the counter.

Before he went, he took the sack and set it by the front doors. Then he got hold of the kerosene lamp, and made his way around the counter.

It was a bad enough sight there that Jason pulled down his mask and let go some breakfast.

When he was done, he didn't bother putting the mask back up. He didn't think the pickle juice would help him a bit, faced as he was with the befouled remains of a fellow Jason was pretty sure used to be Lionel Dempsey.

He guessed that more because of the clothes than anything else. The body still had its apron on, and the white shirt with the arm-bands on it. The little shopkeeper's visor still dangled over the slick forehead. The body was sprawled along the floor. One hand held the leg of a wooden stool in a very determined grip, and Jason could imagine what had happened: Lionel had been sitting on his stool, waiting for a customer an afternoon back in February when none were coming. A spell came over him. He got dizzy enough that he fell off, and knocked the stool too. And thinking that it was just a little dizzy spell, he got the idea he could grab the stool, right it and use it to pull himself back up. And he got as far as grabbing it before he got too sick to move.

Because he didn't have a boy or girl to watch over him, he would have died there of thirst and fever. And then because there was no one to do anything else, he stayed there on the floor of his general store, smelling up a bit until the fire in his stove went out, then freezing, and then, in the last couple days as the thaw came, thawing out himself.

Which point, the creatures got at him.

His face was a dark colour, and bits of the flesh were gone, revealing stuff of a blacker hue still underneath. One eyeball was mostly gone too, and the other stared up lidless and dried. To account for all that, Jason suspected mice or something like them had got at him, gnawing little holes in the half-froze flesh and feasting on the eyeball that was gone. And lately, judging from the things that moved where his lips drew from his teeth, and in that one empty eye socket, the maggots had hatched.

Jason wiped his mouth with the vinegary face mask and bent closer to look.

It was a funny thing: now that he'd seen what happened to Mr. Dempsey, the fear that'd possessed him evaporated, and he was just sad. Looking at Mr. Dempsey like this made him compare with the memories he'd had of him alive. And because all those memories included his mama, it made Jason think of her again. He wondered how it could be, that folks like his mama and Mr. Dempsey could be taken down by something so little like a germ. Aunt Germaine seemed to think she had the answers to that in her little file box—those eleven numbers and the percentage of how fit they were.

Jason could see how a fellow like Lionel Dempsey might fall based upon those numbers. He was always skinny and pale, and his chin didn't come out more than halfway as far as his top teeth. And he was getting on past forty and hadn't lifted much beyond his stock of cans and foodstuff and hardware in many years, and probably he drank too much over at the saloon which made him weaker still. But Jason Thistledown's mama was strong and fit and beautiful. And she did beget Jason, who was strong enough to not be bothered a bit by the germ that came across the land. That had to count for something in Aunt Germaine's eugenical numbers. It should have meant Jason's mama could stand up to anything, at least as much as Jason could.

And yet, the only difference between her and slow old Mr. Dempsey now was a lick of flame.

Jason shook his head. Before he could upchuck again, he went to the ammunition shelf and got what he came for: plenty of bullets and a good knife besides.

§

Outside, Germaine was nowhere to be seen. The only sign she'd been there was a couple of steaming tubs of water, set out next to one another on the wooden sidewalk.

She reappeared when Jason was in the bigger one, dutifully scrubbing the germy dirt off his winter-white skin.

"Take your time," she said. "We won't leave for Helena 'til morning."

"Where we goin' then, Aunt? Somewhere by train?"

She looked to the west, shading her eyes with her hands and peering hard, as though looking at some distant oceanic horizon.

"Idaho," she said. "The mill town of Eliada, at the very north end of the State of Idaho. We . . . I've an appointment there, one of which I am well overdue in the keeping."

"We going to set a fire on the way out?"

Aunt Germaine looked at him. The sun reflected from her glasses and made it hard for him to look back.

"To clean the place up," said Jason when she didn't answer him. "Get rid of all the germs. Like we did the homestead."

"Nephew," she said, "they *hang* arsonists."

Jason opened his mouth to argue. He wanted to ask her why she hadn't thought of that when they cremated his mama and everything she'd made, just to start. But he recalled his aunt's madness that first night; something in the set of her mouth this day told him not to bother.

"Eliada it is, then," was all he said.

"What is Eliada?

"Well, let us take its measure.

"A thousand or more acres of woodland and scrub, stretching from the banks of the fast River Kootenai to the foothills of the Selkirk Mountains. The soil is rocky and saturated with acids from the needles of the pine trees that have taken hold up the banks. It is a hard ride, two days to the north of Bonner's Ferry if the weather is fair, which is a rarity. It is inhabited sparsely; the children of settlers who'd lost their way seventy years ago—some prospectors who strayed south, fifty years past. Indians pass through it, as Indians do. But Eliada is on the path to oblivion.

"It is, one might say, forsaken.

"Yet, gentlemen, that is not the truth of Eliada. The truth I might only describe using the language of poets.

"Eliada is the majesty of a sunrise, spreading gold across the white water of the Kootenai River. It is clear birdsong. Rising mist. The jumping of river trout. The roar of the grizzly.

"Eliada does not give quarter. It demands, rather, that we rise to its challenge.

"I challenge any of you to make the journey, arduous though it may be, and inhale the clean air from the mountains, look upon their great granite faces, implacable as the gods themselves—and find fault with the conclusion that I drew, when I dismounted my steed, and wiped the sweat dewed upon my brow, and beheld it all in breathless wonderment.

"Gentlemen, I concluded thus:

"If we are to make our Utopian dreams a reality any place in Nature's realm—we could do worse than drain our purses carving it from this stern Paradise."

—From an Account Given of Mr. Garrison Harper, in His Address to the Philadelphia Race Betterment Society, July 19, 1904

4

Utopia's Daughter

The first time that Jason Thistledown encountered Ruth Harper, he did not learn her name and had no reason to believe he ever would.

He spied her as he and Aunt Germaine boarded the train at Helena, and she, a passenger from further east accompanied by an only slightly older chaperone, was taking a stroll along the vast station platform before the train debarked. Jason could not help but stare, and later, as the train crossed a deep gorge but an hour to the west of Helena, Aunt Germaine told him that he would have to learn to be more circumspect when be-spying young ladies in public places. "One does not gawk," she said. "It is a sign of bad breeding. And it offends."

"Then how come she smiled like that?" Jason had been gawking hard he figured, because although he was now looking out the window at a true spectacle of God's handiwork—down what seemed like a mile to a fast silver river wending serpentine through tree and rock—the view was eclipsed by his memory of the girl: the light brown curls of hair that peeked out from beneath her wide hat the colour of fresh cream, her greenish-blue eyes that glanced between her soft hands and Jason's own hungry eye, and the smooth red lips that touched up to a smile at one corner only, near a place where a tiny dark birthmark marred her otherwise unblemished cheek.

"She was being well-mannered," said Aunt Germaine. "That was all. There is a tolerant streak in these modern young girls that sometimes expresses itself in what may seem like licentiousness. Do not take too much from it."

Jason leaned back on his seat. He supposed he shouldn't be thinking about young ladies now anyway. Never mind Aunt Germaine's views; Jason's mama always advised nothing good came of licentiousness, and she was still not dead more than two months. Any of her advice he could still remember, Jason figured he'd better heed.

He thought he might pay particular attention to what little of that advice still applied as he drew far from the homestead and Cracked Wheel. Sure, his mama knew how to strike a camp and had some wisdom that Jason could apply to that. She knew how to talk to strange fellows who might or might not want something that you didn't want to give up.

But if she ever knew how to do up a man's cravat, she'd never let on; if she ever said how to negotiate price for a room in a hotel for a boy and his aunt coming late and on foot, she said so too quiet for Jason to hear; and as for counting up money bigger than dimes—well, she didn't have much to say on that ever. It was a good thing for Aunt Germaine, who was wiser in the ways of the roads and towns on the way to civilization. Yes, it was a good thing for Aunt Germaine.

"I'm going to stretch my legs," Jason said and when Aunt Germaine asked why, he fibbed: "I'm not used to sitting so long. My feet are falling asleep."

As he made his way down the aisle, Jason considered the odd mix of guilt and triumph now welling in his middle. His mama was right saying it: no good ever came of licentiousness.

§

Jason searched the train in a way that he hoped was at once thorough and nonchalant. But it was all in vain; Jason did not find Ruth Harper anywhere.

Much later, he would learn that she had spent most of the journey in her berth in the sleeper car, re-reading her favourite chapters in *The Virginian*, while her ostensible chaperone, Miss Louise Butler of Evanston, Illinois, napped and knitted and gazed longingly out the glass at the passing mountains.

They were in a part of the train where a boy like Jason had no reason to linger. Both times he passed through, he was hurried on his way by the glares, silences, and noisily cleared throats of his betters. He and Aunt Germaine were billeted in another car, further to the front where the beds were stacked like shelves on either side and sectioned off by thick, stale-smelling curtains. As far as Jason knew, the lovely girl with the birthmark and the little smile that stopped just beneath it had jumped off the train some time ago, and fled on foot into the Montana wilderness, never to be seen again.

It disappointed him, but not bitterly. In the course of his search Jason was able to observe a great many things about the train, the railway and the people who travelled by it.

Jason figured this would be something his mama would have approved of more than hunting a pretty smile on a locomotive. It would, after all, lead him to self-sufficiency.

Coming upon civilization as he had, all at once through the haze of grief, after spending his short life on a Montana pig farm, and with no one but a new-found aunt to guide him, Jason Thistledown was a boy in need of bearings. Nothing made that clearer to him than the fascinating, loud and stinking machinery of the Pacific Northwest steam engine and the cars it hauled. The thing's engine made a noise like thunder that didn't ever stop, and threw out fat clouds of black coal-soot as evil as anything Jason had ever smelled. The locomotive, as Aunt Germaine called it, scared hell out of Jason and he knew he'd have to conquer that fear (along with the fear brought on by all those strangers in their suits and skirts and high leather boots, and their peculiar expressions) if he were ever going to have a life beyond Cracked Wheel.

When he got back to Aunt Germaine, she looked right at him.

"Are your legs well-stretched?" she asked, and Jason looked away for only an instant before he told her they were, which was at least true.

§

The train pulled in to Sand Point two days later. They debarked, but not because that was the end of their trip. As Aunt Germaine explained it, they would next take a short line ride to a place called Bonner's Ferry, where they would be met by a man from Eliada who would take them the rest of the way by barge and horseback, down the Kootenai River to the town.

As they debarked and waited for the short line train, Jason happened to spot Ruth Harper for the second time.

This time, he tried to be mindful of Aunt Germaine's advice and his mama's wisdom, and made an effort not to gawk.

It was quite an effort. Jason felt his heart thundering in his chest, and a profound quaking in his stomach, and those parts along with every other part of him seemed to be hollering: *There she is! Look over there, you damn fool! Perhaps she's smiling!*

Once or twice—for an instant each time—he obeyed, glancing down the platform, under the overhang where all the passengers gathered against the cold spring rain, to be-spy her sitting on the bench next to her chaperone, reading from a book in her lap. She would stir, he imagined, feeling the heat of his look even though she didn't look up to meet it—just smiling a little more each time.

Later, Jason would learn that he was off the mark but not entirely. For while it was true that his gaze drew notice, it was not from Ruth Harper, but Miss Louise Butler, who sat near to her friend but beyond the scope of Jason's attention. At only his second glance, she whispered to Ruth:

"We have an admirer."

"Do we?"

Miss Butler's hands remained folded in her lap, but she nonetheless motioned in Jason's direction, with progressively indelicate thrusts of her right forefinger. In spite of this, Ruth did not look up from her book. She did, however, smile a little.

"Is it one of those filthy loggers?"

"He might be. How does one tell a filthy logger from a smooth-faced young man who obviously does not know how to dress himself?"

Ruth sighed. "Is he looking now?" she asked, and when Miss Butler said he wasn't, Ruth spared her a sidelong stare of withering significance. "Well?"

"There." Miss Butler pointed.

"Oh," she said, glancing quickly and then returning her eyes to her book. Her smile was noticeably wider this time than the last.

"*Him.*"

§

The train to Bonner's Ferry was not so luxurious as the one from Helena. It was mostly hauling freight, and the single passenger car was old and cheap, with hard wooden benches instead of cushioned seats, and boot-worn slats on the floor in place of the deep red carpeting of the Pullman cars of the Pacific Northwest.

The passengers seemed generally suited to the humbler appointments. They were almost all men—unshaven, uncouth and probably unbathed fellows of the sort that Jason would watch close if he encountered them with his mama at his side. More than one of them sent leering glances in the direction of Misses Harper and Butler, who this time did not have the luxury of their own car. The men's obvious intentions vexed Jason.

Let them try something, he said to himself. As the train wound through the hills, he found his thoughts drifting back to those nights he spent guarding his mama, wondering about wolves and ammunition and such things as followed from those.

"You figure these fellows have numbers?" he asked an hour or so in.

"Numbers?" Aunt Germaine blinked. "Oh. ERO numbers. It is possible, but unlikely. We have not been at this long enough yet. If any of them had been in prison, or hospitalized . . ."

"I bet a few of them have been in prison," said Jason, and Aunt Germaine chuckled into her handkerchief.

"No doubt," she said. "But please keep your voice down, Nephew. If you are correct, we don't wish to provoke an incident."

Jason sat quiet and tried as best he might to look beyond the window. The land here was not dissimilar to that around his mama's old homestead: low foothills covered thick in pine trees, little tongues of lakes with rocky beaches, but mostly—trees.

For parts of the trip, those trees would draw in on the train, so all you could see going past was greenery and the shadows beyond. Then they would open up, and the green would spread out forever, crawling up the sides of far mountains strange to Jason's eye. Jason understood Bonner's Ferry to be a mill town like Eliada, only one that had been there longer. He figured towns like that would do well up here for a long time, all those trees they had to chew on.

"Is there a prison up in Eliada?" he asked.

"No," said Aunt Germaine. "They don't have a great many prisons up this way, I shouldn't think. What's in Eliada is perhaps even less common."

"Well, Aunt?" said Jason, after a long moment watching her stare out the window, not telling him what was less common. "Are you going to tell me what?"

She smiled. "Here comes the town," she said, as the train whistle hooted. The view out the window went dark then as the wind blew the smoke from the engine down and they started a slow turn. "Get ready for a boat ride, Nephew."

Jason found that he liked Bonner's Ferry, and he was disappointed it was only a way station. It smelled like sap and sawdust and wood smoke, and was dominated by a towering sawmill on a river that was all but covered in floating tree trunks. It was raining quite hard under a rolling dark sky as they got off the train, but that didn't stop the men in this town from going about the hard business of logging and lumber-milling. There was an air of industry here, unlike any he'd seen in Helena or Sand Point—or especially, in those days when its inhabitants still drew breath, Cracked Wheel. Perhaps, he thought, Eliada will be the same as Bonner's Ferry.

"Where do we go?"

Germaine pointed. "With that fellow."

Jason looked. There was a moustachioed man in a black coat and a bowler hat standing very straight at the far end of the platform. He held an umbrella in one hand and a sign in the other, which had painted on it neatly "Eliada."

"Oh," said Jason as Aunt Germaine waved.

As the fellow drew closer, Jason saw that he had more umbrellas rolled up under his arm: four of them altogether. He juggled the sign into the crook of his arm, pulled out two umbrellas and handed one to Aunt Germaine and one to Jason. Then he tipped his hat. "Sam Green," he said.

Aunt Germaine introduced herself and Jason, at the same time as she expertly popped open the umbrella and swung it over her head. Jason watched to see how she'd done it, but she was too fast for him to see exactly, so he had to fiddle with his. He did not get far, though. Sam Green reached down and found the catch, and a second later Jason was dry under his own black dome, still not sure of the trick to it.

"How soon may we be off?" asked Aunt Germaine.

"Presently," said Sam Green. "Mr. Harper's new boat is waiting at dock. But I must first gather the rest of our party."

"The rest of our party?"

Sam Green tipped his hat once more. "Please stay here, Ma'am. I shall return." And he strode off toward the train.

"So there's a boat waiting for us? A new one?" said Jason. He set Aunt Germaine's carpet bag down. "I thought it would be a barge. Maybe that is what it is and Mr. Green simply misstated."

Aunt Germaine smiled. "Mr. Harper is a wealthy man—becoming wealthier by the day. If he has a new boat, it will be a fine one. It was not so long ago that a trip to Eliada meant a long and hazardous march or a horseback ride through wilderness. Not now, though. It seems that Mr. Harper's investments are paying off, and civilization draws northward."

"Who is Mr. Harper, anyhow? Aside from a rich man getting richer."

"Garrison Harper?" Aunt Germaine began. "Why—"

"Why, he is my father."

Jason turned. He found himself staring into a smile that was all too familiar.

The girl it belonged to curtsied, her own black umbrella tilting to one side and a wash of rainwater splashing off it.

And that was when Jason Thistledown learned the thing he thought he never would.

"I am Ruth Harper," said the girl. "May I introduce my companion, Miss Louise Butler of Evanston, Illinois." The other lady—a little taller, with darker hair, a longer forehead and thin, half-smiling lips—likewise curtsied. "Pleased to make your acquaintance," she said.

Ruth Harper glanced behind her, where Sam Green was supervising two porters who were each hauling a large steamer trunk. "Mr. Green informs me that we will all be travelling together—" and she turned back to Jason, her smile fading and her eye catching his directly "—for a short while longer."

Jason nodded and blinked. Aunt Germaine smiled.

"He is cross with us," she continued. "Mr. Green is, I should say—because we dismissed his associate in Chicago. Vulgar man. He smelled so. I believe—" she leaned forward and whispered to Aunt Germaine: "—he *drank*."

"Ruth!" said Miss Butler.

"Mr. Green will overcome it," said Ruth. "We are after all here in one piece. Two pieces." Then she turned and looked at Jason in a direct and discomforting way.

"Well?" she said at length. "I believe, sir, that you have the advantage."

"Thank you, Miss Harper," Jason managed at last. "But I don't see it that way at all."

Ruth Harper's laughter was the prettiest sound that Jason had ever heard. He did not know how he felt about having it directed his way, but he sure did like how it fell on his ears. So he grinned and joined in.

"I am Germaine Frost," said Aunt Germaine when they had quieted down. "This is my nephew."

"Jason Thistledown," said Jason.

"Really," said Ruth. "*Thistledown*."

Her smile faded, and was replaced by a look that Jason had not seen on her before: an eyebrow arched a hair higher than its twin, and her mouth half open, a fold of her lower lip pinched gently in her teeth.

Days ahead, when he had composed himself and knew her a little better, he would learn what that look signified.

Miss Harper's considerable store of curiosity was mightily piqued.

§

Jason found the Harper steamboat not so very impressive. Not more than fifty feet long, it had a shape that reminded Jason of a shoe. The boat was a side-wheeler, with a tall, fluted smokestack coming out the middle, a wheel on either side to propel it, and an interior that was mostly filled with barrels and crates and sacks. It was called *The Eliada*, which, while not imaginative, at least hit the point. Its skipper could take a wrong turn or even two, and it would not stay lost for long before someone read the bow and sent it on its right way home.

Sam Green collected the umbrellas as they stepped on board, then cleared off a bench for them that allowed them to look out the side of the boat without getting rained on.

"It'll be a few hours," he said. "The river gets rough in spots as a matter of course, and the weather today is not ideal for it."

Aunt Germaine smiled in a kindly way. "It is preferable to the alternative—riding horseback through Indian country."

"Oh," said Ruth, "I don't know about that. I always enjoyed the trek. Particularly the horses. And the Indians—the Kootenays—oh, they were never any trouble. Mr. Green and his people were always most helpful in that regard."

"I am just as happy," said Miss Butler. "Indians terrify me."

"There is no reason they should," said Ruth. "Not these days."

"Most of 'em are over in Montana now anyhow," said Jason. The two women looked at him, and he shrugged. "Government set up a big reserve for Kootenays last year. I expect they're all of them headed over there by now. 'Twas all the talk of Cracked Wheel."

Miss Butler giggled. "Cracked Wheel? What sort of name is that?"

"Name of my home town, miss," said Jason. "It is not very large, I guess. Or it *was* not," he added.

"Was?" Ruth looked at him. "Mr.—Thistledown. You speak of your town with the weight of the world on you. Is there something the matter?"

Aunt Germaine caught his eye and gave him a warning glare, but that wasn't what shut Jason up on the subject. He didn't want to stray back to Cracked Wheel, didn't want to pick at the scab forming over his grief. He'd misspoke, he saw, naming it at all.

So all he said was: "Sorry I brought it up. No. Nothing's the matter."

Had Ruth Harper known Jason a little better, she might have known to leave it lie, let him to himself for a few minutes. As it stood, her curiosity got the better of her, and she persisted.

"You," she said, turning a third toward him on the bench, "have a secret, Mr. Thistledown. Is it, I wonder, a secret connected to your infamous surname?"

"My infamous surname?"

"I am sure," said Aunt Germaine, intervening, "that he is unrelated to that scoundrel."

"Well, Madame," said Ruth, "as his aunt, you ought to know. Still—" she turned to Jason "—those are, as they say, 'mighty big shoes to fill.'"

"Ruth!" said Miss Butler, but Ruth rolled her eyes. She looked at Jason, and pointed with her index finger. "Bang!" she said, and giggled.

Jason felt his hands squeezing into fists. He pushed them between his knees, and took a breath.

"Miss Harper," he said. "I must apologize but I cannot make head nor tail of what you are saying."

Miss Butler was trying not to laugh herself by now. "You are not alone, Mr. Thistledown. She has, I daresay, read altogether too many dime novels for her own good. And your name—"

"What about my name?" said Jason.

"You mean to say you don't know?" said Ruth, having composed herself. "Never mind having not heard of the man—it beggars the imagination to conceive that no one would have suggested to you the similarity of your own name to that of Jack Thistledown's."

Jason thought that he might have enjoyed studying Miss Ruth Harper from afar a little longer. He did not like this sort of conversation.

"Oh come," said Ruth. "Jack Thistledown—hero of the Incorporation Wars. Killed a dozen men fighting against Granville Stewart and his vigilantes, over the cattle ranges of south Montana. One of three men to walk away from the shootout at Snake River. Does that not jog your memory?"

"My pa's name was John," said Jason.

"Jack is another name for John."

Jason sighed. This would come up from time to time in Cracked Wheel, when fellows were passing through town and overheard someone calling his name in the store. Jason said now the same thing he'd said then.

"I didn't know him too well. But he was no good."

"The same might be said of Jack Thistledown," said Ruth. "Well—this *is* exciting. The son of a famous gunfighter—right here on this boat! I feel I ought to be swooning."

"Ruth!" said Miss Butler, and this time Sam Green intervened too.

"Leave the boy be, Miss Harper," he said. "It's his own business who his pa is."

This seemed to make an impression on Ruth where her old friend Louise Butler could not. Her face took a more sympathetic cast.

"Of course it is," she said. "And look—my questions have made you positively crimson! Oh, I must apologize, Mr. Thistledown. As my dear Louise attests, I am quite mad for the dime novels. And here on my way to a summer at Utopian Eliada . . . Well. I am too hungry for intrigue and so invent it where there is none to be found. Can you forgive me?"

Jason had not been aware that he was crimson. He was not sure he liked having it pointed out. "I can," he said.

They sat quiet for awhile, watching the shore of the Kootenai River transform from docks to tilled field to wilderness. After a moment, Aunt Germaine excused herself to freshen up. As she did so, Jason caught Ruth looking to him again. This time she looked away quickly, and Jason was fine with that. Let *her* turn all crimson for a change.

"What'd your pa buy this boat for?" asked Jason as they drew around a bend and the river stretched wide before them. "If I am not prying in asking."

Ruth didn't look over when she answered, and she spoke in a cool tone. "I suppose that he told the investors it was to haul his brailles of logs and lumber back to Bonner's Ferry more efficiently. When he invested in the town, Father had hoped that the markets downriver in Canada might take an interest in Eliada wood; and he has always hoped that the Great Northern Railway might finally complete a line south through the town. Given that they have not . . ." She spread her hands to indicate the whole of *The Eliada* ". . . *voila!*"

"*Voila.* That's what he told his investors," said Jason. "You suppose."

Now she did smile. "Yes. But you didn't ask the proper question."

"And what is that?"

"Why, given everything, did not my Father acquire his steamboat much sooner?" She did not wait for him to ask it. "That would be because it is only now that Father feels his grand project is enough of a success to let the world in."

Louise Butler pursed her lips and shook her head. "Really," she said.

"No," said Ruth. "It is true. The fact of the matter is that until now, dear Father could not be certain that regular traffic through his community might not pollute it. Why—if the land were not so well-prepared, venal men might arrive and bring with them their terrible vices! Things such as cards—hard liquor—low women—"

"Ruth!"

She waved away her friend's objections without even looking at her.

"—and worst of all: dancing!"

Jason laughed and shook his head. He didn't have much experience with young women, and at first Ruth had sure thrown him. But it was like learning a fancy a dance step, talking with her. And he thought he was beginning to get the rhythm of her humour.

"Sounds like your pa has some definite ideas," he said.

"Oh, only good ideas. Resolutely, unwaveringly *good* ones. For the betterment of all mankind."

"That so," said Jason. "Then he and my aunt have something in common. Hello, Aunt Germaine."

Germaine took her seat beside Jason and straightened her skirts as Ruth Harper went on.

"For instance: do you know that Eliada, which has just a few hundred men and their families living and working there, boasts its own hospital?"

"That," said Jason, "I did know as a matter of fact."

"Well. Here is something that you do not know. Any man or woman needing a doctor's attention may receive it free of payment. At first, the hospital was only for those men who worked directly for my father, cutting trees or milling them. But in the past year, why—anyone in need is seen to. There are doctors and a surgery and many clean white rooms. And it is not even affiliated with a church! But financed from Father's own purse!"

"Fancy that," said Jason.

"My father is very enlightened. You need only ask him. Or failing that, his investors back in the east. They will tell you he is enlightened to a fault."

"Providing free doctoring for folks that need it? There's not much fault in that."

"Except," said Ruth, "when commerce is involved. Father says that by doing this, he is forestalling any of the ugly labour conflicts that beset so many of his competitors. The others are not so convinced."

Sam Green shook his head, which caught Ruth's attention.

"Why, just ask Mr. Green," she said. "He supervises the Pinkerton men who keep the peace in Eliada. Not that they have much to do. Father does frown on violence so, and the men who work for him are not at all prone to it. Tell him, Mr. Green: all is well in fair Eliada, now and forever, and never must you so much as raise a fist to keep it so."

Sam Green made a fist and cleared his throat into it. "Miss Harper," he said, looking at them from under his bowler hat, "talk like that is a good way to make the Devil laugh."

Ruth stifled a laugh herself.

"What are you saying, Mr. Green?"

"Only that things are not so peaceful as you might think."

Ruth frowned. "Pray tell—?"

Sam Green gave a long sigh. "I am in dutch with your father, I fear."

"Oh no! Why is that? Tell us your tale."

"Well. I suppose that you will like the story better than him," said Sam Green. "Just two days ago I shot three men, me and my fellows did—men dressed in sheets, in the manner of the Ku Klux Klan."

"They were not merely impersonating spectres? To cause you and your men to take a fright?"

"Ruth, this sounds to be serious," scolded Miss Butler.

Green shook his head. "They were readying to string up a nigg—a Negro."

"A Negro." Ruth's eyebrows raised. "Do we have any of those?"

"Yeah," said Sam Green. "One, anyhow. He's a doctor, too. Saved him. That's why your father hasn't run me and the Pinkertons out of town yet. The saving balanced the killing. But I'm not sure that is going to do the town much good. Dr. Waggoner's going to make trouble in Eliada. Once he gets to his feet, he's going to make trouble."

Ruth smiled radiantly. "Splendid!" she said. "Trouble in Paradise! Made by a Negro doctor hired by Father! And Mr. Thistledown, who is *not* a famous gunfighter's son, here to witness it all with us! See, Louise? This will not be a wasted summer after all."

Louise blushed and looked to her lap. Jason felt the crimson coming on as well. He looked to the riverbank, which was devoid of any sign of human touch. They were in wilderness altogether.

And the further they got, the more came Ruth Harper into her element.

Jason wished he could say the same for himself. He found himself wishing again that they'd stayed put in Bonner's Ferry. Klansmen and Negroes and gunplay: Eliada sounded like more of Cracked Wheel again, in its own particular way, and Jason was not sure he was ready for that.

§

Eliada came upon them late in the day. The rains had stopped, and the cloud was beginning to clear as they rounded the bend in the river that hid Mr. Harper's grand town.

It was not a peaceful arrival. The river ran fast at the bend, and *The Eliada* rode it hard. They had been through a few of the Kootenai's rapids by then so Jason was more used to it, but he still hung on tight as the boat pitched side to side, veering through white foam and close past shallow rocks.

He was not alone; even Ruth Harper, who was so clever and brave, so up for trouble at the start of a dull summer, sat clutching the edge of her seat as the water sprayed up high alongside and the beams of the boat complained.

"Huzzah," she exclaimed weakly when the river deepened and the boat became more steady. "Are we home now? We are!"

Sure enough, there it was—contained as it was in a tantalizingly brief glimpse: a collection of rooftops and chimneys that peeked between a now much-thinner growth of trees lining the bank. The boat turned then and Eliada's rooftops swung from view, so Jason made his way to the bow, and up a steep stair he'd found earlier. That stair took him to the top deck where the pilot worked his craft and he could get a look.

The early evening sun showed the town to good effect. It was built on a flat stretch of river valley so behind it, the hill and forest rose to a chain of peaks that were not quite high enough for snow and bare rock. Crawling up those slopes, Jason could make out plots that had been cleared for agriculture—even what looked like some young orchards, their little trees all planted in tidy rows. Closer, the gold light caught taller wooden buildings like the ones in Cracked Wheel—general stores and hotels and such. There were more of them, though. There were even a couple of whitewashed church steeples, climbing a bit higher than the roofs of the businesses.

They were all made insignificant by the sawmill. Near the water at the north end of town, the mill dominated all. It was not as high as that in Bonner's Ferry.

But it was high enough; and it sprawled all the way down to the water and its own set of docks—off which floated a wide crescent of logs, crossing all but a narrow channel of the river and chained in against its fast current.

"That will be all our travelling for a time, Nephew."

Jason turned to see Aunt Germaine climbing out the hatch to join him. He reached down to help her. Her hand was icy cold.

"It sure is a pretty little town," said Jason, "although I wouldn't call it Paradise like Miss Harper seems to think."

Aunt Germaine shook her head. "She is a horrible girl."

"She is all right."

"No. There was no need to press you on that ridiculous legend."

Jason shrugged.

"The legend of your father, I mean," said Aunt Germaine.

"My father's no legend," said Jason. "A name's a name. But my pa was no good. Simple as that."

"Well," said Aunt Germaine, "now that we're here, you shan't have to consort with Miss Harper any longer. Our business is with Dr. Bergstrom. Hers—well, girls like that do not have any business with serious folk. She is but a silly . . ."

She stopped then, perhaps noting that Jason had some time ago stopped paying any attention. He was listening to something else. Something that carried across the water with a strange and compelling urgency.

"Jason? Nephew?"

"What's that birdsong?" he asked her. "Sounds like a fellow whistling who forgot the tune."

5

Baby Wakes

The whistling carried like a scream across the fields—it passed across the land like a wave of wind through long grasses, from the base of fresh-planted crop, through gaps in the roofs of barns, and finally, into the crook of some tree roots at the very base of the Selkirk Mountains—where it paused.

That crook had been home to all sorts of creatures—some squirrels, one time a fox and, as evidenced by the sneers of half-collapsed holes, an entire brood of rabbits. Centipedes too. They had all come and gone, though. All but the centipedes.

Right now, the baby lived there.

If it were in the habit of naming things, the baby would not have picked "baby" for itself. It was, in fact, feeling pretty grown-up, inasmuch as its limited experience would allow. Not long ago, it had separated itself from the parent and its servile brood. In so doing, it finished dealing with a good many of its contemporary siblings, who were all of them nearly as tough and determined as it was. The cuts were healing, and the teeth and nails it had lost in that struggle were coming back in.

Pretty soon, it figured it would be walking upright again, marking its territory—making its own brood. It was getting a coalescing sense of just how grand it could become as it curled there in the crook, munching on bugs and watching the world turn. The last thing the baby wanted to hear right now was that whistling. It wanted no part of the things that whistling told it to do.

It wanted no part of it; but neither could it refuse the call.

So it rolled itself over, gathered its legs underneath it, and crawled outside. The ground was wet. It stank. There was no shelter, there was no clue here as to how one might find the bugs and grubs to which it had grown accustomed. Like all babies, this one was fundamentally selfish, and placed a high value on comfort and a full belly.

But the baby didn't have much say in the matter. The instruction spoke to something fundamental in it, below and beyond even its own unkind nature. And so: as the whistling scream had told it to do, the baby drew air in through its orifices, opened its tiny mouth, and repeated, as best it could, the message that had carried itself this far.

Help, it whistled.

Come, it screamed.

And finally:

Pass it on.

6

The Feeger Girls

There was singing on the shore to send the Devil when the call came upon the Feegers of Trout Lake.

It was the three Feeger girls, Missy and Lily and Patricia doing the singing. They stood in a circle, up to their bare ankles in the freezing water of the mountain lake, naked flesh creeping in the cold, heads turned high in the joy of their praising song. One time it had had words, but in the care of the girls those words had melted off and it was all melody and harmony and some splashing when Patricia, the eldest, set to stomping to bring their rhythm back in time.

Day was finished—the sun long disappeared behind the bare peak of the Far Mountain, while before it the water glowed in the light of a splintered moon. All was still but for the ripples that Patricia's foot sent to Trout Lake's heart and all was quiet but for the sweet voices of the Feeger girls singing their song, when the call came wafting up the hill. Patricia let the song go on for what her grandmother might've called a couple of verses before she lifted her foot and pointed the toe so water drizzled from it, straight as a line of piss.

Her sisters took the cue; Missy gasped and looked from one side to the other; Lily, three seasons older, shut her eyes and listened, sniffed. And Patricia held her stork pose, one foot drying in the night air, and paid heed to the call.

"Help," she said.

"Come," whispered Lily beside her.

By the time Missy shouted "Pass it on!" Patricia was already splashing again. She splashed four more times until the water was deep enough that she could bend forward, put her arms out in front of her, and ducking her head into the icy water for just a moment, flutter her feet behind her.

Patricia moved out bravely and purposefully; she would not let her sisters see anything but confidence. Yet inside, Patricia was filled up with a sharp, delicious fear. She had done this swim before, but never by herself—always bringing Offering. She supposed that was what she was doing now, bringing praise that had come across the land, but as their mother had told them many times: the Old Man hungers for our Love. Praise is fine—but it is not the same as Love and if you do not bring it to Him, why, He may just take it and then some.

Was she bringing her Love now? She would say so to anyone who might ask—yet to herself, here in the cold lake? Truly?

But as she swam, she knew one thing: she could not do anything but what she was doing now. She carried with her as much Love as there was. There were not many Feegers here to love the Old Man—not since the sickness had come upon them all a year ago. How many had they covered in stones, when they'd fallen down all poxy and coughing?

How many were gone? Patricia was not much for counting past fingers and toes. It would be easier to count the ones left—for there were not many of those—scarcely enough to portion out their Love to the Old Man, whose hunger for it was swelling like waters behind a beaver dam.

Some nights, it was all they could do to make it up the ridge and sing the Old Man to sleep.

And now—was she prepared to look upon him? With Love?

Hesitation grew in her mind, fear expanded in her middle, the further she went; but when she finally paused, it was not to turn back. It was because she had arrived. The Father was near. She shivered at what felt like a branch brush against her ankle, another thing caress her hip.

Patricia lifted her head from the water, let her feet fall below her, and gulped the lake air. The moonlight was dim, and not much good even to her night-accustomed eyes. She could make out the sky, its canopy of stars—and she could tell the line where the sky met the mountaintops. She could feel the water moving about her, the Old Man's will working on it.

She drew a shaking breath, and closed her eyes and pursed her lips. She did not so much recite the call as she allowed it to pass through her.

And as she did, the fear slaked away. For in her halting whistles, the simple message she conveyed, was a kind of peace. It felt like forgiveness. She was in the Old Man's hands, telling Him a message from His own child, the prodigal—a message that He was happy or at least anxious to hear. She looked at the sky, at the dark mountain, and even as the line between the two grew jagged, spires like tree trunks emerging from the lake around her and blocking off the stars, as more branches, more vines seemed to wrap her middle, she thought only of Love.

When the water fell away from her sides and she felt herself lifting over the lake, her naked flesh shivering beneath the ancient gaze in the now-encompassing shadow, she thought: *There is no need to take that Love.*

I give it. And there is plenty.

7

The Hippocratic Oath

"Tell me about Mister Juke," were not the very first words Andrew Waggoner spoke after the morphine haze passed. Those were French, almost certainly profane, and in their particulars a complete mystery to the nurses who tended the doctor as he returned to himself. But if "Tell me about Mister Juke" were not his first words, they were the first ones suitable for polite company; the first ones that got any kind of answer.

Andrew was dozing in the mid-morning when the door opened and Dr. Nils Bergstrom stepped through, alone. Dr. Bergstrom was an exceedingly thin man, and recently so. When Andrew had arrived in the autumn, Bergstrom carried his weight around his belly, and his blond-frosting-to-white mutton-chop sideburns drew attention to thick jowls. He'd undergone some sort of a regime over the winter—although what, Andrew couldn't say, for he always seemed to be eating—and now the sideburns hung like drapes. He stole close to Andrew's bedside and bent down toward his face.

Andrew opened his eyes.

"Tell me about Mister Juke," he said.

Dr. Bergstrom did nothing more than blink, twice, to indicate his surprise. He stood straight, crossed his arms and smiled.

"You don't want to know how you are doing first?"

Andrew looked down at his legs, lifted each one a few inches and flexed the fingers of both his hands. One of those hands was at the end of an arm splinted to above the elbow, and moving it hurt like a knife-twist.

"Looks like I'm all here," he said. "It's pretty sore."

"I can give you another shot, if you like."

"Morphine? No thank you." Andrew knew what morphine did for men, and he knew what it did to them. On balance, he disliked it. "Thank you for offering." He sighed.

Dr. Bergstrom harrumphed. "You are welcome, Doctor. Now—as to your health: although you did not think to ask, I will tell you."

"Thank you again."

"You have injuries of the ligaments in your left hip and knee. Bruising and strain is what it amounts to, but I do not recommend you attempt to walk on it for at least a few days—preferably longer. Doing so will change your mind on morphine."

"I'll take that under advisement."

Dr. Bergstrom gave him a stern look. "I am concerned about your kidneys and bowel so will be watching your emissions in that regard. You have taken a blow to your skull which is not as bad as it might have been; you have avoided serious concussion. But the coincident cuts necessitated a good deal of stitch-work. As is the case with your lower extremities, it is only a matter of time and you should be as fine as you were before the . . . attack. The more serious injury is there." He indicated Andrew's right arm—the arm with the splint.

"The bone was broken near the elbow. And that," he said, "will prove a problem. You will not be able to perform surgery for some months. And I cannot say how well you will rehabilitate."

Andrew let that sink in. He knew enough how easily bones could set wrong, to know that Dr. Bergstrom was if anything understating the troubles he might face.

"That could bar me from the surgery," he said quietly. "For good. That's what you're saying."

Bergstrom shrugged. "Or it could heal well. Your hands are undamaged, and that is good. As to how your arm progresses: that is up to you. You and God."

"I guess I'm not going to be much use to you this season," said Andrew. *I guess that's what you're saying in your way*, he added to himself.

Dr. Bergstrom had never been what Andrew would have called a strong advocate. Andrew came here on the recommendation of Dr. Albert Mercer in New York, who had reviewed his credentials on behalf of Garrison Harper. He and Dr. Bergstrom had met face to face only after Mr. Harper had hired him. Andrew suspected that if left to his own devices, Bergstrom would prefer a white doctor to assist here in Eliada, one taught in Germany like himself.

"You are correct on that count." Bergstrom looked down at a board on his lap and cleared his throat. "Andrew—I am profoundly sorry for what happened to you out there. I saw with my own eyes what those hooligans did in the hospital. As to your experience . . . My God, I can only imagine."

"It was no pleasure," said Andrew. "But I am alive, sir. And that is more than I dared hope."

"Quite."

"Now," said Andrew. "I repeat my question: what can you tell me about Mister Juke? How are his injuries?"

"Minor," said Dr. Bergstrom. "He is recovering well."

Andrew drew a breath.

"I understand that he was a patient in the quarantine. But I knew nothing of his arrival or his treatments there. Was I misled?"

Dr. Bergstrom did not answer him immediately. He stood up and went to the window and drew the curtain aside a few inches. He squinted outside.

"You were misled. But only through omission. The patient is something of . . . a project of mine. Can you understand that?"

"So far as you have just explained. But there are questions. This Mister Juke—"

"Please. Do not call him that. It's offensive."

"That's not his name?"

"No. That is what some of the others who work here named him. Mister *Juke*." Dr. Bergstrom spat the words. "As though he is some *degenerate*."

"Degenerate?" Andrew blinked. "Oh," he said. "He's named for the Jukes. *Those* Jukes."

Dr. Bergstrom smiled. "You are familiar with Richard Dugdale's book? I'd not think one such as you would find time for that sort of reading."

"By one such as me I suppose you mean 'Negro,' and by 'that sort of reading' I am guessing you mean eugenics." Andrew chuckled. "Dr. Bergstrom, if we all only read what sat easily with us, how would we advance? I read his book—what was it? *The Jukes*: something-or-other."

"*A Study in Crime, Pauperism, Disease and Heredity*," said Dr. Bergstrom.

"I read it on the ship back from France. I was inclined to toss it into the Atlantic. The notion of a family of congenital criminals struck me as—"

"Dangerous?"

"Improbable. Fanciful. Is this poor fellow thought to be a Juke?"

Dr. Bergstrom shook his head. "No. I am certain he is not. What he is, is a poor man beset by idiocy and infirmity. And certain—irregularities in his anatomy."

"Irregularities?"

Dr. Bergstrom ignored him. "He was brought here in the winter, found wandering in the cold. I—I took him in. But I felt it was best that he remain in the quarantine, until I knew more about him. Others here—well, it became something of a joke. At the poor patient's expense; eventually, I suppose, at nearly the cost of his life. And yours. He's no Juke, though. Whatever that is. That I can say for certain."

"I would not worry about his infirmities," said Andrew. "He had a queer look about him. But I saw that fellow survive a hanging."

"Did you?" Dr. Bergstrom tucked his clipboard under his arm, dropped his hands into his coat pockets. He regarded Andrew quietly.

"I saw it."

"I shouldn't worry," said Dr. Bergstrom, "about things that you think you saw at the hanging tree. The patient suffered some injuries about his neck. But obviously, the hooligans did not have the opportunity to tighten the noose much before Mr. Green and his men came upon you."

"I—"

"You are mistaken, Andrew."

"I think I am not," said Andrew, adding pointedly: "*Dr. Bergstrom*." White men had too easy a time addressing him by his Christian name; Nils Bergstrom was not the first. But Andrew was not going to let it pass.

Dr. Bergstrom cleared his throat. "Well the important element is that the patient survived. As did you. That is more than we can say for Maryanne Leonard, though. Isn't it?"

Andrew didn't answer that one.

"Oh, I am not accusing you of anything," said Bergstrom. "Do not fear that, Dr. Waggoner. You had jotted a theory in your notes, that someone had attempted—how shall we say it—kitchen table surgery on the girl?"

"A home abortion," said Andrew. "That was my diagnosis. Someone had taken a knife, or a hook, or something like it, and used it to scrape her uterus. In so doing, they had—torn her. Punctured her abdomen."

"Did she tell you this? Before she succumbed?"

"No. She wasn't coherent. But you must have examined the body by now. You can't dispute—"

"I have seen her," Dr. Bergstrom blinked rapidly as he spoke. "And before you work yourself to an upset, know that I don't entirely disagree with your diagnosis."

Dr. Bergstrom took the clipboard from beneath his arm and flipped through pages until he came upon the one that evidently held his notes.

"If you are correct, however, this was an abortion like none other I have seen. I examined her last evening, before the rigor mortis had entirely set in. And yes, I noted the laceration. Or eruption, as it might better be described."

"Eruption?"

"Yes. Whatever made that incision did so with great and deliberate force," said Dr. Bergstrom. "Tell me, Doctor—have you ever performed an abortion?"

"That," said Andrew carefully, "would violate our Hippocratic Oath."

Dr. Bergstrom smiled. "That wasn't what I asked. But inasmuch as you've raised it: the oath we all took prohibits a great many things—including, you may recall, the application of the knife. Now I have seen you violate that stricture many times. So tell me, Dr. Waggoner, honestly. Have you ever violated the other one?"

Andrew sighed. "Not often," he said. "But yes. As the need's arisen."

"We are fast in one another's company then," said Dr. Bergstrom. "I have practised in this part of the country many more years than you—in logging towns and mining towns and railway camps—and do not be shocked when I tell you that most of the women who arrive at a doctor's doorstep with child are neither fit nor inclined to bear it. Performing the procedure *as the need arose* has given me a somewhat wider experience than might be found in, say, New York. Or Paris."

"I see."

"Do you?" Colour was rising up the other man's neck. He snapped his board behind his back and turned abruptly. "If I may observe, Dr. Waggoner, the sheltered arrogance of the east coast is not confined to the white race."

Andrew let the words sit in the air a moment before he answered. "I'm not to judge," he said. "Better that you do it than someone like the one who took a hook to Maryanne Leonard."

"Quite."

Bergstrom swung his arms in front of him, as though summoning his own energy for a jump. "Well," he said, stepping toward the door, "I shall, I think, leave you to rest a time. I needn't say it, I hope, but you need not worry about either paying for the treatment you receive here, or the receipt of your pay over the time you remain."

"That I remain? Do you mean in this bed? Ah. You don't."

Bergstrom stopped, his hand on the doorknob. "No," he said. "I thought that we had come to an understanding. Once you're able to travel, you must go. Your not-inconsiderable skills are no longer required, and your injury prevents their application in any event. We will make arrangements for your return to your family in New York, where you can recuperate in relative safety. But you cannot remain here—not with the Ku Klux Klan at large. It is unsafe for everyone, as I am sure you'll agree."

And with that, Dr. Nils Bergstrom slid behind the door, pulled it shut behind him and left Andrew alone in his room.

§

The pain got worse as the day progressed. Several times, a nurse came with a tray offering a shot of morphine for it. But Andrew refused.

"You are only agonizing yourself," said the nurse. Her name was Annie Rowe. She was a tall, thick-faced woman who, Andrew had discovered, had trained in a hospital in St. Louis where she had for her own reasons not elected to remain. It had to have been her own choice: she was one of the better women who worked beds at Eliada, and she'd have excelled in any city hospital.

Andrew smiled. "Pain," he said, "is how the body communicates with the mind. Lets it know what it's up to. What its limits are. Why would I quiet all that good communication?"

Annie smiled. "Communicating's one thing. I can see by the sweat on your brow that it's past that and there's a lot of foolish shouting now. Come on, Doctor. Take a shot. You'll rest better."

"No, thank you," he said. "I had my fill of it last night. Although I don't recall asking for any."

"Oh," said Annie, "I know. I heard your views on it. Ears are burning red in Paris, I'll bet."

"Yes. Sorry about that."

Andrew chuckled and Annie laughed.

"I work in a logging town," she said. "I've heard worse. Here—won't you let me drug you, just a little? No? At least let me wipe your brow. Care for some water in a glass as well?"

"I surely would," said Andrew. Annie lifted the water jug and poured from it into his water glass. He took a sip then set it aside as Annie poured more water into a basin and dipped a cloth into it.

"Annie," he said, "mind if I ask you a question?"

"Not at all, Doctor."

"You ever see Mister Juke?"

She paused, the water dribbling from the cloth and rattling along the edge of the basin. "No," she said. "Quarantine is not on my rounds."

"But you knew about him."

"Sit back," said Annie. She brought the cloth to Andrew's forehead. It felt cool and good there as she dabbed it. "Yes," she said. "I knew they brought in a fellow. I heard some of the fellows start calling him that name."

"They brought him straight to the quarantine?"

"As far as I know."

"Now why do you think they would do that?"

"How do you mean, Doctor?"

"Why would they take a fellow straight to the quarantine? Was he contagious? Exhibiting symptoms?"

"I suppose he must have been." Annie dabbed the cloth down Andrew's cheek. "You could do with a shave," she commented.

"So no one told you what they thought he might have," said Andrew.

"Kept it pretty quiet," she said.

"I'll say they did," said Andrew. "All winter long, I didn't see anyone bring him in. Didn't see it, didn't hear about it."

"Well of course not," she said. "That fellow came in late last summer. He's been there the whole time."

"Since the summer?" Andrew shook his head. "And I didn't hear a word about it."

"Really." Annie stepped back, inspecting his face like it was a canvas and she'd finished painting it with water. "He would have been an interesting case for you—for any surgeon from Paris, I'd thought. What with his irregularities."

"That is the second time I've heard that word used when talking of this fellow. What are his irregularities?"

Annie reddened a little at that. "They are not widely—I mean to say—those of us who had a look at him when he came in—"

Andrew nodded encouragingly.

"Well. He is not entirely a . . . he."

Annie seemed literally about to entirely collapse into embarrassment, then remembered who she was and what she did—her profession—and cleared her throat, stood straighter.

"The word is hermaphrodite. Do I really need to go on?"

Andrew raised his eyebrows. "A person of both genders?"

Now Annie smiled a little. "I imagine you saw those sorts of folk all the time, studying in Paris."

"No, not really. I've read case studies, but that is as far as it went. Hermaphrodites are as unusual in France as they are in Idaho."

"Well you should have been able to have a look," she said. "It would have spared me recounting it. You must be in poorly with the management, for them not to've told you about it."

"I don't doubt it," said Andrew and threw Annie a grin. She grinned back, and told him to rest some more, then started getting ready to leave him for the night.

§

He could put as fine a face on it as he wanted to, but Annie Rowe was right. Andrew Waggoner was in poorly with the management; very poorly indeed. He was in so poorly he was fired—fired for upsetting Klansmen in a mill town, having done nothing worse than applying his meagre skills to a girl who needed more. Fired for hurting his elbow in the course of protecting himself from one of those Klansmen—for hurting it badly enough he might seriously not be able to operate again. Fired, at the core of it, because he was a Negro, who so far as the management was concerned did not belong here from the beginning, who was not fit to consult on the charity case in the quarantine.

Gloom fell on him like a wool blanket on a hot summer's day.

It wasn't, he brooded, as though no one had foreseen this sort of problem. His uncles had been deeply sceptical when Elmore Waggoner announced that he would be putting a year's profits in the Connecticut livery company he founded towards sending his oldest boy to France to study at the Paris School of Medicine. Andrew would not be the first or even the second Negro to lift a scalpel in the United States. But he would be consigned, they predicted, to ministering to the ill in Harlem or other similar neighbourhoods in big cities. To try and find a place in a surgery—a surgery where white men's wives and children might one day lie down under the scalpel—would be throwing good money away, they said. And not helping his boy a whit.

But Elmore was stubborn, and because he had some money he could put behind that stubbornness, he was able to send his boy on a boat to France, and welcome him back with a medical certificate from one of the finest schools of medicine in the world.

Who was right? As the sun climbed past the scope of his one window and the room fell into cool, grey shadow, Andrew thought it might be time to congratulate those sceptical uncles of his. Them, and Nurse Annie Rowe.

Andrew was ready to call for some morphine after all, when a knock came at his door, a face draped in shadow poked around the edge of it, and a familiar voice boomed out.

"Dr. Andrew Waggoner! Bless me, it is grand to find you well!"

When they first met in the autumn of '10, Garrison Harper had insisted that Andrew dine with him and his wife at the sprawling mansion he'd had built overlooking the town. That meal was sumptuous—roast beef in a thick burgundy sauce with good French wine, a sugar loaf soaked in rum, followed by Napoleon brandy in wide snifters and cigars imported from Cuba at the end of it. The meal he brought with him today was simpler: mashed potatoes, some greens from Mrs. Harper's garden and a breast of well-cooked chicken already cut into bite-sized chunks. He carried the plate in himself, withdrawing the silver cover with a flourish, then called out to the hallway when it developed that someone had forgotten to provide any silverware.

"We are," said Mr. Harper, "a hospital in an Idaho logging town, and not a fine restaurant in Boston. I must remind myself of this daily. Is there a chair in here?"

"Beside the bureau," said Andrew. "Thank you, Mr. Harper. This looks delicious."

Mr. Harper scooted the chair over beside Andrew's bed, and settled into it. Garrison Harper was not a fat man, not by any means. But he was tall—well over six feet—and he had complained to Andrew on that first night: "The years add weight to both the soul and the waist." The combined weight made the chair creak precipitously, and that and the memory made Andrew smile.

Mr. Harper was like that, always joking with the help. Andrew understood that behaviour to be an affectation—a rich man's hollow conscience at work. But his own father was the same way, walking through the stables and calling out the men who worked for him by name, sharing a joke or asking after their wives, acting like he was one of them. Andrew couldn't begrudge it.

"Go," said Mr. Harper, passing the fork from the nurse who brought it, to Andrew. "Eat a bit. You have to get your strength back."

Andrew ate. He was famished, but he restrained himself. If he took this too fast it would come up just as fast.

"I am ashamed," said Mr. Harper at length.

Andrew set down his fork.

"Sir, do not trouble yourself," he said. "I will find other work."

"What on earth are you talking about?" Harper gaped.

"Other work, sir. After I take my leave."

"Do you imagine I am here to—to *dismiss* you?"

"There is no need," said Andrew. "It is done."

Andrew explained what had transpired between himself and Dr. Bergstrom that morning. Mr. Harper listened quietly, and when it was done, he said simply, "No."

"Sir," said Andrew, "I am bound to remind you that with my right arm as it is, I will be of limited use in the surgery."

Mr. Harper blinked at him, as though this fact had been just presented him and somehow altered everything.

"My God, Dr. Waggoner, have I misread you? Do you wish to depart Eliada? I would not blame you if it were the case."

Andrew knew there was a part of him for whom that was the case. But it was only a small part—the part of him that had been afraid of leaving his father's home for continental Europe, the part of him that would have settled for clinic work in Harlem rather than take a train to the wilderness of northern Idaho. And that part had not had much say in how Andrew lived his life for many years.

"I would be a fool not to fear the noose," he said. "But I have not offered my resignation either."

"I'm glad," said Mr. Harper. "It is too easy for civilized men to turn away when faced with depravity. When I said earlier that I was ashamed, it is to that which I referred. When I came here those seven years past, to carve this town out of the hills, I did not intend to make just another haven for depravity. When I made the decision to hire a Negro physician to tend to people, it was not to bring him to slaughter. And although I am well glad to see you here and alive, I did not intend to taint Eliada's soil with the blood of my workers."

Mr. Harper looked at Andrew expectantly. He'd delivered the whole speech in the manner of exactly that: a speech, written and well-rehearsed as for a university pageant, or from the stump in an election. This was a thing that Garrison Harper had done more than once since they had met. That first night over cigars and brandy, he had held forth uninterrupted for nearly three-quarters of an hour on his plans to create a paradise for workers and owners alike in Eliada: a community devoid of strife and class warfare where men happily lifted their tools at sunrise and set them down again at sunset, not once tempted by Bolshevism or bad morals—and on and on. It was a rich man's habit, not, in this instance, shared by Andrew's father. Of course, Andrew's father was new to the game of wealth, and so did not have the generations of breeding that had so infected the talk of the Harper men.

"You didn't tie the rope," said Andrew.

"No," said Mr. Harper, "but I might as well have loaded and aimed the guns. Why did I agree to have the Pinkertons of all people come here? This is not how I imagined my legacy."

"They're hard men, no doubt of that. And they left three would-be murderers dead, without trial. But if they hadn't been there, it would have been two innocent men dead." Andrew took a breath. "I'd like to thank Mr. Green and his men for their aid."

"For that," said Mr. Harper, "you'll have to wait. I sent Mr. Green away." He looked at Andrew, and noting something in his expression, hastily added, "I didn't dismiss him. He's off to Bonner's Ferry. To collect my daughter and her friend, along with some visitors that Dr. Bergstrom is entertaining. Have you met Ruth?" Andrew reminded him that he had arrived in the autumn, some time after Miss Harper had departed for school. "Well. She's a wonder. When you're able, you must join us. Perhaps we'll have our spring picnic soon, if the weather holds—in the orchards."

"That would be fine," said Andrew. It was good, if baffling, to see this rich white man talk so easily about introducing him to his daughter. "I would enjoy that, thank you."

"Excellent." Mr. Harper clapped his hands onto his knees and started to rise. "Have you finished your supper? No? I will leave it. Is there anything else you need?"

"One thing," he said. "Have you looked in on the patient?"

"The patient?"

"The one some fellows here call Mister Juke. Your men rescued him along with myself."

"Oh," he said. "No. I haven't."

"He has been here some time, I understand," said Andrew. Harper stood hands in his pockets, no longer meeting Andrew's eye.

"Yes. Dr. Bergstrom has been most *charitable* with that one." Mr. Harper shook his head, and smiled as though recalling a private joke. "One of the doctor's many admirable qualities. Qualities with which," he added, stepping toward the door, "you will have ample opportunity to acquaint yourself in the coming months and years. I am so glad you have elected to remain a part of our project. I will go see Dr. Bergstrom now, to make sure we are all of that same understanding."

"Thank you," said Andrew.

But Garrison Harper had already fled the room. Pondering the speed of his departure, Andrew wondered, did Harper know about Juke's irregularities?

He took another bite of chicken and as he chewed, he reflected on that and other matters arising from their visit. He was glad enough to be still employed. But he was confounded by the deepening mystery of this strange creature that could survive a hanging. A hanging that some men in sheets thought due him, on account of the alleged rape of Maryanne Leonard. What, Andrew wondered, was the precise nature of the patient Mister Juke?

Ask Dr. Bergstrom, Sam Green had told him. *Never mind*, Dr. Bergstrom had told him. And as for Garrison Harper? The man, with whom all responsibility in Eliada ultimately rested, was too spooked to say anything at all. Andrew set his fork down and pushed the dining table aside.

It was a mystery, there in that quarantine. He could not let go of it.

Andrew Waggoner winced as he swung his feet over the side of the bed. When he settled his weight on them, he wanted to scream. But he held it in, for nearly a minute, before he flopped back onto the bed, bathed in new sweat and breathing in hitching gasps. Pain was a message from the body to the mind—a message that a fellow failed to heed at his peril. Andrew knew this.

But Andrew also knew that if he was smart about it and had a good enough reason, a fellow could ignore pain all the same. It was just, thought Andrew as he gasped air and felt the tears welling out, a matter of will.

8

The Lesson of Minos

The hospital at Eliada was busiest Mondays, but as Sam Green pointed out, it stood to be busy any day the mill was running and men were engaged in the dangerous profession of sawing up trees for lumber. Tonight was Tuesday, and the Pinkerton man would not offer any guarantees.

"Mondays are bad because men are coming off their weekend drunks," said Sam Green. "But it doesn't matter. Drunk or sober, they cut their hands and break their bones, and sometimes a chain will snap and a log will swing and one or the other or both will catch a man in the skull. There are saws and axes and mallets, swinging and sawing all the time, and not always true—and if one of those does not get him, why, you put enough men in a room doing nothing but twiddling their thumbs and sipping tea, and even here in this perfect world, before too long one of them's bound to fall down with a bad appendix or a kidney stone or some awful tumour."

Or, thought Jason Thistledown, the whole room of them could drop dead from a strange disease, like Cracked Wheel did in the winter. Would this place, this hospital, have helped out any? If he'd been able to bring his mama here, would that have made a difference?

"Thank you, Mr. Green," said Aunt Germaine.

The three of them stood in front of Eliada's hospital in the deepening twilight. The building was a simple, rectangular box, made of white-painted wood and climbing fully three storeys tall. It was back some distance from the dock area (where a few moments earlier they'd bid fare-thee-well to Ruth Harper and Louise Butler) on what Jason figured was the very south edge of town. The land right around it had been cleared but it backed on thick, shadowy forest.

"What I mean to say, ma'am, is that you may not be able to see Dr. Bergstrom for some time. He may be occupied. If you like, I could send for a boxed meal."

"Don't be vulgar," said Aunt Germaine. "We won't be filling our faces in a waiting room, while others before us suffer."

Sam smiled and shrugged. "As you please, ma'am," he said to Aunt Germaine. He tipped his hat first to her and then Jason. "Will you be all right with that bag, Mr. Thistledown?"

"I expect."

"Then, I shall take my leave of you. Welcome to Eliada."

"Good night, Mr. Green," said Aunt Germaine, and Jason repeated it. Then the two of them headed up the walk to the wide front doors to Eliada's hospital.

Carved into their frame were the words:

Compassion. Community. Hygiene.

"That's Eliada's motto," said Aunt Germaine, and Jason said, "Sounds like a fine one to me."

§

The entry hall to the hospital was not the pandemonium that Sam Green had led Jason to expect. It was a large room, bigger than the town hall at Cracked Wheel by about half, with benches along the walls. The tall windows had their curtains drawn, and the only light came from kerosene lamps set into little brass wall sconces. Aside from Jason and his aunt, there were perhaps a half-dozen other people there: a band of men huddled together on a bench and talking quietly. One, a young man not much older than Jason, looked hard pressed. Jason didn't have to count on his fingers to put it together: someone had died or was dying—a person who was kin to the poor fellow. He knew how that felt, and from seeing himself in the glass those weeks alone in the cabin, he knew how it looked too.

At the other end of the room, next to another set of doors, was a long dark wood counter. Aunt Germaine went there, and pressed down on a little silver bell. Jason set the carpet bag and his own sack down beside Aunt Germaine, excused himself politely and made his way back to the bench. He wasn't intending to eavesdrop, but that wasn't clear to the group of men and the preacher he supposed, the way they shut right up and gave him a look as he went to sit down.

"Pardon me," he said, and skidded farther down the bench until they judged him enough past earshot to start up talking again.

Jason didn't hold it against them; after all, he'd damn near shot his Aunt Germaine in the back, just for looking at his mama's corpse the wrong way. Sadness had a way of changing the rules.

Up at the counter, Aunt Germaine was talking to a woman wearing some kind of uniform. Jason had never seen a bona fide nurse before but he expected that was what this woman was. She wore a white smock and a sort of frilly white cap that held most of her hair in. Jason started to get up as the nurse, nodding, backed through the swinging double doors. Aunt Germaine turned to Jason with a look that was, if he were to be honest about it, more than a little bit smug.

"It is as I said," she said. "We were expected, and Dr. Bergstrom will see us presently."

"Well good," said Jason. "Why don't we sit a spell. But—" he leaned to Aunt Germaine "—not next to those fellows. Let's give them their room."

§

"It is," said the doctor, "a boy."

The sad-looking fellow on the bench stood up and hooted, and the doctor, wearing a white smock, long black rubber gloves and a facecloth dangling by the strings around his neck, strode across the waiting room to clap him on the shoulder.

"Congratulations, Albert," he said. "Baby and mother are fine and resting."

"That is Dr. Bergstrom," said Aunt Germaine.

"And that's a new father. I sure figured him wrong."

Germaine shrugged. "I would have made the same guess, had I not known Dr. Bergstrom as I do. Hospitals are places for the dying and the sick, hmm? Not babies."

Dr. Bergstrom let the other men shake his hand and nodded and smiled at their thanks, before he extricated himself. Dr. Bergstrom looked over to Jason and Aunt Germaine. He was a tall fellow, tall and lean, and he stood to his full height and huffed, as though he'd just finished some heavy lifting.

"Mrs. Frost!" he exclaimed. "Welcome to Eliada—at last!"

Aunt Germaine got to her feet, and Dr. Bergstrom beckoned her over. "Come, we will go to my office where it is a bit more private." And then he looked to Jason.

"And this is—?"

"Forgive me," said Aunt Germaine. "He is my nephew, Jason."

"Your—nephew." An odd expression fled like cloud-shade across the doctor's eyes. "I wasn't aware you had a *nephew*."

"Well, I do. This is he. Say hello to the doctor, Jason."

"Pleased to make your acquaintance, sir," said Jason.

"Hmm. Likewise." Then, to Germaine: "He's a strong lad, Mrs. Frost. Surely he did not travel all the way from Philadelphia with you."

"No. We met along the way. He has experienced a family tragedy."

"I see. My condolences, young man." Dr. Bergstrom turned back to Aunt Germaine. "How is our Dr. Davenport keeping?"

As she explained, Dr. Bergstrom led them back through the doors, along a wide hallway and up a flight of stairs. As they moved deeper, Dr. Bergstrom motioned to various rooms off the hallway: Obstetrics, Surgery, Recovery.

There were laboratories on the second floor, along with a library, and that was where Dr. Bergstrom kept his offices and some spare rooms for visiting doctors.

"You can use these rooms for your work," he said. "There are cots there, and you and young Jason can stay there tonight. Until you find more suitable accommodation in town."

"That will be excellent," said Aunt Germaine.

"But first, I am curious," he said as they stopped outside his own office, and he dug around in his pocket for a little silver key to open it. "What is the manner of the tragedy that befell young Jason's family?" He looked to Jason and Germaine with eyebrows raised, then opened the office.

Aunt Germaine opened her mouth, blinked, and then did something of which Jason did not think her capable: she stammered.

"He—it was—well, it was an illness, Doctor."

"Was it? Was it that—"

"It was that grave," Aunt Germaine interrupted. "Yes."

"Mrs. Frost, we ought to speak privately," said Dr. Bergstrom. "Jason, could you wait in the examination room?" He pointed to a set of double doors across the hall.

Jason didn't say anything, just nodded. There was something passing between the two adults—something that went back a long time, and started, he figured, in a place that was no good. He was not about to step into the midst of it, not without knowing a bit more. Waiting in the hall would be fine.

Dr. Bergstrom beckoned Aunt Germaine into the office and she followed, shoulders slumped a little. The door swung shut, and the latch clicked. Jason stood alone in the hallway.

Mama in Heaven, he thought, *what has your sister got herself into?*

§

Jason felt ashamed at even considering it, but he did it anyway—pressed his ear against the door to see if he could make out anything about the conversation that would explain things. It wasn't a good plan. The doors were thick at the Eliada hospital, and even holding his breath and sitting still, he could only figure so much of their talk.

There was anger on both sides of the conversation. Some words repeated themselves: "female" was one, most often from the doctor's lips, and once or twice punctuated by a bang that Jason guessed might be an open hand on a tabletop. Another was "fool," and another "never" and a phrase that Germaine kept repeating: "had you been specific"—it all suggested a conversation going the wrong way for everyone. If it had been his mama in there, Jason might have just gone in. As it was—and as grateful as he was to his Aunt Germaine—Jason let her look after herself. He crossed the hall, and let himself into the examination room.

It was a big space. Everything—walls, floor, ceiling—was painted white, but the twilight admitted by two long skylights and a tall window at the far end made it purple as a fresh bruise. In the middle of the room was a sort of bed that was on iron stilts with wheels on the base; along one wall were glass-covered shelves filled with bottles and bright silver instruments next to a couple of big metal wardrobes, all behind a long wooden bench covered in strange, curving instruments of metal and glass such as Jason had never seen. There was a glass jar, filled with sliced, dried apples.

And along the other wall were shelves filled with books.

He had never seen so many, not in one place, and not all together. His mama had just a couple at the cabin—and that was only if you counted the Bible—and the Cracked Wheel Town Office had a few more. But there was nothing like this.

Jason walked along the rows. The books were about doctoring and medicine; he read titles like *General Surgical Pathology and Therapeutics*, *History of the German Universities*, and *Account of the Sore Throat Attended with Ulcers*.

His mama would have called this a treasure trove. For the first time in weeks, he let himself remember her.

There was that one night when he was very small for instance. It was autumn, he thought, because the wind was up and the fire was on, and the trees that had leaves in the summer were bare and rattling. All in all, things were what you might call foreboding around the Thistledown homestead, but his mama was of good cheer. If Jason remembered right, she had sold some pigs in Cracked Wheel for a better price than she expected, but it could have been another thing too.

But that was the night she'd cracked open *Bulfinch's Mythology*. The book came out of a chest that she had at the back of the house. She had kept it hidden there until this cold fall day when her mood was right and Jason was big enough, and she brought it out with a flourish.

It was a fine-looking book. The cover was like cloth, a deep red, and on it was a picture of a very strong man with his arms thrust in the air, a great curling beard pushing forward from his chin. The letters were solid gold, although they were chipping a bit here and there.

"Gold!" said Jason, pointing at the letters.

"It is a treasure, that's certain."

"We're rich!" he said, and his mama laughed.

That night, she read him his first tale. It was the story of Theseus and the Minotaur, and it became one of his favourites. He thought part of that may have been because his mama spared him the harder facts of the tale. She stopped reading the moment Theseus emerged from King Minos' maze, the huge bull head of the Minotaur in one hand and the thread and sword given him by beautiful Ariadne in the other. No mention of how subsequently he abandoned Ariadne sleeping on the Isle of Naxos. Then, just to show he was a complete no-good, Theseus forgot to signal his pa that things had gone fine in the maze, subsequent to which the old man, thinking his son was dead, slew himself in misplaced grief.

Jason, who knew none of this, demanded to hear what came next. "Did Theseus go on and stick old Minos with his sword just to show him? What about Daedalus, who made that maze in the first place? He had it coming. How about sticking him?"

"Well," said his mama, "there's only one way to find out."

"What's that?"

"Read it yourself."

Jason smiled to himself as he looked around the library at Eliada. He had flown into such a rage. He told his mama she knew full well he could not read or write, and it was unkind of her to withhold important facts on account of his infirmity. His mama had gotten mad too, or pretended to, and took the book away until he came to his senses.

Jason had stayed mad for only a little while. And now, he knew that the only reason he could read the titles at least in this medical library was because of that night. No way he would have figured out reading and writing near as well if his mama had stuck him in a schoolhouse and made him learn his ABCs with chalk and slate at the foot of some stranger. The temptation of mythology was what did it for him, and she laid it out for him, like the Devil doing good.

Out in the hall, a door slammed, and as fast, the door to the examination room cracked open. Dr. Bergstrom stepped in. He was wearing a face mask like Aunt Germaine's, and he had his rubber gloves back on.

"Well now, young Jason. I see you are a bibliophile."

Jason didn't know what that meant, but he nodded like he did.

"Splendid." He walked over to the table, and pulled out one of the dried apples. He popped it in his mouth. As he chewed on it, he opened a drawer and took from there a box of matches. "Would you," he said, approaching a wall-sconce, "be so kind as to strip off your shirt and trousers, Jason?" He struck the match, and lit the lamp with it. "Now, please?"

Jason unbuttoned his shirt. "What for?" he said.

Dr. Bergstrom turned to him, hands crossed before him. "It is the routine in Eliada," he said. "We must make certain that you are as well as well can be, Jason. And then we must keep you that way."

The doctor lit five more lamps, including one that had been hung in the middle of a bowl-shaped mirror, before he started in on Jason. The room took on a glow under all that flame; it turned everything the colour of gold.

Dr. Bergstrom demanded that Jason turn over his shirt and trousers, and he sniffed at them before setting them down on a chair by the door. Then he made Jason turn around in the light, with his arms out. He asked Jason how old he was and Jason told him seventeen, and Dr. Bergstrom nodded like that meant something. He took Jason by the arm then, and led him over to a big weight scale, and told Jason to stand on it. He moved weights along metal rods until they balanced, then looked at them and wrote down the number on a sheet of paper.

"Over here now," he said, and motioned to a spot on the wall that had been marked off in feet and inches. He made Jason stand against it, and took a book from the shelf and measured Jason's height, which Jason thought was five feet and seven inches but Dr. Bergstrom said was five feet and nine inches.

"Sit on the examination table," he said, the mask puffing out with the wind of his speech.

Jason did as he was told. Dr. Bergstrom went over to the bench, and took something that looked like a hand-scythe, except that it was hinged like scissors and not sharp. Bergstrom told Jason to hold still, and he opened it like pincers on a bug, and set Jason's head in the middle. The metal tips felt cold against his temples, and Jason worried it would poke into the soft skull there. It did not. He lifted it away, took it back to the bench, and set it against a ruler, and marked a notation. Then he repeated the procedure with the pincers at the back of Jason's skull, at his jaw-line, his ears and the back of his neck.

"What are you measuring my head for?" asked Jason, but Dr. Bergstrom didn't answer.

"Smile," he said. And then added impatiently: "So I can see your teeth." He examined those, and asked Jason if he ever had a toothache, and when Jason said no, he nodded. He went back to the bench, wrote more things down, then opened one of the glass-covered cabinets. This time he pulled out a thin metal cylinder, and a brown glass bottle.

"Lie on your stomach," he ordered, not looking back.

"You goin' to take my temperature?" asked Jason. When Dr. Bergstrom didn't answer, Jason went on: "When I was small, the doctor in Cracked Wheel took my temperature with a thermometer up my behind, because he feared I'd bite it and poison myself if I put it in my mouth. Well I ain't going to bite it, so you can just—"

"I am not taking your temperature, Jason," said Dr. Bergstrom. He was coming across the floor. Jason could see that he was holding the cylinder between two fingers. On one end was a sharp needle. A bead of fluid gleamed like liquid gold on its tip.

"Now hold still," he said.

Jason did as he was told.

§

Jason blinked and coughed. He was lying down, on a hard bed very different from the examination table. His arms hurt. His vision was blurry; as was his understanding of exactly how he'd got there.

Memory became fragmented up to the moment. He recalled a sharp pain in his behind, and then a cool feeling, like his foot had gone to sleep. He may have said something.

He may have gotten up off the table. Stumbled around a bit. He may have fallen to the floor. He may have even got up again, made it a short way down the hall, and then fallen over again before the world vanished.

Best Jason could say was that, next thing he knew, he was here. Lying on a table or a bed or, judging from its hardness, somewhere in between the two. His clothes were gone, replaced by a thin cotton sheet. The things that hurt his arms and legs were leather straps tied on top of that sheet. They were tying him down.

Jason had to fight to control his breathing as he put it together. He didn't know much about doctoring—what little he'd seen of it happened at the barber shop in Cracked Wheel. But he knew that sometimes the barber would use the straps to hold a fellow still for awful things like amputating a leg or digging out a stone.

What in hell were they doing tying Jason down like this? What was Dr. Bergstrom doing, sticking him with a poisoned needle without asking him first? Jason pushed against the straps. He didn't expect it to free him and so was not surprised when it didn't. It still made him mad.

He blinked, and his eyes got some of their focus back. He looked side to side. He was in a long whitewashed room, with a high ceiling and windows only near the top. There were other beds in here—maybe ten of them. But the rest were empty. At the far end, he could see two figures, caught in the dim moonlight that cut down through the windows, silhouetted in the glow of candlelight. They were huddled around it, talking to one another, turned away from Jason.

"Hey!" he hollered. "Hey!"

They both turned to him.

"Jason!" It was Aunt Germaine. The other one didn't speak, but Jason figured it for Dr. Bergstrom.

The two of them hurried across the room. Jason, to show his displeasure, struggled theatrically against the restraints. When they arrived, he noted that both were wearing white gowns and masks over their mouths. "What is the matter," said Jason in a low, angry voice, "I got a smell about me?"

Aunt Germaine stepped immediately to his side. She put two rubber-gloved hands on his own. It might have been the effect of night, but she looked paler, older than she had ever seemed before. Her hands seemed to be trembling. "Oh Nephew," she said, "I am sorry."

"Do not apologize, Mrs. Frost," said Dr. Bergstrom. He stood somewhat further off, at the foot of the bed. "This was my decision. I will explain it to young Jason."

"Of course." Aunt Germaine squeezed Jason's hand.

"Jason, you must understand that I would not take these measures lightly. But your aunt told me the story of what happened to your town, of—"

"Cracked Wheel."

"Yes. She told me that a contagion—a sickness—came upon the people there over the winter. It was a sickness that spread very quickly—far more quickly than anything that we know. And its mortality rate—the rate at which it killed—was extremely high. Nearly everyone."

"Except me," said Jason. "Because I am immune."

Dr. Bergstrom's lips tightened in something cousin to a smile. "You seem healthy," he said. "That I do grant you. But Jason—that does not mean you do not carry the disease."

"My aunt and me figured that out," said Jason. "We burned things and I kept bathed, even when it was fierce cold."

Dr. Bergstrom shook his head. "The germ might nestle in your soft tissues. It might thrive in the warm places inside your ear—in your throat. Perhaps waiting for a moment to return."

"That's not how germs work."

"And you are expert in this? No. I am sorry, young man. You must remain here for a time."

"Where is here?"

Dr. Bergstrom crossed his hands behind his back and rocked on the balls of his feet. "Quarantine," he said. "For at least tonight."

"Tied down?"

"There is no other way," said Dr. Bergstrom. "As your, ah, aunt attested: you show a tendency to wander."

"How am I going to relieve myself then?"

"No . . . other . . . way," repeated Dr. Bergstrom slowly.

Jason turned to Aunt Germaine who still held his arm. "Aunt! Get me out of here!" He twisted again against the straps. Panic was moving through him like an ugly liquor, and he could hear it in his voice, and he hated it.

Aunt Germaine looked down at him with pursed lips and a crinkled brow. "Doctor," she said, "leave us a moment. The boy is distraught. I will calm him."

"As you wish, Mrs. Frost."

When Dr. Bergstrom had withdrawn sufficient distance, Aunt Germaine bent down to Jason's ear and made shushing noises until Jason stopped twisting and struggling and glared at her.

"I am sorry, Nephew," she said quietly. "Dr. Bergstrom is wrong. You are fine, and this is *wrong*. But I cannot stop it. It is beyond my authority."

"Wh-what am I going to do then? What—"

"*Shh.* Dr. Bergstrom means for you to be trapped here. But you need not be." Aunt Germaine leaned even closer, so her lips brushed Jason's ear, and she whispered: "You are a hero, Jason Thistledown. Your survival . . . well, it proves that. You are as great a Man as Nature might commit. Dr. Bergstrom does not understand that. But he has not seen what you have lived through. He has . . . *underestimated* you. Foolishly, he has underestimated us both." She pulled back a bit, so her face was now inches from Jason's own. "Now turn your hand, slow and careful."

Jason unclenched his fist, and turned it to meet with Aunt Germaine's gloved hand. There was something metallic nestled in her palm.

"Careful," she said. "You do not want to cut yourself. This is a scalpel—a tiny knife. It is small, but wickedly sharp. Should anything happen . . ."

"What?" he whispered.

"Cut yourself free, my darling hero," said Aunt Germaine, "and run."

9

The Quarantine Obscenity

Jason fingered his scalpel and glared into the dark. Anger was all over him like fleas, nestling anywhere it smelled blood.

He was angry at Dr. Bergstrom, who had snuck up on him, stuck poison in him and put him here, tied like a dog for no good reason, without even knowing what sort of fellow he was. Although she had given him this scalpel and said kind things to him, he was angry at Aunt Germaine for what he identified as nothing but cowardly betrayal. She said she had no power to stop this—but in that bag of hers she had two guns (one belonging to Jason's mama) and a pile of ammunition (ammunition that Jason had, at no small risk to his own skin, stepped into the Dempsey Store in Cracked Wheel and faced the putrid corpse of Lionel Dempsey, to retrieve). Jason thought that she was plenty powerful to stop this if she wanted to.

And then Jason stumbled on another source for his anger—an unholy pit of it that ran so deep it dizzied him to look down:

His ma.

His ma, who, if she had not been so weak and slow, might have lived through the sickness that took the rest of those damn fools in Cracked Wheel; who might then have just invited Aunt Germaine in for a meal that winter's morning she showed up with her two pair of snowshoes; a meal where the three of them would have caught up on the goings-on in Philadelphia and New York, and Aunt Germaine could have told how she was doing eugenical research for Dr. Charles Davenport whose privy was filled with damn gold nuggets he was so fine a gentleman. And then together they could have figured out something more intelligent to do about pulling up stakes than getting on a train for this God-damned supposed paradise in Idaho.

All that they might have done and more, if only she hadn't abandoned him.

But that anger was too deep and complicated to hold long without it changing to something else. And as Jason faced it, he felt his chest hitch up and the tears start in the corners of his eyes. He was crying. For the first time, since the time his mama stopped breathing in Cracked Wheel, Jason was crying.

This time, he let it come. He pushed the scalpel away from his hand so he wouldn't cut himself when his fist clenched, and then he let that fist go ahead and clench as hard as it wanted, and the other one too, screwed his eyes shut, and let the weeping out in big, whooping gasps. He cried for his ma, all right—these were tears of grief, and although he was mad he hadn't finished grieving her, if he ever even would.

But it wasn't just for his ma. He had been selfish in his grief and in that he had done many a bad turn. When he'd gone to collect that ammunition in Cracked Wheel, hadn't he looked into the dead eye of Lionel Dempsey—a fellow who'd always been fine to him whenever they met up? Had he even once thought about some of those times they'd seen each other and it had been good enough? No. Had he once uttered a prayer for Mr. Dempsey's poor unshriven soul? No. Had he ever prayed for any of them—any but his ma, who was but one in a hundred or more who'd died gasping and choking in Cracked Wheel? No, no, a hundred times no.

If he'd thought about it at all, he supposed he'd figured he was being self-sufficient in not doing so. But how self-sufficient is a boy, a man, being, really, when he takes off with his new aunt at the first opportunity, abandoning what plans he had and what responsibilities were left?

Aunt Germaine had called him a hero. Jason had read about plenty of heroes. Maybe he was like Theseus, made for one good turn before he ruined it all afterward. Maybe . . .

Jason opened his eyes. And as he did, he blinked. A shadow capered across the moonlit squares on the far wall of the ward room. Jason swallowed a mouthful of his own tears.

The shadow moved slowly against the silver rectangles on the far wall: one after the other, very methodical, slow enough that it could spend awhile working at each pane. It used its whole body—Jason could make out skinny legs, a torso that narrowed at the hip, and skinny arms that pressed against the glass.

Jason glanced up over his head. He could not see much of the windows—his bed was directly beneath them, head against the outside wall. But he figured the windows at the top of the wall weren't more than two feet tall. That meant that the figure—which in shadow looked like a normal man—would have to be considerably shorter than that.

He looked back at the shadow as one of those windows made a *snap!* and a creaking sound. The shadow ducked, and then it vanished before Jason could look up and see.

Jason unclenched his fist, fumbled for the scalpel, and narrowly avoiding cutting himself on the blade, as he thought again about what Aunt Germaine had said before she and Dr. Bergstrom had left.

Cut yourself free, my darling hero. And run.

Jason set to work. It was not as easy as he might have thought; he had to hold the scalpel in his fist so that the blade came out next to his baby finger, and then position it underneath the middle of three straps that held him down. Then he had to start flicking and sawing.

The leather bit into him fiercely as he did so but he would not stop. The thing, whatever it was, had fallen to the floor. He could hear it scurrying. But he could not see. He could not tell how near it was.

What was it? It was shaped like a man, but no more than a foot or two tall. Bulfinch's would say it was a dwarf. A better explanation might be that it was a monkey. That would explain its size, and also its speed.

But as he sawed and picked at the leather, struggling to keep a grip with his sweat-slicked hand, listening as the scrambling sound made its way to and fro across the floor, Jason realized it wasn't just the appearance of the thing.

There was also the whistling.

It was mournful, like an Irish tune about dead lovers—but absent any melody. Jason could not say when it started. The sound seemed *in* him—like the ringing in the ears that came during long silences—a ringing that might always have been there. Jason listened. As he did, he was dimly aware of the scalpel, slipping from his grip. He took hold of it again, so it would not fall away, but he could not imagine how he would begin cutting.

The door opposite him swung slowly open. How long had it been that his aunt and Dr. Bergstrom had disappeared through that door? Jason thought it might have been just a few minutes ago. He thought it might have been a day ago. He did not have any clear notion.

Could it be that the small creature—whatever it was—had let itself out? To run through the rest of the quarantine? He stared at the door, and listened for more scrabbling. He could not hear any but that proved nothing—the whistling was growing louder, and more pervasive.

It must have fled. Jason let out a breath, and turned the knife back to the strap.

Working it was easier now that he'd calmed himself down, and found the notch. The leather was thick and somewhat stiffer than a blade like this was used to cutting, but it was making it through all right.

Jason thought he might have been halfway done when he felt the tugging on the sheet.

The tugging pulled the sheet tight over his ankles and his toes and sent a chill up Jason's back. Something—the thing from the window—was climbing up from the base of his bed. It pulled the sheet tight, first on one side, then the other, as though it was coming up hand over hand. Jason tried to pull his feet back from the edge, but it was no good. The straps were tight—so tight they pushed his legs into the mattress. He stared down, unable to blink or breath, watching as the sheet between his feet rose up in a bulge the size of a man's head. He felt a sharp tickling at his ankles—as though bare branches drew across his flesh.

"Oh mama," he said. He started up the slicing again. It might have got easier, as the strap peeled back a bit from over his arms and gave him a bit more play. But staring down at the thing between his legs, swaying back and forth under the sheet like a tiny little ghost undid any mere physical advantage. He twisted his legs and hollered at it: "Git! Git out of there! Git!"

The thing did the opposite. It started to move up toward him—toward his middle. Jason could feel his nuggets start to pull back, the flesh crawling over them, and he tried to hitch himself back away from the thing, even as it crouched down and pushed against the strap that was tied at Jason's knees.

Jason could feel other parts of the thing between his legs now—a cool flank like leather that pushed against the inside of his left knee—what might have been a forearm, reaching up through the belt and then a claw, touching him halfway up the inside thigh and drawing back slow—the brush of what might have been a foot, pushing against the bed next to his right calf—a tiny damp touch, right at the edge of the strap, that Jason feared was the thing's tongue. Jason sucked a tremulous breath. *Mama*, he thought, *it is tasting me. And Mama, it is aiming for my privates.*

It was aiming for them, but it couldn't quite reach. The belt at his knees was keeping it back. For the moment anyhow, Jason was saved by his restraints.

He knew that protection wouldn't last long.

Jason gritted his teeth and pushed the scalpel back into its groove. His wrist was cramping from the unusual angle, but he went at it hard all the same. At his feet, the sheet was writhing. Something stinging drew across his knee, and the thing between his legs reared up.

The belt at his arm snapped then and Jason let go of the scalpel.

He wasted no time, reaching around until he found the buckle for the highest belt, over his shoulders. He yanked, unclasped it, then sat up as the buckle clattered against the side of the bed. Jason drove his fist into the sheet between his legs. He hit something hard like bone, and heard a crunch like thick, crumpling paper. A high squealing followed and Jason caught a whiff of something sweet and foul—a smell like the dead at Cracked Wheel.

The thing was still moving, though. So with his other hand, Jason grabbed down on the sheet, pushing the thing into the bed. Holding it so, he unstrapped the final belt, and pulled his knees back so he was kneeling on the bed, still holding the struggling creature underneath the sheet.

All right, he thought. *Let us see what it is that goes after me like that*; while aloud he spoke to it softly, little calming wordless coos, like he would a panicked sow on the homestead.

On the bed beside him, he found the scalpel. It was blunted by the leather but still sharp enough. He held it ready like a dagger in one hand while with the other, still making his calm-down noises, he unwrapped the tiny creature.

He blinked. It was hard to make the thing out in the night. It did seem like a tiny person—perfectly formed, not more than a foot or so tall, and clothed in dirt and leaves. It struggled in the sheet, and started making that high noise. The smell was strong—stronger the closer he drew to the mysterious little beast, trying to make it out in the dark ward room. He was very close indeed when it came into focus.

This time, when he dropped the scalpel it fell to the floor—as did the tiny creature with the impossible face. The beast landed near the foot of the bed, and Jason watched, transfixed, unable to breathe, as it skittered first back under the bed—then, gathering its strength, drawing back to leap maybe, it took off on all fours like some hideous rat—shooting through the half-open door and into the dark of the corridor.

Jason fell back. He drew his knees to his chin and wrapped his arms around them. He rocked back and forth, holding the shaking inside, and he tried to make sense of what he had seen leering back at him:

Miss Ruth Harper, her smooth round face and light brown curls reduced to a size as might fit on a doll; her wickedly charming smile not at all improved by the addition of two rows of sharp, glinting teeth.

§

The whistling changed. To Jason's ear it became almost melodic—or perhaps it shifted subtly, to make the harmonies more apparent. Jason thought he might be able to make out three or four different sources, coming from variously the ceiling, somewhere underneath the beds, and somewhere in the dark of the hallway. As he listened, he developed another theory—that whatever it was that Dr. Bergstrom had given him to make him sleep, also brought on waking dreams. Dr. Bergstrom was enough of a no-good bastard to do something like that.

It was a lot more likely than some tiny, saw-toothed cousin of Ruth Harper prying its way into the quarantine.

At length, Jason unwrapped his arms from around his legs, lowered his feet to the floor and lifted the sheet onto his shoulders.

Run, Aunt Germaine had said. Jason was not sure he had a run in him right now—his legs were stiff and slow, and once outside—he'd be barefoot and naked. Jason bent down and scooped up the scalpel. He headed to the door, then, seeing how dark it was past it, turned back to the ward room to see if he could find a candle and something to light it with.

Jason found a melted-down candle in a dish on a table near the door. On another table, near the little iron wood stove, he found a box of wooden matches, and within a moment, he was back to the hallway with the glow of candlelight to guide him.

The hallway was like a narrow gorge, cut by a single axe stroke. The ceiling rested higher than the light would reach, and the space itself was narrow. It carried in each direction an unguessable length. Candles had their limits. Particularly in a quarantine building that seemed bigger than the actual hospital it was supposed to serve.

Because there was no better reason for him to head right, Jason headed left—the candle in one hand, and the scalpel clutched in the other. Only thing missing, he thought, was a ball of thread to help him find his way out of the maze.

§

At first, Jason thought the quarantine gigantic, it took him so long to move along the hallway, through a wider room and into another corridor narrower than this one. The narrower corridor bent, and presented a short flight of stairs up.

Jason stopped at the top of the stairs and listened. There was a sound that a man might make, faced with unimaginable grief. It had a rhythm to it, a cycle: first, a keening, high sound, wavering only minutely; then, as the throat constricted, a sound like a growl, if something signifying such pitiful surrender could be so named.

Yes, Jason was familiar with that sound.

He stepped into the new room, and said, "Hello?"

This room was filled with furniture more akin to the Cracked Wheel Town Office than it was to a room in a hospital quarantine. Jason stepped around a file cabinet and a wide wooden desk to see other things: what looked like tall wardrobes and bureaus and wide shelves. The crying stopped. And something moved—something in white, maybe a fellow wrapped in his bedsheet like Jason was.

"Hello?" said Jason again. "Were you trapped in here too?"

"*Forgive me.*"

Jason crept forward, trying to locate the voice. The man was hoarse from crying, and he gasped noisily after he spoke. No telling where he was, except not in sight.

"All right," said Jason, "I forgive you. Now are you all right? You in here because you're sick?"

"*Forgive!*"

The unseen voice snuffled, and there was the sound of something heavy dragging fast across the floor. Then the place went quiet.

"Hello?" Jason continued forward, to where he thought he saw that flash of white. There was another desk, this one with an odd glass bell jar in its middle. He stepped past it, and as he did, his foot came down on something different than the pine board that had made the floor in the rest of this place. It was cloth. A swath of cloth, dropped there on the floor.

Jason bent down to have a look. It looked like it might be a pillowcase, although Jason didn't think it was quite big enough.

He set down the candle on the table, and played out the fabric. It was a pillowcase, in that it was a white cloth sack—except, as he looked more closely, for the two holes that had been cut in it. They were perfect eye-holes.

Jason set it down and picked up the candle again. He held it out at arm's length, and turned around. "Hey," he called, more loudly now. "You forgot your ghost mask, sir. Why don't you show yourself?"

He made almost a complete circle with the candle looking for the fellow but stopped before he finished. That was when the candlelight fell on the huge wall that climbed high into the dark, with a set of double doors on it that were so high the candle could not see their top.

"Well," said Jason, setting down the sheet on the table, "I'll leave it here for you."

He stepped up to the doors and started looking for a handle. Maybe this was the way outside.

It wasn't. The doors were huge—the size of barn doors—and about as well-made. Where the rest of the quarantine seemed newer, designed to keep the bad air of one room from leaking into the next, the boards that made these doors were warped and decayed with gaps as big as fingers or wider going through them. And the breeze that came out did not carry the smell that Jason associated with a mountain town at night.

The air had that same thick sweetness, the smell of his mama and Cracked Wheel in their dying time, the smell he'd sniffed earlier. The air that wafted out was warm, too. Jason could not find a handle for these immense doors, but after a time he stopped trying. He pressed his face against the slats, and, one eye closed, used the other to peer inside.

He smiled in disbelief. There was some terrific party going on in there—filled with some of the most beautiful creatures he'd ever seen. There were what looked like hundreds of them, dancing and spinning—laughing as their hair whirled out from their heads, their arms akimbo. Every so often, one or the other of them would leap, into an arc twice the height of the others' heads, spreading fairy dust behind it. And in their centre . . .

In their centre a figure sat that Jason had difficulty looking at. He was tall—a giant among the other revellers—with arms skinny like a scarecrow's, and a head that was long and bent kind of funny in the middle, like it had been smacked with one of those mill logs that Sam Green talked about—and hair, that grew from his skull in tangles like branches off a deadfall. He looked around him, then up at Jason's single eye staring through the wood—and then Jason stumbled forward as the doors swung inward, and the candle fell from his fingers and went out on the floor—and when he looked again, he stood in darkness.

The whistling enveloped him, and Jason felt an odd queasiness in his belly. Things moved close to him, nipping at his heels like cattle dogs—moving him forward. And he found that although it was dark, he could see—that the giant that stood in front of him was opening itself up, as though preparing for an embrace.

He realized then that his hand was wet. Warm and wet, where he clutched the scalpel at his chest. And it *hurt*.

He opened his hand, and delicately pulled the scalpel away from the wound it had made in the webbing at his thumb.

The pain must have done it. Jason was loose, from whatever odd spell had held him. Now it was a matter of taking the next step.

Hand bleeding into his sheet, pain thrumming up his body, Jason Thistledown turned on his heel and ran back into the dark depths of the Eliada quarantine.

§

Crossing the strange room with the desks and the cabinets was like crossing a continent. Several times Jason almost lost his sheet as it caught on corners of desks or warps in the floorboards. Finally striking the far wall, he was able to find the stairs again to return to the hallway, but if he had not thought of that he might have been in the room forever.

When he made it to the hallway, the whistling grew louder and he felt certain that as he made his way along tiny hands were grasping at the edge of the sheet. The pain in his hand grew stronger.

As did the anger. Jason thought he understood how it was that people got mad enough to kill. It was not a matter of defending your dead mama and her homestead from bandits: that was not what made you pull the trigger. It was rage—keening rage that went along a fellow's nerves and mingled maybe with some physical pain that was there already, to make something truly powerful.

The good thing about that rage was it helped a fellow push down the terror. So as he worked his way down the hall, with tiny creatures perhaps dogging his steps and trying to draw him back to that—that leering *thing*—he stoked it, let it build, started to make himself some plans.

There were two guns in Aunt Germaine's possession now—the Winchester, and the revolver. *Well*, he thought, *I'll only need one to do the trick. And it will be the revolver because it's easier to stash under a coat.*

He stumbled and nearly fell down the stairs when he came upon them, but quickly found his balance and continued. The blood in the sheet was slick against his bare chest, and he felt like he might faint or upchuck or both.

You will not stop me, Aunt Germaine. For I am about to do what you lacked the courage to. And I will not forget your betrayal neither.

She might try to use her authority—those terrible eyes of hers—to dissuade him, but Jason would not heed them.

I mean to kill him, he would say. *I mean to kill him before I burn his evil quarantine to the ground. Yes. Just like you did to my mama's homestead. I am going to burn this place and everything in it and they can damn well hang me for it if they can catch me.*

Aunt Germaine would shrivel before the onslaught of his venomous rhetoric, and thus unencumbered, Jason would stride down the hall, to the office where Dr. Bergstrom lived. He would kick in the door rather than open it, and when Dr. Bergstrom opened his mouth to shout, Jason would raise the revolver, sight down its barrel, and before he put the bullet between the doctor's no-good eyes, he would say . . .

He would say . . .

The corridor opened up into a larger room that Jason remembered. But this time, without the candlelight to blind him, he was able to apprehend a rectangle of light, or lighter darkness at any rate. A window? No—as Jason stumbled toward it, he saw that it was more than a window. Cool night air—air unsullied by that strange sweet smell—wafted in through an open door.

"Ha!" Jason left his scheming for a moment and hurried toward it.

He stumbled a moment over some carpeting, but regained his footing and continued, wondering: *Who opened that door? Maybe that fellow in white, on his way out?*

Maybe—maybe those things?

Even as he wondered that, the lighter dark flickered for a moment, as a shadow drew across it. Jason stopped dead. He pulled the sheet close around him, pressing it against the cut in his hand.

The shadow came back. This one, at least, was not in miniature. It was nearly as tall as the door—definitely a fellow—but hunched peculiarly.

"Mister—Mister Juke?" said the shadow.

Jason said: "Who?"

The shadow stepped to the door frame, and reached out a hand. There was the sound of a match being drawn, and then, a tiny glow of light. Jason squinted and looked at the dark face behind the flame.

"The Negro," he gasped.

"Who are you?" said the Negro, holding the match forward and looking Jason up and down. "And what happened here?"

And then the match went out and the darkness closed back in on them. That did it.

"You better step out of the way, sir," said Jason, "because this place is filled with Devils from Hell and I don't want to stay here a minute longer."

10

The Autopsy

Andrew Waggoner stepped out of the way, and let the boy out. He looked like a performer in a Greek play—robed in a blood-spotted sheet, face twisted in agony. Andrew was in his own kind of pain. Two nights after his incident, and he had still managed to keep off the morphine, and here he was, gallivanting in the middle of the night outside the quarantine. But one look at this boy, the blood, the wild expression in his eye, ignited his physician's instincts and let him set his own troubles aside.

"Come on," he said, leading the boy over to a little stone bench. "Sit."

"I want to get as far from here as I can."

"That's fine. But not before I get a look at you. Don't worry. I know what I'm doing."

The boy squinted at him. "You're the Negro doctor," he said. "That right?"

Andrew let himself crack a smile. "Dr. Andrew Waggoner," he said. "I prefer that to Negro Doctor, if you don't mind. Particularly coming from a boy wearing a sheet."

The boy nodded. Andrew was glad to see he seemed to be calming down.

"I'm Jason Thistledown," he said. "Pleased to meet you, Dr. Waggoner. Sam Green says you're going to make trouble here. That's good, far as I'm concerned." He put his hand forward. It was covered in blood that welled from a long slice up the palm.

Andrew lit a match on the stone bench and took a closer look at it. The wound was deep, like he'd cut himself with a straight razor. "How'd you get this?"

"Scalpel," said Jason.

Andrew looked him in the eye. "What are you fooling with a scalpel for?"

"My aunt gave it to me."

"Well, I'll have to give your aunt a talking-to. This is going to need stitches."

"Fine by me on both counts, Dr. Waggoner. Now can we get away from here?"

"Of course we can," said Andrew. "I think we're going to have to help each other getting back, though. Neither of us is in very good shape tonight."

§

That was an understatement. Andrew had not been in very good shape for two nights now. The first night he'd tried to get outside, have a look at the quarantine in the cover of the moonlight, he had been in such poor shape that he had only gotten as far as the south staircase before the pain forced him to turn back. Tonight, it had taken him half an hour to make it downstairs and out the back of the hospital. The best that he could do for it was stay still, work the bruised and pulled muscles slowly back to health.

But he knew that something was odd in the quarantine. And there were questions to which he'd received no satisfactory answer.

He had been standing outside, staring at the open door in the front of the great building, willing himself the strength to go a little farther, step inside, when the boy appeared in his bloody sheet.

Well, he thought as he tore a strip from the sheet and tied a bandage around Jason's hand, *there'll be no more exploration tonight.*

"You want help walking back?" said Jason. "My hand's bad, but I can sure walk all right. And you—"

Andrew nodded. There was no point in standing on pride. "I'd appreciate it," he said.

"The Klansmen do this to you?" asked Jason as they moved away from the quarantine, across the clear lawn between there and the back of the hospital.

"You know a lot," he said.

"Sam Green told me," said Jason. "I don't know much otherwise."

Andrew pushed open the door and guided Jason to one of the examination rooms, where they lit a pair of lamps. At Andrew's instruction, Jason sat down on the examination table. Andrew took a chair with wheels on the legs, and that made things better. He could roll back and forth looking for the things he'd need: primarily, a bottle of iodine and a sterile needle and thread. As he pulled that out of a cabinet, he caught Jason looking at it apprehensively.

"Don't worry," he said. "I've done this before."

Jason motioned with his bloody hand. "With your arm like that?"

Andrew smiled. "Well no," he said, "not with my arm like this. But I can manage. This is simple work. Unless you want to wait for Dr. Bergstrom in the morning?"

"Hell no!"

"All right then," said Andrew. "Hold still. I'm going to clean your cut out first and that might sting. Try not to shout."

Jason didn't shout as Andrew splashed iodine on his hand, but Andrew could tell that the boy wanted to.

"Very stoic," Andrew said, dabbing the wound clean. "Now tell me—how'd you happen to cut yourself in the middle of the quarantine this fine spring night?"

"Bergstrom did it to me."

"Dr. Bergstrom cut your hand?"

"No. Bergstrom locked me up in there—on account I might be infectious, even though I got no symptoms."

"Infectious?" Andrew put a wad of cotton on the wound and pressed down. "Infectious with what?"

"Fever," said Jason. "The fever that killed my mama and took about all of my town this winter past, I expect. But that's bunk."

"Wait a moment. A fever killed *all* of your town?" Andrew rolled back on his chair, and started to thread the steel needle. "Over one winter?"

"Over one week, more like," said Jason.

Andrew frowned at Jason. "Are you making up stories?"

Jason shook his head. "Wish I were," he said.

"Before I start, you want a little whiskey? It helps dull the pain."

"No sir."

"Then why don't you tell more about this sickness that had you locked up in quarantine tonight? It'll help distract you—and I'm curious."

"All right."

And so, as Andrew took the boy's hand and started to draw the thread through the wound, Jason Thistledown told him his story. He teared up almost immediately. And Andrew wasn't sure whether it was the pain of the stitches or the sadness of the memories that made him cry.

"Well. I am sorry for your loss," said Andrew. "It's a lucky thing your aunt happened by."

Jason nodded. "I thank the Lord every day. I just wish she'd stopped Dr. Bergstrom."

"All right, this is the last one." And he pierced the skin at the very inner edge of the cut. Jason flinched more this time—as though he'd been holding it in until now.

"Can—can I have that bit of that whiskey now?"

"Sure you can." Andrew wheeled back to the cabinet and got the little whiskey bottle. He poured a capful and handed it to Jason, who slugged it down and coughed.

"This supposed to help?" he finally managed.

"Get enough whiskey into a man, you can saw his leg off."

"Don't get any ideas."

Andrew chuckled at that. "Don't worry, Jason." He wrapped the wound in gauze. "I'm done for tonight."

Now that he was done stitching and bandaging, Andrew got a good look at the boy, assessing him as something other than a patient. He was most of the way to being a man, tall and lean with none of the awkwardness that came on a lot of boys at that time of life. His eyes were pale in the light, but they had a cast to them that Andrew had not often seen, like they looked right through a fellow. Overall, Jason Thistledown just looked strong, and Andrew thought he must be.

This boy, if he were to be believed, had survived an outbreak of something worse than cholera, worse than yellow fever, maybe as bad as Black Plague . . . Some sickness that had killed everybody in a town this past winter. Not a third or a half, but everybody. Everybody but one.

What kind of fever did that?

"Jason," he asked, "can you tell me what the symptoms of the fever were?"

Jason handed back the cap, and Andrew screwed it back onto the whiskey.

"I only know what happened to my mama."

"Tell me that."

Jason nodded. He was quiet for a moment, looking down at his re-bandaged hand. Then he drew a breath, and started talking.

"She started getting sick a day after we got back home from Cracked Wheel. It was a clear day, all right for travel we figured. We were laying in some more supplies, was all. First thing she complained about was a headache. Then she had trouble with the runs, you know what I mean? Then she got all hot with fever, and she said 'Why, Jason I think I shall lie down a moment.' She had a hard time getting up after that, so I saw to her."

"You feel anything during this part?"

"Not symptoms if that's what you mean."

"That is what I mean."

"After that, things took a bad turn. She told me her stomach hurt, and she was sweating something terrible, and when I went to clean her off I saw that she was bleeding."

"Bleeding? Where?"

"From her nose for a bit, and also—also from the skin around her fingernails."

"And then—"

"Well," said Jason, "she got worse and worse, until she seized up—and died."

"Were you able to take her temperature? With a thermometer?"

"No."

"Was she bleeding from anywhere else?"

"I don't know. I think there was some around her toenails, and her eyes were awfully red."

Andrew sat back and thought about what he'd told him. It was nothing he'd ever encountered—not clinically, certainly, and not even in the case studies that he'd read in Paris.

"And you didn't have any symptoms."

"Like my aunt says—I'm immune."

"And you haven't had symptoms—for how long?"

"About two months."

"During which time, you got on a train, and on another train, then made your way up here to Eliada. Meeting all sorts of people at every stop."

"That is right."

"So why, I wonder, did Dr. Bergstrom order you into quarantine tonight? It seems as though your aunt's right—you're immune. You're not carrying it either or others would have surely come down with it. So why lock you up now?"

"That is what I want to know."

Andrew was about to ask his next question when he heard a gentle rapping at the door.

"Dr. Bergstrom?"

"Annie?" He turned his chair around to face the door. "Come on in."

"Dr. Waggoner." Annie Rowe stepped in. "What are you doing up? Oh," she said, looking at Jason. She blushed and averted her eyes. "Hello, young sir."

"Nurse Rowe, meet Jason Thistledown. Jason, cover yourself, would you?"

"Pleased to make your acquaintance," said Jason, pulling the sheet over himself.

Annie Rowe raised her eyes and got a better look at the blood-slick sheet. "What happened here?"

"It is not as bad as it looks," said Andrew. "The boy cut himself. I saw to it."

"You should've called someone," she scolded. But it was not heartfelt. She peered at the boy. "He doesn't look well."

Andrew cleared his throat. "You know what you might do? Could you find Jason a robe or some clothes—something to cover him up better?"

Annie stood straight. "All right," she said, "as you please, Doctor." She spared Andrew a tight smile. "Good to see you back practising so soon."

When she'd left, Jason finally did it, and asked Andrew the question he'd been dreading.

"What were you doing out there tonight? And who's Mister Juke?"

"Mister—"

"Yes, sir. You thought I might be him, when I came out of the quarantine. Remember? Well, I'm not. So who is he?"

Now Andrew found himself brought up short. It was a simple question but a difficult one. Who was Mister Juke? He'd seen him, on the hillside waiting for the hangman's noose—a creature with two faces or so it seemed—one congenitally distorted; one, beautiful. He'd seen Mister Juke hanged, by the neck. And Mister Juke had lived. So who was he?

"That," said Andrew, "is the question I have been trying to answer. He was with me at . . . at . . ."

"The lynching?" Jason pulled the sheet tighter around himself. "Sam Green told what happened."

"All right. He was with me at the lynching. They hung him first—they seemed to think he was a rapist, although I doubt that. They pulled him out of that quarantine building. And they hung him. They tried to anyway."

"Because they thought he was a rapist. Who they think he raped?"

"Sweet girl," said Andrew. "Her name was Maryanne Leonard. She died, this past Sunday. Right here in hospital. Complications from her pregnancy."

Jason didn't ask another question right away. He just sat there and looked at Andrew, and as Andrew looked back, he thought: *The boy is dancing around this*

topic. Just like I am. Because the boy has seen something in there—Devils up from
Hell, he called them—that he cannot explain any more than I can explain anything
I have seen. And neither of us will be able to figure it out, until one of us takes that
step—openly, into that place.

Jason finally asked his question.

"How big is Mister Juke? Is he skinny and tall with a strange bend to his
face, like he's been whacked? Or is he just little? Like a baby, or maybe a bit
smaller than a baby? But with . . . teeth?"

They sat quiet again, as Andrew took that in. Andrew's answer, when it
came, had no words. He nodded.

"So both," said Jason, and Andrew said: "Yes. Both."

Annie Rowe returned with a hospital gown for Jason, and once he'd
changed took the sheet and stuffed it into a sack for washing. As she folded
it and stuffed it in the bag, she nagged Andrew a bit about getting back to his
room, but Andrew put her off. "Just seeing to my patient," he said.

"You are the patient," she huffed. "And a terrible patient at that. Why is that
truer with doctors than anyone else?"

"Annie, I promise to return to bed once I've seen to a few things."

"Why don't you let me see to them? I am on duty tonight."

"You must have enough to do," said Andrew.

"Oh," said Annie, "it's not so busy. We have a new mother and her baby
staying the night, but they're resting fine. Other than that, there is just a certain
doctor who is recovering from an unjust beating, yet prone to wandering. . . ."

She stuffed the cloth into the laundry bag and hung it on the peg outside the
examination room door. The whole time, she did not take her eye off Andrew.

"Now what can I take off your hands, Dr. Waggoner, to get you back to bed
any sooner?"

Andrew sighed and looked in her eyes and, reading the expression there, he
made up his mind.

"All right," he said, "you can go into the autopsy. You can light up the lamps
in there, and you can pull out Maryanne Leonard's remains and set her on
the table. Then you can go up to my room, and you can set up another cot for
Jason, and leave the two of us to our work for a moment," he said. Annie's eyes
widened and she prepared to say something else, no doubt to point out some
other damning aspect of Andrew's obvious infirmities, but he pre-empted her.

"*That* is how you'll get me back to bed the quickest."

§

"Why do you want to look at that lady's body?" asked Jason as they made their way slowly down the corridor to the autopsy. "Why now?"

"The truth is, I want to find out as much as I can before I talk to Dr. Bergstrom next. I have my suspicions about what has been transpiring here all this time—and I want to see, so I can get some good answers from him. You want to wait outside, I understand."

Jason pondered. "You don't get on with that Dr. Bergstrom either, do you?" he said finally.

"No. I guess not."

"Well then, I got stomach for whatever you've got to do. It's not like I ain't seen a dead body before. And you still look like you could use some help."

"All right, then."

As they came upon the door to the autopsy, Annie Rowe emerged. Seeing her gave Andrew pause. She looked older, the lines in her cheeks standing out in sharp relief, and the shadows around her eyes deep. Those eyes were wide, though—not this time with disapproval. She looked at Andrew and gasped, started to say something, then shook her head.

"Annie?" Dr. Waggoner leaned on Jason's shoulder. "What—"

"I did what you asked, Dr. Waggoner," she said. "I brought her out. But—"

"But?"

"Just go do what you got to do," she said. "But leave that boy out of it."

Then she turned and fled into the shadows at the end of the hall.

Andrew and Jason looked at one another. "I think you'd better wait here," said Andrew. "I'll go see what has Nurse Rowe so upset."

Jason nodded. "Just don't cut yourself. I'm not so good at stitching as you are."

"I'll be mindful." And with that, Andrew let go of Jason and headed into the autopsy.

Andrew had been impressed with the Eliada autopsy from his first visit. The fact that there was a hospital in a place this remote was enough in itself; but the Eliada autopsy was also set up with tables like a surgery. The tables were on rollers, and exactly the height of drawers in the wall where the bodies of the deceased rested and there was at hand a full surgery of equipment for the purposes of examination. But for the absence of electric light, the autopsy here would not have been out of place in New York or Paris.

Annie had set things up for him as he'd asked. She'd lit the kerosene lamps that hung from the ceiling beneath big conical reflectors, and placed the table underneath them. And on the table, she had placed what Andrew assumed were the remains of Miss Maryanne Leonard.

They were under a sheet—but without even drawing it back, Andrew could see what got Annie so upset. It draped like a covering of attic furniture—tenting high where the body's face and shoulders lay, and over the up-pointing toes, and the knees. But in the middle, where the hips and belly should have made an impression—there, the fabric held closer to the table. Because there, Andrew realized, there was practically nothing at all. He stepped up closer and drew back the cloth.

Maryanne Leonard had been butchered. The flesh of her chest, her ribcage, everything down to her pelvic bone—it was all removed, nothing but a yawning, blackening space. Looking down at her, he could see her spine, the ribs of her back that shot from it, lying empty. Her viscera had been scooped out; she had been gutted, cleaned like a fish.

Except she was no fish. She was a young lady. As if to give evidence of that, her face floated with the unblemished serenity of the dead above the emptiness of her middle.

Delicately, Andrew drew the sheet back over her face.

Bergstrom must consider the discussion closed, thought Andrew, now that he had so tidily carved away the evidence. Andrew turned around to call Jason in—but saw the boy standing at the door.

"How long have you been there?" asked Andrew.

"Long enough to see," said Jason. He swallowed and shut his eyes a moment. "Where's the rest of her?"

"Why don't you sit down," said Andrew. "Look away. Let me see to this—"

Jason held up his hand. He opened his eyes and stared hard at Andrew.

"No sir. You think I'm upset like a girl or a baby or someone from a city, because there's an awful thing here. Well, I ain't. I've seen awful things already and this is another one. You think we should start looking for the rest of her? Can't be far."

Andrew drew a breath. This boy had depths to him—he was no baby or girl or city person, that was true. "Yes," he said. "I think we should. And I've got an idea."

"You need a hand walking?"

"No," said Andrew. "I better get used to doing that on my own."

Jason stepped aside. "I'm here if you need it, Doctor."

Andrew smiled as he started across the room. "Someone raised you well," he said, and pointed to a door at the far end of the room. "Fetch a lamp, then. We'll check here."

The door led to the closest thing one could find to a cellar to this place. The nurses called it the root cellar, because it was cool and tight, and probably could keep a good store of potatoes and carrots until winter if that was what the place was for.

But there wasn't room in this cellar and anyway, the shelves here were full of things you wouldn't want next to your supper.

"What's the smell in here?"

"Formaldehyde," said Andrew.

"Smells like pickle juice," said Jason.

"You must be used to some awful pickles to say that," said Andrew. "But it works the same as pickle juice—preserves things that left to themselves might rot away. Come on down, bring the candle."

Jason brought the candle down the steps. The space in here had been dug out of the ground and lined with fieldstone and timber. The ceiling was a low, whitewashed arch. Air circulation was bad in here, and the few times Andrew had been down before, he'd always had the uneasy sense that he was about to suffocate.

"Sure are a lot of jars here," said Jason.

"This is where the hospital keeps its specimens," said Andrew. "Someone's foot gets amputated—we pull out some kidney stones—even if we cut out an appendix. It all goes here in a jar."

"Every time?"

"Not every time." Andrew squinted at a line of jars filled with stones of various sizes. Thin sheets of effluvia drifted in the yellowish liquid. "But when there's something remarkable about it. Something worth writing down. Then yes, we keep it."

Jason looked hard at the jars. "Should be a lot of jars like that around here. They're labelled and everything. What're we looking for?"

"Not kidney stones from M. Cunningham," said Andrew.

"Nor a testicle from L. Wharton," said Jason. "A testicle! He can't be too happy with how his life's carrying on."

Andrew chuckled. "I remember that one. I think he's happy enough these days. See how big it is?"

Jason looked closer. "I thought that was just the magnifyin' effect of the glass."

"Oh no. In fact, it looks like it has contracted since the surgery."

Jason whistled. "How'd a fellow walk, dragging something like *that* between his legs?"

"I wondered that too. And so I removed it."

Jason was quiet a moment, considering this. He pulled the candle back.

"What's the matter, son? Too much for one night?"

Jason didn't answer, and when the candle drew farther away Andrew turned. "Jason? Are you all right?"

The candle was glowing at the far end of the little cellar, making a silhouette of Jason, and illuminating a high shelf that was filled with big glass jars.

"Doctor," said Jason, "I think I found Maryanne Leonard. Or the rest of her. You need a hand coming over here?"

§

Andrew made it over on his own but Jason did most of the work moving the jars out into the autopsy where the light was better. There were eight of them that were labelled *M. Leonard*, and each one was big—a good half-gallon. Andrew was doing all right walking, but with one good arm and a limp, he was sure he'd drop every one of them. So Jason hauled them out and arranged them for inspection.

The jars were all labelled with the name of the particular organ that was inside. It was a good thing—because whoever had removed them had done an inept job. The intestine and stomach were both badly perforated, one of the kidneys was almost liquefied, and the liver . . .

Andrew leaned in close to examine the liver. Its surface looked as though someone had drawn a table fork across it—or in some spots, a spoon, scooping parts away like custard. Jason leaned in beside him.

"What happened to that?" he asked. Andrew looked where he was pointing— into the jar that was labelled *Uterus*.

At first, Andrew took it on faith that this was what he was looking at, because Maryanne Leonard's uterus was a ruin. Andrew could see where the rip was, but there were also cuts, radiating out from it. Other parts had holes of a variety of sizes, like a slice of Swiss cheese. The fallopian tubes and ovaries were kinked and ragged, as though they'd been gnawed by rats.

And there were . . . other things.

They looked like tiny pustules, attached to the inner lining of the uterus. They were each perfectly round, whitish, not more than a sixteenth of an inch in diameter. There might have been hundreds.

"Look at those."

"What are they?"

"One way to find out," said Andrew. "Let's have a look. Could you unscrew the jar, Jason?"

"This is going to smell worse."

"I'm afraid so."

Jason wrinkled his nose, took the jar in the crook of his elbow and twisted the top off.

Andrew found a set of forceps and a steel tray, and when Jason set the jar back down he reached inside and carefully pulled the organ out.

"A uterus. That's the same as a womb."

"Very good." Andrew unfolded it onto the tray as well as he could, using only his left hand. "Jason, could you bring a light near? Thank you."

Jason took the candle near and set it on the table beside the organ, while Andrew brought a magnifying glass to bear on the problem.

"Tiny people did this," said Jason.

Andrew was only half-listening, so he nodded. He prodded the pustules with the end of a needle. They were attached all right—and they were hard.

"Tiny people," repeated Jason. "From the quarantine. That's what I saw there—never seen anything like it before. But they had sharp teeth and I bet they did this. I *know* it."

At that, Andrew sat up and looked at Jason. "Jason," he said levelly, "we don't *know* anything. We've both seen things—and we've seen the same thing in one case. So it gives it some credence, this idea that some little cousin of Mister Juke did all this. But we don't know. Not yet." He sat back. "Unless, there's some story about what happened in that quarantine you haven't told me."

"Those things in there—they looked like folks. Small folks but that weren't all. The one I saw up close had pretty sharp teeth and a hungry way about it. It went after my—" he hesitated, and reddened "—my privates. Think if it were smaller—younger—it couldn't cut a hole in a woman's insides? Chew it? Looking for food?"

"That's good, Jason. You are asking questions. And they're good ones too." Andrew looked back through the magnifying glass, focused it on a cluster of the pustules.

"Thank you," said Jason. "And what're you going to do about those questions?"

Andrew frowned. He focused in closer. They looked like nothing so much as a cluster of tiny fish eggs . . . roe.

And they certainly could be. As he looked, he saw what appeared to be tiny fractures along the surface of the pustule—like veins, perhaps, but infinitely smaller. And there—he wondered—might that even be a shadow of a form inside?

Andrew blinked and sat up, set the magnifying glass down.

"Right now, we're going to take some of these things . . ." He shook his head. "We'll put them in a jar, and keep them to look at through a microscope tomorrow. And then we're going to put things back, and we're going to climb the stairs to my room." Andrew drew a deep breath before continuing:

"You're going to stay there the night. By my own bedside. And I'll make sure you don't ever end up in that quarantine again."

Jason glared at him. "Are you putting me off?" he asked. Andrew started to answer, but the boy waved him down. "It don't matter," he said. "I owe you thanks for fixing my hand up and you're right. I don't think I can stay awake much longer and you sure don't look it. We ought to clean up this place and get rest."

"Rest is definitely what we both need right now," said Andrew. He pushed himself up and winced, and looked at Jason. "A tiny person tried to bite your privates?" he asked.

Jason nodded. "Let's get to work," he said.

§

Nurse Annie Rowe met them upstairs, and she was grateful to learn that Andrew and Jason had closed up the autopsy. "I am not squeamish but I have never seen a young lady—her remains—in such a state. What happened? Do you know?"

"Better you ask Bergstrom," said Jason before Andrew could shush him.

"Better not to ask Dr. Bergstrom," said Andrew and Annie nodded and said she understood all too well.

"I don't want to stir the hornet's nest anymore. There will be enough trouble with this one out of quarantine," said Annie.

"Oh," said Andrew, "there will be more than enough trouble, on more than one count there. Kings will fall. We will make sure of that."

Nurse Rowe smiled gently as she prepared to leave them. "Don't exaggerate, now, Dr. Waggoner. Dr. Bergstrom will be in a state in the morning. But things will be fine by lunch again."

11

Love Among the Feegers

The two Feeger sisters waited through the night for Patricia. By the time she came back, Feeger men had joined them. Feeger men often tried to join them for the singing, or more to the point they tried to interrupt it, by grabbing at one or the other of them, or just staring at their nakedness with hungry enough eyes to put them off harmony. Patricia was the one with the knowhow to shoo them off. Now it fell to Lily, second eldest.

So when El Feeger put his hand on her shoulder, Lily said: *Scat!* Which was the first thing you said when a Feeger took a liberty. El took his hand away but he didn't move too far, nor take his dark eyes off her, nor lose that awful grin.

That was fine for the moment but it would not last. Lily hummed a little prayer that the Old Man might release her big sister soon so she would not have to face El and others alone.

The Old Man heard her prayer. Looking out on the lake, which was dimpled with slanted rays, Missy pointed out the little ripple in the waters, spreading like a line from a middle point. As it grew nearer, El's gaze removed itself from his cousin's behind and joined the rest of them watching at Patricia came back from her night with the Old Man.

She was changed. Although she'd spent a night in water cold enough to paint a girl blue, her skin was ruddy and cheered. Was she any plumper? She soon would be, and that may have been why Lily thought she was now. But she smiled as she squinted against the sun at the family, and walked out of the lake.

Missy ran up and threw her arms around her sister, who absently stroked her hair. The men, guessing what had come upon her, stepped back and fell to their knees.

"Patricia," whispered Lily. "You're an—"

"Oracle," whispered Patricia, then, loud enough for everyone to hear: "I am all Oracular now, and I have words from Him in the Lake. So heed, and keep your hands off me 'n' mine 'til I say."

She did not say anything else then. For the whole town had not gathered. So El went down to fetch some weave for his cousin, and they all wrapped her up in it, took her back down the ridge to the crèche where, Oracle or not, Patricia would be staying until the Old Man's issue was done with her.

§

They drew straws that afternoon in the village. Lily was happy to see that it was not El who drew the short straw, but his younger brother Lothar. He was quiet and nice to girls, handsome enough, and Lily figured that he would not much harm her older sister when he laid table for her.

As much as all the Feegers wanted to hear what their Oracle had to say, they knew that this ritual, of laying table, was important. An Oracle would only live short if she carried the issue without sustenance—the issue would turn to her, tear her out from the inside.

So when the Old Man sent an Oracle back, someone had to lay table—fill her up with seed for the issue's larder. To forestall bloodshed, for it was no chore offering this prize, the Feeger men-folk had long since drawn straws.

Lothar drew the shorter straw only second up. He held it in front of him in wonder.

"Old Man favours you," said El, all trace of his smirk gone now.

Lothar swallowed and said, "Oh," and then on shaking legs he headed off to the crèche.

Patricia waited, tucked well beneath the rock overhand. She was trembling, with the memory of the cold and a bit of a fever, but also with a bit of worry. Her memories of the night with the Old Man were not too clear, but happy. She'd given her Love and seemed to get as much back again. She knew how the Feeger men could be with her and her sisters. She thought about bruising and bleeding and being made to feel small again. She worried, like her sister, that it would be awful now.

Then the door opened on the wooden front of the crèche, and in the noon-hour light she saw who it was. She smiled.

"Lothar," she said.

"Huh," said Lothar.

"Glad it's you," she said. Lothar held his hands at his middle, and stumbled in. His trousers and shirt and boots were gone. "Close the door," she said.

Lothar nodded. He turned around and closed the door. Outside, there were sounds of disappointment. But the crèche was dark. Patricia shifted. She heard Lothar shuffling in the dark, moving around the crèche.

"I'll talk," said Patricia, "so you c'n find me."

"Hum," said Lothar.

"It is going to be a good time for us," said Patricia. "That is what the Old Man said."

Lothar stumbled, and there was a clattering sound.

"You hit the table, now, didn't you," said Patricia. "You're going the wrong way. You're not scared, are you?"

"Um," said Lothar. "Um hum."

"Well don't be. This will be—" she paused, looking for the right word "—not mean."

More stumbling, this time closer. Then Patricia felt the heat from Lothar's flank, next to her. She pulled the furs aside, and she felt as he scrambled to get underneath with her.

"You're shaking," she commented.

"Um," said Lothar.

"Well I'll calm you," she said. She reached down and took hold of him. He was slick and warm down there, and he gasped as she pulled and worked him. "Now," she said, "get ready. Babies are hungry. And they will need food for the long walk. So you go plant your seed, Lothar. Plant it for harvest."

"Long—" Lothar made a sound as she lifted her leg and guided him inside "—walk?"

"That," sang Patricia, "is how it is going to be." She thrust down on him, and Lothar made a strangling sound at the base of his throat. "That—that's the message. The Old Man's sending us on a long walk. Down the mountains to that river place. To see about His son. Show the folk there how to treat him right."

Lothar took his breath in sharp, and whimpered, and she felt his release in her. She welcomed it, the way she'd welcomed the Old Man. It was more love for Him.

She would need that love and more—because the Old Man had made it clear. There was heavy work ahead of them, if they were to do his bidding: find the Son, and make things right again. To do that, she would have to preach—preach to strangers, and make them see how the Son was their Father—make them raise up a Cathedral to him.

And if she couldn't convince them . . . if they turned from their calling?

Either way, it would be heavy work.

12

Aunty's Tears

Jason sat up in bed and gingerly touched his sore, bandaged hand. Dr. Waggoner was still sleeping, so he was quiet as he got out of bed and padded to the window, looked out. It was early morning and he had a good view of Eliada. The hospital was on a rise, and looking down he could see the low wooden buildings spreading along two muddy roadways. People were up and getting set for work—a couple of wagons were loading sacks outside a store. Farther along, he could see gangs of men moving around the sawmill, a team of horses in their midst hauling a pile of logs up to a ramp on the mill's edge. The two smokestacks at the far end of the mill building sent out a long white cloud of wood smoke. Muffled by distance and wooden walls, Jason was sure he could hear the chugging of a steam engine, the whine of saw-blades.

He let the curtain fall, and stepped out the door, into the corridor and to a tall window at its end. This view was better. It gave him a look at the quarantine. In daylight.

It was not as big as it'd seemed, but it was big enough, built a little better than you'd build a barn, but shaped like a horseshoe. It looked new. It was nestled right back against thick woods and its wooden walls were painted a deep green—as though it might blend in better that way. And there was one other thing about it that Jason noted especially.

It looked like it would burn.

Jason swallowed and leaned against the wall. Was that what he was thinking? Putting torch to the quarantine? Deliberately murdering whoever was in there? Or not caring who was in there and who was not, and doing it all the same?

Last night, he might have done it. The same way he'd been thinking about picking up a gun and using it to shoot Dr. Bergstrom, he could easily have thought about putting torch to the quarantine. It was filled up with Devils after all.

This morning, that urge was gone. Maybe Dr. Bergstrom's poison had run its course—had made him mean for awhile, like too much liquor or Coca-Cola. Maybe . . .

Jason drew a sharp breath then and forgot his musings, as a pair of figures emerged from the middle of the horseshoe. It was Aunt Germaine—and Dr. Bergstrom. They were talking to each other. But they did not seem angry—not like last night in his office, or at the quarantine. They seemed more like old friends now. As Jason watched, Aunt Germaine actually laughed at something the doctor said. Dr. Bergstrom did not seem as pleased. But he reached up and patted Aunt Germaine on the shoulder, and she did not flinch away from him.

Jason pulled back from the window. The easy part of the morning was over now. The rest of the day, he figured, was going to be a hard fight and nothing better.

§

Jason got Dr. Waggoner awake soon enough that they could talk about a plan for confronting Dr. Bergstrom. They figured they would not talk about the tiny people that Jason said he'd seen in the quarantine, the strange man in white and the other man behind the door, and concentrate on the question of why Dr. Bergstrom thought it was safe to strap down a healthy boy alone in an empty ward room.

"You going to talk to him about that girl?" asked Jason. "All butchered like a hog as she was?"

Dr. Waggoner shook his head. "We fight one battle at a time," he said. "If we tidied things right, he won't be sure we even looked at her. No, I will deal with that next time I can speak with Mr. Harper. Which," he said, looking significantly at Jason, "I intend to do as soon as I am able."

That was about all the planning they had time for, before the door swung open and Dr. Bergstrom, followed by Aunt Germaine, stormed in.

"What are you doing treating patients, Andrew?" he demanded.

Dr. Waggoner leaned back on the pillows they'd propped behind his back, as Dr. Bergstrom approached him closer.

"The boy was cut," he said. "He could have become infected."

"Do you have any notion," Bergstrom said, "of the risk that you took in removing this patient from quarantine? He could be carrying an illness that might wipe out the town!"

"My," said Andrew. "The entire town you say. That is quite some ailment."

"And you removed him."

"I did not remove anyone. He was already out when I met him."

"Not possible."

"How is that?"

Dr. Bergstrom drew back at that question, because Jason figured he had no good answer. Dr. Waggoner must have figured that too, because he showed the faintest trace of a smile as he nodded.

"You are not supposed to be practising," said Dr. Bergstrom finally. Your *arm*, Andrew."

"It works well enough for stitching a cut." Dr. Waggoner looked at his hand coming out of that splint, waggled the fingertips. "And however you choose to address me, *Nils*, I am still a doctor here. At least according to Mr. Harper."

"Yes. Mr. Harper." Dr. Bergstrom regarded him with a squint. "Your benefactor."

"I wonder, should we perhaps speak with him about this *breach*?"

"Do not be so quick, to run—"

"Yes?"

Dr. Bergstrom glared silently, not answering.

Jason wanted to stay for more but he felt a hand on his shoulder and looked up to see his aunt standing close. She bent to whisper in his ear: "Come, Nephew. This is a matter between these men now. Not us. Not now."

"But—" Jason did not care for the idea of leaving Dr. Bergstrom alone with his friend. But when he caught Andrew's eye, he nodded, as if to say, *Go on. I will be fine here.*

Dr. Bergstrom looked at Jason too—and that, more than Dr. Waggoner's encouragement, was what made up his mind, because Jason had never seen a man look hungrier than did Dr. Bergstrom looking at him then.

"Good bye, Dr. Waggoner," he said. "Thank you kindly for the stitching."

Dr. Waggoner smiled. "Take care of yourself, Jason."

And out they went, hurrying down the hall and past the window overlooking quarantine.

"Why did you leave me in there?" said Jason as they moved to the stairwell. Aunt Germaine glanced at him with a queer half-smile.

"In the quarantine?" she said. "I am sorry, Nephew: I could do little else. Dr. Bergstrom is the senior medical official in Eliada."

"*Senior medical official.* Is that the same as the law?" Jason didn't let his aunt answer the question. "Because if he is the law, like a sheriff or a judge, then I guess he has a right to inject a fellow with poison, tie him up and leave him to die. Otherwise . . ."

"Jason," said Aunt Germaine, patting him on the shoulder, "the important thing is—the truly important thing is, that you fared *magnificently*. You—"

"I could just leave, you know."

Germaine's eyes widened in the dark of the stairwell. The two stood on a landing, she a step below Jason, and he towered over her. Perhaps that is what gave Jason the courage to say that thing. Because after having said it, he could scarcely believe it had come from his mouth. It was a region of thought he had not come near—even when his temper was at its hottest.

But he found it was a region with a clear path through it. So he went on.

"You got me out of Cracked Wheel when things were bad, and I'm grateful for that, and glad to know I have kin yet. But when I was sitting in the cabin with my mama, I figured on carrying on with what I could. A fellow willing to work can find it anywhere I figure. I'm surely big enough."

Aunt Germaine opened her mouth to speak. But a sound came out that was unfamiliar to Jason. "Why—" she began, and "My nephew—" she went on, and finally, she opened her arms and flung them around Jason's shoulders, and Jason realized with a hitch that he'd done something that nothing—not the death of her sister, nor the wasting at Cracked Wheel—nothing else had yet done in his presence.

Through his selfish words, he had made his Aunt Germaine cry.

§

"Why did you do that to the boy?" said Andrew when Jason and his aunt were well gone. "He's not sick. From what he told me, any exposure to the illness that took lives in his home town happened long ago. And if he were somehow contagious . . . Well. He spent a long time on train and boat and foot without quarantine. What would be the point of containing him now?"

Dr. Bergstrom pulled up a chair to Andrew's bedside. "You feel that you are qualified in some manner to question my decisions with regard to this boy? That's interesting, Andrew," he said.

"That boy was in danger, and you put him there," said Andrew. "Deliberately. You tied him down and locked him up with that rapist, Mister Juke."

Dr. Bergstrom leaned very close to Andrew's face, and as he did so his expression underwent a change. And that was the first true sense that Andrew got that he might actually be in physical danger from this man.

"Do not," he hissed, "call him that—you damned meddlesome *nigger*. Do not *dare*."

Andrew drew back against his pillows. All he could think about was Maryanne Leonard, the things that had been done to her corpse. What could this man's hands do to living flesh?

"Doctor," he said as levelly as he could. "Control yourself."

His words seemed to have some effect. For a moment, Dr. Bergstrom looked as if he would strike him, but the moment past. The doctor sat up, ran a hand through his hair, then looked deliberately into his lap for a moment before shutting his eyes tight.

When he opened them again, he drew a deep breath. He stood fast enough the chair rocked at his calves.

"What an error it was," he said softly, "bringing *you* to Eliada."

Andrew did not say anything to that. He could do nothing but stare at the man across from him.

"Well. I have other business to attend to. So if you will excuse me—I will leave you to your rest."

Dr. Bergstrom lifted his hands from his side—with a flash of silver in one of them. Before Andrew could react, he grabbed Andrew's good arm, pulled it out straight and pushed it down onto the mattress, then pausing not an instant to find his mark, jabbed the hypodermic needle into it. Andrew moaned, as the drug found its way into his veins.

"Rest," said Dr. Bergstrom again, wagging the spent hypodermic in front of him and backing away, he slipped out the door and hurried down the hall.

DAVID NICKLE

§

Aunt Germaine was set up in a room on the third floor, not far from Dr. Bergstrom's own offices. There was a table, a couple of wooden chairs, and five big boxes full of papers.

Aunt Germaine, having dried her eyes and calmed her nerves after Jason contritely explained he was not going anywhere, said, "Those are like larger versions of my file cards. They are all the records that Dr. Bergstrom has kept of the people here in Eliada. From the time that it began."

"That must be a lot more than those ones."

"Not so much more," she said, whisking her skirts aside as she sat down. "Eliada is a young town. It was incorporated in 1887—just a quarter of a century ago. Currently, some eight hundred souls call it home. But its population has grown only in recent years—since Mr. Harper and his foundation arrived and began their work in earnest."

"That the Utopian paradise business that Ruth was talking about?"

Aunt Germaine smiled wryly. "Near enough the mark," she said. "Let me see if I can explain it a little better. Mr. Harper comes from a family that has done well for itself in timber and mining. Most of their more profitable holdings are farther west of here—in Seattle and California. Mr. Harper came into—shall we say, *possession* of this town, inasmuch as he took control of the sawmill, at the turn of the century. So we are properly regarding just a decade of medical records."

"Because the hospital came with Mr. Harper."

"Correct."

"And so what is it that makes this place so Utopian? The hospital?"

"Utopian. Those are that young Ruth's words." Aunt Germaine shook her head. "The hospital is not the cause of it. It is, however, a signpost."

"A signpost."

"It is an indication that the community cares for the health and hygiene of its members. However remote—this is a safe place. Do you know what Eliada means?"

Jason frowned. "It's from the Bible. One of King David's sons? I got that right?"

"Very good. And it means, 'Watched over by God.' That is the principle upon which Mr. Harper governs."

"What was it like here before Mr. Harper came along then?"

Aunt Germaine shrugged. "I really cannot say. But," she said, patting the top of one of the boxes, "we will be able to say a great deal about the last decade here. Once we have looked through these, and conducted our interviews."

"I guess you want to get started."

"In time," said Aunt Germaine. "To begin with—I think we ought to find a good breakfast. I have your clothes here. We can go into town, eat our fill—and you can tell me all of what happened last night."

Jason did not tell all of what happened. In fact, he left out important parts and that changed the story utterly. He was not sure when he decided to withhold these things from his aunt, but decide he did. As they left the hospital and made their way along the wide roads to breakfast he told her a story: how, left alone in the ward room, he had panicked when a large raccoon came into the room and had gotten curious about him. So he'd cut himself loose, he told her, as he ate a plate of fried eggs and thick-rinded bacon, and run off into the dark, where he had cut himself on the scalpel something terrible. Dr. Waggoner had found him outside, bleeding and naked, and taken him inside and stitched him up.

"So we went up to his room, where he said he would keep me until morning, on account of neither of us thought it was a good idea going back into that quarantine building." He pushed his plate away. "On account of the raccoon. And just generally."

Aunt Germaine patted a napkin on her lips and regarded him. They sat in the dining room of the Eliada Empire Hotel, which had in it five tables, each round and covered with identical red-and-white checked tablecloths, and they had it to themselves. In fact, from the way the old man who ran the place greeted them coming in, Jason got the idea that fixing breakfast at ten in the morning was a real *travail*. Now, he could feel himself being watched.

"A raccoon," said Aunt Germaine.

"Or something."

"It must have been quite something. You do not want to talk about the things that happened in there, do you?"

"We *are* talking about them."

"No we are not," she said, smiling sweetly. "Not truly. But that is fine, Jason. It was an awful night. You will speak of it in time."

There was a rattling behind them then as a door opened. Sam Green walked in, hatless but well-dressed. Aunt Germaine pursed her lips and looked at her hands. Jason nodded back hello when Sam Green waved.

"Good morning," he said. "Trust everything went well at the hospital?"

Jason thought about speaking, but before he could, Aunt Germaine spoke up.

"Thank you, yes, Mr. Green," she said. "Fine."

"Fine," he said, and sat down at a table near the door, a respectful distance from the two of them. "Glad to hear it, Mrs. Frost. You able to start your work, determining all our fitness and whatnot?"

"Not yet," said Aunt Germaine. "Thank you."

Green's moustache spread like a fan over his smile.

"And you, Mr. Thistledown? You ready to assist?"

Jason nodded.

"Well today looks like a fine one for it."

"Yes," said Aunt Germaine. "Thank you."

Sam Green nodded, reached into his coat and pulled out a little black book, stuck his nose in it to signal the conversation was done—or he was finished trying to start it. He took out a pencil and began underlining. At length, Aunt Germaine leaned forward.

"You saw something in there other than a raccoon," she said. "You did. Didn't you?"

Jason swallowed. "I—guess I did," he said.

"It is important that you tell," she said. "Not anyone—" she glanced over to Sam Green, who was now scribbling something on a piece of paper he'd used to mark his place "—but me."

"You."

"You should tell me, so I can protect you."

And as she looked at him in that way, her eyes wide and generous, her hand resting lightly on his shoulder, Jason almost did tell her everything. She was family, after all, and if you could not trust family with your secrets then who could you trust? And had she not given him that scalpel—that little knife that had saved his life as far as he knew, in the quarantine?

But as he tried to put it into a sentence, he found that he couldn't.

"Just don't let him put me back in that quarantine," he finally said.

Aunt Germaine nodded. "I have an idea," she said. "Why don't we go explore a bit? My work can wait a few more hours. Why not see what we can find in this little town—well away from that dreadful quarantine."

"All right," said Jason. "That sounds fine to me."

They got up to leave, and as they did, Sam Green stood as well.

"Ma'am," he said as she stepped through the door to the street. As Jason passed, Sam Green was more demonstrative: he clapped him on the shoulder and shook his hand. "Pleasure to see you once more, young Thistledown. Enjoy your tour of the town."

Jason swallowed as he let go of Sam Green's hand, did his best to avoid making a face.

"Thank you, sir," he said, meeting the older man's eye.

"Hurry along, Nephew," called Aunt Germaine from the street. He did. It was only at the end of the block, as Germaine rooted in her handbag for a fan, that he opened his hand and looked at the scrap of paper that Sam Green had left him there.

BE AT NORTH DOOR OF SAWMILL AT AFT SHIFT CHANGE, it read.

And underneath, in big letters underlined twice:

LEAVE AUNTY BEHIND.

13

The Mercy of Sam Green

The sawmill's north door was at the edge of a vast and shadowed lumber yard—a whole town made of stacks of square-cut timber, whose avenues and alleyways were choked in sawdust so thick it might have fallen in a storm. Jason Thistledown waded along its main thoroughfare as the hour neared four o'clock. A bell was ringing to signal the shift change, and because of this he was not alone on his march. Men were walking to and from their work. A couple of them made eye contact with Jason but just one of them, a heavy bald man whose beard dangled well past his neck, spoke to him, from across the crude avenue.

"Hey fellow," he called, and beckoned him. Jason cringed inside. He was sure he was going to be found out, told to scat and then he would never learn what Sam Green wanted with him and *not Aunty*. But there was nothing for it, so over he went.

The man looked at him. "You new here, heh?"

"Yes sir," said Jason. "Just came in yesterday, sir."

"You name?" The man had a strange way of talking; like his tongue was stuck in his mouth sideways.

"Name!" he repeated.

"Jason," Jason said.

"Nowak."

"Pleased to meet you."

"Is good place in Eliada," said Nowak. "Godly. You like."

And then he slapped Jason on the back and laughed deeply, and gave him a push forward hard enough to make Jason stumble.

"Thank you, sir," Jason said, and waved as he stepped away from Nowak. Jason swore to himself. Telling his name to a strange fellow on his way to a secret meeting was probably a bad mistake. But it too was done.

Soon enough, they came upon the sawmill itself, and met with another group of men who were coming out. In this chaos, Jason stepped to one side, into a little alleyway between two long stacks of lumber. MEET AT THE NORTH DOOR, the note had said. AT, it read. Not INSIDE it.

Jason settled into shadow as the lumber yard cleared out, and waited. He'd positioned himself to have a view of the door without being too conspicuous— or worse, seeming like he was hiding.

He did not wait there long. The Pinkerton man showed up only a moment after the whine of the saw blade started up, and just preceding the first plume of sawdust that flew out a high opening. He was wearing his hat now, but no coat. His suspenders were showing atop a dusty white shirt. The revolver holstered at his hip was in plain sight.

He came out of the same door they were to meet by, and without so much as looking left or right ambled over to the spot where Jason figured he'd hidden himself so well.

"Aunty back there anywhere?" he asked, and when Jason shook his head he nodded. "What did you tell her?"

"Nothing," said Jason. "I left her a-napping back at the hospital."

"Good. Anyone else see you come? I should have told you the same about Dr. Bergstrom and other folk too, but by the time I'd thought of it you'd left."

"I didn't tell Bergstrom. No one else either."

"Good." Sam Green stepped around Jason and set his behind against the lumber. "I thought you might have good instinct. Turns out I was right."

"I don't trust Dr. Bergstrom," said Jason. "He locked me up in the quarantine with some kind of Devil, left me to—"

Sam Green raised his hand. "Hold on," he said. "You don't trust Dr. Bergstrom and that's smart thinking. Why'n hell do you trust *me*?"

Jason looked at him. "Because—"

"Because I invited you here to meet me by yourself, and not tell anybody?" Sam Green shook his head. "Boy, I wanted to, I could kill you right now and probably get away with it. You just told me nobody knew you came here, then started spilling everything after I buttered you up about your good instincts."

"But—"

"But nothing." Sam Green grabbed Jason's shoulder and leaned close. "You're in some trouble, Jason Thistledown. You're right Doc Bergstrom locked you up in the quarantine with something else—maybe a Devil, maybe a freak of nature . . . but for certain something that has no business being there. He did that last night and he put you at grave risk, son. What do you think he's going to do tonight?"

"I—"

"*I* nothing. *You* listen, and I'll tell you. What's going to happen tonight, it's got nothing to do with you. But it has a lot to do with our friend Andrew Waggoner. He's not going to wake up tomorrow, if he stays in that room in the hospital through the night."

Jason twisted his shoulder and Sam Green let go.

"All right," said Jason, stepping back a bit, "I'm listening. You tell me what's what."

"Good." Sam Green sat back, blew out his cheeks. Sawdust was falling on them now, light golden snowflakes, and the whine of the saw was steady. "First thing. I know that you and Dr. Waggoner met outside the quarantine last night. I saw you, because I was watching the quarantine under orders from Doc Bergstrom."

"I didn't see you anywhere—"

"You didn't see me because I didn't want you to."

Jason glared at him."You tell Bergstrom?"

"About last night? As it happens, no. No I did not. You and I are of a mind on Dr. Bergstrom, and that mind's made up. I didn't tell, but I did talk to him. Him and your aunt, early this morning."

"My aunt?"

"Yes, son, your aunt. He did most of the talking but she was there for all of it. And he—" Sam Green looked at his hands, and huffed. "He asked me to do something. Or not to do something."

"What?"

"He told me to keep clear of Andrew Waggoner tonight."

"And that is it?"

"Son, you remember how I told you I was in dutch?"

Jason remembered. "On account of shooting those fellows at the hanging tree?"

He nodded. "That is why I'm in dutch with Mr. Harper. Doc Bergstrom is none too happy with me, either."

"And why's that?"

"I'm in dutch with the doctor," he said, "for showing up at all."

Jason gaped, and Sam Green nodded. "Or at least when I did."

"You mean—"

"Bergstrom thinks that the Juke was never in any danger of hanging, or at least of dying from it. He said the important thing was for those fellows to try, and then to fail. Teach 'em a lesson, he said.

"He was more than happy to see the Negro doctor die on the end of a noose. It would have solved some problems for him if he did.

"And so he asked me to keep clear of the top floor of the hospital. He made sure to tell me that everyone would be keeping clear of the top floor of the hospital tonight. He told me that Dr. Waggoner needed his rest—and that if someone came by, to make sure they understood—why, he wanted to make sure no one who knew how to use a gun was there to stop whatever's going to happen."

Jason sat back and absorbed that. In the mill, the saw had stopped its work a moment—maybe while the men were positioning more logs. So the lumber yard became quieter, but the sawdust still fell.

"Why do you think he's doing that?"

"Two reasons. First one: Bergstrom is the kind of man who cannot abide a nigger in a white man's job, and Harper's the kind of man who can't abide denying a smart nigger his due. And second: that smart nigger's learned more about the Juke than Bergstrom would like."

"You know about the Juke," said Jason. "You know what that thing is in there."

"I know it is a freak of nature," said Sam. "It doesn't die from a hanging. It does not speak but makes itself understood better than any man I have met. And it gets . . ."

There was quiet again.

"Yes?"

"It gets bigger."

"Bigger." The air cleared now, as the last of the sawdust plume settled on the brim of Sam Green's bowler hat.

"Yeah," he said. "It grows. When Bergstrom found it, just in the summer—the thing was only as high as my elbow. Now . . ." Eyes down, his voice trailed off. But he put his hand level a good six inches over the top of his bowler.

"Were you there when he found it?"

Sam Green looked up from the hands he was examining so closely. "Boy," he said, "here is what you've got to do. You get up to Andrew Waggoner's room. You tell him that if he sleeps tonight, he won't wake up, because Nils Bergstrom aims to see him dead. You tell him he's got to get far from here. No one will suspect you—because I am the one supposed to be watching you, and I will say you were someplace else. And if you head up there around—oh, let us say seven—you will find you can make a clean escape."

"Think I should go with him?"

"I think," said Sam, "that you ought not trust your aunt to protect you. But you shouldn't leave, either. That will draw things back to me, and that won't do anyone any good. I'll do my best to keep you safe if you stay here. But stay you must."

And at that, Sam Green got up.

"That is all for today," he said. "You think I have done you a favour but I haven't. I'm doing my friend Dr. Waggoner a favour. You are not my friend."

"How can you trust me to carry it out then?"

"I trust you," he said, "because you owe that doctor a debt, and you are not the sort of man to leave a debt unpaid. And," he added, "you won't leave, or tell of this, or anything else, because you owe me now, for giving you a way to repay it." And then he turned and stomped off. Jason watched him go, across the avenue and into another passage between the lumber. Jason had no reason to stay, but he waited all the same, until the saw started up again, to make his way out of the lumber yard and back to the hospital.

He was gone before the sawdust stormed again, which was a good thing, because Jason knew he would have to clean the residue off before he got back to the hospital, and went to work settling all those debts.

§

Andrew Waggoner blinked and coughed. The boy—Jason—Jason Thistledown—was in his room again. He had left the room at some point, but Andrew was not clear on exactly when or why, or on the things that had come after. Now he was back and he was talking. Or whispering. His mouth was moving, anyhow.

Andrew worked his lips, which felt numb, and blinked, and as he did, things started falling into place. Jason leaned closer, and Andrew became aware that the boy had his hands on his shoulder and was talking, somehow more clearly now.

"Dr. Waggoner, you have to wake up now. You're in very bad trouble. You have to walk out of here, because I cannot carry you and the things I've got for you."

Andrew licked his lips. "Wha—"

He tried again. "What are you talking about, Jason? What things?"

Jason looked relieved. "Good. I thought they might have already got you. Why're you like that?"

"Bergstrom gave me a needle of something," said Andrew. He looked at the window, the purple-orange sky outside it. "What time is it?"

"Quarter past seven," said Jason.

Andrew let out a slow whistle, counting hours until he got to ten. What had Bergstrom put in that needle? It wasn't morphine. Veronal, perhaps? Put enough of Emil Fischer's hypnotic drug into a hypodermic, and it could knock a man out for a day. Put a drop too much, and it'd kill him.

"You were saying something about the trouble I was in. I may have missed the beginning of it," said Andrew.

Jason took a breath, and started over again. By the time he was finished, Andrew was fully awake, alert—and convinced. He had to get out of that hospital room. There would be no stopping at his house for things. There would be no dallying here waiting until his wits were all returned to him. He had to get away from Eliada. And he had to do it now.

§

A few moments prior to eight, they were out the back door of the hospital. Andrew wore a pair of workman's trousers and boots, and an oversized woollen coat—one big enough to admit his splinted arm and still let him move. Jason carried the doctor's bag and another satchel containing food and a knife, a canteen for water and what other things a man might need on foot in the wilderness.

There was no gun in the kit, an omission for which Jason apologized several times, but as he explained: "Aunt Germaine keeps a close watch on both our guns and would miss them. Then you'd be done for."

I may be done for anyhow, thought Andrew as he and Jason made a wide circuit around the quarantine, towards the tree-line. Whatever Dr. Bergstrom had put in him that had knocked him out, seemed to have the effect of numbing the pain enough for him to move right now. But he knew enough about anaesthetic to know that would only purchase him so much time, before all that pain came back at him. He would have to pace himself—and then rely on some good luck to get him through the next couple of nights.

For now, though, he kept on moving. The going got tougher the closer they got to the trees, and finally, maybe a dozen yards into the thin woods—out of direct sight of the hospital but still in good view of the quarantine—they stopped. Andrew sat down on a log. Jason handed him the doctor's bag, and the other bag that could be thrown over a shoulder.

They sat still and quiet for a bit. Then Jason spoke, his voice soft and quavering.

"Why would they lock me in with that thing?"

"I don't know." Andrew squinted at him. "You sure you won't come with me? I'm not sure this is a safe place for you right now."

Jason shook his head. "Sam Green said: I go, it points straight back to him."

"Ah," said Andrew. "I don't know about that. There's a game going on here. Has to do with Mister Juke. Harper. Bergstrom. Sam Green now. And I wonder how your aunt's involved."

Jason hunched his shoulders. "I wonder that myself." He looked right at Andrew Waggoner. "Sometimes, I wonder if it wouldn't have been better I just got left alone back in Montana, my aunt never showed up. Or maybe if that germ had took me—"

Andrew stopped him. "That is not something to wonder about."

"I know." Jason sighed. "You better get moving. I'm sure sorry I couldn't get you a gun."

"Don't apologize. I'm not much good with a gun right now anyway."

"Well—" Jason stood up, and cleared his throat. "Well, it would still be a greater help to you than that knife. I hope this goes a little ways towards repaying you for helping me last night."

"That is no debt," he said. "Helping a boy who's hurt in the night is a doctor's work. I am sorry that we won't be able to learn more about Maryanne Leonard, and those things inside her."

"You can," said Jason. He put his hand on the bag. "I wrapped the specimen jar with those eggs in it in cloth. You get back to someplace with an eyeglass, you can have a look at them and see what's what."

Andrew smiled. "Thank you," he said.

Then Jason's expression, something in the tilt of his shoulders, shifted. He finally looked Andrew in the eye.

"No," he said. "You got no reason to thank me, sending you off alone to die." He took a look back at the hospital. "Hang Sam Green. I'm going with you."

Andrew put his hand on the boy's shoulder. "No," he said. "You made an agreement—a promise. You go too, attention will come back to Sam Green, who'll suffer for no reason other than doing a fellow a good turn. I'll be fine."

"You won't be," said Jason.

"You don't have a say." Andrew made himself smile, and lied. "I'm feeling much improved, anyhow. That knife and the food will be a help, and I can remember the way back to Bonner's Ferry fine. You go back to your aunt, and keep your mouth closed, and lie low for awhile. Like Sam Green said to."

Jason didn't answer. He turned away and tromped back through the underbrush. Andrew watched him as he headed past the quarantine, paused to look at it for only a second, and returned to the hospital and his aunt. By the time the boy was inside, the smile was not even a memory on Andrew Waggoner's face.

With a grimace, he pushed himself up off the log, gathered the things that Jason had brought for him, and headed into the dark sanctity of the woods.

§

Aunt Germaine was waiting for Jason as he came through the door to their rooms at the hospital. A single candle burned in a dish beside her. She held a small envelope between two fingers of her right hand, tapping the edge of the envelope against the palm of her left like the blade of an axe. Those eyeglasses made her expression inscrutable.

"Good evening, Aunt."

"Nephew," she said, nodding sternly. "Been busy?"

Jason felt something fall in his gut—something that had stayed put through the whole adventure of stealing medical supplies and clothes and what else he could find, and sneaking Dr. Waggoner out the back. Through it all, he had attributed the ease of it all to improbable luck. Now, all he could think of was how improbable it was that he'd get away with the escape—how vastly improbable. Aunt Germaine knew of his conspiracy, and he felt like a bandit, caught in the act.

He looked away from her. Germaine leaned forward. "Nephew," she said, her voice low, "I am trying to protect you. Do you understand that?"

"Yes," said Jason. He felt very small then. Were he a couple of months younger, he thought he might've started to cry.

"Well," she said, "then why do you feel the need to go to another?"

"You mean—" Jason felt as though it were all going to spill out. Aunt Germaine—who, if Sam Green were to be believed, was at the very core of this plan to murder Andrew Waggoner . . . she had Jason in a corner. She had him figured out. Her next words would surely be about Sam Green, he thought.

"I mean that dreadful girl," she said. "Ruth Harper."

Jason gawked, and Aunt Germaine took his expression as something else. She held the envelope, and pulled a card from it. "Do not play the innocent, Nephew," she said. "This came for you whilst you were gallivanting—no doubt signed after you had met." She tossed the card on the floor in front of Jason. Perplexed, he bent down to pick it up.

It was written in a fine script on paper so thick it almost felt like cloth. It was addressed to *Jason Thistledown*. It requested the *Pleasure of Your Company* at a *Celebration of Spring* in the company of *Mr. and Mrs. Garrison Harper* this *Sunday the Thirtieth of April*, following *Worship*. It was signed, *Miss Ruth Harper*.

He took a long, even breath, then looked up and met Aunt Germaine's gaze.

"First I heard of this, Aunt," he said. But all he could think of was his improbably good fortune.

§

Just as Sam Green said they might, men came to the hospital in the evening. They wore ghost-white cloaks over their shoulders, and white hoods like pillowcases over their heads. There were five of them and they all strode purposefully to the front of the hospital, up the steps and in through the waiting room like Hussars.

One of them hollered: "Where is the nigger rapist?" which brought the duty nurse as far as the door to the clinic (she fled back into the depths of the hospital when she saw who was there) and set the newborn infant sleeping not far in a room with his mama yowling.

They were not perturbed by the sound of a crying baby, not these men. They did not even look to each other as they pushed through into the corridor beyond, up four floors to the very top of the hospital—to the floor with a few private rooms for the important ones, where nurses and doctors had not been for some hours.

Although there were many rooms upstairs, there was only one occupied now, and the men in white went straight to that one. The one with the rifle pushed open the door. He held up the gun, aimed it at the form in the bed, and stood still. One of the sheets with a club nodded at him, went to the foot of the bed and raised his club over his head. The sheet with crossed arms shifted, looked one to the other, like he was trying to suss some secret communication between the two of them. The rifleman motioned with the barrel of his rifle and the club fell, with murderous force.

"Fuck," said the rifleman. He raised his rifle and strode over to the bed. "Fuck," he said again, as he pulled the covers aside and saw naught but a stack of pillows artfully arranged.

"He was warned," said another sheet. "Nigger got warned, now he's off."

"Treachery," said a third.

And: "Blasphemy," said the one with his arms hid.

"Don't overstate matters," the rifleman said. But his hands shook. He gripped the stock of the rifle harder, until the shaking stopped.

14

The Faerie King's Bride

"I'm not going to fight you," Andrew Waggoner said. He raised his hands palm out to display the splintered arm to full effect. The hill man holding the rifle nodded. He was a tall, black-haired fellow with a patchy beard over a thick chin, gangly but for disproportionately wide shoulders.

"You ain't gonna fight," he said. "You ain't gonna run, neither."

"I won't do that either."

"Well get up."

Andrew lowered his good hand and propped himself up with it against the bare rock. He drew his feet under himself and stood. He had been resting on the lichen-covered shelf of rock, partway up a steepening slope he'd spent the early part of the morning scaling. It should not have been a difficult climb, and—reflecting back on it with the perfect wisdom that comes to a man staring down the barrel of a rifle—Andrew thought it was not a necessary one either.

But Andrew's exhausted mind had fixed on the idea that he could find the riverbank he had lost the day before by climbing above the tree-line and looking for it; and his exhausted body had made that walk up the slope of a hill into an ascent of a mountain. He was thinking about opening the doctor's bag, sticking himself with a syringe full of morphine, letting it work its magic, when the man with the rifle came upon him.

"I am up," said Andrew. "Now tell me what you want."

"You the nigger doctor," said the hill man. He glanced down at the bag, which Andrew had not gotten around to opening when he came. "From the log town. You got your doctoring fixings there. 'M I right?"

"Dr. Andrew Waggoner," he said. "Yes. I'm the doctor."

"Pick it up," said the hill man. "I'll get the other one. You come now. Got work for you."

They climbed for a short distance, then came upon a beaten path through the underbrush that followed the contour of the hillside. Andrew was glad: it helped him catch his breath, put his thoughts together.

"What's your name?" he said then.

The hill man said something that sounded like "Ink."

"Well, Ink," said Andrew between gasps, "you said you had work for me. Someone sick?"

"Sick," he said, nodding, and prodded Andrew's back with the gun barrel. Andrew took the hint: he didn't ask any more questions, although he had plenty.

Over his time in Eliada, Andrew had only had a little contact with the folk who lived in the hills to the west. They were old families—some of them here since the 1830s, settler families whose wagons had travelled north—and they did not come to Eliada much. When they did, the hospital would see to them; Andrew himself had stitched up a couple of cuts, splinted a fracture or two.

As they climbed over rocks, he wondered: might not some of those Klansmen who tried to hang him and Mister Juke have come from shacks up the hillside from Eliada? How did Ink know that he was the "nigger doctor?"

"Here w'are," said Ink, and they climbed a short rise in the path, and stepped into the compound of Andrew's captors.

It was a homestead, built on a cleared-out plateau and surrounded by tall pine trees. There were four buildings, all cut from logs with low sod roofs, arranged in a semicircle with their front doors facing downslope.

Ink hollered something that Andrew couldn't understand, and the front doors of two of the other buildings swung open. An enormous man strode out from one, and two younger boys came out the other.

"Set your bag down," said Ink. Andrew did, and found himself falling to his knees.

The boys took up the bag. One of them opened it and had a look inside. He reached in, pulled out a scalpel, turned it in a filthy hand and set it back. Then he pulled out a bottle of iodine, twisted off the top and gave it to the other to sniff.

"Put it back," said Ink. "This here's the doctor."

The boy did like he was told, and squinted at Andrew.

"Don't look like the doctor," he said.

"Different doctor, but he do the job," said Ink. He sounded irritated to Andrew. "Take his bag inside. To Loo's bed."

Andrew looked back over his shoulder. Ink had lifted his rifle so its barrel pointed up to the treetops. Seeing Andrew turn, the hill man nodded.

"You can get up," he said. "Look like you're going to wet y' trouser."

Andrew got to his feet. He was shaky and his vision greyed a bit, but he was feeling better. He was certainly not going to wet his trousers because this was far from the worst he'd imagined. These weren't Klansmen.

These were hill people with a sick relation.

Ink motioned with his hand, and walked ahead of Andrew to the doorway. He disappeared into the dark, and Andrew followed.

The house was a single room, with light coming in mainly through the spacing between badly fitted timber. A little kettle-shaped stove warmed things, and next to it was a crude mattress, held in a box made of pine, like a great crib. Or a casket.

One of the boys opened the wood stove and stuck a candle in. He brought the flame near the bed, and Andrew bent down.

"Oh my," he said softly, peering down into the sweat-covered face, the skin that even in the warm candlelight seemed deathly pale. "How long has she been sick?"

"Two week," said Ink.

"This is Loo, am I right?"

"Loo," said Ink.

Andrew looked close. Loo's dark hair was thin—Andrew could make out patches of bare white scalp. Beneath it, her face was slack—so much that at first he feared that she was in a coma. But her eyes were open, and they followed him as he examined her. Andrew put his fingertips to her cheek, and found it warm to the touch. He asked if a window might be opened, and one was.

"Hello, Loo," he said, as the girl's eye squinted in the light. "Can you tell me how you're feeling?"

Loo licked her lips with a tongue that seemed swollen. She took a breath. Then she closed her mouth and looked away.

"She can't," said a woman's voice. "She's too simple. She's feeling awful though. You should be able to tell that by looking."

She stood beside the open window, wearing long dusty skirts and her hair tied in a dark bun from which individual hairs strayed like thin branches. This woman was lean, and quick, and old. Lines were on her face like rivers.

"You are feeling awful too," said the woman, looking at him, glancing in particular at his bad hand. "Hank do this to you?"

"I—I'm sorry," said Andrew. "Hank?"

"Ink," said Ink, who was standing by the door, rifle tucked away at his elbow now.

"Hank," said Andrew. He smiled weakly and turned back to the woman. "No. He didn't."

"Well you're in no shape to do us any good now," she said. "Look at your hands. They shakin' like a drunk's, and one's bound up. No cuttin' for you, Doctor sir."

Andrew sighed. "I know. I'm not going to do anything but look right now. Look, and ask questions. If you could tell me, ma'am, what you think's ailing her, that would help. Then I can get a look, and we can talk about what to do next."

"Sounds fair," said the woman.

"Fine then. First things. This is Loo. She's the patient. My name's Andrew Waggoner. I'm the doctor. And you, ma'am . . . ?"

"My name's Norma. I'm Loo's cousin, let's put it that way. And you asked what's wrong with her?"

"Yes?"

Norma tucked her chin into her blouse.

"Raped," she said, her face pinched angry.

"Raped," said Andrew. "By anyone—"

He didn't know how to put it gracefully, but Norma spared him.

"No one in this room," she said. "No one here now."

At that, Hank spoke up.

"She was raped by the Faerie King," he said, standing on his toes so he could see over Norma's shoulder. "He planted his seed, and now—now, we got to stop that."

"That's enough, Hank," said Norma.

"Got to stop it," he said, eyes wider than they should be. "Before it eats her up. 'Fore it turns us all *Feeger*."

§

Andrew Waggoner set to work on Loo Tavish. He checked her fever, and it was a shade over 100. Her heartbeat: regular. She was breathing easily, and although she wasn't talking, her eyes followed his fingers when he moved them and her foot jumped when he tapped her knee. He started to look under the blankets, to see about this rape, this pregnancy—the talk of the Faerie King and Feegers and everything else—but that was when Norma put a stop to it.

"No more 'til you get some food in you and your hands stop shakin'," she said.

Andrew's hands *were* shaking—and he had to admit, thinking straight about the problem was beyond him now. If he did anything, it would be as likely to harm her as help her.

So he accepted Norma's invitation to come up to her cabin for a bowl of fiddlehead-and-rabbit stew. Apparently, the hill folk saw nothing wrong with a Negro having a meal alone with their lady cousin, because he and Norma hurried alone through the rain along a path that wound between some woodsheds and up a little slope to a small log building with a bowed roof. Even Hank and his rifle let them be.

As he stepped inside through the low front door, Andrew remarked on that fact. "Suddenly, I'm no longer at gunpoint," he said. "It's refreshing."

Norma shrugged as she opened her own stove, lit a twig and brought the flame to candles mounted along the walls. "Up to me," she said, "wouldn't have brought you here at point of a gun. Would've asked nice. But Hank's jumpy, and don't care much for the folk in the mill town."

"You know better."

Norma laughed. "You're hurt," she said. "Not much trouble, and not much use either. Why don't you sit down, Dr. Waggoner." She motioned to a table with a couple of chairs.

Andrew sat. He liked this little house. It wasn't exactly civilized—but held against the shack where Loo was staying, this was fine. It seemed cleaner, more orderly—and the rich smell coming from the stove promised a fine meal.

Norma pulled out a couple of metal plates and cutlery, and ladled the stew into them. She put one in front of Andrew, and watched as he set to it. It was delicious, and it warmed him through.

"You manage to get out of town without them killing you," she said as Andrew spooned another mouthful.

He sat up, swallowed and looked at her. "Now why do you think they were going to kill me?"

"Look at you." She pulled a small bone from her mouth and set it on the plate. "You di'n't get that from fallin' down a hill. Fact is, a nigger in that place shouldn't have lasted any time at all. A doctor nigger? My."

"Wasn't a problem," he said, "until the end."

"Never is," she said. "Not 'til the end."

Andrew let out a breath, and leaned back. He thought he was coming back to himself, now the food was working its magic. More than anything, he wanted to go to sleep. But as he sat back, the question formed itself and he spoke it before he knew:

"What does 'Feeger' mean?" he asked.

Norma set down her spoon.

"Hank said it. Before I started the examination. He said, what was it? . . . get rid of it, before it eats her up—and turns all of you . . . *Feeger.*"

"He said that?" she said. "Maybe he meant feeble. Maybe he thinks it's catching. Hank tends t' mumble."

"Mmm." Andrew didn't think that Hank had been mumbling. But he didn't press her on it. "Faerie King. Was that more mumbling?"

Norma made a humourless smile. "You'll think we're crazed," she said.

"No," said Andrew, "I don't think I will." He waited for Norma's reply, and when it didn't come, he smiled and shrugged.

"Let's finish eating," he said. "How about that? When we're done, I'll help you clean up and then . . . I've something to show you."

Andrew cleaned his plate and stowed the bones in the garden bin, and good as his word, after helping clean the dishes he went to the doorstep, where he'd stowed his doctor's bag.

Norma watched with interest as he dug among the ampoules of morphine and jar of iodine, and finally pulled out the small glass jar that Jason had given him before he fled.

He brought it to candlelight. Norma drew close, squinted through the glass.

"Where'd you get these?" she asked.

"A woman," said Andrew. "After she died. They were on the inside. In her womb."

Norma took the jar from him and twisted open the top. She made a face as a whiff of formaldehyde came out, and before Andrew could say anything reached in and pulled one of the tiny spheres out on her fingertip. "Ah," said Andrew, "best leave the rest."

Norma nodded. "She alive?"

"No," said Andrew. "I told you. She died."

"All the way dead, I guess you meant. Well that's too bad. No baby inside, then."

"I—beg your pardon?"

"In years past, when the Faerie King took a bride, he left the mother half-dead when he done with her and her babe. That's only if she's already with child. Takes most from the baby, only a bit from ma. If she be barren . . ."

Andrew stepped back and stared. He must have been making a face to frighten children, for this grown woman took a look at him, set the jar down on next to the candle, folded her arms and stepped away.

"You want to sit down?" she said.

"If she's barren," said Andrew, putting together this story with what he'd found in the autopsy, "the Juke eats her from the inside, killing her completely."

"The Juke?"

"The Faerie King," said Andrew. He followed the notion further. Assembling it together with what he had observed in Loo's cabin.

"Is that the trouble with Loo?" he asked. "She's barren?"

Norma nodded. "Not born barren. But thanks to your hospital and that fine doctor there, she be so now."

Andrew picked up the jar and screwed the top back on. "Norma," he said, "I think it's time to talk about Loo's case in more detail. I'll sit down now, if you will."

Norma talked. And through the rest of the afternoon, at Andrew's gentle prodding, they put together a case history of Loo—who's proper name was Lou-Ellen Tavish, and who had never done a wrong thing in her life save on her birthday, when she killed her mama.

§

Her mama's name was Rose, and she'd had three other children, all by her husband Will. That may have been part of the trouble. Rose was old, near forty, when she lay down with Will in the summer of 1894. It was winter when the child came due, and Rose was that much older, and more things went wrong than the midwife could make right. She bled to death on the earthy floor of their cabin, while Will held his quiet baby girl close at his coat and screamed blue murder to the rafters.

As the days wore on, old Will's screams quieted, and little Lou-Ellen—she stayed quiet. Lou-Ellen didn't cry in her blankets, she didn't laugh or coo when her brothers and sister would wiggle their fingers at her. By the time she was two, everyone had worked out that Lou-Ellen had been born simple and she might never be able to look after herself. It led to some awful talk among the families, about how a girl ought to be able to pull her weight. But it was only talk and it didn't go on for long. Lou-Ellen was kin, everybody'd liked Rose and only a few didn't care for Will. So they all cared for Lou-Ellen as she grew. They fed her even when food was scarce, gave her hugs and played with her, and when she got so she could make some words, they rechristened her Loo, which was something she could say back.

She managed to make herself useful, too. By the time the folks from Eliada came, she was tending goats and cleaning kills and minding the garden patch.

There were three men that made the trip up the hill. Two of them carried Winchester rifles on their backs and made it clear that they were not to be trifled with. A third was a fat old doctor (when Andrew asked if the name Nils Bergstrom rang a bell, Norma thought that might've been it).

The doctor talked to a couple of them and said he was there to provide free medicine—that some people out east had decided it was a good way to spend their money, to make sure that folks who couldn't afford it got properly looked after by doctors.

There were some in the families who were suspicious, but they were quiet about it. The two riflemen looked like they had other friends besides this doctor, and no one wanted to have those ones drop by. So the riflemen set up a tent and started inviting folk inside for examinations.

No one was sure what sort of conversation went on when Loo was in the tent, but others from the families reported that the doctor just asked a lot of questions, looked into their eyes and listened to their hearts with a stethoscope.

The doctor heard many complaints, but by the time he packed up his tent and headed back to town, he'd offered little to cure them that the family couldn't figure for themselves.

He did, however, offer what he called "preventative medicine." His last day there, he invited a few people back, who'd had no complaints at all. It was mostly the younger folk—Loo, her sisters and brothers, and the two boys. He was, he said, going to give them a special operation that would make it easier on them. Loo, he said, would go into the tent first.

She would also be the last to go in.

Loo never spoke of that operation, but her cousin Jacob got the whole story for them. Jacob was little for his age, but fast and smart. While he was waiting his turn outside the tent, he managed to slip away and get around the back side, and stick his head underneath the cloth to see what was going on.

Loo was strapped down to a bench, and struggling a bit. The doctor held what looked like a shoe over her face, and she stopped moving. Then he took a shiny knife, and started cutting away at her middle—her privates. There was a bit of blood, and although she was quieter, Jacob could tell by the way she moved that it still hurt.

Before the doctor was done with her, Jacob had relayed all this to the rest of the family—and when the doctor came out, he found himself faced with Norma, Hank, and Karl (the giant that Andrew had seen coming in, Norma explained).

There might have been shooting, but the doctor seemed anxious to avoid it. He begged the families to trust him, that he was doing this work for the good of everyone. When Karl wondered what he meant by that, he explained:

"I am doing you a service," he said. "Your daughter Lou-Ellen was born feebleminded. If she had children of her own, the chances are that they would be feebleminded too. Now, there is no danger of that."

"What d' you mean to do to the rest of 'em?" asked Norma.

The doctor shrugged. "You are all family," he said. "You all carry the germ. You all need to be cleaned."

The doctor and his men left not long after. For as the talk went along, guns and knives and axes started to appear among the families, and the two men with rifles took the measure of their hosts and whispered to the doctor that a fast leave-taking might be the best.

And so the doctor made sure that Loo's cuts were properly dressed, set her out and set his men to rolling up the tent. On leaving, he told the families that he thought they would thank him for the work he did on Loo. In the end, he said, they might wish that they took him up on his offer.

"In the end," he said, "it might save you all a lot of grief."

§

"So if I understand, the doctor—Dr. Bergstrom—sterilized Loo two years ago."

"That's the word he used," said Norma. "Sterilized."

"Did he ever come back?" asked Andrew.

"Not him. Couple time, his friends with the guns came up. Them and some others." Norma looked at her hands. "They come up with their guns and rope and horses . . . They take a few folk back. To the hospital."

Andrew was horrified. "They *kidnapped* people?"

Norma said she didn't know that word. "But they took 'em. They always brung 'em back."

"Have you—"

Norma smiled thinly. "I haven't," she said. "Too old to worry about, I expect. But it's been a long time since a baby's been born to the families."

"Until now," said Andrew.

"*Huh.*"

"And this one was . . . fathered by the . . ."

"Faerie King. That's what we call it."

"You believe—" *in faeries*, Andrew was about to say. But he stopped himself. The fact was that he'd seen them too. It would be insulting and worse, unreasonable, to feign scepticism.

So he took a breath and started again.

"Tell me everything you know about the Faerie King," he said. "Then tell me what happened."

§

The families had never held much to religion. There were some around who did—but they lived further up the hill and grew stranger by the season, and although they seemed happy it was not the kind of happiness you wanted to share in. Families here on the slope had nothing but bad to say about the clergy they'd left behind and had not much to care for a God you couldn't see or hear. But they knew the old stories of the creatures that lived in the forest. The stories all pointed to a simple warning—don't expect help from them without paying a price worse than the help was good.

And though they may speak fair and smell sweet, don't walk off with one if it beckons, and don't ever lie with one.

It was this last thing that the family thought had happened to Loo, from the simple story she told over the days.

Loo said she had been digging for leeks with her knife in the early spring soil, when she met the fellow. He was fast and no bigger than a baby, but she thought he was fine. In the early days, she would listen to birdsong as though it were speaking to her, and nod or shake her head or say, "Ho!" or "Yep!" or just laugh, and no one thought anything of it.

But as the days got longer she took to bed more and more. And then the elder members of the family, folk like Norma, started to pay more heed—both to her and to the birdsong.

"You listen to it in the right frame of mind, it's like words," said Norma.

"Can you hear it now?"

Norma looked at her hands. "Always," she said.

"What does it say?"

Norma snorted. "Preacher talk," she said.

"Preacher talk," said Andrew. "You know, I've seen some things that've had whistling attached to them. I don't hear the words."

"That's because you ain't kin," said Norma. "And you're a nigger. Ain't even the same race."

"I'm the same race."

"Oh," she said, seeing his expression. "M' apologies. It's just . . . the whistling seems to come clearer the closer kin you are."

"And it talks like a preacher," said Andrew. "To kin of the woman that was pregnant with it." Andrew leaned back. "Not pregnant," he said. "I should have said the woman carrying its eggs. Does it normally attack pregnant women?"

"It does, but not always," said Norma. "Doesn't happen often enough to really say." Now she sat back and thought about it. "But it's queer—you hear stories, how after the Faerie King picks a virgin bride, she goes off and lies with her sweetheart."

"Ah."

So the Faerie King would lie with a woman, and put his seed in her—his seed in this case, not spermatozoa—but something like an egg. He would choose pregnant women preferentially, and they survived better. That made sense. Women who were with child went through many changes that allowed them to carry a foetus—really, another animal—not only without casting it out, but providing nourishment through the umbilical cord. Andrew wondered: did the tiny creatures latch onto the cord and steal food from the withering foetus?

Ingenious, so far as it went. But what if the mother was not pregnant? What if—

Then Andrew recalled Mister Juke, and the one thing that Dr. Bergstrom had let slip.

Mister Juke was a hermaphrodite.

And that drew his consideration to Jason Thistledown, and the night he had in the quarantine.

"You ever hear," he finally asked, "of the Faerie King lying with a man that way?"

She did not answer that question but looked at Andrew, her fingers drawing into a loose fist on the table, and asked: "So can you help Loo or not, Dr. Andrew?"

Andrew said he could—although he was less sure of that than he was of his own desire for a serious look under the blanket—a look at one of those things *alive*. And for the second time since he'd fled Eliada, Andrew felt himself fill up with a terrible shame.

He made himself smile around it—pushed that shame down, and to make sure it stayed there said again:

"I can help her. Perhaps."

15

A Wicked Cut

Andrew rose early in the morning, and took stock of both his equipment and his circumstance. He had not, since departing Eliada, done a close inventory of the physician's bag, so he did so now and was pleased to find the bag well-equipped if not precisely modern.

There was morphine and alcohol in a row of phials, packed alongside several thick rolls of gauze. There were other things as one might expect: a flexible stethoscope and a hammer; a small concave mirror and scissors; a roll of suture thread and steel needles. At the bottom of the case was a mahogany box containing a surgical kit that Andrew thought might have dated back to the Civil War, given the rust-specked bone-saw and the ebony-handled trepan tucked among the scalpels and clamps. Andrew would have liked more gynaecological equipment—all he could find was an antique speculum tube that'd been carved from ivory and might be adaptable for vaginal examination. But given that he was not precisely aborting or giving birth to a child—given that he was not entirely sure *what* he was going to find inside poor Loo—he thought he might make do.

The circumstance was more troubling. His bad hand was only a part of it. In the relative darkness of the dawn, the cabin where Loo rested was nearly pitch black. And it was filthy. The risk of sepsis was enormous in the confines of this place. He asked the woman who was staying with Loo to throw open all the windows, but it was not enough to resolve either difficulty.

There was nothing to do about his hand, either—other than enlist Norma, who had some experience with midwifery, to assist where she could.

As to the cabin?

"We will have to perform this procedure outdoors," Andrew finally declared, and Norma agreed.

"I'll find a table," she said.

"And clean bedclothes."

"Clean bedclothes. Anythin' else?"

By mid-morning, Andrew counted a dozen people helping set up the outdoor surgery. He supervised for part of it, but it soon became apparent that Norma was a quick study, and he wasn't needed. So at her urging, he took his bag and went back inside to look in on his patient.

She was awake and more alert than the night before. The two of them were alone in the cabin, and it seemed to Andrew that she was smiling at him.

"Hello, Loo," he said. "Do you remember me?"

She mumbled at him, in a slow, damp drawl. She was definitely smiling. He could see her teeth—short, plaque-covered stumps that peeked out under glistening lips. She mumbled again, and grunted.

"I'm Dr. Waggoner," he said, and pulled up a stool beside her. "Going to try and make you better. Do you understand?"

Loo made that grunting sound again, and her eyes squinted as though she were trying to pass stool, and Andrew shocked himself by flinching, a sliver of disgust and horror pricking his middle. The girl was enfeebled through no fault of her own; and she had been raped by—by some inhuman thing—and here he was, trained to heal all infirmity, turning away in what? Disgust?

Horror?

He bent forward. "I am going to check you," he said. "Can you lie still for me?"

Then he set about her second examination.

Loo was still running a low fever, her heart sounded fine, and there wasn't much congestion in her breathing.

"Good girl," said Andrew, and Loo mumbled back. "Now," he said, "I am going to look at your belly."

The sheets and blankets were stiff and stank from days of stale sweat. He had to literally peel away the tattered bottom sheet.

Andrew gasped. Even in the dim light, he could see the mottled discolouration across her, dark bruising from beneath her breasts to her pelvic bone. He traced with a finger one of the two thick scars that Nils Bergstrom had left. With his other hand laid flat, he felt for movement—anything, any sign of the thing in her uterus. He felt nothing but the girl's breathing.

So he took the stethoscope, and after warming it first in his hand, set the chest-piece against the flesh above her navel. And he listened.

§

The two things missing from the physician's bag that Jason Thistledown had stolen for him were the two things that Andrew dearly wished he had: a pencil and a proper notebook. With those two things, Andrew might have written down a proper clinical description of the thing he heard twisting and gnawing inside the belly of the poor idiot hill girl.

As it was, Andrew Waggoner took the stethoscope away, looped the rubber tubing and put it back in the bag. He returned to Loo's bedside. He felt her forehead for fever, checked her eye movement with a finger, and even tapped her knee to see if it might jolt, which it did.

Then he sat by her, and waited, until Hank opened up the door and told him they'd finished everything he'd asked and there was no more reason to tarry.

"So 's time," said Hank. "Get doctoring."

§

It was just past noon when Andrew Waggoner cut into Lou-Ellen Tavish. They had laid her out on a clean sheet on the table, pots of steaming boiled water next to her and Andrew's surgical kit laid out on a stool beside her. He had set his mirror between her legs, which had been strapped apart, one to each table-leg. Her breathing was slow and steady, as a result of the morphine he'd given her. Next to the mirror was the ivory speculum, fresh out of the boiling water. He lifted it, because he did not intend to cut yet, and brought it to her vagina. The speculum had two pieces: a conical wedge, which fit perfectly inside the cylinder. If things were as they should be, the first step of this operation would be to insert that between the patient's labia, gently forcing it open. Then he would remove the wedge, and have a two-inch diameter tube through which to operate.

But Andrew set the speculum back down as fast as he'd lifted it. He bent forward, positioning the mirror to get a better look.

"What's a matter?" asked Hank, who was standing with his brothers and sisters and cousins at the agreed-upon distance of ten feet. "Your arm hurtin'?"

Norma, the only one allowed close, leaned in closer to look herself. "What's it?"

Andrew touched the labia with finger and thumb. "Look," he said, drawing them apart. Between the pink flesh was a yellowish membrane, stretching the length of Lou-Ellen Tavish's vagina. "There's no opening. Or rather—there's an opening, but something is covering it." Andrew prodded it. It made a crackling noise, as though it were part calcified. "It's as though her hymen regenerated somehow."

"Hymen?"

"Maidenhead."

Norma nodded. "Ah. The child skin. That don't come back once you've lain with a—"

"No, it doesn't," said Andrew. "I'm going to need a scalpel."

Norma didn't know what that was, so Andrew took it and showed her: "Scalpel," he said. "For next time I ask. Now I need you to get around there and spread the—" he was about to say *labia*, but again, just showed her: "These."

Norma leaned over and did as she was told. Lou-Ellen made a soft whimpering noise, as Andrew leaned in, positioned the mirror, and set the blade of his scalpel against the tissue.

"Need somethin' else?" asked Norma finally.

"No," said Andrew, "I'm fine."

Which finally was true enough. His hand did not shake at all as he pressed the tip of the blade into the strange yellow tissue.

Although the scalpel was keen, it took surprising force to break through the membrane. It became fibrous once the scalpel breached the brittle surface, and Andrew had to saw at it.

But once that pierced, Andrew did not have to complete the incision. It was like breaking a seal on an overturned jug; once the scalpel pierced all the way through, the pressure from a thick flow of brownish liquid tore it the rest of the way open. It splashed up Andrew's arm, stained the sheet to the edge of the table, and filled the dish of the mirror with a foul broth.

Loo shrieked, and her back arched, and the table-legs creaked as she tried in vain to draw her knees together. Andrew lurched back, pulling away just in time to avoid slicing her thigh with the scalpel. Norma moved as well, to take hold of Lou-Ellen's shoulders, hold her down and try to comfort her best she could.

Andrew took a breath. If his patient were genuinely pregnant, this might be explained as amniotic fluid, but Loo was not, and this was not. It was something strange.

And it smelled . . .

The smell was a cousin to the stench Lou-Ellen had left in the cabin. *It could be a sign of infection, just that*, Andrew thought. But it reminded him of something else, that skirted at the edge of memory. He sniffed at his hand, which was covered in the mucous-thick liquid, trying to recall—and as he did, he chanced to look closely at it. It was not, he saw, entirely pure—suspended in it were tiny dark objects of various shapes. They might have been insects, or pieces of insects.

You have a patient, he reminded himself. *See to her.*

Lou-Ellen was still screaming but she had slowed her struggling enough that Andrew could get close again. The sheet was soaked now, with glistening puddles here and there. Andrew shook off his hand, and reached in to pick up the mirror, clean it off and begin again, this time sliding the speculum into the open space to see what he could see. Which would be a problem, Andrew realized, because in her struggles she'd knocked the speculum to the ground. It would have to be sterilized. He shook his head as he started to pour the juices out of the mirror's bowl. Then he looked at it more closely.

At its deepest point, the bowl held about a quarter-inch of the liquid. And it, like the stuff on his hand, was impure. But the particulate that had gathered there was bigger. Andrew held it in the full sunlight and squinted. Was there something like a hand in it? No bigger than a man's fingernail? Wispy effluvium trailed in the murky liquid, making it impossible to tell.

"Does anyone here have a jar?" he asked. "A clean jar I mean?"

"Sure," said Norma. "In the root cellar there's plenty." She turned to one of the children, and ordered her to fetch a couple.

Andrew set the mirror down carefully. He motioned with his splinted arm to the ground, where the speculum lay. "That will have to be washed," he said. "Clean it with boiling water and alcohol."

Norma stayed with Loo, so it was Hank who bent to pick it up. He, and the rest of them, had drawn closer. Any closer, and they'd be blocking out his light. "Wash your own hands first," said Andrew. "Don't want Loo to get sick. Not now she's through the worst of it."

"Worst of it?" It was Norma. "You mean you're done?"

Andrew looked back down at the bowl—the grotesque pieces of tissue—the strange shapes they made in the liquid. "Maybe. I don't think I had much to do. Looks like whatever was in her died on its own. There are pieces of it in this." He held the mirror out so Norma could see. Her eyebrows raised and her nostrils flared as she sniffed it. "I'd call it a miscarriage if I didn't know better. As it stands, I'll still take a look inside. See what troubles this awful sickness has caused her."

"But you think she's better," said Norma. Loo did indeed seem better. The morphine, still in her blood, was back to work now that the panic was over.

Andrew gave a smile he hoped was reassuring. "We'll see," he said.

"All done," said Hank, and handed Andrew the speculum. Andrew took it, and dribbled some of the alcohol on it and through it for good measure. Then he bent back down. "All right, Norma. Same as before."

Norma reached down and pulled the labia apart, and Andrew leaned closer to insert the speculum. He barely touched it to the girl, however, before the second eruption. This time, Andrew didn't lurch back, because this time, the fluid coming out was something that his surgeon's reflexes understood.

This time, it was blood. Lou-Ellen Tavish was haemorrhaging.

§

Andrew had encountered this circumstance four times in his career as a physician. Three of the women who had bled out in the afterbirth had died. The last of those was Maryanne Leonard.

The fourth survived—because the French hospital where she was being seen employed a surgeon who had studied blood typing with Landsteiner and knew enough to pick the correct plasma for transfusion.

If he could find the source of the haemorrhaging and stem some of it, Andrew thought he might be able to save his patient with the blood of a close family member—if he could transfuse enough of it, with the single brass syringe in the doctor's kit.

But he needed to work swiftly. He shouted to Norma to keep Loo's vagina open, and he quickly inserted the speculum into the opening, then cleared the tube. Unmindful now of what happened to his specimen, Andrew poured the fluid from the mirror onto the sheet. "Out of the light!" he shouted, and when the families obeyed, he positioned the mirror so the sun lit the opening. He demanded a narrow set of forceps and a swab of cotton dipped in alcohol, and he took it in his injured arm, ignoring as best he could the shooting pain. And he peered up Lou-Ellen's canal, and transferred the forceps to his good hand. He meant to staunch the bleeding with it, if he could spy the source.

And if he could manage it at all, with his hand-and-a-half. It was one thing to take a temperature and listen to a heartbeat; to tell these hill folk how to wash a table and boil water; even to stitch up a farm boy's cut hand. It was something else again to save the life of a girl bleeding inside.

It's even harder, Andrew scolded himself, *if you keep thinking about all those troubles and not your patient.*

Blood began to flow out through the speculum now, like a drain pipe. Andrew twisted the mirror, so he could see the red-flushed wall of the canal in an inch, but the rest was dark. So he set down the mirror, propped himself painfully on his damaged elbow, and inserted the forefinger of his good hand. He felt for the telltale pulsing of an open wound.

He was not in there long at all, before the thing inside Lou-Ellen Tavish bit down.

Andrew shouted, and pulled his finger out, and transferred his weight to his bad arm so that he cried out again. The finger was covered in Lou-Ellen's murky blood. At the pad, a dark blood-blister grew.

Now Andrew did stagger back, taking the alcohol-soaked cotton from the forceps and pressing it against his finger. He swore under his breath. If that bite had broken skin . . .

A shudder ran up Loo's body. And the speculum pushed from her vagina, and fell into the mess below, and Andrew thought to himself as the labia spread, this time pushed out from within: *I am watching the Devil's birthing.*

And then he thought, as the twig-thin appendages emerged, pushing it wider for the bloody, snot-covered head to emerge, and Loo shuddered and rattled, one last time:

I've lost her.

§

The thing pulled itself from Loo's middle, spewing a fresh stench and emitting a high, furious whistle. Andrew cast about the crowd. The adults were no good—they covered their faces and whimpered, held one another or just onto themselves. One by one, they fell to their knees and prostrated themselves.

But the children were back with the pickle jars. Andrew grabbed one from a slack hand, and pulled off the top. When he turned back, the creature was crouched on hind legs that articulated in two places, like a horse's, while clawed hands scraped mucous and blood from a wide mouth that was lined with sharp teeth (and somehow, despite its orifices being blocked, it kept screaming). Its eyes were small and black, its skin bedsheet white, the only colour being the tiny rivulets of Lou-Ellen's lifeblood shearing off its forehead. From buttocks to skull was a span of no more than eight or nine inches.

The jar was big—it would hold four or five quarts of liquid and the mouth was wide. It was only a little smaller than the ones that had held Maryanne Leonard, in her parts.

Andrew held it in the crook of his bad arm, and as he stared the little creature in the eye, and inched towards it, it dawned on him that a point had come and gone in which he had not only given poor retarded Lou-Ellen Tavish up for dead, but that he had ceased to care; because what he was truly after was this . . . this thing that had killed her; this thing, whose cousin had jumped onto his chest, the afternoon he was nearly hanged outside Eliada, and maybe driven him a step nearer to madness.

The creature spat a gob of bloody phlegm in front of it, and reared back on its haunches. Andrew tried to reach for it but he could not. The God-damned arm hindered him. The thing was too quick, too quick . . .

Norma was quicker. She let go of poor Loo's shoulders, and lunged across the table. The creature made ready to leap, but Norma grabbed it, two hands around its narrow chest. As she did, it seemed as though a dozen mouths opened up along its side, and a terrible whistling rose up. But Norma did not let go, even as she slid down along the blood-slick edge of the table and grasped the twitching thing to her.

Lines of blood beading like a necklace rose up along her face where the creature had slashed. But she did not let go—just yanked her head back so the tendons stood out on her neck, keeping her eyes clear. Yet as Andrew watched, it seemed that she became both Norma and Loo at once, his perception crossing time and memory and making a single thing.

Andrew shook his head as if that might dispel the madness. This was some narcotic that the creature spewed from its orifices and it made him and the others hallucinate. Was that what caused the families to fall into prayer as they had?

He stumbled around the table to where Norma struggled with the creature. It was face-down on the sandy ground with her half-pinning it. She looked up at him, her eyes wild, and as he got closer he saw that her knuckles were nearly as white as the creature as she struggled to crush it.

Andrew intervened. Setting the jar down on his side, himself on his knees, he grabbed hold of the thing and pushed its head through the mouth of the jar. It squealed, painting the glass with a shifting fog. Norma squeezed harder, and Andrew heard a clicking sound that he felt sure was a tiny rib cracking, and Andrew then realized that if he meant to collect a live specimen—and he did—that Norma would be as much hindrance as a help.

She was trying to kill the thing.

Andrew took his good hand and twisted Norma's wrist. She cried out and let go, and Andrew was thus able to stuff the Juke into the jar. It scrabbled furiously as he found the lid and jammed it on top. The creature lurched back and forth, claws clicking against the glass.

Shaking, Andrew stood up and faced the families. They were still prostrate, most of them, but they looked up at Andrew in a strange way. Andrew could not tell if they meant to tear him apart, or worship at his feet.

He drew a breath.

"You," said Andrew, motioning to one of the children. "Fetch me a nail. We will have to make holes in the lid, if this thing is to live."

§

The creature did live, for a time. They watched it through the day, keeping it safe in its jar while Andrew tended the cut on his own good hand with alcohol and gauze, then looked to Norma's injury. Andrew could not say for sure that he wanted it to live—Norma certainly did not. But he insisted they keep it near them—probably away from the others—and watch what it did.

"I need to know what it is," he said when she complained about keeping it.

Norma said she was pretty sure she did know what it was, and it was better dying there.

"It's gonna take over the soul of my folk, you don't deal with it." She winced as the gauze settled over her cheek. "Look at them outside."

Andrew was more interested in looking at the thing that slumped and squirmed behind the fogged glass. But he got up and cracked the door open.

The families had built a bonfire in the middle of the village. When he and Norma had stolen off back to the house, they were already gathering sticks for it. Andrew objected—he wanted to examine Loo's body before they cremated it. But Hank had insisted the fire was not to burn poor Loo.

"We ain't to burn the Mother," he said, as though that explained everything.

And before Andrew could say anything else, Norma whispered to him: "Don't fight him. You got wounds to tend, Doctor."

Now the fire was roaring, billowing smoke into the pines, over the roofs of the other shacks up here. The forest was filled with the sound of it crackling, of it whistling.

"They're fightin' it best they can," said Norma. "Smoke distracts them. But . . . it's goin' to be a hard fight. They could be headin' to the hill, before too long. Worshipping." She said the word the way other old women might say "fornicating."

Andrew shook his head. "I thought you folk didn't care for God and priests."

"Faerie King's changing 'em. Working 'em."

"Why are they like that and you all are free?"

"I'm older," said Norma. "They're younger. They're all more one family then I am."

Andrew nodded. Norma was older—in terms of her own germ plasm, she was a generation or two removed from most of these others.

"And the Juke does best in a family."

She shrugged. "If I let it, over time it'll get to me too."

"I met one of those things, you know," he said. "At the hanging tree."

She didn't say anything—just squinted at the smoke coming up.

Andrew thought back, to that small face he'd seen for a moment, the thing crouched on his chest. He thought about the creature that had gone after Jason in the quarantine. The quarantine where Dr. Bergstrom had hidden away his own Faerie King, the strange hermaphrodite Mister Juke. Hidden away, like, Andrew thought now, some secret, mystical treasure. A treasure that he would not let an outsider—an infidel—a nigger—like Andrew Waggoner lay eyes upon.

"If they fail . . . They're going to want the baby Juke," said Andrew. "Aren't they?"

"They think you're carin' for it," said Norma. "That's the only reason they're leavin' you alone. Soon, I'll be able to help them. But soon ain't now."

He let the door close slowly and turned to look at her. "You have a pretty good idea about how this goes. Norma, have you seen this happen before?"

She looked back at the jar. From inside, the thing might have been peering out. She nodded slowly.

Andrew took another stab in the dark. "Feeger," he said. "That doesn't mean feeble, does it?"

Norma shook her head. "It don't mean feeble," she said. "It's a name—a family, lived here as long as us."

"And Hank doesn't want to 'turn Feeger.' That means—this family, they fell into the thrall?"

"We should kill that thing," said Norma, stepping toward it and staring at it. "Cover its air-holes and let it smother."

§

Andrew kept Norma clear of the jar, but he wasn't trying save the thing's life. He was being a scientist, he told himself: staying near, watching it through the glass, wishing again he had something to write on to record his observations. Because damnation, they were inconstant.

Was it elongate, mantis-like? A fat toad, with silvery-grey flesh pressed against the side of the glass like bloated fruit in a preserve?

A baby?

Light?

It might have been all of those things at one time or another. Notes might have helped, later.

It sat still for an hour, staring out with black and unblinking eyes. Then it became agitated, throwing itself against the sides of the jar. Andrew held it still so it wouldn't shatter; this made the creature angrier. It whistled—that sound that Andrew had heard before, and he surmised was the thing's speech. He sent Norma to the door, to see if anyone were coming but no one was—they were all in their mystical trance around the bonfire.

"You make them see God," said Andrew as the thing slid down the side of the jar, like it was falling into despair. "That's how it works, isn't it? You make them see God with your narcotic fumes, and so they think they're special, and that makes them think you are special. They start to worship. That how it works?"

The thing ran a clawed hand down the glass.

"Then what happens? You get bigger, with all the food they give you—and you go lay your eggs in one of their girls? And so it goes?"

"Hey," said Norma. "Don't be talkin' to it. That's how it starts!"

"Shhh," said Andrew. He felt an awful black thing welling in him—a deep hatred that he could barely put a name to. He saw Maryanne Leonard, he saw Lou-Ellen Tavish . . . he saw Jason Thistledown, trapped in the quarantine. Dr. Nils Bergstrom, driven mad by it he figured, pulled from his course of sterilization. And he saw this thing in the jar, a dim angry shape, ever-changing, like a djinni in a bottle.

His hands were shaking as he lifted the jar off the shelf. He sat down by the stove, with the jar on his lap. The thing was moving in circles now. Spinning. Let it spin, he thought nastily, wear itself out. \

"All because we're willing to believe," said Andrew. And with his good hand, he covered the air-holes, but he couldn't bring himself to keep it there. He half-turned back to Norma.

"You were right to want to kill it," he said, as the thing flopped and struggled and cursed, its whistles muffled by suffocating glass.

§

Andrew did not kill the thing right then. But it died on its own all the same. If it were older it might have made it—like the Juke that'd hung and lived in Eliada. But this was a baby—a newborn. It sent noise from the jar as it expired— tapping and scratching and whistling. It was hard to see what it was doing, because the glass was so streaked with mucous and blood. But its death was not quiet.

As the creature died, Andrew huddled like a boy in the arms of the old mountain woman, curled around the raw spot in his middle where so far as he could tell, his soul had once resided; while around them, the forest whistled and screamed the baby Juke's dying lament up and down the mountainside.

PART II

NATURE

16

Saint Lothar

The Oracle woke a-screaming that night.

Before she was done, she was joined by her sisters—Missy, who was waiting up during that part of the night anyway, hunkered in the crook of a fallen tree—and then Lily, who slept on the flat of a creek-side rock.

The three girls screamed until they lost their wind and paused, looking around blinking to see what attention it brought them.

It took time to find out. The rest of the Feegers were camped downstream, most all of them out cold from the labour of the past days, preparing the march and making that first hard climb, down rock-face and scrub slope, carrying all they needed. By the time they got down to the stream, a spot in the crook of two mountains like the bend of a lady's middle, they curled up and slept like the dead.

And you don't wake the dead with just a shout. So it took time, and that did not make the Oracle happy. She demanded to know where the Feegers were. Just to show she meant business, she swatted Lily a good one across the ear.

"I have word from Him," said the Oracle Patricia. "Gather my people."

And so Lily and Missy took off for the camp, and the Oracle was left alone a moment before they came. She calmed herself, hand on belly, walking into the rushing stream that was made dim silver by the moon. She caressed her belly, which was still small.

She dropped to her knees in the cold mountain water, felt the ice travel up her thighs to her middle, where the Host waited for their larder to fill. If it weren't filling, they'd start in on her straight away—but they were wise enough to know that there was a proper time of things.

Oh soon, she thought, and smiled a little. *You can thank old Lothar when the time comes. He will be a Saint for the part he plays in making you strong. . . .*

And her smile fell away, as she recalled the cry that had awakened her—not a cry for help, but one of dying. A dying son; a dying grandson.

Murdered by the hand of ignorant heathen. Like those others, maybe, who stole the Son. Those ones though—those might be sinners: folk who, with strong application of word and stick, could be made to see to their God. To see to Him right.

Not like these killers. . . .

She stood now, and stared down the stream, where around the bend she saw the light of lamp and torch, as her Feeger kin made their way up the bed, to see what their Oracle wanted now.

When they got there, she made it clear that it was only a little thing, a few drops of blood, scarce an ounce of courage, and doing it would not take them long from their path.

"But there ain't a choice," she said. "Wicked heathen folk did a thing. They got to be *shown*."

The sleepy-eyed Feegers didn't know what to do with that at first, and for that instant, the Oracle felt a sliver of doubt.

But that doubt vanished, as a cry rang out. There in their midst, Lothar, eyes shining in the starlight, lifted his blade above his head.

"Wicked heathen!" he shouted, his voice cracking, and shouted again: "Wicked heathen!"

And the Oracle smiled upon him, and Lothar hollered some more. And before long, the rest did too.

He will be a Saint, all right, thought the Oracle. *Lothar will do it for us fine.*

17

The Dauphin's Women

The first morning after Loo's death, Andrew Waggoner went to see her body intending to perform a post mortem examination.

He might even have done it. Good as their word, the families had neither burned nor buried her, but wrapped the girl up in a blanket and placed her back on that foul bed in the awful shack where he'd found her. He brought his physician's bag and a candle to see her by as he went into the single room that stank so sweet of death; he shuffled in like an old, sick man, and he fell to his knees, as though in prayer.

He was not in prayer—not precisely—but as he crouched there he realized that he would not be able to cut into this girl's body and learn anything from it. It was as much as he could do to lift the cloth from her head and look at her face. And even that, he could not do for long.

In some, death brings a final serenity. That was how it had seemed for Maryanne Leonard, whose face had been so pure and clear in death, above her mangled torso. One could have imagined that her fleeing soul had paused an instant to show a hint of the transcendence it sought. One could take comfort in such a thought.

There was no such comfort looking on Loo. Death had etched a final, leaden idiocy to her: no joy, no redemption signalled in her face. There was not even the pathos of surrender. In the end, she was just insensate meat.

Bergstrom meant to spare you from this, he thought.

Andrew knew, of course, that Bergstrom meant to do no such thing when he travelled here with his armed surgery. He meant to spare the race, *his* race, more abominations like Loo. But as for Loo?

The doctor was not caring for his patient; he was not caring for the unborn children she might make. He was caring for a larger body of patients than this girl and her young.

Which was something Nils Bergstrom had over Andrew Waggoner. When Andrew had made his cut, he hadn't even been sure he could help her; he was in fact fairly certain that he could not. Andrew was looking after his own curiosity and nothing else.

And now, crouched in the darkness of the cabin, he was tending it some more. How hateful, he thought.

Norma came in to get him at lunchtime.

"Come on," she said, laying a cool hand on his shoulder. "You're in no shape for this."

He looked up at her as she guided him to his feet.

"No," he agreed, "that is true."

He went back to Norma's house, and drank down a tea of rose and mint and something else he couldn't identify. He lay down in the bed while she changed the dressing on his older injuries and packed them with a compound of mud and twigs.

"What is all that?" he asked.

"Remedies," she said.

"What kind of remedies?"

"Wild onion and ginger. Fireweed. Some yarrow. Rose and mint in the tea. Other things." She squinted at him. "Good for body and for soul. Don't argue. You'll do better with them and a bit of rest. Now I got to go see to my kin."

Andrew didn't argue, and he did rest, and Norma was right: he did better by it all when he woke, in the pre-dawn of the second day.

He lowered his feet to the earthen floor and stood, flexing his hands in amazement. There was pain, but it felt as though it had aged, as though bones were knitting, wounds were closing. Norma was nowhere to be seen. That was fine—Andrew didn't need to talk.

He thought that he might try another look at Loo.

Quietly, he pulled on his coat and found the physician's bag, and made his way to the death house.

Standing outside in the crisp mountain air, Andrew thought a storm might have passed in the night—a storm that stirred up the scents of the forest floor—that somehow refreshed things, washing away the old. He shivered and gave his head a quick shake, and felt himself smile.

It didn't take him long, however, to see that he might have a hard time conducting his examination. Lamplight flickered first between tree branches, and then as he drew nearer, from the windows of the house. Andrew could hear something like singing coming from inside, faint but certain. He slowed his step and crept closer.

In spite of his good feeling, he was not anxious to intrude, so he moved near one of the windows and tried to peer inside.

The space was almost as crowded as when he'd first arrived. But this time, things were busier. A couple of the women were going at the sheet with needle and thread, sewing it shut. Some others were sipping from mugs.

And it seemed like everybody was humming—some tune that Andrew couldn't make out. He raised up on his toes to get a better look around, and that was when he felt the hand on his arm.

"Hem."

Andrew turned. He was looking at Hank.

"I—I'm sorry," said Andrew.

"You already paid your respects," said Hank. "Time for us."

"Of course."

"Then go on."

He let go of Andrew. Andrew nodded, and stepped away.

It was fine. He would not dissect the body at its funeral. He would not bother the families. He took a walk.

As Andrew walked, he found himself humming. Cheerfully. There was a tune to it, but Andrew did not think to try to place it. It was more like he followed it, as though he were listening a song some minstrel might have been playing in the woods downslope. A minstrel, or a choir.

He stepped around a copse of tamarack, onto a little shelf of rock, and when he was through that, the sun came up. There was no missing it, standing as he was on the east slope of the mountain. It gilded the rock-face—brightened the green of the moss and lichen and daubed the tops of the trees below with honey. Andrew blinked and squinted in the light, and fell back, and watched, as the breadth of the Kootenai River Valley below him was obliterated—by Heaven.

He blinked and his breath hitched, as he caught himself using his good arm against the rock.

There were gates in the sky: gates marked by two tall monoliths that bent toward one another at their peak. The gates themselves were covered in hammered gold and pinkish-white stonework and they hovered like storm clouds over the river valley. The sun rose beneath them like a straining bloody red bubble; yet within the gateway, another sun shone—this one of purest white, a light that tickled Andrew's flesh where it touched. Andrew looked into its naked brilliance. He could not look away.

Things moved in that light—they moved, and they sang.

Andrew hummed along, and he realized that he was humming that tune that he'd half-heard in the forest, and as he did, it occurred to him that this was the same tune that he had heard coming from Loo's death house.

Of course, a small part of him observed. *It is a trick of the mind. The Juke is working on you and pulling things out of memory. The song's part of the trick.*

It was one thing to observe that in small measure, another for Andrew to entirely accept it, particularly faced with the spires and arches, the manicured gardens of the City of Heaven. A great Ferris wheel turned in its midst, carrying laughing cherubs nearer the sun, letting them fly at its crest. Marble bridges arched over canals lined with tall trees, carrying long boats painted a brilliant green.. Atop a great flight of stairs, a beautiful Dauphin sat on a throne of hammered silver in robes of white, surrounded by a dozen maidens wearing thin shifts with fine yellow hair tumbling to their waists. Wings emerged from behind him—great white expanses that Andrew first took to be part of the throne, then as they spread, he understood to be coming from the shoulders of the Dauphin himself.

As Andrew looked at him, so the Dauphin looked back. He must have been miles off—but it was as though they stood face to face, as though Andrew could feel his warm breath on his cheek. He looked into his eyes, the irises of which were at first a brilliant blue—then into the pupils, which were black as night sky.

Free thyself, Andrew Waggoner, of thy Earthly bonds.

And as Andrew listened, the irises narrowed, and the blackness of the Dauphin's pupils became absolute, and he did as he was told.

§

Higher and higher, Andrew fell.

§

Shadows appeared and shortened on the mountainside and as they shifted, the colour changed too. Pink turned gold turned silver turned to nothing but the colour of tree and rock and blue, clear sky. There was a scream. Andrew Waggoner's right hand twitched in its splint. A hundred wings pounded the air not far off, and then—another scream.

Heaven had come, Heaven had gone. Andrew had stayed put.

He blinked, and drew a breath, and squinted toward the sun. No gates. No city. No Dauphin.

Andrew let out a long, slow breath. "Redemption," he said aloud. The Juke had offered him redemption. It had brought him low, and lifted him high, and it had offered him redemption from a Heaven of Andrew's own devising. And that last trick . . .

His knees trembled as he stood up. He looked at his hands; flexed the fingers on both; his broken arm gave off waves of pain, but it was as though he were listening to the pain rather than feeling it. As though he were a larger thing now, that encompassed the trees and the rocks and the sky, that sun that was too bright to look at.

That last trick . . . that glimpse of *forever* . . .

"You clever beast." The Juke—the creature in the jar that killed Maryanne Leonard, that had led him to the killing of Loo—the bastard had figured a way to a man's soul. Or at least to the parts of a man that got agitated when he started thinking of his soul.

But it wasn't a soul that a man would be thinking of—any more than it was sleep a man thought of when morphine moved in his veins. It was all chemistry; chemistry in the service of these animals, chemistry that they used to hold a man's attention and hold it for the kill.

Andrew stood up. Whatever chemical smell this thing had put in him, it had passed. He was here in his body—his arm did hurt, his joints did crack. And as to his soul—he felt only muddle-headed, as he would in a morphine aftermath. He stretched his legs and headed back upslope, looking for the path through the trees to the homestead.

"*Nigger.*"

Andrew stopped and turned.

The voice was a girl's. It had sounded close, as though the girl stood next to him and leaned nearer as he spoke.

"Nigger."

She was not that close. She stood in the midst of a close cropping of young pine trees, maybe a dozen yards off. The needles intersected her nakedness, rustling as she moved in them. Her hands strayed up and down her thick naked middle like spiders.

"You the nigger that killed me," she said in a voice clear as sky. "Killed the young one."

"No I am not," said Andrew. "A girl got killed. You're just part of a clever trick. You here to show me the way to Hell now?"

Loo was not in an answering mood. The pine needles rustled and shifted, and Loo's shade shifted and was gone.

"I guess not," said Andrew, and he smiled grimly. This trickery—it wasn't so different really than Klansmen, dressing up like ghosts, thinking they could put the fear in foolish Negroes.

Andrew made his way over to the baby pines, looked for the tracks, the trampled path through the underbrush that he knew would not be there. He knew, but he had to check, and check again. He was under the influence of a powerful hallucinogen—one that placed credulity on him. He pushed aside branches and looked down, and sure enough, there was nothing but needles and dirt.

"Doctor."

Once again, the voice seemed right in his ear and it was the voice of a young girl, though not Loo. Andrew stood, and turned—and as he did, he stumbled and choked.

Thin, cold arms were wrapped around his neck from behind. A wet torso pressed against his back and a mouth blew warm, damp words into his ear with breath that reeked of formaldehyde:

"It's me, Doctor," whispered the shade. "Maryanne.

"Tell my brothers it's good here."

Andrew reached up with his good hand and locked it around the narrow wrist, tried to pull it away. The more he pulled, the tighter it seemed to grip. Sharp ribs broken by a bone-saw scratched at his back.

The voice giggled. "I won't tell," she said. "Don't worry, Dr. Nigger.

"I won't tell—how you came to me that night—how you put your filthy piece in me—how you made your little nigger baby in my belly, then ripped it on out with a pair of pliers—I will not tell, Dr. Nigger," she said. "I will not tell what an awful surgeon you are—one-armed and weak and stupid like a nigger was born. It's between you and me, Nigger. Oh I won't tell I won't tell I won't—"

And with that, Maryanne Leonard snaked her hand free from Andrew Waggoner's fist, and her fingers cupped over his mouth and nose—and Andrew fell to a powerful sleep.

§

"Hello, Andrew."

"Hello. It's dark here. Norma?"

"It is dark. Yes. Norma."

"Am I blind?"

"It's dark."

"Didn't answer my question."

A laugh for an answer.

"What happened?"

"You're safe."

"You're not answering any questions, are you?"

"You haven't asked a good one yet."

"All right—here's a good one. What part of the trick is this?"

Norma didn't answer right away, but Andrew heard a rustling, as of wings. In the distance, he saw a pale bluish light—like a star.

"Well, I'm not blinded," said Andrew.

"Follow the light," said Norma. Her voice sounded farther off—as though she'd set off through the dark toward this light and were still walking. "Only there is your salvation."

"Only there, hmm?" Andrew pushed himself up from the ground and stood straight in the void. "Will that take me to the Ferris wheel? The Dauphin, with his giant wings?"

"Follow the light."

"Yes, the light. It's the sort of thing you'd say if you were dead, Norma—a soul guiding me on. But you aren't. You're alive right now, looking after a dead girl's funeral. You have been working me with such lies, such lies."

"The Dauphin awaits," she said.

Her voice was near now—he could smell her breath, which was sweet. And she had lost the rasp of years.

"I think," said Andrew, "that maybe I'll stay here. You can tell that to the *Juke*, Norma."

He blinked as he spoke. It was later in the day: the sun was higher than it was when he'd seen Heaven in it. And he had moved a distance in that time. He sat next to a low stump on a plateau of stumps and small pine trees. His shirt and trousers were filthy.

The day had also marched on since he'd last looked. Andrew thought the sun had moved a good three hours. Andrew was tired—deep, soul-tired—but he was elated.

I defeated it, he thought. *I faced that thing down, and I defeated it.*

Andrew pushed himself to his feet with a wince. The land here was clear for four, five hundred yards around him. Downslope, he saw wide paths cut in the trees, starting to grow in with underbrush. Harper's men had been at work here, but they had not been back in some time.

Still, he could follow one of those paths and eventually find himself back at Eliada.

Andrew marched upslope a few dozen yards. His doctor's bag lay where he'd dropped it as he twitched and stumbled down the hillside. Miraculously, it was intact.

No, Andrew corrected himself. There was no miracle because there had been no battle. He had not been attacked by her, any more than he had encountered Loo in the trees.

The mechanism of this thing had simply preyed upon his own doubts and fears and aspirations. It had somehow aided him in isolating something that for lack of a better word might be called "sin." And for a physician, sin was failure.

Andrew shut his eyes. Oh yes—the Juke had done its work with the brainless cruelty of a clockwork. It had done everything that it might, to draw him into its web—to ripen him for what amounted to a religious conversion.

All of which gave rise to another question: why hadn't the strategy worked?

It should have. Andrew thought himself clever enough. He had been a good student and, recent experience notwithstanding, a competent physician. But he was under no illusions that he possessed heroic will or genius insight. What was it that saved him?

Norma said the Juke tended to make its deepest mark upon close families— through the amniotic fluid and germ plasm of the host mother, no doubt. And

Andrew was far enough from the stem of that family tree that he was barely affected at all.

He flexed the fingers of his broken arm, and thought then about another possibility.

Perhaps it was something in Norma's remarkably curative tea.

What was it she had said? Good for the body and the soul. Might she have discovered some root, some concoction that lessened the ability of this thing to rob men and women of their wills? It would explain how it was that she and her ilk had lived in this place for so long, without falling into the thrall of these creatures.

I will have to ask her for the recipe—as soon as I find my way back, he thought as he hefted the bag in his good hand and started to climb back up the slope. It wouldn't be hard—there was a good plume of wood smoke climbing into the sky. *Perhaps*, thought Andrew as he climbed, *they are cremating Loo now.*

§

Or perhaps, Andrew thought as he first took sight of what was left of the Tavish's homestead, *the Juke hasn't finished with me yet.*

At the opening of the path was a body of a man, his intestines torn from his middle and stretched through the blood-quickened dirt, mingled with pine needles. More corpses were stacked in the middle of the common, in the same place that just a day ago, Andrew had worked his meagre skills to try to save Loo. The table was gone—perhaps locked in the still-smouldering ruins of the house where Loo had been kept in her last weeks.

Andrew knelt down by the first corpse and took a good look at the cut. Nothing had clawed its way out of this one and no creature had torn it either. The cut was crosswise across the gut, and it was neat enough to be from a blade, not neat enough to suggest a sharp one.

Andrew touched the man's face. He stared with wide milky eyes up into the pines. Blood flecked his beard, and flies buzzed in Andrew's ear. He let go of the man's face, and touched his fingertip to the cooling tube of intestine, and drew a deep breath of the smell of this place—and uncertainly at first, he stood up, shaking with the realization: this was no chemical fakery. This was not something that Norma's tea would drive off.

Andrew left the single corpse and made his way through a thickening cloud of flies to the others. Eyes stinging, he made a count: there were seven here, among them what was left of Hank, his skull split from the side. One eye hung out, its orb crusted with dirt where it touched the ground.

He wanted to cry out, to call for Norma—but he didn't. The ones who'd done this weren't in sight, but they mightn't be far. So Andrew picked up his doctor's bag, and propelled by the slimmest hope he struggled his way up the hill as quick as he might, to Norma Tavish's cabin.

§

He didn't have to get that far to find her. She was on her back, a great slash across her throat, beside a rain barrel next to the barn. Her hands were still clenched in fists, as though she were still alive, waiting for another fight to come.

Andrew reached down with trembling hands and opened those fists, uncurling each finger. He smoothed her hair back. He tried to lift her but that was beyond him. So he reached down and shut her eyes—the last grace he could give her. He left her there under the trees, and made for her house.

The door hung open when he came upon it. He approached it slowly, under the sensible assumption that whoever had done this could well be still inside. But the cabin was uninhabited. It had been ransacked; blankets tossed onto the floor, furniture overturned.

Just as Andrew had heard the call drawing him away from this place, the killers had heard a call drawing them here.

And they'd found what they'd come for.

The dead infant Juke in its pickle jar. All that was left of it were shards of glass and the now-familiar stink of it. Otherwise, it was as if it had never been there.

Andrew didn't have to search long for the other thing he sought: the tea that kept the Juke at bay.

Norma kept a bin near the fire, and the killers had missed it. It made sense, as Andrew thought about it. They might not have any idea about what the mixture signified. And once they had the Juke—well, they had what they sought.

But the scent of the herbs was unmistakable—sweet and earthy and fine. He found a cloth, wrapped the concoction into a ball the size of a small roast, and put it into the medical bag. Then he went back outside.

He walked through the village not looking down or to the side, back to the path that had brought him here. He would make for the clearing where he'd fought off the Juke, and then the logging road beyond it back to Eliada.

It took all his will not to look down as he passed the barn—not to wonder whether it really was Norma's spirit, freed from flesh by a slash across her throat, who had come to him at the conclusion of his battle with the Juke. A man might conclude such a thing; that the visitation coming after a true but yet-unknown demise, was evidence that Andrew Waggoner really had seen Heaven, really had been offered his salvation.

Andrew spat as he entered the woods. He would not entertain such thoughts. He would be no good to anyone—not himself, and certainly not Jason Thistledown, the boy to whom he owed his life and who, Andrew was certain, was in very grave peril indeed.

18

Compassion. Community. Hygiene.

"It's not infected," said Annie Rowe. "Even with a half-working hand, Dr. Waggoner did well by you."

She pulled the bandage back further, and Jason flinched, though the pain turned out less than he feared. "In a day or two we can take out the stitches," she said.

Jason peered down at the wound. It was the morning of the third day since he'd sliced his hand in the quarantine, and it was indeed looking better; the flesh was pink and tender where the black stitches held it together. It itched more than it hurt.

"Hold still," said the nurse, as she dipped a ball of cotton into a jar of alcohol and dabbed it on the wound. Now *that* stung. Jason looked away, up at the skylight of the operating theatre where Nurse Rowe had brought him to do the work. It was, she said, the cleanest place in Eliada, this operating room. It was also—next, maybe, to the storeroom behind the autopsy—the quietest.

Neither of them wanted to go down to the autopsy. So here they were.

"Thank you," said Jason, and Nurse Rowe said: "Just doing my work here. Stop moving."

"I'm not moving," he protested. "I didn't mean thank you for looking at my cut. I know that's your job. I mean—"

"Hush. I know what you meant." She eyed him over the spectacles she wore for fine work. She set his hand down on the table and reached around for a roll of fresh gauze. "He got away all right?"

"He did," said Jason. It had been two days since Nurse Rowe had helped Jason gather the doctor's bag and everything else. Jason had figured he could trust her, owing to their adventure the night of Dr. Waggoner's escape, and she hadn't betrayed that trust. But he hadn't felt safe coming to see her after he saw Dr. Waggoner off. It might tip off Bergstrom, or those fellows who were responsible for breaking into the doctor's rooms. Sam Green had promised to protect Jason best he could—but he'd given no word as to Annie Rowe's safety. So Jason decided he wouldn't talk to her again without an excuse.

That excuse came this morning, when after breakfast in the apartments he shared with Germaine Frost, his aunt suggested he have his hand seen to.

"I would change those bandages myself," she said, as she straightened a stack of fresh index cards on the roll-top desk she'd been given for her work. "But I'm quite occupied with the catalogue. There are more than a thousand souls here. You should avail yourselves of the facilities."

"You want me to go see Dr. Bergstrom?" Jason had been avoiding Bergstrom, lest he find some new pretext to toss Jason back into the quarantine.

Aunt Germaine might have been worrying about the same thing. "No," she said. "Aside from everything else, Dr. Bergstrom has more to do than inspect stitches and change bandages. Go, Nephew. Go find a nurse. And then find some fresh air and exercise."

So Jason went—and made it a point not to find a nurse until he located Annie Rowe, seeing to a couple of new mothers in the maternity ward on the first floor. They made an appointment to meet in the operating theatre an hour later.

Now, Nurse Rowe listened hungrily as Jason told the story of Andrew's escape. He told her everything, except how he found out that Andrew might be in trouble. "That's a promise I made," said Jason, "and I keep my word."

"I won't make you break your word," she said, and cut a square of gauze. "I just pray he's safe."

"Safer than here," said Jason. "Everybody keeps talking about this place as Utopia. I don't know about that."

"You don't like it here?"

Jason laughed. "Oh it's fine," he said.

He'd spent the previous day out of the hospital, wandering the town while Aunt Germaine did her eugenics work. He could see how someone had set down a plan for it. The workers all lived in fine little houses in three roads, not one bigger than another, with space in back for a garden and some livestock. The roads were muddy, but they were wide—wide enough for little gardens in the middle. What he'd first thought was a church was a town hall, with space inside for big meetings and that motto—*Compassion. Community. Hygiene.*—repeated again and again where the walls met the ceilings.

The fellow who seemed to run the place told Jason they ran lessons for the young people two days out of the week from there. When the children of Eliada got a little bit older there'd be a proper school for them. In the meantime: would Jason like to stop by and learn some things?

Jason got out of there as fast as he could. He spent a little more time inside the sawmill. He would have stayed longer, watching the men run logs across the great whirling saw-blades, thinking how this was a kind of family he could join, something he could *be*. But a foreman spotted him and ushered him out into the road and Jason put thoughts of being a lumberman aside for another day.

In the end, he had wandered the town like he had wandered the train from Butte—hoping to catch a glimpse of pretty Ruth Harper, and finding other things instead.

"It's a fine town," said Jason. "Yet look what happened."

Nurse Rowe gave a wry smile. "There's no such a thing as Utopia, really. Not on earth. And for a Negro, that's doubly true."

"If that's right," said Jason, "I have to wonder why he'd come here. Why you'd come here, come to think of it. Seems like a long way to go to live a life as hard as you'd find anywhere else."

"Wise boy," said Annie.

Jason shrugged, and she laughed.

"Just because this place isn't Utopia now, doesn't mean it can't be," said Nurse Rowe. "There are ideals at work."

Jason looked at Nurse Rowe sidelong. "Ideals. Like eugenical ideals?"

"Eugenical? Did you make that word up?"

"Maybe I did," said Jason. "Eugenics is how I heard it. You know about eugenics."

"I do. Mr. Harper speaks of it sometimes, as one of the pillars of Community. It's all tied up with Hygiene." She pointed to the door they'd come in. There were those words again, hung over the frame: Community. Compassion. And Hygiene.

"Mr. Harper?" Jason held out his hand so Nurse Rowe could wrap bandage over the gauze. "Haven't met him yet. I met his daughter. Not him. I suppose I will at that picnic on Sunday. You two talk a lot?"

The bandage wrapped quickly, and Nurse Rowe cut it with a pair of scissors.

"Oh no," she said. "But I listen to him speak. He's an inspiring fellow, is Mr. Garrison Harper." She sat back on her stool, smoothed down her skirts. "It weren't for him, I wouldn't be here."

Jason flexed his fingers and looked at the bandage. This one was better than the one Dr. Waggoner had put on him. That first bandage had started to peel back almost immediately. Nurse Rowe knew her bandaging.

"My aunt says she got inspired by a fellow like that," he said. "Dr. Davenport was his name. He was lecturing at nurse school."

"Well Dr. Davenport never came to lecture at my 'nurse school.' I heard Mr. Harper speaking in Chicago, in . . . the summer of 1907, I believe."

"Didn't know he went around making speeches. Did he have a tent like a preacher?"

"He might have in some of the other places he visited," said Nurse Rowe. "He could get worked up as any evangelist. This one was in a hall. At the old World's Fair grounds. I was accompanying my father, who had thought he might like to invest some money in Mr. Harper's project."

"Your pa was a rich man?"

"No," said Nurse Rowe, and she tucked her chin against her neck as she rolled the remaining gauze back up and considered. "Not for lack of trying. But it seemed my father only ever had enough money to lose. He didn't play cards, thank Heaven. But he fancied himself a speculator. When I was a little girl, he lost a great deal of money buying a stake in a gold mine in Montana that wound up a fraud. He had more success with real estate in the crash, and he was better at being a landlord. But that is not a rich man's avocation. Not always."

"So he got you worried," said Jason, "that he might go and give Garrison Harper all the rest of your property—and you came along to see that he didn't."

Nurse Rowe covered her mouth to stifle another laugh. "You *are* a wise boy," she said. "Young man. Excuse me. You're a wise young man." She looked up to the skylight, and leaned back on her stool. "I went along with him for exactly that reason," she said. "And I wanted to see the World's Fair, or what was left of it, one more time. You'd be too young to remember it—I am barely old enough. But my goodness . . . what a fantastical place it once was. The whole affair was strung with wires. Wires and electric lamps. It glowed like a fairyland after dusk. And in one of the pavilions—a scientist called Tesla put giant steel globes on poles and made lightning jump between them. You don't forget a thing like that."

Jason could see how. He'd first seen an electric light at work less than a month ago, in Butte. That tiny spark of brightness was enough to drop a fellow's jaw. A man directing lightning from one ball to another? That was the business of old Zeus.

"Of course, by the time Mr. Harper set up his podium there, Dr. Tesla was long, long gone. The entire place had gone to seed. Many of the buildings had been torn down, and the pavilion that Mr. Harper had hired . . . well, it had seen better years. The paint on its entryway was peeling, and inside the plasterwork was crumbling. The pavilion still had some electricity, though. Enough to shine a very bright spotlight on Mr. Harper, and to run a projector to show some photographs on a sheet he'd hung from an archway."

"Sounds fancy," said Jason. Nurse Rowe smiled, like he'd been joking.

"I went in there thinking I'd just get my father out of there as soon as possible. As it turned out, I didn't have to worry. Nothing Mr. Harper said did anything to convince Father that the mill-town in Eliada was a sound investment. I remember the tram ride home; he listed off all the problems. Eliada would be a logging town with nowhere to market its wood: the Kootenai flows north into wilderness in the Canadian territory The railway stops fifty miles or more south of Eliada, and Sand Point was already filling whole trains with wood. And stacked against all that, he said that Harper's scheme to pay and look after his workers—it amounted to charity! He figured Harper for a mad socialist. He used those words. 'He's just another mad socialist, Annie. Best keep clear.'"

"You call this keepin' clear?" Jason gestured with his bandaged hand.

"Well, when he said that, it caused me to think maybe Garrison Harper was a mad socialist. And maybe I was too. It was a fine speech. You haven't met Mr. Harper yet, so you don't know how he can be."

"He's a convincing fellow is he?"

"He convinced me," said Nurse Rowe. "I'd just finished learning nursing at the American Medical Missionary College and was starting work at the Hinsdale Sanatorium. Don't suppose you know about those places either, coming from where you do?"

"I know about missionaries. They spread the word of Jesus."

"Word and deed," she said. "The college taught me what I know about nursing; the Sanatorium taught me the need for it. They were still working on it when I left it for Eliada, later that year. Made by good Christians, in a lovely well-off village, to minister and cure the fallen women of south Chicago. Some would come to the sanatorium. But we'd go visit more than that, in their homes . . . in their slums."

"Slums?" That was a new word to Jason.

"Jason, I watched more babies born into filth and squalor—put those babies into the arms of their mothers, and left them in their cold, filthy shacks . . . more than I'd care to say. I don't know if it was worse if their man had left, or if the cad was still sharing the roof. It broke my heart to see it, I swear."

Jason put his hand on Nurse Rowe's. "Better if they leave, if they're that kind of pa."

Nurse Rowe took a breath, and slipped her hand from under Jason's. "And so," she said, "when Mr. Harper stood in front of us, and said those three words—*Community. Compassion. Hygiene.*—it struck a chord in me. I remember how Father fidgeted beside me, when Harper explained how we could fiddle around the edges all we wanted—babies would still die in their mothers' arms, until we got to work in the middle . . . fixed society up, top to bottom."

"Or start a new one," said Jason.

Nurse Rowe nodded. "That was when he had me. The missionaries . . . for them, the meek are rewarded in Heaven. It seemed to me that Mr. Harper was fixing to make a little bit of that Heaven right here. Before we left, I took down the address he gave—it was a lawyer's office in Chicago—and a week later, I went there. To offer my services."

"And you've been here since then. For—" he counted it in his head "—four years."

"Nearly, yes."

Jason thought about that. "You must've seen some things in that time," he said.

Nurse Rowe shook her head and chuckled. "You are fishing, Mr. Thistledown," she said. "You ask why I want to stay here in Eliada, and that's a fair question. But I could ask the same of you."

"I haven't been here but two days," he said.

"And yet—the things you've seen." She bent forward and put her hand on top of his now. Her eyes found his, and he couldn't look away. It may have been that, it may have been a shift in the cloud . . . but it seemed as though Nurse Annie Rowe was bathed in a strange light, like gold shimmering down from Heaven.

She went on: "You went into the quarantine," she said, "and you drew your own blood. And you saw. And now you're trying to find a way to talk about it."

"I ain't—" he began, but she stopped him.

"It's all right, Jason," she said, and gripped his good hand in hers.

Jason yanked his hand away. "No," he said, "it ain't."

"It's all right," she said again, but she kept her hands to herself. "You've seen so much. You can let it go, in here. I won't tell. It'll be between you, and me, and Jesus Christ our Lord."

"Jesus ain't here," he said.

Annie laughed once more and said, "Of course he is. All around us, Jason. Always. You know what Eliada means, don't you?"

And then, for an instant, Jason thought that funny gold light showed him a row of teeth . . . Then he thought, *No, I got her confused with someone else* . . . and Jason pushed his bandaged hand underneath his arm, and pressed down hard.

"My aunt," he said, through gritted teeth, "said I should see a nurse and get some fresh air. I have to go get some air now."

Nurse Rowe nodded. And a cloud moved above the skylight—perhaps—and dimmed whatever light it was that rained upon her.

"I didn't mean to press my beliefs," she said. "I'm sorry. I thought it'd give comfort."

"Don't be sorry. I'm glad you like it here," said Jason as he got up and headed to the door.

He spared a glance at the skylight—at the even ceiling of deep grey cloud—and he added, "Thank you for the bandaging and all." He stepped out the door, and headed down the hallway toward the town, for his second tour of "Utopia" in as many days.

He wouldn't run into Ruth Harper this time either, and Jason was fine with that. For the first time in many weeks, he thought of the solitude of winter on the farmstead, the quiet of Cracked Wheel in early spring . . . both places without God, or man.

Both places, right then, that he missed, with a soaring and unreachable ache.

19

The Rite of Spring

Nowhere on the invitation sent from Ruth Harper to Jason Thistledown could Aunt Germaine find the words . . . *and Mrs. Germaine Frost*; and as the hours and days passed, no second notice arrived at the Eugenics Records Office in the Eliada hospital. But that did not dissuade her. When Jason awoke Sunday morning, his Aunt Germaine was dressed and ready to go, sitting impatiently in the antechamber to their rooms in the hospital, sour as old milk.

"We are going to worship," she said simply as he buttoned his shirt. "Then to the Harper estate. Comb your hair, Nephew."

He knew better than to argue. Aunt Germaine was as reasonable as sweating dynamite these days. For a time he thought it was because she disapproved of Miss Ruth Harper, but as the hours and days wore on, he realized it was a deeper trouble. She was offended, more deeply than he would have thought possible, that her name had been omitted from the invitation.

They went to the only church in Eliada. It was called Saint Cyprian's, at the end of a row of workmen's houses, along the road to the Harper estate. The service was underway when they got inside. Jason looked over the slumped backs of the worshippers to see the priest going on in Latin the way they did in this church. He and Aunt Germaine slid into a pew near the door, earning a couple of dirty looks for their troubles. Jason felt his heart twist, but not from that. He happened to spy Sam Green, decked out in a black suit, bowler hat nowhere to be seen, bent forward in fervent prayer. During the whole long service, he did not look over once and Jason was fine with that. It wasn't as though he didn't appreciate Sam Green's help directed through him to Dr. Waggoner; he simply thought that conversations with the Pinkerton man came at too steep a price.

By the time the service was done it was nearly the noon hour and time for the picnic. It was turning into a good day; the sun was beating down and it was warm enough to walk without a jacket.

The road went a quarter mile before it led them to the gate, cut nearly straight through the rows on rows of blossoming apple trees that made up the Harpers' orchards. Some of those trees were pretty tall, Jason thought, to have been planted when the Harpers were supposed to have come here ten years back. He wondered who was here before that, with the leisure to plant apple in fine old rows.

Surely it was not the same folk with the leisure to build a house like Mr. Harper's. That place was something. It was huge—bigger than any two barns combined that Jason had ever seen—in the same class as the sawmill or the hospital.

The house was laid out like a horseshoe, made of cut stone near the ground, square-cut log higher up. Jason counted six stone chimneys, climbing high above the steep-peaked roofs. How many rooms could you put in a place like that? How many kin?

How many servants?

This would have been a sore point with his mama. She had unkindly views on the keeping of servants. *A woman ought not live larger than she can sweep in a day*, she would say. Every servant she used brought her that many steps further from looking after herself in a pinch.

It was hard to tell how many servants it took to run the estate by the time they'd made it through the gate. The grounds were filled with people.

"Looks like the whole town's here," said Jason, and instantly regretted it as Aunt Germaine spared him a severe look.

They walked in silence to the crowd of folk that were gathered on the lawn to the north of the house. The guests fanned out across the lawn, some sitting on blankets they'd brought, others standing and watching. A couple Jason recognized from the mill, but it was hard to tell on account of the lack of grime on their shirts and sawdust in their hair. They all stood quiet, listening to the moustachioed fellow in their midst, propped on something so he was a head higher than the tallest. Although it was sunny out, he was hatless, and his dark hair blew over a high forehead as he spoke.

"Our host," said Germaine dryly, and nodded when Jason breathed: "Garrison Harper."

Harper grinned as he spoke, and raised up his arms. "Rites of spring!" he shouted. "This is one of the things we've lost, in this new world of ours. We move through the seasons, one after another—and how do we mark them? Places on a calendar? The inching of the Earth 'round the Sun? Well not here. Not in Eliada!"

At that, a few voices shouted the name: "Eliada!" and like an echo in a canyon, more caught the gist and threw it back. Harper clapped and beamed.

Jason stopped and craned his neck to look around, and when he looked back down he saw that Aunt Germaine had moved on through the crowd. He didn't hasten to follow—it was, to be truthful, a relief to be out of her sight.

"Some of you are new members of this community," said Mr. Harper from his podium. "A month, two, or three, no matter. You've bent your back to labour through a cold and hard winter; perhaps you've been to see the doctors at the hospital. But you may well have asked yourself: what makes this place so fine? Where is this great community you sought when you travelled so far from family and home? Well I can only say—look around you—to the man next to you, and the one next to him."

Jason looked to his side, his eye caught by a bright flash of red. Two men stood there. One caught Jason's eye. Smiled.

"He," said Mr. Harper, "is Eliada."

Wider and wider, his teeth sharp points beneath his lips.

In the distance, Garrison Harper was on to something else—something about the ties that bind, the height of civilization.

Jason scarcely heard it. Icy sweat broke out on Jason's brow, and he could feel an awful crawling at the base of his spine. For that instant, he was back in the quarantine, looking at that tiny, leering face. Striking at it. Running. His hand itched where he'd cut it on a scalpel, and as he looked at this fellow he also looked into the tall, skeletal Juke's eyes at the back of the quarantine and could not look away.

Finally, it was a touch at his elbow that drew him back. The man looked away, and smiled at someone else. The spell was broken. The touch at his elbow was from an older man, dressed better than most. He was one of those servants, Jason guessed.

"Mr. Thistledown?" he asked, and Jason nodded. "Miss Harper is awaiting your company. Perhaps best to join her?"

§

The fellow did not speak again, but led him to the top of a rise to the north of the main party. Downslope was a cleared-out area that edged on the orchards. Not far off was a barn. There, a small group of people milled together. From the crowd, an iron horseshoe flew out, and as it clattered against a spike sticking out of the ground, a girl squealed. Jason waved at them, and started down.

They were near a little iron table, topped with tall glasses and a pitcher of apple cider. Miss Louise Butler was there, sipping her cider in a light blue frock and looking well, Jason thought, compared to how she seemed on the river boat; and also there was Ruth Harper—dressed as outlandishly as Jason had ever seen on a girl, wearing very baggy pants of a deep green tied near the ankle, and a white shirt like a man's. She was beaming.

"Jason Thistledown!" she shouted, waving the horseshoes above her head as she drew up to him.

"Thank you ever so for inviting me to your party Miss Harper," said Jason, parroting what his Aunt Germaine had told him to say when greeting his hostess. He originally was not intending to follow her advice—the way Aunt Germaine had said to say it seemed prissy and girlish and he was sure it would make him out a fool.

But no one laughed. Ruth gave a little curtsy, and she smiled in a sly way at him—the sort of way that made Jason feel that he was in on the joke, not the butt of it. The smile also washed away, at least for the moment, that memory of a tiny face like hers but not, grinning with sharp little teeth and a perverse shine in the bead-sized eye. Jason felt himself exhale, and set about figuring a greeting for Louise Butler, who stood clutching her cider to her breast and looking stricken.

Ruth set the horseshoes on the ground and stepped lightly to the table, where she lifted the pitcher and began filling a glass. "Cider, Jason?"

"Of course you remember Louise."

"Good afternoon," said Jason. Louise finally smiled properly.

"It's still morning," said Louise. "But good day, sir."

Ruth handed the glass to Jason, then set the pitcher down. Jason took a deep swallow of the cider. It was thick and a little tart, and burned his throat.

"Too strong for you?" she asked.

"I like it fine. Like drinking a pie." Jason took another sip. "This is quite a party your pa puts on."

"The first of many," said Ruth. "Father feels celebration is essential to maintaining community. This summer, he'll have a hundred."

Jason laughed. "He'll run out of Sundays," he said, and Ruth said, "He'll just send to New York for more."

Louise interjected: "Do you play at horseshoes, Jason?"

"I do," said Jason. He drained the rest of his glass of cider and set it on the table.

Horseshoes was a game that Jason played quite some with his ma. When he was small, she'd driven an old rail spike into the dirt behind the house. On summer evenings after supper, the two of them would sometimes haul out a rusted stack of horseshoes and toss them over that spike until the last of daylight had bled off. The Harpers' horseshoe set was nothing like that—the horseshoes had not a speck of rust on them, and not one of them had ever borne the weight of an actual horse.

They played four games of it before the call to lunch, and Jason won three of them without even thinking. The last one, he started thinking—and that did it. He threw one horseshoe wild, and another dropped halfway between him and the spike. Louise took that game, and at the end of it, Jason found he had to sit.

"Why Jason—what is the matter? I've not seen you this pale since I accused you of being the son of a gunfighter!" said Ruth.

Jason shook his head. "Nothing."

A single vertical line formed on Ruth's brow. "Well," she said, "I doubt *that*. What *have* you been up to since we parted ways at the dock?"

Jason might have told it—told Ruth everything of that night, from the creature at the window to the Juke at the back of it, from the sad fate of Maryanne Leonard to the less certain fate of Dr. Andrew Waggoner—his game of cat and mouse with the murderous Dr. Bergstrom in days subsequent—were it not for the exquisite timing of Garrison Harper. He stood at the top of the rise, his coat in his arm and the sleeves of his shirt rolled past the elbow—a huge grin on his face and the breeze teasing a long dark forelock like a torn strand of flag.

"Children!" he shouted. "Dinner! Hop to it please—plenty of time for horseshoes later!"

And then Ruth Harper stood, and between finger and thumb, she took hold of his little finger on his right hand, and by that lifted him to his feet.

"We are summoned, Mr. Thistledown," she said. "Best we do not tarry. The guests shall become restless."

§

"Quite a crowd, isn't it?" said Ruth. "Have you ever seen that many people at once, Jason?"

"Sure," said Jason, although he could swear there were twice as many as there were before they started playing at horseshoes.

"Ever seen so many so fine?" she asked.

Jason looked—but try as he might, he couldn't figure what she was talking about. Were they fine? Finer than others? Mr. Harper seemed to like them—he was striding on ahead, into the midst of a group of men who had the hard look of lumberjacks, bellowing his welcome at them.

And with that, they headed down the hill and into the midst of Garrison Harper's picnic, and as they jostled through the crowd, Jason thought Ruth was right. He hadn't seen a bunch of folk like this before—and the number of them didn't have anything to do with it. This place was supposed to be a Utopia—something like Heaven on earth, designed to fit with some grand idea that Mr. Harper had come upon. And as he wandered through the crowds of people with Ruth and Louise, making their way towards the food, it dawned on Jason that as much as his aunt had talked on about free medical care and good working conditions in the mill, he had never fully fathomed exactly what that idea was.

But as he was moving among these folk, he thought he might be getting a better inkling. They were tall—not one of them who was an adult was any shorter than Jason. They seemed pretty strong too. And as to the ladies? They were lean and comely, in the main—good matches for the men they accompanied. And Jason had spent some time with Aunt Germaine and knew of the infirmities that she looked for doing her work—there was no sign he could tell of idiocy or lunacy in their faces; nothing of the mongrel or the degenerate.

In fact, one might wonder just what profit Aunt Germaine and the Eugenics Records Office might find spending time here. Aunt Germaine told him that they were looking for the bottom ten percent of the world.

And here—at least judging by the strong arms and the clean brows—Jason figured there wouldn't be anyone in that bottom percentage. And then another thought came to him—a recollection not of the quarantine, but of that other awful place, Cracked Wheel. Those days he and his aunt had hid out in the town offices, and she'd told him what was what about Dr. Charles Davenport and the ERO.

Why not look for the top ten percent? he'd asked her.

Why not indeed? That'd been her answer. Jason wondered now if he asked Garrison Harper the same question, he'd say anything different.

§

The sun had passed its height by the time Jason had himself a plate full of some of the finest food he'd tasted, but he had lost sight of Ruth. He spotted Louise Butler, though, at a long table half-full of folk, so went and asked if he might join her. She smiled and said he might, so he set his plate down, put a leg over the bench and asked her a bit about herself. She was more conversational on her own, but only a little, and Jason still had to draw it out of her.

Where was she from again now?—*Evanston, Illinois, thank you.* What business were her folks in?—*Dry goods, Mr. Thistledown.* And she and Ruth Harper attended school together?—*Yes thank you.* In Chicago?—*Not far from Chicago. That is correct.* Did she ever read the Bulfinch's at that school of hers?

"The—Bulfinch's? I am sorry, Mr. Thistledown. I'm not familiar with that text."

"Mythology," said Jason. "The Greeks and such."

"Oh," she said. "The Greeks. I've tried to read some of Homer. Not my cup of tea."

Jason took a mouthful of mashed potatoes soaked in butter. He swallowed and set down his fork. "You figure where Miss Harper's got to?"

"No doubt avoiding that man's speech," said Louise.

"Beg your pardon?" asked Jason. He followed the tines of Louise's fork where she indicated, and added, "Oh."

Nils Bergstrom had arrived. He wore a light summer jacket and a hunting cap, and he'd climbed onto a table in the middle of the crowd. He wavered on his feet, and Louise commented disapprovingly: "He looks drunk."

Bergstrom might have been drunk, but if so, he wasn't drunk in the way that Jason understood a man could get: first too familiar, filled with great love, which could change in an instant to a fountain of murderous rage. Bergstrom seemed to move too easily, his arms swung too slowly.

If he spoke, Jason might have been able to tell from that. For drunk men in Jason's experience couldn't quite say anything without stumbling and slurring. But it wasn't speech that came from Nils Bergstrom's open mouth.

"Is he whistling?" whispered Louise, and Jason shook his head.

"Mouth's wide open. Maybe it's some of those folk."

Jason pointed now, at a couple of men at a table nearer Bergstrom, who were standing up now and swaying as well. Jason could hear the tuneless whistling and soon placed it. His eyes flickered shut, and he stood in the quarantine, before a great pair of barn-board doors—doors that were shut for now, but from which a terrible light might emerge. . . .

The whistling stopped.

"Is that your aunt?" said Louise, and Jason opened his eyes.

"It is," he said.

Germaine Frost took Bergstrom by the arm, and helped him down from the table. Bergstrom shook his head as she patted his shoulder, and led him back toward the house.

"It would seem that she saved the day," said Louise.

With shaking hand, Jason lifted his fork and dug into his mashed potatoes. They were like paste in his mouth, but he made himself swallow them. A fellow could see spectres in all sorts of places, even hear them, in a woodsman's whistle.

"Why don't you tell me about the Harpers?" he said finally, and Louise laughed.

"What an excellent idea," she said.

§

"Well," said Ruth Harper some time later. "Aren't you two a pair?"

Jason looked up. Ruth stood behind and between the two of them. She held a dark wooden box under one arm and rested her other hand on Louise's shoulder. Louise started at her school friend's touch, like she'd been accused of something.

"Oh yes," said Jason. "I have been learning all sorts of things about the Harpers from Miss Butler."

"Have you now?" Ruth gave Louise a light slap on her shoulder. Jason winked at Louise—shocking her, and shocking himself a little bit. Seeing Dr.

Bergstrom finally, in full inebriation seemed to have stoked Jason's confidence. Maybe past what was reasonable.

If that were so, Jason had no problem with it. A few minutes ago, as the table was clearing and the other guests went off to join games that Mr. Harper had organized nearby, the notion had alighted on Jason: he was taking pleasure at the picnic. His aunt, the doctor—his dead mama's ghost—the horror in the quarantine—all of that was tucked away. This was more pleasure than he had ever expected to see.

"For instance," said Jason, but before he could continue Ruth interrupted.

"You can tell me everything another time," she said. "For now—I've something I want to show you. Come."

Jason stood up, but when Louise tried to stand, Ruth gently pushed her back down. "I think you have had enough excitement for today. Jason—come with me. We shall have a walk in the orchard. Would you carry this?" She handed Jason the box, and he took it. It was heavy—Jason guessed whatever was inside was made of iron. But he could not tell what it was.

He hefted the box under his arm, tipped his cap to Miss Louise Butler, and followed Ruth Harper through the crowd. He was grinning like a fool, but he didn't care and figured he couldn't do anything about it if he did. That grin stayed with him—when they ducked through a group of workers to avoid drawing Mr. Harper's attention; when they hurried past the horseshoe spike and down a row of blossoming apple trees, over another rise and to a quiet place beyond.

It stayed on him right up until the moment that he opened the box, and found the gleaming silver Colt six-shooter nestled there, resting up in its blood-red bed of velvet.

20

The Secret Terror

"No one knows," said Ruth Harper, rocking from one foot to the other and grinning madly in the dappled sunlight of the orchard. "Not even Louise. Especially not Louise. I purchased it in Chicago—it belonged to Calamity Jane!"

Jason held the gun in two hands. It was a Colt Single Action Army revolver, and although it was nickel-plated with a fine walnut grip, it showed its age. The barrel was nicked in two places and the finish on the wood was worn where the heel of a hand would touch. Jason flicked the magazine open and sighed. At least it wasn't loaded.

"The ammunition is in a little compartment in the box," said Ruth.

Jason flicked it closed and held it at his side, pointed to ground. "How much did you pay?"

"Twenty-nine dollars," said Ruth.

"That seems dear."

"I know," said Ruth. "But it came with the box—and a certificate."

"Have you fired it?"

"No."

"That's one reason nobody knows you got one, I guess. These things make a racket."

"Like thunderclaps," said Ruth.

"Although it looks like you could," said Jason, sighting along the barrel. "Gun's old, but it's been cared for."

"Would you like to?"

Jason looked up. Ruth had moved off to the base of an apple tree. It was too early in the season for apples to grow, but she must have had one in her pantaloons, because she was buffing it on her shirt now. She stood straight against the tree, and put the apple on her head so that it balanced.

"The bullets are in the box. A compartment near the hinge," she said.

Jason gawked.

"Oh come along," said Ruth, rolling her eyes in such exasperation that the apple nearly fell. "You can deny all you like. But I see how you handle that iron."

"Iron?"

"Gun," she said, and took the apple from her head. "It's quite clear to me that you are simply being obstinate."

"Obstinate, huh?" Jason let the gun dangle at his side.

"Obstinate. As Jack Thistledown's true-born son, you should have no difficulty shooting the apple from the top of my head," she said, and made her finger into that pantomime of a pistol again, pointed it at the apple in her other hand, and bent her wrist like she fired it. "You've got shooting in your blood. It is a eugenical fact."

Jason looked at her. He drew a breath and counted a few before talking.

"First thing," he said, "I have not shot one of these before. I've seen them. And I've seen them shot. So the one eugenical fact is this: if I tried to shoot the apple from your head, more than likely I'd shoot the eye from your socket. Then you'd be dead and I'd be in dutch." Jason flipped the gun around in his hand so he gripped it around the barrel and the magazine, and presented the grip to Ruth. "This is a fine enough 'iron' you bought yourself—though I don't guess it came from Calamity Jane or anyone else famous. You got the certificate?"

Ruth took the gun. "In my room." She said it sullenly. "You know, *everyone* is convinced that your father was Jack Thistledown."

She whirled then, raised her arm and pointed the gun at Jason.

"Ha!" she said. "See? Your nerves are steel. You did not even flinch!"

"It's not loaded," said Jason.

Ruth squinted at him. "Even knowing—a lesser man would have flinched," she said. "The son of a gunfighter? Never."

"You know," said Jason, "you don't know me well enough to make those sorts of guesses."

Ruth stood still, lowered the gun, and crooked her head to one side in a way that was becoming familiar. "Why Jason Thistledown I do believe there is a tear in your eye."

"Something in my eye. Not crying."

"*Ahem.* Nerves of steel indeed."

And she stepped up to him, dropped the apple to the ground and standing very close, touched his cheek with a fingertip. Her eyes held nothing but frank amazement.

"You never answered my other question," she said.

"What question?"

She pulled back. "Whatever have you been up to since we parted ways at the dock?"

§

It came out fast—most of the story, and at the right point, the rest of the tears.

That point came early on, when Jason was telling about burning up his mama and the homestead and all, at the advice of Aunt Germaine. Jason did not want to tell that part, but it was the only way he could explain Bergstrom's decision to lock him up in the quarantine the first night.

"Aunt Germaine figured that washing me down and burning up my mama would do the trick—kill the germ and make it right, and I went—" He was about to say, *I went along*, but he found he could not say anything else. He felt a fist close in his middle, and his mouth filled with salt, and he shut his eyes to try to will it away, but he could not. So he cried, and as he did he found he was no better at it now than he was when he wept at his mama's deathbed.

"I'm sorry," he finally said. They were sitting at the base of a tree, cross-legged on the ground, Ruth facing him. He saw that she was tearing up too.

"Your mother died," she said. "Do not apologize."

"Not just my mama," said Jason. "The town. Cracked Wheel. Everybody died."

Ruth frowned and sniffed and swallowed. "The entire town. From this same illness?"

"A hundred folk," said Jason.

"All," she said, "but you—you and your aunt."

"She wasn't from town."

"Yes. She was just passing through, you said."

"Intending to visit us, she said."

"In the middle of winter. Did she visit often in winter?"

"She never visited before this," said Jason. "Winter or summer. It was a good thing she did, though. On balance, I mean."

Ruth let Jason get on with the rest of his story: about how Dr. Bergstrom stuck a needle in him and put him in quarantine. Jason did not cry for this part, although it was a memory that he had been doing his best to forget since freeing Dr. Waggoner and he thought it might be a thing to make him weep. But thinking about it now just made him mad, and egged on by Ruth's encouraging nods, he told most all of the story the way it had happened. All of it, but the fact that the creature looked like Ruth Harper in miniature. He could not figure out a way to say that.

"Your aunt gave you a scalpel," Ruth said. "To cut yourself free."

"Else I'd have been done for."

"May I see your hand?"

Jason extended it. The bandage was off now, but the stitches were still in place, little black sutures running up the heel of his thumb. She took his hand, cradling it in her own palm, while she ran a fingertip along the sutures. She made a tsk-tsk sound, then set his own hand back in his lap.

"So she knew about the creatures."

"She—" Jason had seen her talking with Dr. Bergstrom like they were old friends. But he had not yet let himself think that she actually knew all the things that were to befall him in that quarantine.

"She must have known about the Juke," said Jason. "Before I got there."

"What a wonderful aunt you have, Jason," she said acidly.

Jason told about the autopsy room and the state of Maryanne Leonard's corpse in better detail, expecting that Ruth would at some point beg him to spare her. In fact, she asked Jason if he'd kept the samples someplace safe and seemed appalled when he told her he'd sent them off with Dr. Waggoner.

"You entrusted them to the Negro?"

"He's a doctor," said Jason.

"He's a runaway Negro doctor. I understand he stole clothing and medical supplies before he ran off."

"He stitched up this cut. He's my friend. I should've done more."

"More?"

Jason looked at Ruth—and wondered whether he ought to omit the next part of the story the same way he left out the little be-fanged Ruth Harper that crawled up his leg that night. He had given Sam Green his word, after all, that he would keep their meeting—his own involvement in this thing—a secret.

"What more do you mean, Jason?" she demanded. "What did you do for Dr. Waggoner in the first place?"

"I helped him get out," said Jason. "Before the attack. I stole those things."

Ruth looked at him hard, and she must have read something in the pained expression in his face, because she did not ask him the question that he could not answer: *who warned him that the Ku Klux Klan were planning to break into the hospital and murder the doctor?*

Instead, she finally asked: "How did you get away with it?"

"Mostly luck and good graces. I did get caught," he said. "When I was fetching the doctor's bag, Annie Rowe came by. Caught me red-handed."

"But she didn't turn you over."

"No. She asked what I was doing—I said I was gettin' something for my aunt. I could tell she didn't believe me. But she didn't stop me, neither."

Ruth shook her head and smiled slightly.

"Otherwise, I kept to the quiet places," said Jason.

"Hum. Move over, Jason."

Ruth got up, picked up the Colt and the box it had come in, and settled against the tree trunk, close enough so their shoulders were touching. Jason shifted to give her room, but she closed the gap. She put the gun in the box, and shut it.

"So what did you find when you returned to the quarantine?"

"I haven't," he said. "Not since that night."

She turned the clasp on the box shut, and set it on the ground beside her. She looked at Jason very seriously.

"Have you been back down to the autopsy room?"

"I been laying low."

Jason looked right into her unblinking eyes. He felt that fist in his middle again, but this time it opened up wide. Ruth Harper's eyes drew closer, and fluttered shut, as her lips touched his, and held them as her fingertips moved up the back of his neck to the base of his skull and teased the fine hair there. Her mouth opened and he felt her moist breath pass his own parted lips. And then she pulled away, her hand resting only a moment longer at the nape of his neck, and she apologized for her forthrightness, and said she hoped he did not regard it as an affront to his manhood.

Jason took a deep breath and swallowed. He had a feeling in his middle that a fellow gets when he is falling in a tumble: one instant, he's facing the ground—the next, the pure blue of Heaven. And the whole short time of it, his stomach's in his throat.

"Do you know why I did that right now?" Ruth was looking at her hands as she spoke. She sounded flustered.

Jason shook his head.

"Because it terrified me."

"More—" he cleared his throat. "More than having an apple shot off your head by a farm boy?"

"I didn't really expect you to. But yes. More than that."

"I don't understand."

"Well—I think it terrified me about as much as it terrifies you—to go back into that quarantine, or go down to the autopsy room, or confront that aunt of yours. Perhaps to face up to—" She looked up at him now, one side of her mouth crooked up in a grin. "Well. You want to do all of those things. It will be better for you if you do. And all that it takes is one reckless moment—"

And then her expression changed, and for an instant her eyes left his and glanced over his shoulder, and narrowed. Jason would have asked what it was, but he had no chance. Ruth turned back to him, parted her lips, and leaned toward him. This time she did not hold onto his head, which Jason figured meant he'd better do his part, so brought his mouth to hers. Her lips were open, and his were too, and their teeth clicked together as he felt the softness of her tongue on his. Her hand this time stayed clear of his neck and rested on the inside of his leg, fingertips playing with a fold in his trousers, inches from his parts.

She pulled back from him then, and rested her chin on his shoulder, and whispered:

"We are being watched."

Jason started to pull away, but stopped when she made a shushing noise.

"Don't worry," she said. "This is what he'll be expecting us to be doing. There won't be more questions if we're simply found doing it." And then she pulled back and said at volume:

"Boy! Come out and stop spying on us!"

Now Jason did turn away, and look up the slope where Ruth was looking. Sure enough, at the crest of the rise, someone was moving. But it did not take long to tell that Ruth had guessed wrong. This was no boy.

This fellow had dark hair, and a wide face, and he was huge. As he climbed up over the rise, Jason saw that he was wearing a white robe that came down to his ankles. He was carrying a thick branch in two hands. Jason thought he might recognize the fellow, and as he started down the hill, Jason figured he knew from where.

"Nowak."

§

The last time Jason had seen Nowak had been four days ago, outside the sawmill just before he met up with Sam Green. Nowak was changed from that afternoon. Watching as he moved stiffly down the hillside toward them, Jason was put to mind of something his mama had taught him early: the way she put it, men-folk could change from one fellow to a completely different one, in as much time as it took to drink a jug of whiskey. And when they did, you had to watch them. You could not let them get too close.

"Do you know him?" whispered Ruth.

"I met him. It ain't right."

"It's not—" Ruth took a sharp breath. "He's wearing a *Klan* robe. Oh *damn*. Let me—"

She reached around beside her. Jason could hear the box with the Colt inside opening. He didn't look at what she was doing. He stood up, and kept his eye on Nowak. He was grinning widely. As he started to close the gap, there was enough of a shift in the breeze, and Jason caught a whiff of something rotten. He was carrying the branch across his middle, bouncing it in one hand while the other gripped it hard, like he was getting ready to swing.

Jason kept his eye on the man. That was the trick, his mama said. Don't let them see you back down or look like you might take what they're planning on giving out. Because they'll see that as an invitation. Show them you'll look them in the eye. Show them you'll fight.

"You want something?" said Jason.

Beside him, Ruth whispered: "Damn. Damn damn *damn* it all!"

Jason heard the metallic click and spin sound that told him she had opened the magazine. He cursed too, but to himself. It would have been better if she'd just handed him the gun empty. Jason thought he might have bluffed. He stepped in front of Ruth, so at least when Nowak rushed them, he'd hit Jason first.

But Nowak stopped about a dozen feet from them. He didn't say anything and didn't move—just stared at Jason. It was mesmerizing.

"What do you want?" said Jason.

"God," said Nowak. "I want to show you God."

"I seen God already," said Jason. "Why don't you run off?"

But as Jason spoke, he saw that wasn't going to happen. It was as though a cloud moved across Nowak's face—and as it passed a whistling came up—and

Nowak said: "God wants to see you some more." And then he stopped bouncing the stick, and lifted it, and started again toward the two of them.

And at that, Jason lost the contest. He flinched, expecting an arm-smashing blow, or something that would end up on his skull, and finish him.

But before that could come, he felt a hand around his right wrist, and the cool walnut grip of the Colt.

He didn't even think past that. He brought the gun up and held it two-handed—waited the instant that it would take to know whether the gun would cause Nowak to stop—with a thumb drew the hammer back, with a forefinger squeezed the trigger—screwing his eyes shut and bracing against the kick—

—then finally, when it was all over, thinking to himself:

You were right, Ruth. It's a thunderclap.

§

They had only a moment to themselves after that. Nowak was on his back, bleeding into the sheet from his shoulder where Jason had clipped him. He was not in such terrible shape that he could not get up again, but the one shot had taught him respect for the gun, which Jason kept trained on his head—so he stayed down.

Which was a good thing, because Ruth had only managed to load one more bullet before she'd handed the Colt over. Jason did not wish to shoot a fellow just for trying to stand up, though he knew he would have to.

During the moment before the riders crested the hill, Jason only asked him one question. Later, he would come to regret that he had not followed that with more questions, because when the two Pinkerton men ordered him to surrender the gun and pulled him away from Nowak, they made sure Jason did not have another chance to speak with him alone again.

For the next few hours, Jason didn't have a chance to speak with anyone alone. Sam Green showed up and hauled Jason and Ruth back to the house, and then Jason found himself in a big sitting room, face to face with Mr. Harper and Mrs. Harper and Aunt Germaine. That was when he found out how lucky he was not to have been shot by the first fellows to arrive at the scene.

"They found you standing over a bleeding man with a gun in your hand, son," said Mr. Harper. "I would not have blamed either of them if they'd put a bullet in you as a matter of precaution. Now tell me, son—why did you bring a firearm to this home? What possessed you?"

"I'm sorry," said Jason, and saying that, he realized that he was willing to lie to protect Ruth Harper. He was willing to because he had—same as he'd shot that fellow without thinking.

"I did it," Ruth blurted. Jason looked at her in amazement.

She confessed to everything—even going so far as having the certificate brought downstairs from her room. She explained that she had brought the weapon out because she wanted to see how Jack Thistledown's son could shoot.

"And as it turned out, he is a remarkable shot," she said.

"Jack Thistledown." Mr. Harper shook his head.

Then Ruth went at her father on another tack. "That man was deranged, father. He was a Klansman! If Jason—Mr. Thistledown had not fired upon him, Heaven knows what he might have done to us both!"

Mr. Harper went quiet and thoughtful at that, and although Jason did not know him well he could see the arguments turning in his head. He wondered when it would come to the point where he asked to know what the two of them had been doing back in the orchards.

Jason regarded Aunt Germaine. She was seated away from them on a high-backed stuffed chair, hands folded in her lap. Light from the tall windows reflected in her glasses, making it difficult to tell where she was looking.

"Jason," said Mr. Harper finally, "look at me."

Jason looked at him.

"Dr. Bergstrom thinks that Piotr Nowak will live. So you have not killed a man today, although you might well have. For that, you can be grateful."

"I am grateful for that."

"And I must tell you that I am grateful you had the presence of mind to use my daughter's ill-gotten *toy* to protect her life and honour."

Jason nodded.

"Now I am going to send you home. You and Mrs. Frost both."

"Father," said Ruth, standing up, "Mr. Thistledown should not go back to the same hospital as that brute!"

"I am not speaking of the hospital," said Mr. Harper. "I mean to say, it is time that both you and your aunt left Eliada. The steamboat is downriver just now. It returns late tomorrow. On Tuesday, you shall both be on it."

Aunt Germaine leaned forward. "I beg your pardon," she said in a tone that suggested anything but begging.

"I'm sorry, Mrs. Frost. You may convey my apologies to New York, if indeed that is your next stop."

"You are suggesting that we leave," she said. "Now."

"I am insisting."

Aunt Germaine stood, and walked over to Jason. She put a hand on his arm.

"He rescued your daughter, sir. From, if I may say, a difficulty that is of your making—not his."

"Is that so?"

"The Klan. They were here before us, sir. They injured your Negro days before we arrived."

"My *Negro*."

Mr. Harper drew a breath and paused, as if collecting himself.

"Madame," he finally continued, "I will not be swayed. Do you not see what danger you are in now? Both of you? Are you not afraid that this fellow's friends will try to take vengeance?"

Aunt Germaine took Jason's arm. "We shall see," she said. "Come Jason—we are returning to the hospital."

Jason stood up, but Mr. Harper shook his head. "I would not recommend that. Ruth is right—the hospital is not safe."

"Then what would you recommend?"

Mr. Harper sighed. "Mrs. Frost, I don't bear you ill will. You or young Mr. Thistledown. I'd ask that the two of you remain here as our guests for the next two nights. We have spare rooms aplenty, and I think you will find that Harper hospitality exceeds that at the hospital. I do not think that anyone would dare strike *here*."

"We shall send for your things," said Mrs. Harper in a kindly tone.

Aunt Germaine was having none of it. "Do not think this makes things right!" she said, so fiercely that Mrs. Harper gasped, Mr. Harper looked away, and Jason felt the blood in his face as he briefly met eyes with Ruth. He recalled as they arrived that Aunt Germaine had not wished to be embarrassed. He wondered now, somewhat nastily, if she even had the wit to be.

§

The picnic carried on long into the evening but Jason stayed clear of it. He had a good view from the bedroom the servants had put him up in. It was an attic room, but pretty fine for that: the bed was wider than the hospital bed that Jason slept in, and softer too. And there was a little window that cut out from the eaves, and a place where a fellow could sit and look out. It was also advantageous, in that the room was a floor up and a wing away from the quarters where they'd placed Aunt Germaine.

He had only two visitors during the day.

Sam Green stopped in about four in the afternoon. Outside, some fellows had gotten with their instruments—one with a guitar, another with a fiddle, and another fellow with a harmonica—and started to play a tune together. Sam Green knocked twice on the door before letting himself in. Jason nodded welcome.

"You ever learn to dance, Mr. Thistledown?" said Sam, bending his head to look out the window over Jason's shoulder.

"Not much call for it," said Jason.

"Are you sure about that? Nothing a young lady likes better'n a fellow who's quick on a two-step."

"Mayhap I should learn that then."

Sam tilted his head. "Mayhap," he said.

Jason slid out of the window. "How is he?" he asked.

"He?"

"Fellow I shot," said Jason.

"Oh," said Sam, "you're interested. That's something. Wouldn't have thought that of a Thistledown boy. Particularly one as you."

"What do you mean by that?"

Sam smiled and set down in the window where Jason had been. "You shot a man today. You shot him right, just where you needed, to take him down but not kill him. And then you held him—kept that gun on him steady until my men could show up."

"Wasn't much else to do."

"Well you did the right thing—exactly the right thing—and that is something most fellows would not have been able to. I know because I've seen how most fellows get when they start to shooting. Some of them keep shooting, doing all sorts of harm and you got to calm them down or shoot 'em to make 'em stop. Others—well, they shoot the once and miss, and then start shaking so bad they can't do it again and they get themselves shot often as not as well."

"And then there's another sort. Like you."

"Like me."

"Ice in your veins, boy. I could tell the minute I showed up, and looked you in the eye."

"What did you see?"

"What I've seen in your pa's eyes." Sam was nodding slowly as he looked at Jason, and things got quiet. Jason did not take the bait.

"You going to tell me how that fellow's doing?" he said. "The one I shot so well?"

Sam smiled and chuckled deep in his chest. "He'll be fine soon as the doctor sobers up enough to work on him. Then I will talk to him. We found some other sheets in the orchard—dropped, like their owners heard the gunshots, dropped the costumes and bolted—not far off. Did you happen to hear or see anyone else?"

"No. Just him."

Sam nodded. "Figured you'd say if you had. That wasn't what I came here for, though."

"What did you come for?"

"Tell you thanks," said Sam. "Thanks for keeping that matter between us. And thanks for taking care of Ruth. That was a near thing."

"Well, you are welcome sir," said Jason.

"And son," he said as he pushed himself off the windowsill and headed for the door, "you might want to take my advice and learn that two-step. More reliable way to impress a young lady than shooting folks with a borrowed six-gun, you want my opinion."

§

The second visitor was a mystery—just a knock at the door, and a wax-sealed envelope slipped beneath it. By the time Jason opened the door, the footsteps were going down the stairs.

So Jason opened the seal and pulled out two folded sheets of paper and an empty, unaddressed envelope. One sheet was blank, one was full of fine handwriting. He did not have to look to the signature at the bottom to know who it was from.

§

Jason read the letter from Ruth Harper twice before he could put pen to paper and make up a reply. Lord, but the girl was verbose. She used up not one but four sentences describing how much she liked being kissed by him and kissing him back. She felt less kindly toward her father, and she took three more sentences to say how awful he was for making Jason leave town so fast. She was also cross with Miss Louise Butler (although on this she did not elaborate), which was why she had imposed upon Harris, one of the servants, to deliver her letter instead. He would be by later in the evening, to collect any reply that Jason might wish to write, which was what the blank sheet of paper and empty envelope were for. She apologized for not sending along a stick of wax, but it would not have fit under the door.

Jason did reply, but not to any of what she had written, other than to say that he had liked kissing Ruth Harper fine too and hoped they might do so again before he left.

On the final points of her letter he was more specific:

You are welcome for saving your life, although I should thank you for loading the gun or else I would be dead. I am sorry you lost your Colt.

I do not want to go to the quarantine again without a gun at least. But I will meet you at the place you wrote in your letter this night and we can talk about it.

And then he set the pencil down and thought for a moment and wrote:

I am terrified of this too but you were terrified of kissing so I will be brave like you.

He thought about changing that sentence—it was not at all as pretty as the sentences that Ruth had set down in her long letter, and it was not made any prettier by his awful handwriting. And there was that other question—one that he should have an answer to by now. So he wrote his name at the bottom, folded up the note paper, slipped it into the envelope, and settled down to wait for the servant's return.

§

Jason kept Ruth's letter and read it over a couple of times more. His eye kept moving to that single question—the one that he could not figure.

She wrote: *I cannot yet fathom why you asked him that question: "Who sent you to murder Dr. Waggoner?" I have been beside myself with wondering—how you would have thought this fellow had gone to murder Dr. Waggoner? Will you not tell me, Jason my darling? Is there another piece to this mystery you have kept from me?*

And what of his answer, Jason? What of that? What is this "old man" of whom he speaks? Is it Dr. Bergstrom? That creature you described in the quarantine? Some other man? Do you know? Pray write me & say!

Jason read the letter over and over, until the hour struck three, and it was time. He folded the letter, put it in his pocket, and with a shaking breath, slipped out through the door and padded down the corridor.

How in tarnation was he supposed to know who the old man was anyhow? All he knew was what Nowak had said, lying in his own quickening blood and spitting through the pain:

"The Oracle is on the march. She deliver God.

"She deliver God."

21

The "Germe de grotte"

"You are ever punctual, Mr. Thistledown," Ruth said.

Jason didn't see her, but he felt a warm hand on his arm as soon as he stepped through the doorway of the cider house. She drew him further along, and the door swung shut. In the dark now, Jason leaned over to where he thought the voice came from with another kiss in mind.

Fortunately, Ruth Harper was deft enough to move aside, so when Louise Butler struck a match and held it to a candle, they stood blinking in the flickering light a respectable distance from one another. Louise granted Jason a bare smile and set the candle on a wooden shelf behind her, and gave Ruth a look of ambiguous meaning. Jason nodded a how-do-you-do and Ruth let go of his arm.

"Isn't it wonderful?" Ruth's voice was taut as a banjo string. "Louise has elected to join us."

"Pleased to see you again," said Jason. Then to Ruth: "You sure you want to go to this place?"

"Soon enough," she said. "But not right away."

Jason's eyes narrowed. "We have only a little while to sunrise. You want to figure out a mystery, we best be on our way."

"On your way where?" said Louise. "I thought—"

"Yes," said Ruth quickly. "There's work to be done here first. Jason, why don't you sit down a moment."

Jason looked around. They were alongside the curve of a huge wooden barrel that he guessed was for pressing apples. There was a bench along the wall underneath where the candle was. As he looked around, he saw a dark shape on the plank floor. He squinted and stepped closer.

"That's my aunt's bag," he said, bending down to touch the handle.

"Indeed it is," said Ruth.

"Ruth stole it," added Louise.

Ruth scoffed: "Oh, hardly."

"She ordered the help to bring it to her," said Louise. "They wouldn't bring the guns though."

Jason looked at Ruth. She wore a pair of dark trousers and high laced boots, her blouse concealed underneath a small woollen jacket, and in the light, Jason might almost have thought he was kneeling beside a fellow.

"We will give it back," said Ruth. "After we've given it a proper search. I trust that won't present a problem?"

"I—I looked through it at Cracked Wheel," said Jason. "She was pretty upset when she caught me."

"Yes. Well, Mr. Thistledown, why would she be upset if she had nothing to hide? I have been considering the tale you told me about your sad adventures at Cracked Wheel—and the more I considered it, the less sense I could make of it. Consider the fabulous coincidence: a terrible sickness strikes your community, and in its aftermath—this long-lost relation arrives to spirit you off to . . . here! Where she consorts with that awful Dr. Bergstrom, who subjects you . . ."

"Subjects him to what?" said Louise.

"Well my point," said Ruth hastily, "is that your Aunt Germaine, if that is who she is, seems a most sinister presence."

"All right, Miss Harper, Miss Butler," he said. "Let's have a good look inside and see what we can see."

§

Jason had hauled that bag across hundreds of miles it seemed, since the winter's end. As they pried open the clasp and began their inventory, he was amazed with himself that he had found so little when he looked inside it the first time—and that he had failed to take a second look during the rest of the journey. Was he that afraid of inciting his Aunt Germaine's displeasure?

Ruth felt no such compunction. She wasted no time in pulling out Germaine's box of eugenical index cards, removing one after another and reading the contents out loud in an unflattering impersonation of Aunt Germaine's overly precise east coast diction. Louise looked at some cards too, but more quietly—her brow creased as she tried to decipher the numeric code.

Jason helped her: "Epilepsy," he said. "That's the fainting sickness. Congenital criminal. That's—that's folks born bad."

Ruth gave him a light slap on the thigh at that. "You've already explored these then," she said, and dug further. After pulling out some garments and a small ivory box that contained small amounts of cosmetics, she reached to the bottom, and looked at her hand in the bag and then at the floor.

"There is," she said, "another compartment in this bag. Between the bottom and the floor, there is a good four or five inches."

"Let me see," said Jason. Ruth leaned away from the bag and Jason took her place. He felt the bottom of the bag. He tapped at it.

"Sounds hollow," he said, and ran his finger around the edge as Ruth smirked and Louise, in spite of herself, moved in closer.

"A secret compartment," Louise whispered.

"Not much of a secret," said Jason as his finger stopped at what felt like another clasp. He twisted it, then when the bottom wouldn't budge moved to the other side of the bag and found another. He pulled the bottom out, and set it on the floorboard. Ruth stood and brought the candle down from its shelf.

Jason peered into the compartment. There were two things there: a sheaf of paper bound in string, and a small wooden rack, perhaps ten inches long and five wide. It had two circular holes cut in it. One was empty. The other held a small, earthenware jug fired with a reddish glaze. Its top was sealed with deep red wax that drooled down its edges. As Jason lifted it carefully from the bag, he could see no writing or seal on it to say what might be inside. Whatever was inside shifted when he turned the jug upside down to look on its bottom.

He set it down on the floor between himself and Louise, while Ruth busied herself untying the string on the papers.

"Careful," said Jason, "to remember how she tied that up. We got to put it all back."

"Quite," said Ruth. She set the string back on the bag and began to leaf through the papers. Many of them, though not all, were in envelopes that had been neatly cut. Ruth squinted at these.

"Do you know of an *M. Dulac*?"she asked.

"No," said Jason.

"Well," said Ruth, pulling a sheet of paper from one of the envelopes, "your aunt appears to. *Ooo-la-la*, he is a Frenchman."

"Let me see that," said Louise, and snatched letter and envelope from Ruth's hands. "Remember I sat alongside you in French Grammar classes." Then to Jason: "She is hopeless at it."

"You are not much better," said Ruth, as Louise squinted.

"Well, I am versed enough in World Geography, to know that M. Dulac is no Frenchman." She held up the envelope, and pointed to the return address. "He is writing from Africa—the Belgian Congo. That means that he is Belgian."

"How do you know?" asked Jason.

"Because," said Ruth, "it is a well-known fact that the Belgians don't let Frenchmen into Africa any more. Particularly not their precious Congo, wherever that is."

"You were correct, however, about Mrs. Frost's intimacy with this fellow— or at least his intimacy with her. See?" Louise pointed to a paragraph. "*Tu*! Not *vous*. *Tu*! He is addressing her as an intimate. And could this be *chère*?"

"Love letters." Ruth gave a low laugh. "Well that is one secret that we've uncovered. Are you shattered, Jason?"

"No," said Jason.

"And what's this?" said Louise. "*Germe de grotte*?"

"Perhaps an affectionate nickname?" offered Ruth.

"It can't be that affectionate," said Louise, frowning. "It translates as Germ of the Cave. Or Cave Germ."

"Well, you know the French," said Ruth.

"I do not," said Louise. "And in any event, this fellow is Belgian."

"Does your French Grammar learning let you read more than a couple words? What's the letter about? Aside from being intimate I mean," said Jason.

Louise fixed him with a glare. "I am more than capable of translation," she said, "but it is not a simple matter."

"No, it surely is not," said Ruth. "Why, I can recall you spending entire nights translating filthy French poetry from that Rimbaud fellow."

"Ruth! I did no such—"

Ruth interrupted. "We do not, however, have time to wait for a translation. It's only a few hours 'til sunrise. So I propose this: you remain here and complete a translation of those letters. We, meanwhile, shall investigate the mysterious quarantine—then rendezvous back here an hour before the sun comes up, and share our discoveries."

Jason could see that Louise was thinking about objecting to this; Ruth was, in her plan, brushing Louise aside. But from the way that Louise kept glancing down at that letter and the other ones still in their stack, Jason could tell that she was maybe more curious about what was going on with M. Dulac and Germaine Frost than she was about what was going on in the quarantine. So when she finally sighed and acquiesced, Jason was not surprised.

"Splendid!" said Ruth, standing abruptly. "Then we shall be off."

She disappeared into the dark for a moment, and before Jason could follow far, returned with a lantern and a hatchet, the second of which she handed to Jason. "It's not a six-gun," she said, "but it's better than nought."

Louise shook her head absently, as she leaned over the first of the letters from M. Dulac, and Jason and Ruth slipped out into the night.

§

They could not have been more than ten paces from the door when Ruth stopped, put a hand on Jason's neck and touched his lips with hers. This kiss lasted longer than the other two, and when they parted, she sighed. "I think that I'm no longer afraid," she said. "Of kissing, that is. Are you still frightened of the quarantine?"

Jason was, but he didn't say so. Ruth laid her palm on his chest and looked up at him. The moon was past full, and low in the sky, and it filtered into a silvered filigree through the branches and leaves of the apple trees. She was smiling, mouth open. He couldn't see her teeth.

"Your heart is thundering," she said. "You are still afraid."

Jason lifted her hand from his chest and stepped back. He *was* afraid. But it was not the quarantine that made him so.

It was that vision of Ruth Harper, small as a doll, mouth filled with sharp teeth and eyes black and mischievous. It was a mad fear; he knew that, but it was a true one—like she was some terrible Gorgon. He could not keep looking at her, but he couldn't look away.

"May I help, Jason?" She closed the distance and took his hand. "Think of the first time we met. Do you remember? On the train?"

"Sure," he said. "Although we didn't meet on the train. It was after."

"That is when we spoke. We saw each other some time before. I've been thinking on that, all this long evening. It was remarkable, don't you think? That the two of us should, amid all those other passengers, lock our gazes across a rail platform?"

"I didn't know our gazes locked," said Jason, and Ruth laughed.

Jason swallowed. Ruth took his hand, opened the fingers and placed it against her cheek. Jason found her birthmark with his thumb, ran his finger along it. She lifted her chin and moved it so she nuzzled his hand, and that was all it took: the panic that had run up and down his back gave way to something finer.

"And here we are," she said, "mere days later, off on a grand adventure—at one another's side."

"That's something," agreed Jason.

"Something," she murmured. "Hmmph. I will tell you what it is, Jason Thistledown. It is fate."

She peeled Jason's fingers from her cheek. "Fate," she said, "has seen us this far. It helped me overcome my terror at your touch. It helped us, through the good fortune of that mystery in your aunt's bag, it distracted Louise from our adventure so we might have a few hours alone before you must leave. Now, let it help you." She intertwined her fingers with his, and twisted so they were alongside each other.

"Come," she said, leading the way along a path. "I know a way past father's guard. Let's be on our way."

They headed into the orchard, along a row and then they turned and went along another, and it wasn't long before he was entirely turned around and lost. He hoped that Ruth was not trusting entirely to fate to see them through the orchard and had some idea where they were going. Jason had read enough of the Bulfinch's to know that not all fate was the helpful kind.

Before he could worry too much about that, they stepped out from the trees and back into moonlight. There was a rail fence in front of them, and past that, a gentle slope leading down to some back gardens, and then to a row of what Jason pegged for worker houses.

Ruth set the lantern on the ground and hoisted herself up on the fence so that she straddled it. Jason followed her over.

They headed down a footpath between beds of vegetables. Jason moved low to the ground and Ruth copied him, and kept up with him when he sprinted for the road. It was only there that Jason took a good look down the slope to the town, and noticed the lights.

Ruth stopped short beside him, huffing and clutching her lantern. "Oh my," she said. "That is queer."

They had a good view of the main streets of the town, and those streets were easy to tell, because they were lit up with lamps, bright like star-points, swinging and twinkling up and down the avenues. More light came from windows, shining squares of light that flickered with flame and intersecting shadows. That was strange—all those lights and activity past three in the morning—but that wasn't what made him worry so.

It was the whistling.

The whistling was everywhere—and it was the same kind of sound as he had heard that first night, that filled the whole of the quarantine and got into the back of his head. The same as came up at the picnic, when Bergstrom made such a scene.

As he listened now, Jason wondered if maybe he'd been hearing it all through the night, since he snuck out from the house and made his way down here—got to wondering if maybe it had granted Louise the fascination with the love letters from Africa and Ruth her sense that fate decided everything. It was the sound, after all, that had nearly robbed him of his will, when he saw the thing—the Juke, whatever it was—in the quarantine.

And then, as fast as it had come, the whistling faded. And there were just the lights. Hundreds of lights.

Another light appeared beside him, as Ruth struck a match and held it to the wick of the lantern she carried. "I don't know what they're doing. But we won't be able to sneak past them. We may as well hide in plain sight."

Jason sighed. He slid the hatchet into his belt, and lifted his shirt so it covered the blade. He wished that fate, if it were watching over them, would have at least seen fit to provide him with a decent gun.

§

The street was empty, but it was lit by the flickering lamps in the windows and on the porches of the worker houses. Jason started, as he saw one of those lights blacked out for a moment—blacked out by something that was moving in the dark outside. Ruth didn't notice that; she was too busy trying to hide in plain sight, as she'd said. She held the lantern in front of her like a banner in some parade.

"Jason," she said, as they approached St. Cyprian's, "I should thank you for your kind reply to my letter."

"You're very welcome."

"And you answered many of my questions. But not everything."

She stopped at the path to the church. "I can remember very specifically in fact, a particular question I put to you that you did not answer."

"That so?"

"That's so, yes. I asked you: why did you think that this fellow was sent to murder Dr. Waggoner? And you wrote me back a fine letter about many things besides that." She lifted the lantern to shine it on Jason's face, and peered into his eyes seriously. "Don't think you can avoid all my questions, Mr. Thistledown, now that we have become *intimates*."

Jason looked back at her. He was on the edge of telling her the whole thing: how Sam Green had warned him of the attempt on Waggoner's life, and how Dr. Nils Bergstrom was tied up in it, and everything else. It would be easier to betray Sam Green to Garrison Harper's daughter, he thought, than it would have to tell Aunt Germaine the truth about what had happened in the quarantine. Jason wondered about that: this was a betrayal, pure and simple— not just keeping a secret from someone he'd stopped trusting anyhow.

But it was betrayal to Ruth Harper, who was, as she'd put it, an *intimate*.

"Well, Jason?"

"I can't," he said. "I'm sorry but I can't."

She narrowed her eyes and looked at him more closely. Jason was sure then that she would become angry and stalk off, leaving him alone in the road. But she surprised him.

"I see that's so," she said. "I'll not press the point. You can tell me about that when you tell me more about your papa."

"All right," said Jason.

"All right," she said, and pulled the lantern away.

The whistling started up again as they passed the sawmill. Jason by this time had one hand clutched around the handle of the hatchet, his grip all the tighter for the fact that he knew it would be of scant help, if all those folks turned their attention away from the mill and its maze of lumber. He leaned to Ruth and said that he thought it was time to snuff the light and she agreed.

The crowd around the mill was prodigious; there were easily as many people there as had attended the picnic that afternoon. Their attention on the mill was absolute; they stood facing the walls and between the stacks of lumber, as though waiting for someone to emerge from it.

"Why are they whistling?" whispered Ruth.

"I don't think they are whistling at all," said Jason, and then looked to his feet when a woman dressed scandalously in a long nightgown, turned to him and made a shushing noise. Ruth shuddered, and hurried toward the hospital.

It wasn't far—indeed, they came upon it sooner than they might have thought, because unlike most of the other buildings in Eliada, the hospital was dark. Jason pulled the hatchet from his belt.

Perhaps they both could feel it: the darkness was only an indication of what was truly going on there. They hunkered low as their eyes adjusted to the lower light.

There was movement around the hospital's perimeter. Maybe more of Sam Green's men, perhaps guarding Nowak. But they moved different. There was a flutter, like a skirt.

Jason touched Ruth's shoulder and pointed. She whispered: "*I see.*"

Jason leaned to her ear, so near her hair tickled his cheek. In a few short breaths, he relayed a plan that he thought might work. When he was done, she nodded, brushed his jaw with her fingertips, and got to her feet.

§

Absent sheets and masks, Jason gave up the notion of hiding in plain sight. Better to creep up on the quarantine through the woods surrounding it, emerge from the farthest point from the hospital, and wait until the guards had moved 'round the corner to make the final rush.

Thinking about it made it seem easy. Doing it was something else.

The underbrush was thick with high, curling ferns that came past Ruth's waist and that combined with the darkness made it difficult to move quickly; nearly impossible to move quietly. So to avoid getting spotted, they decided to go back farther into the woods.

This turned out better or at least easier: under the canopy of the trees, the underbrush thinned, and they were soon walking between pine and fir trees on a floor of needles. Jason's eyes were well-enough fixed to the dark that he could navigate, stepping around a deadfall here and spotting a little spring-bed there—and still keep an eye on the clearing where the quarantine sat.

Finally, he judged them far enough around to make the plunge back. They stood on a small rise of rock and moss, in a spot near a clear sky that made a lonely patch of ferns behind them.

"All right," he whispered. "You ready, Ruth?"

There was no answer.

"Ruth?" he said again, and turned.

Ruth stood with her back to him. He thought she was saying something, but it was hard to tell: her head shook and bent side to side, but the words weren't clear. Jason stepped beside her, and as he did so she bent to her knees, peering down from the rocks. Something was moving down there, in a nest made of crushed ferns. He couldn't tell what it was. He knelt down too, and put his hand on Ruth's shoulder. Her back was twitching, like she was sobbing. He looked at her, but she shook her head, and pointed down. Jason looked.

It was a girl. Jason thought she might be a little bit older than he and a bit older than Ruth. She had dark curly hair. Far as he could tell, she was naked. The sweat on her breasts and collarbone caught errant rays of moonlight as her chest worked up and down. Her eyes were only half-opened, looking up at the little space of star canopy, and she had a sleepy smile like she was dreaming up a fine night for herself, there in the ferns.

Except it wasn't just her in the ferns this night. Looking down her stomach, Jason saw something else curled there. First it reminded him of a raccoon, or some other small animal—but it hunched below her navel, and in between her legs was where it rested—and it seemed to be moving, with the same rhythm that Ruth's shoulder moved when she sobbed.

Jason let go of her and half-slid down the rock. He raised up his axe.

"I've seen this thing before," he said to Ruth.

Oh yes, Jason had seen it before. Last time, it had been crawling up his own stomach, making a run for his privates. Tonight, it had latched onto this girl's parts—and it was eating or tearing at them or fooling them.

Whatever it was doing, Jason wasn't about to let it finish. He made his way up close, reached over and grabbed at the thing's pulsing back. He grasped smooth flesh that felt like pig, and he tried to yank. But the thing wouldn't budge—it had itself hitched in there somehow.

Jason had to restrain himself from taking the hatchet to it; he knew if he did he'd hurt this poor girl. No, he had to get hold. He turned back to Ruth, to ask her to give him a hand.

He couldn't see her.

"Ruth?" he said. He stood up and peered over the rock face. In the distance he could see the squared shapes of the quarantine and the hospital. He thought he might be able to hear the sound of someone scrabbling through underbrush, but it was hard to tell over the whistling.

Jason felt his heart hammering. Ruth had run off. She'd panicked, fled. He looked back down. The girl was writhing, her hands on the rolling back of the thing as it snuffled deeper between her legs. Her back arched and her knees bent.

Jason swore, and turned back to the thing. He buried the hatchet in the ground beside him, got down on his knees, and with both hands grasped the creature. The girl screamed as he pulled, tugging back with all her might, and Jason nearly lost his grip before he reached around and threw his weight backwards.

And all at once, the thing came away. The girl screamed again and scrabbled away—and Jason held the creature to his chest and rolled in the opposite direction. It was like wrestling a hairless raccoon, with claws and teeth tearing at his shirt.

He pushed it away, and found himself face to face with the beast. This time, there was no chance of mistaking the thing for a tiny Ruth Harper. The alternative was nothing short of demonic—the thing's black eyes glittered in the light and its sharp teeth snapped as he held it back.

It slashed out, running a claw down his cheek—and as he held it, something else pricked at his ribs. He pushed the thing away so hard that he convulsed in so doing, and the creature rolled away. As it rolled, he saw briefly something that looked like a dagger, only knobbed and twisted, point into the air. That, he was sure, was the thing that tried to pierce his belly. It may have been the thing that it had used to hang onto the girl.

He reached behind him, found the handle of the hatchet and pulled it from the ground. As he did this, the thing that had previously seemed the size of a raccoon began to unfold itself. It stood on thin legs, a small hunched body and dangling clawed arms, the height of a child. It seemed to convulse then—like it was coughing. Jason's eyes stung, and he felt like he wanted to sneeze.

He didn't. Instead, he swung the axe.

It was a wide swing, and it nearly sent him to the forest floor, but the blade hit the thing where its shoulder might have been. It felt as though Jason had cut into a sapling.

Jason twisted the handle and pulled it free, and for a moment he stood straight, wobbling like a drunk, and the thing stood still too. They stared at each other, as though waiting to see which one would fall first. Jason was sure the creature would go down, but it surprised him. It twitched, and bent, and with impossible speed dove into the shade underneath the ferns.

Jason sneezed. His heart was hammering in his chest as he looked over to the girl, who now sat holding her knees to her chest. She was rocking back and forth.

He turned to her, to see if she was all right, but she hunched her shoulders closer in. He touched her shoulder, started to say something like, "You should get away from here 'fore that thing comes back," but he couldn't get out a word before she looked up at him, opened her mouth wide, and screamed.

The scream was like a slap across the face—the kind of slap that sometimes a fellow needs, to put him back on course.

He had helped this girl on a whim. But Ruth, who he'd met in the middle of the night and accompanied on this dangerous adventure across Eliada—who he'd kissed . . . she was gone.

"Ruth," said Jason.

He hefted the axe and headed up over the little ridge.

"Ruth!"

He didn't even take the time to see if there were any guards before he started across the open. Ruth was there—he could see her clearly, by the light of her newly lit lantern, at the edge of the building itself. And the door closed on her and that light before he was half the way across.

What was she thinking? She'd taken off, lighting up her lantern like she was walking back to her pa's house and not that Devil-Infested quarantine. She stepped in through a door, leaving Jason outside to deal with that thing in the forest, help that poor girl. What a no-good—that was his first thought.

He didn't keep it long in his head, though. Because about the time he was thinking back to his own dizzy time in the quarantine—when it had taken a cut to his hand so deep it still hadn't healed to bring him back to himself—he thought how quick and easy it was to give yourself up to old Mister Juke, giving not a thought for anything other.

If that is what had happened to her—if she was following some wicked siren call from within—

—like mayhap he was himself. Jason took a sharp breath, and reminded himself of where he was: out in the open, in a yard where men wearing sheets were keeping guard. That thing he'd fought had coughed something in his face, and sure he'd fought it, but now wasn't he walking into another kind of trap?

He figured he should maybe go back to cover, and thinking that chanced a glance over his shoulder.

The thought was enough to save him—he saw the first of the things mid-leap, before it had a chance to hit him.

This one was almost as big as he was, though skinnier by far. Its scarecrow body blacked out the sky as it jumped over him, scythe-claws spread. Jason ducked and slashed up with his hatchet. He felt the blade graze something and the thing landed a few feet beyond him—one hand clutched at Jason's middle as it steadied itself.

Jason rushed at it and slashed out again, but this time the creature ducked to the side and it was all Jason could do to keep his feet beneath him. He didn't get a third swing, because at that moment, something bit into his ankle. He looked down—a smaller creature, no bigger than a newborn, had latched onto his foot and was gnawing at his Achilles tendon. He didn't let it get far, first kicking out then stomping down on his ankle. The thing squealed and dislodged, rolling back. Jason thought he could see things like porcupine quills roil across its back.

The big one had meantime recovered its wits, and slashed out at Jason's back. Jason was expecting it, however, and whirled around with the axe at arm's length. He caught it in the chest more by chance than anything else, then yanked the hatchet free and swung it again. This time it bit into the thing's head—and as Jason pulled the blade out again, he drew the head close to his.

"God-damn you," he swore as he looked it in the eye and saw the thing that it had become. His mama's eyes rolled in sockets that looked like hers, and a black tongue emerged from between lips like hers. He swore again and pushed it to the ground, then kicked it hard with his bad foot even though that hurt like hell to do it.

"God-damn you!"

He turned back to the woods and raised the hatchet.

That was how they did it, these Jukes: they put the face of the thing you loved or wanted most at the top of your mind, and using some kind of magic put it on their own flesh. Or maybe just made you imagine it. Jason felt his eyes heat up with tears. And even if you know it can't work—if you know it can't be true—it doesn't make it any less hurtful, to put an axe-blade in your dead mama's skull.

Another of the things leaped out of the darkness at him, and Jason swung at it—too wide, and the thing latched onto his arm. The pain was bad enough that Jason's hand opened without his meaning and the hatchet fell to the ground.

"Damn!" he shouted, and tried to yank the tiny Juke off his arm. It glared up at him with Aunt Germaine's tiny, magnified eyes and held tighter. But if that was meant to make him pull his punch, it was the wrong trick. Jason punched it straight on the back, and it came undone like a leg trap.

But by then two other things had hit him in the legs, and there was nothing for it. Jason went over. The ground came up fast and he coughed away his wind, and then he felt another thing on his chest, while something else forced his fist open on his good arm and another thing, no bigger than a barn cat, jumped onto his groin and started scrabbling there, like it was trying to hook a claw into his belt.

And then there arrived one other—a big one, like the creature he thought he'd finished.

It had the girl's face—a face covered in dirt, with pine needles in her hair—and that face leaned over him, to look in his own face. The creature had made those eyes wide and angry, and its lips curl back with a kind of mad hunger—and as a hand lowered over his mouth, and two fingers pinched his nose to cut off his air, and she said, "You the boy who drove the Baron from my bed." It dawned on Jason then that this was no Juke at all.

This was the girl—and she was finishing the Juke's work. He tried to pull away, but his strength was sapped. She leaned close to him, so they were eye to eye, and said: "I ain't never going to forgive you that, so quit your begging."

I was helping you, he thought, as the rest of his wind ran out.

22

The Prodigal

A long sleeve of cloud had scooted across the Kootenai River Valley in the early hours of the day, so that when the sun approached the horizon, it made but scant impression. Andrew Waggoner was fine with that. He'd been marching through the night as best he could, but it was slow and dangerous going in the pitch black. He needed light, but not the sort of light he'd seen the morning before. That light was a lie; it would not take him where he needed to go.

The dull, sickly light that came through the pine trees now . . . that was fine. He could see the deadfalls before he came on them, he could tell when the slope turned too steep and he had to go around. He could see if there was anything pacing him, or know it was just his fevered imagination at work in the midnight forest. Just to be sure, he kept a mouthful of Norma's herb mixture—proof against the ache in his healing bones and, he was reasonably sure, the trickery of the Juke.

He hoped it were so. There were no voices that whispered in his ear as he made his way through the dark woods. They were easy to dismiss. But as the light grew—sickly as it was—Andrew wasn't going to assume the same about Heaven. That . . .

§

That was a lure; a sharp, shining lure the same as the real Paris had been, when he boarded the steamer in New York. His father had taken the train with him to Manhattan, and waited with him and his trunks in the gathering crowd at the East River docks for nearly three hours in drizzling rain as the steamer prepared to let its passengers aboard. Elmore Waggoner had never been so proud, and he didn't mind saying so.

"It's always a fight for men like us," he'd said, exhaling a lungful of apple-scented smoke from his pipe, "and we've fought it hard. Now, Andrew . . . for a little while, it's not going to be such a fight for you."

"I don't know about that," Andrew replied. He was not twenty years old then, and his French was mostly from books, and he couldn't imagine a harder job than learning the ways of the scalpel from Frenchmen. But his father explained it, how much easier it would be there than here: starting with just three words.

"*Liberté*," he said, looking Andrew in the eye. "*Égalité. Fraternité.*"

The French, Elmore Waggoner firmly believed, stood by those words. And in taking that stand, in casting down their aristocracy in their revolutions, they'd made a society where men might enjoy opportunities not much different from one another, regardless of the station of their birth, the colour of their skin. A place where a smart Negro had as good a chance of becoming a physician as any other man.

"It may not be a perfect society they made," said Elmore, "but it's nearer than anywhere this side of the ocean."

Andrew chuckled to himself as he picked his way down a rock-fall, and held his splinted arm ahead of him to keep the branches of a stand of young tamaracks from his eyes. Not long after he said that, Elmore Waggoner had given Andrew a hug, and helped him haul the trunks he carried up the gangplank, and into the crowded steerage berth, that was the best accommodation an American Negro could expect on his way to the welcoming harbours of the enlightened Third Republic—and in that airless, low-ceilinged barrack, he'd seen nothing but opportunity—*égalité*, like the French would say.

Andrew stepped out onto a shelf of rock. It was getting light enough now that he could see his goal, not far now, over the tops of the low, neat orchards. Eliada spread before him, its rooftops spreading like a span of dark stones, smoke rising like river-reeds from their chimneys. At the river's edge, Harper's steamboat was pulling away.

Andrew bit down on the sour herbs and made himself swallow. He shut his eyes a moment, and squeezed the hand of his injured arm into a fist until tears rimmed his lids. Then he set out again.

He was nearly there—and much as he wanted to, Andrew couldn't let himself rest. He had to deliver his warning; and meet Sam Green, and settle some other things that had occurred to him, as he walked in the near dark.

§

The fence marked the western boundary of Harper's orchard.

It wasn't high, but it was high enough. Andrew had set his bag on the other side of it and was halfway over himself, when he heard the hoof-beats, muffled as they were by the soft dirt of the orchard. He winced, pulled his other leg over the fence, and waited, as the man in the slicker with a rifle under his arm rode between the trees, bowing his head now and again, but never taking his eye off Andrew. As he got closer, Andrew thought he recognized the fellow by face, but not name. As he got closer, he shifted his hand to the trigger guard. The horse stopped, and the man sat high in the saddle, and he raised the rifle and aimed along its barrel at Andrew. Then he glanced down at Andrew's feet, and the rifle went down.

"Dr. Waggoner?"

Andrew looked at the doctor's bag at his feet.

"I am."

"What're you doin' here?" The fellow threw his leg over and climbed down from the saddle. "There's Klan on the move in town. You should be long gone, sir. Ain't safe."

"No," said Andrew. "It's not safe."

And in spite of himself, he started to laugh.

"You all right, Doc?"

"I'm fine," said Andrew, then added: "Not entirely, obviously. But—you're right—it's not safe."

"Where can I take you, Doc? To the hospital, by the looks of you."

"No," he said. "Not the hospital. I need to see Sam Green," he said. "Then Mr. Harper."

"I can do that. Here, let me help you up on the horse." He bent down and lifted Waggoner's doctor's bag. "I'll carry this, and lead."

§

Sam Green looked tired as he came down the path to the cider press—and Andrew thought he must have made the same impression on the Pinkerton here in the dawn.

Green waved his rifle over his head, and told his man: "Go on now. Leave me and the doctor be."

When he was gone, Sam Green came over and set on one of the chairs. He took off his bowler hat and set it on the table, and laid the rifle across his lap.

"Thank you," said Andrew finally.

"Thank me?"

"It does sound odd, doesn't it?"

Sam shrugged. "Figured you'd be long gone. This place is no good for a Negro—particularly not you now. Why'd you come back?"

"I think you might have an idea about that, Sam."

"Might I?"

"I'll save you the bother," said Andrew. "There's worse trouble than men playing at the Klan in these parts. I spent some time up the hill, and I'll tell you: Loo's dead."

Sam kept quiet, but a shift in his shoulders, a slump really, told Andrew what he needed to know.

"I tried to save her," he said, "but she needed more help than I could give her. She had one of those monsters in her—one of Mister Juke's children. And it tore her to pieces, on account of what you helped Dr. Bergstrom do out there a year back. I don't think I have to go through every tiny detail of that, now do I, Sam?"

Sam looked away, and now Andrew nodded.

He'd put this together through the long night march he'd made down the mountainside—parsing the odd coincidences together. The family had stumbled upon him, as if by pure happenstance, as he rested on a rock that he'd stumbled upon, after marching straight in the direction that Jason Thistledown had sent him. And Jason had sent him that way, thanks to Sam Green—who sent him the warning at just the right moment. He put all that together with a guess, but he thought a pretty good guess: that perhaps one of those fellows with guns that had accompanied Dr. Bergstrom on his mission of sterilization, might have fit the description of Sam Green. Who, if he were accompanying Bergstrom on his hellish mission, might have concluded that the Tavishes and the others deserved kindlier medical attention than Bergstrom would ever give them.

"I put you to use, Dr. Waggoner," said Sam.

"You did. But I wouldn't have made it through the night, if you hadn't sent the boy to drag me out of there. So don't waste breath apologizing. Just don't waste breath lying, either."

"I won't, then," said Sam. "Answer me, though, what are you doing back?"

"The Tavish clan—they're dead."

Sam sat quiet at that. Finally, the Pinkerton ran his hand across his broad forehead, smoothed down a tuft of hair, and looked up. Andrew felt a heavy drop of rain on his forehead as he said: "Better get to shelter. Can you walk, or should I fetch a horse?"

Andrew pushed himself up. "I look worse than I am," he said. Sam picked up his bowler, took Andrew's arm, and they headed up the slope.

"Bergstrom stopped sterilizin' a few months before you came," said Sam finally. "And not because he finished the job, neither. There're mayhap a dozen families living on the slopes of these hills up and down the Kootenai—kin of settlers whose wagons fell too far off the trail. Got to no more than half before he gave up on it."

"You always in his company?"

"Often enough." They crested the hill, and looked on the house. It squatted huge on the land, blocking out the river and the sawmill both. Andrew could still see the roof of the hospital, though, over the tree-tops. "The Tavishes were good folk. It's true—I sent word you were on the road, and that you could perhaps help. What killed them?"

Andrew shook his head. "Didn't see who did it. But it happened—it happened after we killed the Juke. I was away. So I didn't see it."

"Away, were you?" Sam Green stepped a little faster as they headed down the slope. Andrew watched his back as they headed to the main entrance of the house. All was, then, as Andrew had begun to suspect; Sam Green had spent more time, considerably more time, with the hill people around Eliada than Dr. Bergstrom had. He had seen a great deal of this. And he knew enough about Mister Juke, and the way the creature reproduced, not to look too surprised when Andrew had told him what he'd found in Loo Tavish's belly.

One of his men met them at the front door, which he was guarding like a castle gate. He stepped aside, and Sam opened the door himself. They stepped into the entry hall of Harper's house silently, and then he shut the door.

"What killed them, Dr. Waggoner?" he said.

"It wasn't an animal," said Andrew. "It was men, but not men with guns. The Tavishes were butchered. That's why I'm back here—I think the attackers might be on their way."

Sam might have been about to say something else, but he stopped himself at the sound of two pairs of footfalls overhead. They both waited as the footsteps started down the stairs, and at no great length Garrison Harper appeared unaccompanied on the landing. Even at this early hour, Harper was dressed in a dark wool jacket and trousers; his hair combed impeccably.

"My God!" exclaimed Harper, hurrying down the remaining steps. "Dr. Waggoner! You have returned to us! Pray you've returned unharmed!"

"I am a little worse in some ways," said Andrew. "Better, thank you, in others." He pushed himself to his feet. Harper strode close and took his good hand in a typically resolute handshake.

"Yes, yes, I suppose that you are," said Harper. "First, however, we must get you cleaned and fed." He pulled back and looked Andrew up and down. "Food and water first, I think. Yes, sir? I apologize, but given your state I think the kitchen—"

"—will be fine, sir," said Andrew. "I would appreciate some fresh water."

Harper made a harrumphing sound and turned on his heel. "Harris!" he called, and the butler emerged. "Let's repair to the kitchen. You can arrange for Dr. Waggoner to have an acceptable breakfast, I presume?"

Harper's man led the three of them through an archway beneath the stairs barely acknowledging Andrew's presence, hurrying through the dining room and nearly letting the door to the kitchen hit Andrew's arm as they made their way into the vast, stove-hot space. Harper settled on one of several wooden stools next to a wooden table. Andrew took another.

"We'll take our breakfast here," said Harper.

"As you wish, sir." The fellow gave Andrew a disapproving look and hurried off.

"I have to apologize again, Dr. Waggoner. Eliada, despite my best efforts, seems to resist your kind at every turn."

"Eliada's not unique that way." Andrew shrugged and Harper nodded, and in the silence Andrew wondered how was he going to broach this discussion?

Do you remember that strange patient we discussed? The one with the remarkable neck? I believe, sir, that he is of an entirely different species . . . A monster, Mr. Harper, it is very true! His young burrow their way into the wombs of expectant mothers— they issue forth—and they seize the very souls of men! Andrew Waggoner thought he would never be clean enough, or well-enough dressed, to broach the subject to a fellow like Garrison Harper with anything approaching credibility.

As it developed, he did not have to. Harper smiled sadly at Andrew.

"Eliada is not unique now," he said. "But with the help of that patient we discussed before you left—the fellow they tried to hang before harming you—I hope that one day it will be."

"The patient—Mister Juke," said Andrew.

Harper nodded. "Mister Juke," he said. "Ah, Dr. Waggoner, how over this past week I wished I had been more forthcoming with you, that evening we met. You asked me about him then, didn't you? And I evaded."

"I've seen more of them," said Andrew.

"Have you?"

"I've developed a theory about their nature."

They were interrupted as one of Harper's kitchen servants, a stout young blonde-haired girl brought over a chrome platter of china and silverware, and another who might have been her older brother, bearing a steaming pot of coffee which he poured into two delicate china cups. Andrew took his with sugar and thick cream; Mr. Harper drank his black.

"They are," said Andrew, after swallowing a long pull of the hot sweet mixture, "fundamentally parasitic."

Harper raised an eyebrow. "Parasitic. Like a tapeworm, you mean? The tapeworm lives inside us. Yet this patient—he exists outside the body."

"No, it does not," said Andrew. "It's born from eggs that are laid in the wombs of women. Once hatched, the young compete for food inside the womb—either from the nourishment travelling along the umbilical cord to the foetus, or, if there is no foetus there, from the mother herself." Andrew felt a palpable release as he spoke—drawing together as he was the culmination of a day and a night's thought and correlation, as he crawled down the mountain slope toward Eliada. "As they do so, they develop an affinity for the mother's blood and that of her family. And using that affinity, the ones who survive and emerge are able to . . . manipulate the family."

"Using the affinity," said Harper. "I see. How does this manipulation manifest?"

"Like a narcotic. It causes hallucinations—visions that are indistinguishable from what spiritualists might call the *transcendent* experience. Those visions cause men and women to believe that the creature is something other. A spirit. A god."

Harper looked away.

"You don't believe me," said Andrew.

"Oh, quite the contrary. You've said nothing that I haven't heard in as many words already. Our friend Dr. Bergstrom has followed your line of reasoning quite as far along as you have—and beyond."

Andrew set his coffee cup down. "Beyond," he said. "So you know what threat the Juke poses to this community?"

Harper smiled. "The threat," he said. "There is no threat to this community, young man, that its constituents do not manifest upon themselves. The Juke is nothing more than an opportunity for this community. For this one, and all others."

"An opportunity? Sir," he said, "the Juke is a . . . it's a rapist. And a *leech*."

The kitchen went quiet at that—just the low burbling of a boiling pot of water carried forward. The half-dozen others in the room—including Sam Green, who, Andrew noted, had made his way closer so as to better hear the talk—were all staring at him.

"All right!" said Harper over his shoulder. "Back to your duties, please!"

The staff turned away, although Sam Green just leaned against a wall. Harper shook his head.

"It may be that the creature in the quarantine could inspire religion. But although I've allowed churches here—and in spite of its name—Eliada is not a town raised to God."

"If not God," said Andrew, "then—"

"Man," Harper finished for him. "The perfectibility of Man. That was our goal when we built this place. Do you know what was here before we came?"

"I do not."

"Savagery," said Harper. "There was nothing here—naught but hill folk barely possessed of language, never mind wit, surrounded by the Kootenai Indians—who although savage themselves at least had the wherewithal to make good use of this land's bounty, in fish and land and stone."

"And you have carved a fine place from it," said Andrew.

"It is not I," said Harper. "It is the fine men, and their wives and their sons, who have done the work. Many of them we selected for the task based on their strength and intellect—but it is not just strong men who make a community. They must be motivated—to a common purpose."

"Yes," said Andrew. He recalled discussion along those lines when he first arrived. "What has this to do with Mister Juke?"

Harper drained his cup and set it in its saucer. "Why everything," he said. "This—discovery, of Dr. Bergstrom's . . . it is . . ."

"An answer to your prayers?" interjected Sam Green. Harper scowled at him, then turned his attention back to Waggoner.

"You must share your observations about these creatures with Dr. Bergstrom," he said. "He has not spoken to me about the creature's reproductive habits—but we have spoken extensively, about the positive influence the creature has had on the hospital staff and those who work with him."

"The *positive* influence?"

"I suppose one might mistake it for religious feeling. But really, it is much more efficacious than simple superstition."

"How do you mean?" asked Andrew.

"What does this creature do, but infuse a sense of community, of belonging, in those it infects? Assuredly, combining this—well, shall we call it patriotism?—let us do so—this patriotism with firm, wise and benevolent leadership—a strong sense of societal ethics—and what have we? Nothing less, Doctor, than Heaven on earth. True Utopia."

Andrew finished his coffee, which had grown cool in the bottom of his cup. Heaven on earth. He thought about the vision that the Juke had given him—of his own Heaven on earth, in a way, that crazed and idealized vision of a Parisian cityscape. With a mad Dauphin at its centre, demanding supplication and sacrifice, offering forgiveness for sins that in the glimmer of hindsight seemed entirely manufactured. What, he wondered, had Mr. Harper seen when he met the Juke? Some well-run factory—some town of dutiful workers who sang their employer's praises rather than plotted strikes and sabotage? Strong, smart and loyal all at once?

"You are building a religion," said Andrew.

For an instant, this seemed to take Harper by surprise. But only an instant. "It is not a religion. It is simply a community—a place, where the creature might rest comfortably and according to its needs. Because as we both know—" he leaned forward "—the creature does have needs."

"Yes," said Andrew, "it does. As I believe we discussed. It rapes young women, destroys them from the interior or starves their babies—then in adulthood demands and receives utter loyalty."

Harper pretended not to have heard. "It needs to be fed, of course," he said. "But are we not well-suited to do so, a community of several hundred strong men, and the machinery of industry to create surplus in all regards? You must agree that it is one thing for these subsistent folk to offer up livestock and grain and whatever else the creature desires, when they can barely scratch together enough to feed themselves. Yet something entirely different, for us to do so."

"Here in Utopia," said Andrew, shifting on his stool. Harper was playing with fire.

"Indeed," said Harper. "Now see here, Doctor. I understand that you've been through a horrifying ordeal, at the hands of those who would see this experiment fail. But I brought you on because I thought you'd make a contribution. You are no naysayer. You've had your share of them, I'll wager, pulling yourself up into the medical profession as you have. But you're saying nay now, aren't you? You think this is a lot of bunk."

Andrew started to rise. "Sir, if you had seen what I've—"

Harper put up his hand. "Enough. There is no harm in that. In fact, a day from now, the riverboat *Eliada* will be casting off for Bonner's Ferry. I am already sending back two others who unwittingly stand in the way of this enterprise. Would you like to join them?"

"Two—"

"Jason Thistledown," said Sam Green, "and that aunt of his."

Harper turned to look directly up at the Pinkerton. "Yes," he said. "Mrs. Frost's nephew. Mr. Green, why don't you make yourself useful around here, and go rouse them?"

Sam nodded slowly and gave Andrew a wink. "Take care of yourself while I'm gone, Doctor," he said and turned to leave.

When he was gone, Harper noted that their cups were empty. "Would you care for more coffee?" he asked.

Andrew shook his head. "If it's all right," he said, "I'd like some tea. I've got the fixings for it in my bag, if you'd care to join me."

Andrew pulled the cloth from his bag, and pulled free a handful of the mixture he'd rescued from the Tavish clan.

He found a clay teapot that was empty on a sideboard, and he wasted no time filling it with the mixture, and hot water from the stove.

The tea was steeped and ready to drink just as the servants brought their breakfasts—fried eggs with bread and a generous helping of bacon. Andrew downed his quickly, as he'd learned from Norma, and advised Mr. Harper to do the same.

Harper sniffed at it, and made a face. "Perhaps later," he said.

"As your physician," said Waggoner, "I'd advise it sooner than later. You see, there is something else—something, I believe, that is on its way here."

Harper sighed, and brought the cup to his lips. Andrew was considering how he'd explain the next part—the massacre he'd escaped; the sure sense he had, that the dying baby Juke had called that massacre down—when Sam Green, ashen-faced, hurried back into the kitchen.

Harper set the tea down and glared at the man.

Sam spoke very quietly as he relayed what he'd learned. Jason Thistledown, he said, was missing from his room.

Also absent, said Sam, was Mr. Harper's daughter Ruth and her friend Louise Butler.

"And it appears," said Sam, his moustache tucked close over tense lips, "that Mrs. Frost is also abroad this morning."

"Abroad?" demanded Harper, half-standing. "Where?"

"No one will admit to knowing," said Sam Green. "I'm sorry sir, but that's the full of it."

23

The Incident with the Shotgun

The old man sitting back in the chair across the room did not affect to notice Jason. The wooden chair legs creaked as he pushed back on two of them, leaning the back of the chair against the wall beside the window. He smoked as he sat there, his eyes focused on the glowing bowl of the pipe. The stem of it disappeared behind a thick moustache, over a whitening beard that drooped down onto his shirt. Hanging from a peg on the wall was a long white sheet that reached the floor.

Jason lay very still on the cot. The only move he'd made, he figured, was his eyes opening up and there was nothing to be done about that. He kept them narrow, so maybe this fellow wouldn't see, and think him still unconscious.

Jason had in fact been awake off and on for some time. He first came to slung over the shoulder of a sheet-backed man, as his own shoulder banged against a door jamb that he thought might have been part of the rear door of the hospital. He'd gasped and passed out again, and then thought his eyes might have opened in a brighter room, looking up at a couple of ghosts in sheets talking about something. He might have seen Dr. Bergstrom at one point, or he might not have. Because here in this little hospital room, with a window just starting to lighten with the pre-dawn sky and the light just so and the quiet man who had no obvious gun on him, Jason thought that he was finally coming properly back to his own mind. Those things outside—the first one and maybe the others—they'd done something to him, whether with the whistling or the stuff the first one had coughed at him.

Whatever had happened to him, he'd had a chance to shake it off. Now he just had to figure out how to take this fellow. That sheet on the wall made it clear that he was no friend.

The man took the pipe out of his mouth and examined it.

"You're a smart boy," he said, still not looking up, and Jason's heart fell. There was no fooling this fellow.

Not with any simple ruse, anyhow.

"Don't know how smart I am," said Jason, swinging his feet around and sitting up. "I'm here, ain't I?"

The fellow looked up. His eyes were deep-set under thick, silvered brows. He took a puff on that pipe of his as he looked Jason up and down. "Smart mouth on you too," he said in a flat voice. The two front chair legs made a sound like a coffin lid closing when they hit the floor and he leaned forward.

"That's all right, young Mr. Thistledown," he said. "You can be just as smart as you like. Ain't nobody going to hurt you."

"Late for that." Jason looked down at his trouser leg, which was torn and stained in blood and dirt, and at his arm, which was also cut from the attack out-of-doors.

The man shrugged and said, "You had worse, I expect."

Jason looked at the fellow. He had a long face, with cheekbones sticking out far as those brows, like ledges on a cliff. Jason got to his feet and the fellow stood up as well. He was a tall man, six foot or more Jason guessed. He moved in an easy way that Jason knew should make him afraid.

"I don't know you," he said. "You sure seem to know me."

The skin on those cheekbones wrinkled and the moustache rose up in a smile. "James Bury," he said.

"James Bury." Jason took a step to him, and Bury held his ground. It was ludicrous, the two of them facing off in this little room. Jason knew it and he could tell that Bury knew it too. But Jason wasn't going to let this man stare him down. . . .

Bury lifted his pipe and sucked on it, and his smile vanished in smoke. "You won't leave here right now," he said, pipe-stem clenched in his teeth. "Looks like you're fixing to, but you won't."

That was as much warning as James Bury gave, before he drove his fist into Jason's gut.

Jason bent over, felt the air whooping out of him and then he was back on the cot, and on his side, curled around his stomach, and Bury was standing over him, fanning the fingers of the fist of his left hand open while in his right he held the pipe. His eyes were bright now, watching to see if Jason might cry or beg or whimper, or perhaps shit in his trousers or lose his lunch.

When Jason did none of those things, Bury bent over and sat back down in his chair. He leaned it back again, so the rear legs creaked and he resumed smoking. But he kept his eye on Jason, as the pain faded and Jason was able to get his legs straightened out again.

"Best stay abed, young man," he said.

"You—" Jason didn't like the whimper he heard in his voice, so he pushed it down. "You're the one tried to murder Dr. Waggoner."

The chair creaked like a question, and Bury followed it with one: "You say that . . . why, now? 'Cause I hit you, and you're all fired up about it?"

Jason nodded to the sheet on the peg. Bury looked up at it, made a face like he was impressed with Jason's keen mind, and nodded back at him.

"But you're no Klansman," said Jason.

"Oh, ain't I?" He squinted at Jason. "If I ain't a Klansman, then what am I?"

"I don't know what you call yourself. But I saw you . . . or maybe someone like you . . . in the quarantine that night."

"That night." He snorted. "Must've missed each other, boy."

They sat in silence for a moment. Had he and this James Bury fellow met up in the quarantine? The voice might've been the same—he might've been as tall. Or he mightn't have been, of course.

But something in Bury's stare said he wasn't far from the mark. So Jason kept up.

"You were beggin' forgiveness. Not for trying to kill a Negro doctor, I'm guessing."

Bury looked at him hard, and Jason thought: *I'm not the only one bluffing.* He went on. "Because you tried to again, didn't you? You were one of the ones who tried to kill Dr. Waggoner."

Bury's face hung still in the morning light. "In a minute," he said, "I am going to ask you a question, and I want you to answer it truthful."

"I ain't tellin' you who—"

"Not that." James Bury set the chair straight and stood up and came over and sat down beside Jason, who could not help but flinch. Bury pretended as not to notice. "Before I ask you a question, I'll tell you some things. That'll help you give a better answer than this shit you're speaking now."

Jason didn't say anything—just kept himself steady.

"I came to these parts before there was an Eliada. Why I came's not your business in the particulars. There was some trouble up in Canada, put it that way. This was a good place to be; a quiet place. I learned my way around the hills, and the folk who lived here. And when Eliada came, with its hospital and its sawmill and its moneyed fucking fools . . . I learned to make myself useful. Know what's most useful in Eliada?"

"Not woodcutting," said Jason, and Bury laughed humourlessly.

"It's tracking the folk that live here," he said. "And I mean tracking. They live like animals, these folk, and they ain't the kind of animals come running when you whistle."

"You kill them too?"

"Be easier if we did," said Bury, then corrected himself: "If the doctor did. No. He's a scientist. Doesn't kill folks if he can help it. So I and a couple other fellows'd climb up the mountain with him, and show 'em where the folks lived, and watch his back whilst he finished his business."

Jason listened, and he watched too, and he saw that as the old man went on, it seemed more the old man was just that—a bent-over coot, telling stories over pipe smoke. Less a danger. Jason wondered if maybe he could take James Bury yet. And then did his best to hide that wondering.

"A year back, we climbed one of the mountains. There's a clan living at the top of it. Folk call them Feeger. They don't come down much, ever. And there were stories about them. The doctor—he got excited. There's a book he's got—*The Jukes,* it's called. He started wondering if this family weren't another of those . . ."

He went quiet at that, tucked his chin into his chest, and looked away. Jason might have been able to jump him then, but instead, he asked: "So is that Mister Juke out there . . . one of their children?"

Bury looked at him now. His eyes were wide and wet (almost, Jason thought, pleading).

"It was a child," said Bury. "A beautiful child, full of light. I found it—me, James Bury . . . not the doctor—and I tell you, son. I could see the sky in its eyes. It went on forever." And then, he made a fist, and Jason was sure he was going to strike . . . but he closed his eyes instead, and shook the fist in the air, and coughed.

"I got lost that night," said Bury. "I been lost for most of the year. You said

I tried to hang your nigger doctor, and you're right. Because every so often—once every couple weeks, maybe—I could come up for air. And I figured, as things went on and got worse—that Mister Juke that Bergstrom was keeping, it wasn't a beautiful child at all. So when it got out that night—when it went ranging . . . when that girl got sick with its seed . . ."

"Why'd you try to hang Waggoner?"

"Because, boy, no one in this town will hang Mister Juke. Hanging a nigger . . . I don't care how many sermons Garrison Harper gives out about compassion and community and good fucking manners. . . ."

"You got them riled enough to forget their manners," said Jason. "Long enough to string up Mister Juke at the same time."

"Almost long enough."

Jason made his move before he even thought about it—rolling back and kicking with both legs. He connected, but not as well as he needed to. One heel hit Bury in the jaw, just inches higher than his throat; the other, hard in the shoulder. It knocked Bury to his side; but he was able to roll, and twist—and like that, he had two hands at the base of Jason's throat.

"Yeah," said Bury, his fingers digging in under Jason's collar bone, "we're comin' to my question now." He pulled him close, and looked him in the eye as he hissed: *"How do you get him out of your head?"*

Jason cried out something that wasn't a word and Bury held him tighter, if that were possible. "Don't try to slip out of this one, boy. You see what I am capable of. Now you came here with something special. You got a gunfighter's blood in you, and you are pretty clever but this thing—this thing talks like *God* in your head and you have seen it, and you have turned away from it. And stayed away. Somehow.

"Now, *how*?"

Jason felt hot flecks of spit on his face. Bury's eyes, no longer hidden beneath his craggy brows, were wide and blood-rimmed. He looked old all right—older than God-damned Zeus. His hands were closing around his neck. This old man was going to strangle him. Jason twisted, tried to get free but Bury held tight.

"Damn it, boy!" Bury lifted his hands higher, and clamped them tight around Jason's throat. And at once, Jason felt his wind cut off.

"I do not have much God-damned time, boy," he growled. "I'll snap that neck if you don't—"

"You will do no such thing," came a voice from behind him.

Jason looked over his shoulder at the open door. Aunt Germaine stood there. She was holding the revolver she'd carried onto his homestead at Cracked Wheel. It was levelled at both of them.

"Now unhand my nephew," she said. "And raise your hands, Mr. Bury. I will not hesitate."

"You wouldn't—"

Germaine drew the hammer back.

"Mad cunt," he said. But he let go of Jason.

"Now," she said, "James Bury: you are relieved."

The old man, Bury, took the white cloak from the peg, and slung it over his back. He and Jason met eyes once more before he hurried out the door. This time, there was no challenge, no fight to it. The mad look was gone—he was looking at a place far away. He blinked, and hurried off like a man with an appointment; an appointment he had no choice but to keep.

Jason wondered if that were not truly the case. Bury wanted to know one thing from Jason: how to stop Mister Juke from talking to him. Jason would have told him if he knew; he thought the shock of being cut turned it off. Maybe if he'd let Aunt Germaine shoot him in the belly, that would be enough of a jolt to quiet the voice telling him what to do.

Aunt Germaine shut the door as Bury's footfalls turned hollow on the stairs and began to diminish. The revolver fell to her side, although she did not let go of it.

"Aunty, you ought put the pistol down," said Jason. "Your hand is shaking, and I fear . . ."

Germaine smiled wanly in the thin light and nodded. But she did not let go of the firearm.

"Did he hurt you, Nephew?"

"No, but he was fixing to. These cuts—" he motioned to his leg "—I got them outside."

"Did you?" said Germaine. She was wearing her travelling skirts—long, deep blue swaths of wool that held stains of grass and muck gathered from countless miles of Montana track and they had a smell to them, of must and mildew that would not launder free. Unpacking here, she'd vowed to burn them, but had obviously not gotten 'round to it. With her empty hand she picked at them now, as though pulling off invisible burrs. She seemed to catch herself, smoothed the cloth and looked up at Jason.

"Who was that?"

Germaine shook her head. "A common thug," she said.

"In a Klansman's sheet," said Jason. "And you knew his name. He work for the Eugenics Records Office too?"

Her eyeglasses caught a flash of sky-slate in reflection and lost it again as she tilted her head.

"What do you take me for?"

"What do you mean?"

"You were outside with the Harper girl," she said. "In spite of everything that transpired at that picnic—in spite of all the things that Mr. Harper said— you were outside. Skulking about in the night. Weren't you now? And you met with some *things*. Didn't you, now?"

Germaine was waving the revolver around as she spoke, so strenuously Jason was sure it would go off sooner or later. His expression must have communicated that, because she stopped, looked at the gun in her hand as though she had only just realized it was there, nodded to herself and set it on the windowsill.

Then she turned back to Jason.

"Do you take me for a fool, Jason Thistledown?"

Jason stared at his Aunt Germaine Frost. He thought about the way her chin twisted as her thin and pale lips pursed, and he thought about his mama. He thought about how Aunt Germaine knew to call that fellow Mr. Bury—and how she worked so close with Nils Bergstrom. He thought about some of the very smart points that Ruth and Louise had raised, after listening respectfully to his tale of the tragedy and woe in Cracked Wheel.

And then, because he didn't want to be a fool himself he thought some more before he decided what to say.

"No more a fool," he said, "than Mama did, when your pa shot his own foot outside Boston back when she was a girl and I guess you were too." And then he made himself smile a little.

She softened at that—smiled back, like she was remembering how it'd been, Jason's grandpa cleaning his shotgun on the road outside Boston, only it'd gone off, and filled his boot full of shot that penetrated through some leather and gave him a funny limp until he was older.

"You remember that?" he asked. Aunt Germaine nodded and came over and sat down on the bed beside him. She squeezed his knee and Jason let her.

"Oh, Nephew, I am sorry for that. I know that you're not being disrespectful."

"I'm not," he said. He stood up and walked over to the windowsill. "Just like Mama was nothing but respectful when Grandpa hurt himself like that."

"I remember it well," said Aunt Germaine.

He lifted the gun, turned to Aunt Germaine, and as surprise widened her eyes, he said: "No, you don't."

"What—?" she began, but Jason could see by her expression that she understood.

"Far as I know, my ma's pa never shot himself in the foot. You were really her sister, I think you'd know that."

Germaine Frost was without words. Her mouth worked in little *oh's*, like a river trout on the rocks.

"You lied to me," said Jason. "From our house to Cracked Wheel to here. You ain't my aunt, but you went to a lot of trouble to make me think it were so."

"Jason," she finally managed, in a high, frightened voice, "I only wished to help you."

Jason held the gun steady. A moment ago, he'd been ready to shoot her—put a bullet in this woman, who he ought to have figured sooner for an imposter. Hell, she didn't look like his Mama or him or anybody in his family. She'd shown up in the middle of the winter just right after a terrible plague—like some sneaky old vulture, a hawk, swooping in and carrying him off to this place. And there was the thing she'd let Dr. Bergstrom do . . . And then there were those letters they'd left with Louise. . . .

"The Cave Germ," he said.

And with those words, all the fear melted from Aunt Germaine—Mrs. Frost. In its place rose an expression that Jason could only describe as glee.

"Yes," she said, nodding. "It is up, isn't it? You've divined my purpose, my hero."

If Germaine Frost were afraid of getting shot this morning, she showed no sign of it.

"Stop calling me your hero," said Jason.

"All right," said Germaine. "Though it's true."

"Truer than me being your nephew maybe." Jason braced his arm against the weight of the gun. "Why don't you tell me how you came to tell me you were my aunt. How you know my mama to pretend at bein' her sister."

"Oh, from the Cracked Wheel Town Hall," said Germaine. "I knew her, and your father, and many others."

"What you mean by that?"

She leaned forward. "Records, Jason. I had ample time to peruse them all—in the long days that the Cave Germ took to finish its work."

She smiled at that—or maybe at Jason trying to work it out. Whichever it was, Jason didn't care for it, having this lying old woman, who'd abducted him (that was the only word for it) smirking at his ignorance.

"The Cave Germ from the Belgian part of Africa. That Mr. . . . *Dew Lake* sent you all those letters about?"

"*Dulac*," corrected Germaine. "From the Belgian Congo. You're a clever boy, Jason. But you are not quite clever enough to translate my private letters—not unaided, hmm? Why don't you give me that gun. You're shaking, Nephew—"

"Don't call me that!" The gun had been lowering, and Jason held it up and drew the hammer back. That got Germaine's attention. She held up her hands in clear surrender.

"All right." Her voice had a bit of a shake to it. "May I call you Jason?"

"You may," said Jason. "You can tell me about those letters now. That Dulac fellow—you fixin' to marry him?"

Germaine's hands lowered slightly. "Marry?" In spite of her predicament, she chortled. "Oh, no. Maurice is not the marrying sort. No, Neph—*Jason*, my correspondence with M'sieur Dulac is strictly professional. He is an operative at a plantation in Africa—not too far up the Congo River. We have never met face to face."

"How do you know him then?"

"Correspondence," said Germaine. She shrugged. "We had, I suppose, become intimate sufficient to trick the eye of one with schoolgirl French. But we are professional colleagues, Jason."

"You mentioned that."

"I prefer to make myself clear," said Germaine. "M'sieur Dulac would not relish any confusion on the matter either. He has already risked so much, so much. . . ."

"How'd he do that?" Jason had spent long enough with Germaine to know that she told her stories in her own time—and he could tell by the way she perched, her thick shoulders arched like a child's by fireside, that she was building towards an important one now—but he was getting impatient.

"M'sieur Dulac had been working on this sugar plantation for some time. He was on the one hand managing the vast crew of jungle niggers that his company employed—but he also made a study of them. For these were not like the niggers you find in America—weak and foolish and prone to crime—but proud savages. Still you could not trust them, for crime and deceit is congenital to that race. But Dulac conspired—conferred with the physician there to make good records of their health. And as he told me, there was one nigger— particularly tall, with teeth strong and thick and endowment prodigious even for his species—he who walked alone. No wife, nor mother, nor sibling, did he have—and he rarely spoke to others. This nigger came from a village some miles back in the jungle—a village that, the stories told, had been ravaged by a fever that came from the earth—" she chuckled "—from a dank cave inhabited by Devils! Only this nigger—only he—had walked away from it. The superstitious darkies—they all thought it was Devils at work, but Dulac—he, like myself, was a man of science. Devils do not bring up sores, or stop hearts with congestion or drive fevers high. No. It was a germ at work."

"A germ." Jason shifted the gun's weight from one hand to the other. "That's the Cave Germ," he said.

Germaine nodded, her smile broadening. "It took not nearly so much doing as you might think to take that lucky, strong nigger back through the jungle roads to the ruin of his village. Oh, Maurice described it in such detail, I recall it though the letter's not before me. Burnt circles lay where grass-made huts had been prior, only discernible from the fire pits by the presence of so many bones. . . . The nigger didn't weep, though Maurice could tell it weighed upon him mightily. But they knew the nigger had nothing to fear; not there—not even, although they had to whip him to it, on moving aside the branches and stones at the entrance to the cave from whence the sickness came—nor when they forced him into it, one final time. For he was immune! He, of the scores of people in that village, was immune to the terrible, killing illness."

"M'sieur Dulac," said Jason, his voice quavering, "sent that nigger into the cave to collect some Cave Germ," he said. "In clay pots. Ain't that right?"

Germaine nodded. "He was a good nigger, as much as the species is capable. He plucked it from bat guano in that cavern. He was even so kind as to seal the pots with wax, and douse them with alcohol. Maurice," she added, "was kind enough to let the nigger finish the bottle of brandy, before he shot him and collected the jars."

Jason felt like he was going to upchuck. He leaned against the windowsill. "And he sent you a jar."

"Or two," said Germaine. She stood up from the bed, her hands wringing in front of her, her smile wider now.

"And you—you opened one of them in Cracked Wheel," said Jason. "You—" *killed my mama*, he was going to say, but of course she had done more than that. She had murdered an entire community—every man, woman and child with the misfortune to set foot in Cracked Wheel that winter's day, and then every man, woman and child who'd met them before the disease showed symptoms. Killed his mama she might have—though Jason felt the pain as acute now as he did that night she died—he knew that his mama's death paled against this woman's larger crime.

Germaine Frost had killed a town.

"Yes," said Germaine. "I opened one in Cracked Wheel—and by its grace, Jason Thistledown—" she stood so that the gun's barrel nearly touched her shoulder "—I found *you*."

Jason squeezed the trigger. But Germaine had already pushed it to the side and before Jason could squeeze off a second shot she had the gun from his sweat-slicked hand, and driven her fist into his groin so hard he slammed against the window hard enough to crack glass. Jason didn't fall out, though—just slid down to the floor, the pain in his gut and middle renewed and amplified. When he opened his eyes, Germaine was standing over him, the gun trained on him.

"I can't see any reason for me to apologize," she said coldly, "but I shall in any event. *Nephew*."

"You killed—" Jason choked and pressed himself higher "—you killed all those folks."

"Culled," said Germaine. "That's what I did—what the germ did. By my own hand, I only killed one person—a sickly old man, who tried to gain entrance to the town office. And I may not have killed him. Do you recall that window pane? The one that you remarked upon, with the bullet-sized hole in it?" She smiled, and let out an incongruously girlish giggle. "Oh, it was all I could do to keep from laughing aloud, when you pointed that out. Laughing aloud. Do you remember?"

"I remember."

"The fellow may not, of course, have died from my bullet," she said. "He disappeared from the window, and when I checked later on, there was no body.

Oh stop looking at me like that." Germaine motioned with the gun. "Get up," she said. "Get into bed. You're hurt."

Jason did. He hobbled over to the bed, as Germaine motioned with the gun. "Now, take off your shirt." When Jason hesitated, she added: "I need to examine you! Please, Jason—I am a nurse!"

Jason did nothing to comply. He had thought about what she said. "You were culling them, you said. . . . You were culling them to find the folks that might survive this sickness, figuring there would be just one or two. That right?"

Germaine's eyes widened, filling the glasses, and her lips parted. "You are bright, as is to be expected."

"As I think of it, I do recollect that bullet hole, said Jason. "I also recall you telling about Charles Davenport and what an impression he made on you. You said something about him wantin' to get rid of the bottom ten percent of people. What's he think of you tryin' to get rid of the bottom ninety-five? 'Cause that's what you were doing, wasn't it?"

"Dr. Davenport is the bright face on our movement. There has never been a need for him to know the whole of what we are doing. And in any case—we do not aim to get rid of, as you say, the bottom ninety-five percent of humanity. If I'd wanted to do that, I would have unscrewed the jar in the middle of New York City."

"Then—"

"For us it was simply a matter of finding that top five percent. Finding—" Germaine smiled, looking Jason right in the eye "—the hero. And look . . . here he is."

"Here," said Jason, "in Eliada."

He felt dizzy at the revelation: how Germaine Frost had with evil foresight come to Cracked Wheel, unleashed a plague and taken the one boy left standing as her own. Taken him . . . here. To Eliada, this place where the creature they called a Juke lived. "Tell me something," said Jason. "About Dr. Bergstrom—is he one of your eugenicists? Like M'sieur Dulac?"

Germaine nodded and said, "For that I *will* apologize. Dr. Bergstrom had been engaged in promising research here, I'll warrant that. When he contacted me last, it seemed as though he had found something beyond a hero. Something like a god: a creature that seemed resilient to dismemberment and illness—a hermaphrodite, inter-fertile with humanity. I was supposed . . ." She looked down. "I was supposed to find a girl."

Jason looked up, aghast. "So you could breed her with the Juke?"

"When it was you, you who survived, I should have taken you straight back to New York." She sighed. "Dr. Bergstrom has fallen into madness. Sheer madness."

She lowered the pistol and leaned back against the wall, eyes still downcast. Jason briefly thought he might be able to overpower her; launch himself across the room, knock the gun from her hand as she had knocked it from his. Either shoot her or, more likely—for Jason was not so good at shooting folks as that—just get out.

But the moment passed. Her eyes looked up at him, over the tops of the glasses. They were small, curiously pig-like without the magnifying effect of her spectacles.

"It doesn't matter," she said. "We'll find a strong sow for you, my prize hero. Before the day is out, we will have you bred."

"What're you talking about?"

"Ruth Harper," she said. "I am not so old, *Nephew*—" she said the word like an epitaph "—not so old, that I can't smell the rutting urge."

Jason barely listened.

Ruth! He hadn't forgotten about her, but in the cascade of revelation, her predicament had fallen far from the top of his mind. And her predicament might have been dire indeed—for hadn't he lost track of her, going into the quarantine, where Mister Juke—

"Where is she?" he demanded. "You know where she is—"

"Oh, don't worry," she said. "Ruth is tucked away safe. We found her after we located Louise Butler, by the light of her lamp, reading my letters while the two of you played at footpad. The two of them are very . . . safe."

"Safe?"

"Well—relatively so. They are safe as pickles in jars. We'll see how safe soon, hmm?"

Jason lowered his feet to the floor. He was thinking not of the letters now, but of that jar that was hidden at the bottom of Germaine's bag—the earthenware jar sealed in wax, that now Jason was certain contained another piece of bat guano from Africa . . . another piece of the cave germ, that killed nearly all it touched.

"Think of it, my Nephew," said Germaine. "By day's end, we'll know for certain. Either Ruth, or Louise. One of the two will be a fit sow for a hero such as yourself." She giggled. "Bergstrom can play with his monsters if he so wishes—but we . . ."

Jason thought for a bit, then stood up. Germaine glared at him, and waved the handgun. "Nephew!" she scolded. "Sit down! Take off your shirt! And your trousers!"

Jason shook his head. He took a step toward Germaine. He fought to keep his voice steady. "I ain't playing your game no more, Mrs. Frost," he said.

Germaine held the gun high, so the barrel pointed between Jason's eyes. Jason took another step forward.

"You ain't going to shoot me," he said. "You killed too many folk to find me."

"I warn you—"

Jason shook his head, said: "You won't," and reached out slowly to take hold of the gun's barrel.

Germaine's thick finger caressed the trigger, and watching her, for a moment he thought that this strange woman—this monstrous *witch*—might do it. But Jason kept moving, and the hammer did not fall, even though Jason took his time pulling the gun from her hand.

When he had it, her arm fell limp to her side. It was as though all the fight went out of her.

Jason opened the chamber of the revolver and shook the bullets, of which there were four, out into his hand. He looked at Germaine, who was now sobbing quietly.

"Oh, Nephew," she said, her voice weak and tremulous. She shuffled toward him, and he shuffled back. "It's true—I could never harm you, my darling—"

He didn't let her finish the word *hero*, before bringing the butt of the gun up against the side of her head.

Its impact sent her stumbling against the wall. He hit her twice more, to make sure of it. She finally fell to the floor, and to his shame, he kicked her, hard in the middle. She was not moving—but she was not dead either. Jason watched her as he reloaded the pistol. When he was done, he raised it up and pointed at her. He stood that way for maybe a dozen heartbeats, then finally sighed; let it drop to his waist and let himself out of the room. Maybe he should become a killer; but he wasn't one yet, and that was all there was to it.

And he had a more immediate worry.

Ruth was in here somewhere—Louise too—locked up, in a place where the Cave Germ would work only on them, and no one else. A place where the air would not move—where the smell of things could choke you because of that.

Pickles in a jar.

Jason had a good idea where such a place would be.

24

The Test of Faith

The song rose over the Kootenai where it wended close to the hospital. A small dock extended into the river; on the bank above it, a wooden canoe turned over. The men in their sheets stepped gingerly around it as they moved to the bank of the river. There were several dozen of them. Some had known each other, once. They all listened as the song rose up.

Lothar Feeger watched them from the water. He had swum ahead of his brethren; he alone, promising to scout out things and give a signal if there was likely to be trouble the Feegers ought know about. When Feegers had met strangers in the past—well, there had been good meetings and there had been bad ones.

And on balance, more had gone badly. The Feegers had once had rifles and pistols, but they were only a few and that was long ago; and now, it seemed that the rest of the wide world rattled with iron.

The Oracle had proclaimed that they ought just go ahead, march into the place where the Son had been entrenched, and preach the word to the people there; bring them in line with what the Old Man wished, and set them to work.

"Folk who worship need be learned," said the Oracle. "Else they praise ignorant, and their God might go astray with 'em."

And her sisters had nodded, and Missy said: "Can't suffer one go astray," and Lily went on: "That's heresy, ain't it?" and the Oracle nodded, and bowed her head, and held up the swaddled Infant before her.

No one debated much—one didn't argue in the presence of the Oracle and her sisters. But Lothar worried; although the scent of her had long washed off, Lothar still could never be far again from her, from the memory of the time with her, when her soft, lake-wrinkled fingers had took hold of him, and drawn him inside. The Old Man spoke through her now, but she was still just a girl—a Feeger—and Lothar would not let her walk into peril blindly.

So it was that when she ordered them to climb the hill, and take the heretics' homestead for the thing they had done, Lothar had been in the forefront of the raiding party, scouting the town to make sure that no one guarded with rifle, and quietly killing that one who had. He would have wished it had been he who had found the Infant, martyred in a glass jar. But Lothar hung back and made certain that not one of the folk of the 'stead lived, to return one day and take revenge on the Oracle and her brood.

And so it was, that when she ordered them forward to spread the gospel, Lothar nodded—then later, when they crouched in the cold dark by river's edge, he stole up to a cousin, and told him that he would scout ahead an hour before the rest came, and if there was danger of gunmen, he would whistle a signal so they might all approach more carefully. The cousin grinned at him, and hit him on the back, and told him to go on ahead.

Lothar moved his fingers to his lips now as he watched the men in white mill about the dock. There were a number of them, maybe half as many as all of the Feegers. But they did not carry guns, or even blades and axes like the cousins.

He squinted around the tree-covered bank, and seeing nothing else, lowered his fingers.

They were strangers—but at least they posed no threat.

And so Lothar waited quietly, for his family to catch up.

§

The song grew over the water as the sheeted men watched and listened. They'd all of them come this morning, even the ones who weren't watching over their Lord, Mister Juke—even Nowak, who had been resting in a lower ward in the hospital, his shoulder tightly bandaged from the surgery a day before. The call had been building through the early morning, carrying on the scented breeze. A girl's voice, high and lilting, singing words that though unclear, beckoned— the same way that Mister Juke had beckoned, but with a greater insistence somehow—a sound as insistent as it was insensible.

It grew as the rafts appeared around the river-bend. There were three of them, crowded with folk—tall and beautiful, bearing blades that gleamed in the morning light. The men in sheets raised up their arms in welcome as the rafts drifted closer, and spread out in front of them.

In the middle raft, a girl stepped forward. She wore sheets of her own, her long dark hair tumbling down them. In her arms, she held an Infant. The men gasped at her beauty, and fell to their knees as she opened her mouth and sang to them.

She sang and sang, until she was hoarse—as the music washed over them, some of the men thought: *She is singing the same song again and again. It is growing more shrill—it is as though we haven't heard it properly.*

But the thoughts were passing, and not a one spoke of them. The music was too great a thing, and its majesty confounded them; whether they felt joy or rage, it mattered not. They knelt in dumb rapture, uncomprehending, before the greatness of God.

§

Beside her sister the Oracle, Missy grumbled: "They're heretics. Kill 'em."

The Oracle drew a breath. They *were* heretical, these strange men in sheets—but they were worshipful too; they had been touched by the Son, and they'd felt the touch, and they listened. But the song . . . they only bathed in it, like water. When the Oracle sang for Feeger, how better it was. Feeger knew the song—they knew who they were—and in the end—they would obey their Oracle.

These folk—they were obstinate. They were . . .

Lily found the words that the Oracle could not. "They were let be too long," she said. "They hear your song—some other Oracle's words."

"And it'll send 'em mad," said Missy—and the Oracle nodded, and hefted her bundle nearer her breast—and she sang again, this time, not to the Heathen in sheets. But to Lothar—and his brothers.

The axes and blades came down in a flurry. They caught the men at the shoulder, the neck; an arm was sheared off, and one of the heretics shrieked, and fell into another blade. The white sheets stained red, and the screaming stopped, as the Feegers stepped away from the steaming circle of the dead.

And that, the Oracle feared, was how things would need go from here. They'd had a false Oracle—they wouldn't hear her; they thought her foolish, because that other one had poisoned their minds.

"Lothar," she said, and Lothar came to her. She smiled. He never missed instruction; never asked questions; never disrespected her.

"Find me that false prophet," she said, "and cut him up the middle."

25

The Gospel According to Nils

"Bergstrom is coming," said Sam Green to the Harpers. "Ben says he's carrying a lamp."

They were all of them in the kitchen by now—Mr. and Mrs. Harper and of course Andrew Waggoner, as well as some of Sam's men.

"A lamp?" said Andrew. "It's broad daylight outside."

Ben, a young man with a short-cropped beard and the beginnings of baldness, looked sheepish as Sam explained: "I'm guessing a lamp."

"A bright light, Mr. Green," said Jake. "Can't say it was a lamp."

Mr. Harper sighed. "I don't care if he's got the God-damned sun in a sack. What's he doing here at this hour?" Then he straightened, as a thought occurred to him: "D'you suppose he's an idea where Ruth has got to?"

"Did anyone send word to him?" asked Mrs. Harper.

Garrison Harper looked to Sam, who shook his head: "Not us, sir."

Ben looked over his shoulder. "Doctor's here," he said needlessly, before stepping out the servant's entrance.

Andrew took another gulp of his tea and sat up straighter on his stool. It was absurd, given everything that Bergstrom had done to him—but he didn't want to appear dishevelled in front of his peer.

"We are in the kitchen!" shouted Garrison, then turned to Andrew. "I'm sure Dr. Bergstrom will be delighted to know that you're well, in any case."

"If he's sobered up," said Mrs. Harper, under her breath.

"Hush," said Garrison again, as the door from the front of the house swung open. It was an instruction that none of them disobeyed.

Andrew gaped.

The doctor had undergone a complete metamorphosis since last they'd met. This morning, he had managed the difficult trick of looking at once cadaverous and bloated. His lips were flushed red as a whore's painted mouth, and his eyes were shadowed with deep rings. He wore a long coat, into the pockets of which he'd jammed his hands.

"Good morning, Mr. Harper," said Bergstrom. "I trust you are well this morning?"

Harper didn't say anything for a moment; he simply stared, as they all did. "Sir, you look ghastly," he finally said. "How can you even be about?"

"A man can find reserves, sir. Vast reserves, when the times call for it."

He stepped nimbly around a low butcher's block, and drew nearer the table; and as he did, Andrew's nostrils flared around a familiar, and awful stink.

"Mr. Harper, Mrs. Harper, I come with joyful news," he said. "Just from in the docks, I can report that the final juncture's reached."

"I beg your pardon, Doctor," said Harper.

"The men—the men have met the host—as I have instructed."

"Host? What are you babbling about?"

"The—yes. I'm here to tell you, Garrison—something is coming. And it will change—it will change, if I may say—*everything*."

A quiet fell on the kitchen then: it was as though Bergstrom had mesmerized the room of them. Andrew sniffed the air, and blinked, and shifted.

And for the first time since his arrival, Bergstrom seemed to see Andrew. His mouth twitched into something that might presage a smile. "Why look. Good morning, Andrew."

"Nils."

"You are well."

"Better than I'd have been if I'd stayed."

Bergstrom seemed taken aback at that. But it was only for an instant. He smiled, and reached into his coat, and scratched at his stomach as he turned to Harper, and said, as though Andrew was still missing in the hills and not there beside him: "Garrison—forget all this a moment. We are at the dawn of a marvellous day. The Gods are tumescent. They are joining!"

"Are you drunk now, Dr. Bergstrom?" Harper asked coolly.

Bergstrom shook his head. "Only the opposite."

Andrew, meanwhile, was watching that coat. It was not just moving—

it seemed to be roiling, as though something lived under there, clinging to Bergstrom's middle and irritated by the commotion. Andrew caught Green's eye, indicated the coat. Sam Green nodded.

"I apologize for my state yesterday," said Bergstrom. He thrust his fists deeper into his coat pocket, like he was holding himself in. "I was not myself—I understood things only part-the-way. So I had something to drink after . . . after worship, when I should have been still in contemplation. It is the weakness of flesh, Gar', when faced with the fact of divinity."

"Ah," said Andrew, as matters came together. The smell—it was near enough the stink that Loo had given off, in the last stages of her illness, of her infection with the Jukes.

Bergstrom looked at him and blinked. His gut rolled and churned.

"You're very ill, Nils," said Andrew. "You know that, don't you? I've seen something like the thing that's infected you—in the hills. You've seen her too—remember? Loo Tavish?"

Bergstrom nodded slowly; that seemed to be reaching him.

"You have been to see the imbecile. Is she doing well?"

"She's dead," said Andrew.

Bergstrom adopted a thoughtful expression. "She was past her time when we met," he said. "God has taken her."

"No. Just dead."

Bergstrom smirked. "You really have no capacity for it, do you, Dr. Waggoner? You are just a low nigger, after all."

"Dr. Bergstrom," said Mrs. Harper in a sharp tone. "There are other matters at hand. Perhaps you could assist us in determining the whereabouts of my daughter."

Bergstrom withdrew one hand from his pocket, and fanned his fingers out on the tabletop. The nails on three of his fingers had been torn, and the quick under them glistened darkly. "Your *daughter*. Ruth. She is with God." Mrs. Harper gasped and clutched at her husband's shoulders. Bergstrom's coat flapped open.

"Oh, not like that. No. Sorry." He smirked. "She still breathes, still breathes. All is well. And that is why I came here." He withdrew his other hand, and leaned on it too. "To prepare us all—for as I said . . ."

Andrew stared at Bergstrom's exposed mid-section. Nestled inside the coat were the things that Andrew had seen once before. On the hillside, crawling out of Loo Tavish. These were smaller than that creature, barely the size of a child's hand—but they were unmistakable, crawling like thin, long-limbed rats across Bergstrom's scarred, infected gut.

"The Father rejoins the Son today!" said Bergstrom.

Mrs. Harper shrieked—and Andrew counted five small creatures before they dropped like ripe fruit and scurried across the floor, before the whistling took up. Bergstrom straightened and cast off his coat, and tore away at his shirt. His flesh was bruised and swollen in places. It seemed to move with inhuman musculature. It only confirmed what Andrew had been thinking—it was the answer to the question he had asked Norma Tavish on the mountainside: *Do these things ever lay their eggs in men?*

Andrew was now sure that they did. The writhing flesh on Bergstrom was testimony to that. These things had laid eggs beneath that skin. But there was no umbilical—no uterine wall from which to feed. So they had immediately begun to feed off—what?

Andrew shuddered. Bergstrom had been a fat man in the fall. And that—his fat—is what they'd fed on. He had been their regimen . . .

. . . those tiny cherubs . . .

Andrew took a breath. It was hard to hold his eye on one of them as they drifted up onto the table, laughing in high voices that might have been whistles. He felt what seemed like a great, hot wind upon him, and when he looked up, it seemed as though the ceiling, the very roof of this house had been torn away—and above, the sky opened into a great vortex. If he looked at it long, Andrew was sure he would overbalance and fall up. But he looked up again, and the ceiling was as it was, bare pine boards, with great hooks for pots and other implements sticking out of the wide beams that criss-crossed it. The cherub that seemed to have been prancing on the table turned small, and squat—a greyish-pink thing, with no fur but a thin baby-fuzz, and long curved claws that clicked on the table. Andrew lifted his plate and swatted it. The creature howled and scurried off.

Then Andrew coughed, and bent, and looked around again.

Nils Bergstrom stood before him, arms spread and belly reshaping itself while Mister Juke's demonic offspring scurried and danced around him. He glared across the table at Andrew, with what he must have imagined was divine wrath in his eye.

Andrew could understand that. Of everyone whom Bergstrom had caught meeting in this kitchen, only Andrew Waggoner had dared not bow down before his delusion. The rest—even Sam Green—had all bent low to the ground, trembling. They thought—believed—*knew* that what they were seeing was God manifest in man. Only Norma's drug, and the things he had seen already, let Andrew see Bergstrom for what he was.

"You're sick," said Andrew. "You're going to die from this."

"I am reconciled," said Bergstrom, his arms extended to either side and trembling, "to my God. Unlike yourself, Dr. Nigger. You cannot even look upon Him."

"I don't see God here," said Andrew. "I see a trick—I see . . ." he motioned to one of the juveniles, perched like a Notre Dame gargoyle on a pine shelf behind where Mrs. Harper bent and wept. "I don't see God."

"Then you are blind." He smiled. "Outcast."

"Nils, you're in grave danger right now, said Andrew. "Those things in you—they'll kill you. Just like they did Maryanne Leonard. Only I think it'll be worse for you. You're going to need surgery—"

"Shut your mouth."

Bergstrom held his hands out and shut his eyes, as though he were listening to some unheard voice. Then he opened them again and looked straight at Andrew. "Why are you alive, Dr. Waggoner?"

"I'm alive," said Andrew carefully, "because I'm clever enough to know when I've overstayed my welcome. Nils, pull yourself out from this insanity. Drink some damn tea—" he offered his cup "—and sit down, and think about what you've done to yourself. Then we'll go and cut those things out of you—as many as we can."

His hand was shaking awfully as he extended the cup. Bergstrom, encumbered but still nimble, reached across and with a flick of his wrist, knocked it from his hand. The cup shattered on the floor.

"Keep your poison!" he snapped. "You cannot cut me out—that was among the first things that Nils learned when he began to study my effects."

"Ah," said Andrew. "So you—so *Dr. Bergstrom*, has been making a proper study of this."

"Bergstrom has always sought truth in nature. That is why I came to him."

Andrew chose his next words carefully. Bergstrom had tried to kill him—he'd thought, from pure wickedness. But he was vulnerable now, trapped in a delusion, speaking of himself in a disassociative way . . . as though it were someone else speaking through him.

But delusion or no, Bergstrom certainly came here with a message. Andrew thought he might have a better time drawing that message, and more, from the thing that Bergstrom believed possessed him.

"All right," said Andrew. "Why don't you tell me, how it is you came to Dr. Bergstrom. Why don't you deliver me your *gospel*."

Around them, the whistling grew. In a distant wing of the house, something that sounded like a gunshot rang out. But he didn't let himself become distracted by any of it.

"Sit," said Bergstrom. "I command you."

Andrew pulled up a stool amid the grovelling others, and got ready to listen.

§

"My father," said Nils Bergstrom, "is the mountains. He is the trees and the sky and the forest. All this." He spread his arms above him to indicate the whole kitchen, and by implication, Andrew thought, pretty well everything else. "So has He been for as long as men have walked this land, He has been their protector."

The Harpers had managed to climb as far as their knees, draw their hands together in prayer, and they looked up at Nils Bergstrom. Andrew didn't have to guess; it was clear they were looking not at but through Bergstrom, at nothing but pure eternity. Sam Green was still bent over; his shoulders shaking, forehead pressed against the flagstone floor. The Jukes had withdrawn to shadow; they only revealed their presence by their soft whistling, the clicking of their talons on the tops of hanging pots and the beams of the ceiling. Andrew fought to keep his eyes off them all—all but Nils Bergstrom.

"Praise your Father," said Andrew.

"And so men do. Those who praise. The Feegers."

"Feegers," said Andrew. "What do they have to do with—"

Bergstrom didn't let him finish. "Yet lo, do they wither. Sickness and weakness and their own animal natures—lo, do they wither. Such a withering came upon the Father's men, and their women and young also, not a winter's past. They grew hot and cold and their chests filled with water and many died. The Father wept for them. And he cried out—and his angels, for there were many, cried with him. And in the depths of his despair—came a wandering man—this one." Bergstrom jammed a thumb into his chest, while Jukes chittered from the rafters. "Come did he, with balms and knives and blankets, up the mountain-slope, and see to those folk as best he might.

"The Father's folk were fools—they tried drive him away, and nearly they did, swinging sticks and axes and knives of their own. They chased him 'round the great lake atop the mountain, nearer the Father. And there—the Father picked up his scent, he did. And he knew, though the people were fool enough then—he knew that the wandering man had a place for him. So—so he sent me."

Andrew could no longer keep silent. "You," he said.

"Mister Juke."

"I thought you didn't care for that name."

"Nils does not, but I—" he stood straighter, glared down at Andrew "—I take the name my worshippers give me."

"Your worshippers. You don't mean the folk in the hospital."

"Those who would have destroyed me came to love me," he said.

Norma and her clan knew about that; knew how to defend against it. Nils Bergstrom would have had no opportunity to share that wisdom. So when he went to the place where the Juke came from, and stole it away . . . he would have been defenceless.

And now he was gone, his mind twisted into what he believed was a personification of the Juke.

"I came," said Bergstrom, "to this place but a babe—swaddled in a crib, carried by this one. He wanted to know me, but was not yet faithful. And so he kept me away in a place cold and bright—and he did feed me and question me and watch me as I grew. I was his secret."

"I had thought you came here on your own," said Andrew.

"That is a false gospel."

"And why would you allow a false gospel to be spread?"

"The folk had to meet their God quiet."

Andrew considered that phrase: *meet their God quiet.*

The thing was a secret, because it had secret work that early on the folk of Eliada would not agree to: it would have to sneak out in the night, meet up with girls, and plant its seed.

For what was it that Norma had said before she'd been killed? The thing did not preach to someone until it had a taste of their kin; until it maybe had such a taste as only could come from the inside of them.

"And so you walked the land here in secret," said Andrew.

"And so I did."

"And Maryanne Leonard?"

Bergstrom smiled. "I came to her in the night—while Bergstrom watched from a perch—I came upon her in secret, as she walked through the night, and she met my eye, and knew my love."

The one part of things that was true, then—Mister Juke was a wandering rapist.

And Bergstrom—he had aided.

Andrew imagined how it might have been: whether Bergstrom had taken the young, small Mister Juke from the quarantine one night, led him over to the Leonard house; or perhaps just followed the creature through the snow, checking his pocket watch to mark its progress, then merely crouching down out back of the place, while the creature mesmerized and ravished the child. He wanted to strike him for that, as much as he did for the thing that he later did to Jason Thistledown; the thing he'd tried to do to Andrew. But he contained himself. Nils Bergstrom was in deep with his fancy; he had been as much a victim of this creature as a fine dog is of rabies. Bergstrom's head had bent back now, as though he were looking to Heaven and not just the rafters.

"Maryanne," he whispered, and Andrew followed his eye to the rafters.

From those rafters, Maryanne Leonard stared down, her face a ghastly, necrotic ruin. She grinned at Andrew with a mouth too wide, teeth bent and pointed. Andrew felt his breath freezing in his chest.

"She bore angels," said Bergstrom, his voice taking a hideous, doting tone as Maryanne drew down, moving like some immense and bloated spider toward Andrew. Over her head, the ceiling opened up to light—pure and celestial—bursting out between floorboards.

Andrew tried to look away. "That's not right," he said. "There is no God here. There is not—"

Andrew felt it pressing him down—to the floor, to join those others already deep in their worship. There was another pressure in his heart—an expansive feeling, as though he might grow immense within himself, and be so joyful as to only sing the praise; another thing, that feared the apparition above him like a tornado, like a sandstorm—like nature, made manifest.

He swallowed, and shut his eyes, and drew a sharp breath, and when he opened his eyes again, it was only rafters overhead. And there was Nils Bergstrom, shirtless and bruised and emaciated, like a refugee from a war. His flesh crawled with the maggoty young of Mister Juke.

"Nils," Andrew said, standing and reaching to him. "Let me get you under a knife. I don't know—but I think it's the only hope for you."

Bergstrom looked back at him, and reached out his own scabrous arm.

Maybe this is the benefit—the good thing that comes from the Jukes, thought Andrew as he reached, and the two touched. Weren't there good works done by churches around the world? Didn't religious feeling fundamentally provide for those things of value? Compassion—pity—forgiveness—community? That was Garrison Harper's theory—and maybe . . . maybe wasn't there something to it?

But Heaven wouldn't leave them alone. As he stood there, the door behind them flung open and light flooded in.

A giant stood at the door.

He was big enough the frame barely contained him. His hair was black and a beard hung down over his home-sewn buckskin coat. He stepped inside, looking around with an almost childlike fascination, as light from the doorway haloed him. He carried a sword, long and dark and curved slightly like a sabre.

Another God-damned hallucination. Andrew shut his eyes to it.

Bergstrom's fingers touched Andrew's; and he said, in a high, childlike voice of his own: "You see, Nigger? They *come*."

"No," said Andrew. "This is another lie, Nils—another—"

He didn't have the opportunity to finish the sentence. Bergstrom's finger jerked away, and there was a sound like an axe-blade splitting kindling, and when Andrew opened his eyes, he saw—there was Bergstrom, on his knees, bright arterial blood spraying from his shoulder. Andrew couldn't look away from his eyes—wide and wet, first pleading and then diminishing, as what life was left in him drew back and away into whatever the Juke had tricked him to thinking came after.

Andrew stumbled back, in time to avoid the tip of the giant's sword-blade as it cut the air at the height of his throat. For an instant, he met the giant's eyes, and he thought he could read the disappointment in them—

—disappointment, at having failed such an easy swing at the nigger doctor's throat.

The giant raised the sword for another try, but Andrew was on the move. He half-ran, half-fell to his left, toward the door. He screamed in pain as he did so—the move pulled his bad arm in a way that it did not want to go—but the sudden move was enough to once more bring the blade up short.

This time, the giant didn't look disappointed: Andrew could swear he heard him giggle.

It's a game, he thought. And it was an easy one. Andrew had to cross a dozen feet to get to the back door; the giant had to cross half that distance, to cut Andrew's throat open.

The giant knew it too. He stepped slowly toward Andrew, the sword held in front of him like a torch.

"Feeger," Andrew said.

And the giant said, in his high, child's voice, "Feeger."

Then it was that the room rolled with thunder and the Feeger's halo returned, in a spray of blood and bone and brain that reached as high as the rafters. He fell to the ground, and behind him was Sam Green, up on one knee now, his Russian revolver smoking.

When Andrew met his eye, he saw nothing there at all.

"Get the fuck away from here, Dr. Waggoner," said Sam. "Get far." And he raised the revolver, resting it on his forearm, and fired another shot past Andrew as a shadow briefly filled the door.

§

Andrew didn't go out the back door—not after just a glance outside. There were maybe a dozen men like the first—not as large perhaps—crowded behind the house. There were more blades, and axes, and spears standing in the muddy garden behind the estate. He shouted a report of this to Sam Green, and Green motioned him to the other door, leading into the dining room and the rest of the house.

By this time, Garrison Harper and his wife were on their feet. "I'll cover you," said Sam. "Get them safe."

Andrew didn't wait for them. He slipped through the swinging door into the Harpers' dining room. The last time he'd spent any time here, it was sipping brandy and listening to Garrison Harper boast about the fine conditions in his fine young town. Now, he pressed against the stained-oak wall, the light filtering through rain-streaked glass, flinching at every report of Sam Green's revolver. He counted three shots before the door opened again, and Mrs. Harper came through. It was quiet as Garrison Harper finally slipped through. "He's reloading," he whispered needlessly.

Andrew touched Garrison Harper's sleeve. "We have to move fast," he said. "Are you able?"

Harper nodded. "Mrs. Harper?" he asked.

She indicated she was fine, but Andrew wasn't sure he believed her or her husband. The Harpers had moved when Sam Green told them to, and here they were. But Andrew remembered how he had been, the first time the Juke had infected him. What were they seeing when they looked at him?

The gunfire resumed: three quick retorts from the kitchen, and other shots outside. Somewhere in the house, glass shattered.

At that, Garrison seemed to find himself. "Dr. Waggoner is correct," he said. "We have to move."

"Where?" said Andrew. "Do you have a store of firearms?"

Harper nodded. "The study."

"Across the hall?"

"Afraid so."

Two more gunshots came from the kitchen—a volley of gunfire outside— and a hollow, splintering sound.

"Oh God!" said Mrs. Harper. "That's the front door!"

"We don't know that," said Garrison. He beckoned Andrew and started towards the arch that led into the central hallway.

"Sir! That may not be safe!"

"Damn sight safer than here in the dining room," he said, "unarmed."

Harper took two steps forward, looked around the corner, and took a hasty step back. "Damnation," he whispered. "Mrs. Harper was right. The front door's wide open." He pushed Andrew back into the dining room. "Are you strong enough to move furniture?" He gave Andrew an appraising look. "No. Never mind. I'm fit enough. We are not going to let these God-forsaken degenerates destroy what we've made—this enterprise, this *family*," said Harper, as he lowered to his haunches and lifted the long table with one shoulder.

The table crashed onto its side, and the small amount of china and silverware set there shattered on the floor. It made a terrible moaning sound as Garrison pushed it to the door. After that, two more shots rang out from the kitchen, but that was all. Perhaps, thought Andrew, the fellows outside are simply reloading.

"What is that?" whispered Mrs. Harper. Andrew cocked his ear. "Someone's in the hall," she continued.

Andrew strained to listen, and then nodded. There was the sound of footfalls moving steadily up the hall. Andrew thought it was only one set. Mrs. Harper clutched Andrew's good arm as they drew nearer.

They slowed, and stopped outside the door.

"What're you?"

It was a high voice—a child's voice. Andrew squinted. He could see the shape of a figure in the dark hallway. It didn't come up more than a foot higher than the top of the overturned table. A young girl.

"Hello dear," said Mrs. Harper, trying to sound cheerful and friendly. "Are you lost?"

"You in there—what sort're you?" The girl stepped forward. Her hair was down to shoulders, and it was matted thick and black. She raised her face, and her lip twitched as she sniffed the air.

"We're the Harpers," said Mrs. Harper, cajoling. "Aren't you a pretty little girl. What's your name?"

"Lily," said the girl. And she boosted herself up and flung one leg over the dining room table.

"Hello Lily," Garrison Harper said.

She gave him a sniff, and then she dropped to the floor. She was wearing a filthy slip of a skirt; her feet were splayed and callused. She approached him and Mrs. Harper, and sniffed again.

Lily looked straight at Andrew Waggoner. "You," she said, "got some song to tell."

And then, she started to sing.

§

There were four tall, rain-streaked windows in the dining room and men outside, flinging rocks. The windows all smashed at once. One of the rocks struck Mrs. Harper in the side of the head; it cast her to the floor amid a lawn of broken glass. Andrew dropped to his knees to see to her, but he didn't get much chance; strong arms reached down and yanked him to his feet, bending his bad arm hard and sending long spears of pain up his spine.

Men stepped through: big men, in buckskin, armed with blades and sticks.

The fellow who had hold of Andrew lifted him like he was nothing, and hauled him over the sill of the window and Andrew couldn't see, but he could surmise. The men went straight for Garrison Harper. There was a sound that might have been a scream, and then a smashing sound, and what sounded like more gunfire—

—and then Andrew's face was in mud, and he was struggling to breathe. He was lifted into the air again, and a thick finger dug into his nostrils and his mouth, clearing an airway for him. Andrew blinked, and looked up into a long face, with patches of beard and some discolour, and wispy black hair that snaked across a broad forehead.

He saw other things too. A man face down in mud, a Remington rifle a few feet off his splayed and grasping fingertips; the sky, roiling with storm; the ground itself, seeming to move with the wet, scrabbling backs of things that whistled and cried as they fled; and at last, flames, licking the sides and crossing the roofs of the Harper mansion, while the girl sang a song whose words blended together into a long and triumphal note.

26

The Pickle Jar

Jason made his way by candlelight from the room where Germaine Frost lay bleeding, down the dark stairwell to the hospital's basement. The pickle-juice stink of formaldehyde carried along the corridor there, and grew unbearably thick by the time he reached the autopsy room. Jason didn't heed the stink, though, as he hurried into the room and saw what he suspected. There was the door to the storeroom—the one place in Eliada that Jason knew was cut off from all the others, even better than the quarantine.

The door was padlocked. And as Jason stepped to it, someone pounded weakly from the other side.

He set the candle down, and put his ear to the wood.

"Help us!" It was unmistakably Ruth's voice. "We're trapped!"

"Hold on, Ruth. It's Jason. Don't tire yourself out. I'm getting a crowbar."

Minutes later, Jason had the lock off and the door open. The room was dark, and damp, and he held the candle over his head he saw them: Ruth, crouched as if in prayer, hands held together and eyes wet—and behind her, Louise; lying on the floor, curled around herself.

Ruth stumbled to her feet and ran to him. Jason caught her in one arm, as he stepped inside and pulled the door shut.

Ruth pulled back and looked at the door. "Wh-what are you doing?" she said. "We have to get out of here—warn my father and Mr. Green and the Pinkertons! Your aunt—"

"Just a minute." Jason squinted around the room. The shelves were still filled with jars containing the grotesqueries of the Eliada surgery. It didn't take him long to find the other, tiny earthenware jar, sitting on a shelf near the door, its lid removed.

"We can't leave," said Jason, letting go of Ruth and stepping up to the jar. He peered into it—there was a tiny twist of something that looked like a root, but streaked with white. He carefully picked up the lid and screwed it back on—and then, although he knew it was pointless, Jason dribbled some candle-wax over it. He looked at Louise, who was beginning to stir from a very deep sleep, and turned back to Ruth.

"We have to stay here," he said. "It ain't safe outside."

Louise sat up and coughed. She regarded Jason, or at least the candle that he held, with narrowed eyes. "You shouldn't leave that going in here, if we're to stay, she said sleepily. "There's not much air circulation here."

Jason blew the candle out. "We're to stay here," he said. "So we'll leave the candle out." The darkness was suffocating and disorienting. Jason groped in it, until he found Ruth's arm. He drew her to him.

"You do mean to stay," said Louise quietly. "That's kind of you."

Ruth stood close to Jason. "I'm sorry," she said. "I'm so sorry. You—"

"It's all right," said Jason.

"I so pushed you to come out last night; mocked you for being afraid. But I know—there are some things that you should be afraid of."

"It's all right."

Jason led her away from the door, taking care not to knock anything over. "But as dangerous as it is out there—we can't wait here. They'll come back!"

"We have to wait here," said Jason. "No choice."

"Jason is right," said Louise weakly, in the dark. "No choice."

A shiver went through Jason. "Hey Louise," he said, "you remember what happened to you?"

Louise sniffled. "Yes. I took the material back to my room and was reading it by lamplight. Your—your aunt came in. She was accompanied by—"

"Say it," said Ruth, acidly. "She was accompanied by Mr. Harris. The very fellow who had brought us her bag in the first place. What a traitor."

"She didn't say anything," said Louise. "I tried to apologize, but she struck me. I woke up here."

"You all right?" asked Jason.

"No," said Louise, miserably. "No."

"She hit Louise on the head," said Ruth. "It's a wonder she didn't kill her."

Jason didn't think that Louise was being troubled by a sore skull right now. And he thought she knew that as well as any of them.

"Louise," he said, "how far did you get in Germaine's letters?"

"Not far," she said, a little too quickly. In the dark, Jason nodded.

She knows, he thought. *She knows that we're locked in here with the Cave Germ. She knows what it did to Cracked Wheel; she knows what it is likely to do to both her and Ruth, and she's probably figured out what it is already doing to her.*

And for whatever reason, she's not told Ruth a thing about it.

"That's too bad," he said to Louise. And to Ruth: "Let's go sit down and rest a spell. You can tell me what happened to you."

"Ah, of course," she said as they settled down against the cool stone of a wall. "You must have so many questions."

"Last I saw you, you were bustin' into the quarantine," he said. "Did you— hey!"

Jason rubbed his shoulder where she'd punched it.

"So *many* questions," she repeated.

"Sorry," said Jason, and she hit him again—not as hard this time, but still firmly.

"Stop apologizing. All right, then—let me set an example. This, Jason, is how one answers a question honestly put. I didn't *bust* into the quarantine. I fled there. The forest—it seemed to me that it was filled with beasts. That thing that had attached itself to the girl in the woods . . . there were more of them. Countless . . ."

"I know."

"I suppose that you do. My God, how did you escape them?"

I didn't, he thought.

"Well. I bolted across the green, and as I fell against the wall, I was fortunate enough to see a crack with light coming through. So I tried my luck—and fell inside."

After a moment, Jason asked her what she saw in there.

"Light," she said. "Brilliant light."

"And what else?"

"It—" she paused again. "It's hard to say, because . . . sight was not a part of it. What I saw was—well, something larger."

Jason decided to help her along: "Like a very tall man, with tiny creatures dancing around it in a circle?"

"Now you're making fun," she said. "No. No tall men. No tiny pixies.

Just—a kind of brilliance. A kind of basking warmth. I felt as though I were—not vanishing, that's not precisely the word . . . but—cut loose, perhaps." She paused. "*Are* you making fun of me?"

"No ma'am," said Jason.

"Then what do you mean, some tall fellow, with creatures dancing around it?"

"It's only—that is what I saw, when I went—when Bergstrom locked me up in that quarantine. Don't you remember? I thought I told you about them back in the orchard."

"Did you?"

"I'm pretty sure of it."

Ruth sat quietly for a moment. "Yes," she said, "you did. I remember now. Why would I have forgotten that?"

"Maybe all that brightness shook you up."

"Maybe. Things took a turn then. I felt—I felt as though in the midst of this, someone—some*thing*, perhaps—glimpsed me. That I stood naked before . . . something that was . . . *vast*. As big as a mountain. Perhaps that was your tall man?"

"That sounds a lot bigger—" Jason stopped himself. He remembered what Sam Green had told him: the Juke was growing. "No, no. It could well be."

"And then . . ."

More quiet. Ruth leaned against him, rested her head on his shoulder. Finally, Jason prompted her to continue, but it wasn't Ruth who answered.

"That's all she remembers," said Louise. Although she sounded weaker before, her tone was firm "If you are going to remain here, you should let her rest."

"All right," said Jason. He shifted so that she rested against his chest and not his shoulder. She snuggled close and wept quietly, her tears cooling on his shirt, and Jason struggled to control his own.

"Do you believe in fate, Jason?"

"We talked about this." Jason was having a hard time keeping his eyes open; the air in here being as stale as it was, and with the sickly fumes from the pickled innards all around them, he wanted to pass right out. "Back at the party."

"It was outside the cider house actually," she said. "And I believe I told you *I* believe in fate. But *you* never answered me."

Jason was quiet until Ruth said, sharply: "Jason!" and he sighed.

"There are Fates," he said, "sure. That's what the Greeks called them. Ladies who wove the strings of your life together, who knew the lay of things before and after." Other races, he recalled, had the same idea, so he mentioned that too. "The Norsemen called them Norns. I don't know if I believe in them." He yawned. "You like to hear a story about them? I can recall a couple."

"Hmm. From the Bulfinch's?" Yawns being contagious, she joined him a moment before continuing: "No, Jason, I don't think that is the story I want to hear. Not now."

"What story, then?"

"The important one," she said. "The story of Jason Thistledown and his mysterious father."

"Aw, damn you," he said. "Pardon my French."

She laughed softly. "If Louise were awake, she'd tell you *damn* is not a French word. Not damn, nor hell, nor . . ." she paused, as though drawing a breath: "*Fuck!*" And she laughed.

"Ruth Harper!" said Jason. "I'd wash your mouth with lye, I had some handy."

"Well you don't," she said. "And you owe me a story. A true story, about your father. The gunfighter."

He owed her a story, did he? The rough stone of the cellar wall scraped against Jason's shoulders as he shifted. He had moved away from Ruth, but didn't realize until she remarked upon it. For Jason felt as though he were in two places: here, in the cellar of the hospital at Eliada—and hundreds of miles away, in the single room of the cabin he and his mama had occupied most of his entire life. He'd owed her a story too, he supposed.

"You want to know about my pa the gunfighter," he said finally. "All right. My pa was no gunfighter. Not that I saw."

"He was retired," said Ruth. "You are not old enough to've seen Jack Thistledown when he fought in his prime."

"You seem to have an awful high opinion of Jack Thistledown," said Jason. "You sure you want to hear this story?"

"No, I'd rather you recite a tale from *the Iliad* instead. Or perhaps not. Continue," Ruth said imperiously.

Jason pulled his knees up to his chest. "You're not—" he felt his voice starting to tremble, and drew a breath to still it "—not quite right to say he was retired. Just I don't think he was ever what you would call a gunfighter, 'cause there's no such things. You don't fight with guns. You kill folks with them."

Ruth gasped. "So John Thistledown *is* Jack Thistledown!"

"Sometimes fellows would come to Cracked Wheel," said Jason. "I was only small, so I didn't get to see much of them. My pa would hear word that someone or another had come around looking for him. Sometimes, that fellow would go away no wiser. Sometimes a fellow would make it up to the mouth of the pass, and Pa would be there waiting for him."

"An ambush!"

"You can see fellows coming a long ways off," said Jason. "Pa picked this place careful, when he decided to settle with my ma. He made himself what he called his trapper's cabin, with a good clear view of the slope. If he were lucky enough to get word someone was coming, he'd sit there with his rifle, watchin' for them—shoot them dead before they'd even seen him. You think that's gunfighting?"

Ruth paused before answering: "He was defending his family," she said. "His kingdom."

"Where he spent most days drunk insensible, while Ma did all the work," said Jason. "And he wasn't always that good about defending his kingdom, neither."

"How is that?"

Jason pressed his chin into his knees. *It don't matter*, he said to himself. *She can't tell anyone. Not trapped here.*

But "Etherton," was all he said. Ruth prodded, then scolded him and begged him to continue, but Jason kept quiet until he had it under control enough, to tell Ruth the story of that very bad week, when Bill Etherton came to call on his pa.

"What was this fellow Etherton?" asked Ruth after the longest silence yet. "He sounds a monster."

Jason could see how Ruth might feel that way. He'd tried thinking of ways to tell the story any number of times over the years, and each time it started with figuring out how to talk about Bill Etherton in a way that did not make him sound like some wild beast. He knew how his mama had told it, not long after it had finished and Jason's face was healing up:

Bill Etherton was a wicked man from your pa's past. That's why he did that to you—hit you like that. No excuse. No blessed excuse.

That was comfort to Jason when he heard it, the cut on his little chin starting to itch rather than hurt and his shoulder still aching where it'd been twisted. But it was no good at all to Jason Thistledown thirteen years on, trying to make some sense of the memories for the likes of Ruth Harper.

"One day," said Jason, "a man came out of the bush and hit me hard. He was tall as a tree and wore a long coat of brown leather. I think I asked him something—I was playing with a couple sticks—and he looked at me and said something and hit me. That fellow was Bill Etherton. He knew my pa one way or another."

"He came out of the bush," said Ruth. "Your father—your pa would have been watching the pass, correct?"

Jason shrugged.

"And Mr. Etherton stole up behind the homestead. Which was unprotected."

"We were unprotected," agreed Jason. "I must have cried out loud, because my mama came running. I remember some of that but not all of it."

Jason remembered more than he would tell. He remembered vividly the tree branch that Etherton had used to whack Jason with across the face. He did not remember getting hit, but he remembered the tears and screaming, for he was just small when it happened.

His mother cried out, and then Etherton said *Good mornin', Ellie,* like he knew her, and Jason's ma tried to get back into the house, but Etherton was fast and got in her way, and told her there would be no getting the gun this time. *No gettin' the gun this time, Ellie, nuh-uh-uh-huh.* . . . That was one thing that Jason remembered clearly, because even though he was small and had only lived through four winters then, those words had the ring of history—ancient history between his mama and Mr. Etherton and somehow wrapped up with Jason himself.

Jason drew his knees up to his chin. It was warm here, but he shivered all the same.

"Jason."

It wasn't Ruth this time. It came from across the room, and before Jason could stop himself he said: "Ma?"

"Jason, just tell her the story. Tell *us* the story. Stop fussing."

Jason sighed. "Sorry, Miss Butler. It's hard in the tellin'—"

"Yes," said Louise sharply. "It is hard. For *all* of us, Mr. Thistledown. Forgive me if I don't—"

"Louise!" Ruth was just as sharp, and she took hold of Jason's arm tightly. "Let him tell the story in his own time."

Louise cleared her throat, and cleared it again. Soon, Jason figured, she would be coughing. He put his hand on Ruth's, and was relieved to find it cool. For now.

"All right," said Jason. "Etherton was a bad fellow. But I can't recall everything that happened."

"It was long ago."

"I know my ma got herself hit too. In the stomach. Made her sick up. I remember watching that—never saw my ma sick up before."

Ruth gasped. "He struck her? Jason . . . tell me. Was your father murdered by this Etherton? When he came back and found his family terrorized by his old enemy? When he confronted him?" She wrapped an arm over his shoulder and leaned close—like *she* ought to be comforting *him*. "Oh my dear Jason."

Jason shook his head. "No," he said. "My pa came back, but he didn't confront anybody. Ma'd cleaned herself up and put a dressing on my cut, and when pa came back, he just gave that Etherton a big hug and the two of them set down to drinking. But . . ."

"But?"

"My mama said it was Etherton that pushed her to do it. Not him—but watchin' *them*, Etherton and my pa. After what he did to both of us."

"Mr. Thistledown," said Louise in a low tone.

"She—" began Ruth, but Jason finished the sentence: "Took care of my pa."

There was a silence, and Jason felt embarrassed by it, so he started talking faster: "It was not only that day that drove her to it. My pa would run off whenever he felt like it—he would get himself drunk and do bad things to my ma—he hit me same as Etherton did, for even less reason sometimes. He had it coming; he was no good and so my mama did what she had to, on account of our safety and her dignity and . . ." He stopped again, feeling as though the words were running together. Ruth took his head and drew it down to her breast, and held him there, and he could feel hot tears coming to his eyes as the image of that night, outside the house as the November wind blew black leaves up off the ground and the sky turned colours like bruised flesh and he had watched his ma . . .

"I'm sorry," he said, and in his ear, Ruth hushed him, and her fingers entwined with the hair on the back of his head, and her other hand brushed down the side of his ribs. He tried to say more—how knowing it or not, he'd brought this fate down on her and Louise, and this whole town, how that sealed-up jar of sickness on the floor was the curse he'd carried here—how in bringing this curse, he'd killed her. He tried to say it, but it was too much for words: even having passed the story, or most of it, of his pa and his mama. Saying he was sorry to Ruth was the same as saying he was sorry to his ma, whom he hadn't even buried—and saying that right, was more than he could say in words. So all he could do was lift his cheek from her blouse, and try and face her in the pitch black. It was too late after that; her mouth was on his, lips parted, and they were sharing the hot breath of fever.

Hush, darling. No regrets.

Ruth's fingers danced like the legs of a spider down to the belt of his trousers, and then below, and Jason held back a gasp, as her hand formed a cup, and held him in it. He pulled away from the kiss, swallowing a mouthful of her, and slipped his own hand up to her blouse. He could feel her heartbeat, fluttering like a bird's through the cloth and the flesh, and he could feel her grow momentarily rigid at the contact. They both knew that the only thing guaranteeing their privacy was the dark; the slightest noise would leave poor Louise with little doubt as to what they were doing.

So they made quiet work of it. Ruth found the buttons of Jason's fly, and in no time she had undone the top two of them, which was enough: the cool, soft flesh of her wrist touched him first, and then she drew him into her palm. Jason could not breathe a moment—yet somehow he managed to find the buttons at the side of Ruth's drawers and with only a little help from her, was able to loosen them enough that she could wriggle free. Louise might have heard that, but she must have been coughing at that instant; there was no comment from her. Jason trembled as he traced the smooth curve of Ruth's hip with his fingertips; he drew a sharp breath as she twisted her wrist somewhat, in drawing him between her thighs. He thought—he was sure—that he heard her declare love for him, as she gasped, and pulled him deep inside her. But Jason could be no surer of that, than he was of Louise. Jason drew a sharp breath, and in doing he felt Ruth do the same thing—and he recalled—

—the moment on the rail platform, a cool spring breeze catching her as he spied her standing next to Louise, the tiny half-smile that touched only part of her face—as he wondered: did she spy me too?—and now knowing, that yes, it was, as Ruth herself had said, a moment of Fate. And so it was, when that smile widened, and—

Hush, my darling.

He clutched both her shoulders with his hands, and in so doing thrust himself deeper inside her. Her pantaloons were tangled around one ankle, and the fabric wrapped the back of one thigh as she pressed her legs around him, and drew him inside—

—widened, and reached—

Jason thrust in deeper. He fell into an easy rhythm—he was surprised at how easy. It was like he'd been doing this all his life. In his ear, Ruth whispered things that he could not understand; and he whispered them back, and they moved together more quickly, and finally, although they both fought against it, they cried out—first Ruth, and then Jason.

They lay quietly for a moment, wet with each other's sweat and juices, and slowly returned to themselves. Jason pulled away enough that he could sit up, and as he did so, he was overcome by a sudden shame. He was not a complete fool; he knew what they'd done was private, better kept behind the doors of a saloon, or best yet, the vows of a marriage. But his will had fled him in her embrace, and here he had taken Ruth Harper, in the dark, in a sick room, right next to her good friend Louise.

The same thought might have occurred to Ruth, but she responded differently—with a laugh that only slightly betrayed her embarrassment. "Oh my," she said, running her hand down Jason's forearm and entwining his fingers with hers. "Oh Louise," she said, "I can't imagine what you are thinking."

Jason could—and he waited in the dark next to Ruth for a few heartbeats, for the rebuke.

"Miss Butler?" he finally said. "I'm sure sorry about that; I sure wasn't brought up to . . ."

"Louise?" Ruth let go of his hand then, and scrambled away from him. Jason, slower on the uptake than she, didn't work it out until he heard Ruth's gasp, and then a sob.

"Oh," he said. And he rolled to his knees, and crawled over to where Louise lay. He found Ruth first, and took her shoulders, and brought her to his arm as she let go of the cooling, lifeless hand of her friend and chaperone.

"What have we done, Jason?"

Jason swallowed, and with his other hand reached over to touch the wax-sealed jar that had travelled from Africa, to Cracked Wheel, and now, in secret, to this cellar. "We haven't done a thing," he said. "Not a God-damned thing."

Not you.

"Not us."

But that's not to say you're not going to do anything, is it my boy?

"No mama," Jason whispered.

Ruth pressed in close to him, and he held her tight. And She, come from the shadow of Montana, tall and beautiful and strong as the sky, held them both in her arms.

27

Gods and Oracles

They've gone Feeger, thought Andrew as the quarantine appeared through the trees. That was what Hank had said, back in the Tavishes' little village on the mountainside. They were afraid of going Feeger, and so they kept to themselves, and—until the end—the Feegers kept from them. Then one day, Sam Green sent them a doctor to kill a Juke. And the Feegers came down the mountain, and they killed those stubborn Tavishes.

And now . . . now, the Feegers were upon Eliada. And the folk here were losing themselves . . . going Feeger. He saw it as they hauled past St. Cyprian's—and a crowd of folk, who stood faces upturned to the rain, hands reaching for the sky beyond it. He heard it, in the off-key voices that sang along with the whistling dirge that seemed to come from every cranny. Fifty of them, maybe more, shuffled outside the sawmill as they passed it.

Andrew gasped, and shut his eyes a moment against the pain, which was beyond anything he'd felt before—even at the moment of his beating by the Klansmen. When they pulled him from the mud, the men who'd attacked the Harpers' mansion had spread his weight between two of them—without any consideration for his injuries, particularly not his elbow. The pain from it was brilliant—it drowned out any song he could have heard, and blinded him to anything but its own light.

Just like it had for Jason, when he was locked in this building with Mister Juke and had sliced his hand—agony brought Andrew back to flesh.

They let go of him at the front steps to the quarantine. The door hung off one hinge, and it was clear the two men who had carried him this far wouldn't go further. Andrew stumbled and nearly fell against the wall, but he managed to stand.

The little girl Lily stepped into the doorway and looked at him. "You got an honour," she said seriously. She extended her hand. "Walk wi' me."

Andrew looked back at the men. The two who were hauling him had stepped back among the rest: about twenty of them, all told. Any one of them looked powerful enough to kill him—but all of them were staying well out of reach of the door. And the little girl.

What would happen, he wondered briefly, if he tried to hurt her?

She took his good hand in her thin, cool fingers. "You kin walk, caintchya?"

"I can walk," he said.

"Then come," she said. "Oracle's waiting."

The girl tugged at his hand, and Andrew followed obediently. As they passed over the threshold into the quarantine, Lily squinted up at him.

"Don't be crying," she said. "It's only darkness."

§

It *was* dark. Once they got through the entry hall, the quarantine swallowed memory of day, of sunlight. It was only Lily's hand, her sure foot, that gave Andrew any bearing at all.

They travelled down a corridor where the walls seemed to chitter with birdsong. At a point, they wandered into a room that stank like a privy. Andrew gagged and Lily, leading him forward, giggled. They climbed stairs for a step or two or ten, and Andrew felt a cool breeze on his cheek, and caught a smell like the sort of river that might run through a grand city. It was when the texture of the floor became soft, like a mown English lawn, that Andrew made a point of flexing his elbow, and gasping at the pain of it. Lily started to sing then, and stroked his hand in a mothering way, and Andrew heard trumpets behind her voice—and as that happened, the darkness began to dissolve like spots of ink, and he saw that he was in a great chamber lit by ten thousand candles. At the far end, a woman sat demurely, long raven hair combed down as far as her waist.

He had arrived in the presence of the Oracle.

"Might wan' t' bow down," said Lily.

Andrew grimaced, and bent his elbow once more.

"Think I'll stand," he said.

§

Seen through the lens of pain, the Oracle wasn't all that demure.

She stood tall like her brothers, and her black hair hung near her waist, and she seemed strong, with thick hips and large, full breasts and flushed cheeks and lips. But the Oracle paid a toll, and Andrew could see it in her eyes, at once wide and sunken, ringed dark; and her odd posture, bent and swaying in the dark cloth of her homespun dress. She held a bundle wrapped in cloth and twigs, the way a mother might hold a baby. The room was not lit by ten thousand candles or even a hundred, just four kerosene lamps that cast scant light in the wide room. It looked as though it hadn't been put to use as much but a storeroom for broken old furniture. She stood by an old roll-top desk, not far from a tall blank wall with two big barn doors. Lily pushed him: "Go see 'er," she said to Andrew, and across the room to the Oracle: "Smell 'im!"

"No need," said the Oracle. "I c'n smell him from here. Need a look, though."

Lily pushed him again, making it plain that there was no option. "Go see 'er," she whispered. "An' try bowing. She's the Oracle."

Andrew made his way forward, jostling painfully against the furniture as he did so. Lily followed close.

"Yes," said the Oracle, "come to me, black man. Let me a look at you."

Andrew kept the desk between them. "I think I'm close enough," he said, and the Oracle nodded. She sniffed the air, and looked him up and down. Then she bent and sniffed the bundle in her arms.

"What is that you got?" asked Andrew, and Lily smacked his arm. "Hush!" Then, to the Oracle: "He got the smell of Him! Of the Lost Child. So I brung 'im."

"I know you did. Good girl." The Oracle squinted at him. "You ain't like th' others here, are you? Black man."

"I guess I'm not," he said, carefully, studying this girl. She was just a girl—he didn't expect that she was any older than Jason Thistledown, and might well have been younger. And yet, they called her Oracle. "And you aren't, either. Can I see your baby?"

The girl took a possessive stance, sheltering the bundle with her body.

"Ain't my baby," she said, her voice going high. "Ain't larder."

Andrew made a hushing noise. "May I see?"

For a moment they stood still, the only sound being the pattering of rain on the quarantine's roof. It sounded like it was coming harder. At length, she looked up at Andrew.

"It's the Lost Child," she said in a small voice, and reached over with a hand, and pulled aside some cloth. "Like you."

A tiny claw revealed itself, talons gleaming in the lamplight.

"We saved him," said Lily.

And the Oracle said, "Too late, too late. So we brung 'im here."

Andrew stared as she removed more of the cloth, drawing the bent claw out, caressing the thing's chest.

"Heathen did this. So this is our reminder—of what we do with Heathen that bring harm to the Old Man. To the Son." The Oracle pulled the cloth back over the corpse. "And you—you smell of him."

Andrew bit down on the inside of his cheek. No wonder, he thought. This was the thing that'd ripped itself from Loo Tavish. And these girls had it—they had it, because of course they were Feegers, and the Feegers had torn through the Tavish village with knives, and now . . .

"What are you going to do with the Heathen here?" asked Andrew.

"Same thing," said the Oracle, "but we can tell the difference. There's the ones that hurt him. They got one smell. There's the ones that don't know yet. They got another."

"Kill the one," said Lily. "Learn the other."

"Then there's another kind," said the Oracle. "Smell different. Not one of either. And then—there's you."

"Smell of the Lost Child."

"Black man. With that smell."

"A *mystery.*"

"So Mr. Harper—the people in the mansion—the big house—they were harming him?"

"Took him away," said the Oracle. "Not this one. An elder. They twisted him around, hurt him. Made him do things. That ain't the order."

And so they were murdered—cut down by old swords and axes, and the house burned, by this entire community—this extended family—of criminals, bowing to service this animal—this Mister Juke.

How apt, he thought, that the folk of Eliada had named the creature Juke. Apt, but off the mark. The real Jukes were these Feegers—men and women if not congenitally criminal, then made so by the spoor of this parasite. And so it became with anyone who encountered this beast, and its young.

"You have one inside you," said Andrew to the Oracle, "don't you?"

At that, the girl beamed.

"And a baby," said Andrew. "It's early, but you have a baby too."

"No," she said. "*He's* got the baby. Larder. It's better for Him, with larder. As might you know."

Andrew opened his mouth to speak, and shut it again. This was as he'd surmised and as Norma Tavish had explained to him—the Jukes did better in a womb with child than on their own, by killing and eating the child, stealing its nourishment and so on. It was one thing to understand the behaviour, another to see these . . . children, apparently understanding what was before them, well enough to deliberately set it in motion.

To make a child for food. A deliberate sacrifice.

And what did they mean: *as might you know*?

"Why would you?" he asked.

But it wasn't only the thought. He felt a deep vibration up his back: a deep, basso rumbling, or a moan, as of great timbers drawing against one another.

The Oracle and Lily heard it too. The two girls bent their heads back, and began to hum and sing, in high, broken voices. They mingled with the deeper noise into a harmony as Andrew had never heard before. He flexed his elbow, and the shooting pain drew him back from reverie.

The sounds mingled and bent, and slowly, the room filled up with a cool light. Andrew looked to its source, and saw: the two tall doors were opening.

§

Two things dwelt there.

One was luminous: a tall, slender man in robes, flesh of buffed mahogany, his brow unfurrowed and gaze open and loving.

A Dauphin.

He stood in a great glass dome, as high as a cathedral. His head nearly reached the apex; doves flew about him, and settled on his shoulders.

When he spoke, he sang, and the doves joined him in harmony. It was a song of forgiveness and welcoming; its lyric spoke straight at Andrew Waggoner.

Come on to Heaven, said the man, raising his hand to touch the glass over his head, and bringing rays of gold where his fingertips tarried. Looking up through there, Andrew felt certain: the shades of Loo Tavish, Maryanne Leonard, might never reach him from this exalted place.

And then there was the other. That one was harder to see—Andrew had to work at it. He took his bad hand in his good, and twisted—and he saw the Dauphin's head loll to the left, and that fine brow grew quill-thick hairs, and the colour fled and it was the pale white of a fresh-dug grub. Andrew bit down hard on his tongue—and the dome vanished, replaced with weathered beams and cracked roofing, through which rainwater fell and pooled on the packed-earth floor—and high, filthy windows that let in the damp light, to cast upon a shape that was like a shoulder but bent as a wrist. He jammed his elbow against the corner of an old cabinet, and the gentle gaze of the Dauphin became the idiot stare of the Juke, two great black eyes, sunk in folds of mottled flesh, which shifted and faded, into the dark eyes of the Dauphin . . . which opened up into an infinity that Andrew had glimpsed once before.

And the Dauphin whispered . . .

Andrew smashed his arm into the corner of the cabinet. The things that leaped and capered at Mister Juke's side shifted from dove and angel, into small dark things that scurried through the shadows—and back, to beauty.

Love Me.

"No." Andrew drew back.

Spread My word.

"No," he said again, and allowing himself one last glimpse of Heaven, drove his head into the corner of the cabinet.

§

"Dead?"

"No."

"Oracular?"

"Don't know. Maybe."

"Need to know."

"There be only one way to."

"Leave him to it?"

"With the rest."

§

And so, higher Andrew Waggoner fell.

Not so high as Heaven, though. Not so high as that.

§

"The Negro wakes."

Cool water on the forehead, a damp cloth mopping it up. "Annie?" The sound of water wrung from cloth into pan. A laugh.

"Oh, no. Not her."

Andrew blinked in the light. He was on his back, on a soft-mattressed bed, staring up at a high plank ceiling.

"Mrs. Frost?" said Andrew. He pushed himself up in the bed. Annie Rowe might've stopped him, but Germaine Frost kept her distance. She sat on a metal stool near his bed. On the right side of her forehead, someone had taped a thick pad of gauze. The reddish-brown of dried blood frosted its edges.

She sat with hands folded, and nodded. "You're not addled, Dr. Waggoner," she said. "That's good."

"I'm addled," he said, looking around. They were in a ward room that he'd never seen before. He wasn't alone. The room was filled with beds—and patients. Beside him, a woman stirred underneath her sheet, pulled it to her chin.

"You must be in great pain," said Germaine.

"I am," said Andrew, and he wasn't lying.

"Yet you don't flinch." She nodded, slow. "You are really a fine specimen."

He looked at her levelly. "I'm not a specimen, Mrs. Frost."

"Of course you're not. It's just this—place. And I meant it kindly, in any case. You're a man of resource, Doctor. I can see why Mr. Harper selected you."

"Mr. Harper is dead."

She pursed her lips, stood and dipped the cloth into the pan of water. Wrung it out, and examined it an instant before handing it to Andrew. "Hold it to your forehead," she said. "You've taken a trauma there." Andrew took the cloth and pressed it there, and Mrs. Frost sat back on her stool. "Dead, you say? Well, given the march of events these past few days, I shouldn't be surprised. Yet I am. He was a visionary."

"The march of events." Andrew snorted humourlessly. "I take it we're in

EUTOPIA

the quarantine—one of the wards." She nodded. "Who are those women?" he asked, indicating the other beds.

"I don't know them," said Mrs. Frost. "They were present when I woke up here; and they're not so conversational as you, so I couldn't learn as much of them as I'm sure I can of you. But to be honest, I don't care to interrogate you, Dr. Waggoner. I presume you came here much as I did—beaten by some sheet-wearing thug into unconsciousness. Although I daresay you look as though you put up more of a fight." Her mouth twitched into a tiny and, to Andrew's eye, thoroughly unpleasant smile. "You would think that the people here would have more gratitude, for the society that we—that Mr. Harper—provided them."

We. "You work for the Eugenics Records Office," said Andrew. "Your people had more than a hand in this town, didn't they?"

"Not in a way that we like to advertise," said Mrs. Frost, "but yes. The ERO watched this place with interest. We even helped it along. Do you know that Eliada means 'watched over by God'?"

"Really."

"It's a fine statement of the middle of our aim," said Germaine, "to make a perfect society of strong-backed men and their wives, who would never stray far from the healthful path; of children, who were disposed to be healthful by dint of their inheritance. But we were foolish in its application. I hope you won't take great offence if I tell you that your hiring here was a matter of some controversy at the office."

"You had a hand in my hiring?"

"Not I. But if I had known and been placed to intercede, I like to think that I would have been one of those who advocated on your behalf. As matters stood, the ERO was in the main opposed to the hiring of a nigg—a Negro doctor. It was Garrison Harper's intercession, I gather, that brought you here. He believed that excellence in a man is not dictated by race or creed—but by the strength of the lineage. Great men come from all corners of the Earth. It is a belief a few of us share."

Andrew tried not to laugh. "I'm flattered you—or at least Mr. Harper—thought so highly of me," he said.

"You ought to be," she said, and: "Oh. *Hush*."

The door from the ward room swung open as Mrs. Frost lifted the cloth. "Lie back," she said. Andrew reclined, but he watched as the small figure stepped through. It was a girl—very young, this one—with long dark hair tied into an off-centre braid. She wore a grey frock, and a serious and wide-eyed expression

284

as she went to the bedside of one of the women at the far end of the room. She delicately put her hands on the woman's belly, rubbed them in circles, and began to sing.

She's singing to Jukes, Andrew thought. *Because all these women are carrying Jukes. Just like Maryanne Leonard, and Loo Tavish.*

The woman responded to the child's song, the circling touch—writhing obscenely beneath the sheet, stretching as though waking from a long and restful sleep. The woman didn't wake, but she did join in—and the strange, wordless song became a duet.

Mrs. Frost set the cloth on his forehead again. She drew it across his brow, down his cheek. The damp tip of it stopped at the corner of his mouth. She leaned over him.

"You ought to be flattered," she said softly, her breath sour as the night. "You are a fine, strong, smart Negro. I know they didn't appreciate that in Paris—in New York, when you tried to find internships there. They look at skin, and they think—inferior, by dint of darkness." She huffed, and spat: "*Prejudice.*"

Andrew reached up and took her hand. Her eyes widened, and she snatched the cloth away, and for barely an instant, she looked quite fierce.

"They can scarcely tell," she said, "when Gods walk among them."

Gods. Andrew thought about that. Gods were what these people thought they were making: people like Bergstrom, like Harper . . . like the people who worked with Mrs. Frost. How susceptible they all must have been, to the alluring lie of the Juke, which put worms into the wombs of virgins to make saviours; into the flesh of men, to make prophets of them. . . .

Did any of them ever mark the day, he wondered, when they fell from reason into madness?

And then he wondered: *Did I?*

"Mrs. Frost," Andrew said, "I must find your nephew. Jason Thistledown. Can you tell me where he is?"

"My nephew," she said thoughtfully. "Jason. You need to find him, you say?"

The little girl had moved on to a second patient, three beds away from them. Germaine Frost glanced over her shoulder, as she bunched the cloth up into a ball in her fist, then back at him.

"To what end?" she asked.

Andrew lowered his voice. "The boy is in as much danger as any of us here," he said. "I don't know where he might be—I've come back looking for him, but had no luck. But he's your nephew, Mrs. Frost. If you're hiding him from these people—these Feegers—you don't need to hide him from me. He may be with Miss Harper."

Mrs. Frost looked back over her shoulder. The little girl was making circles on the new woman's belly, same as before, singing a song with a slightly different cadence. She regarded Andrew with a twitch of a smile.

"I don't know where he is," she said, "but I can guess. He's an intelligent boy—a fine boy—and he will have known where to go. There is not much that gets past a boy of Jason Thistledown's stock."

"Where, Mrs. Frost?"

"We would have to go together."

"All right." Andrew glanced at the little girl. She had moved around so as to face away from them. "She can't be the only one here. Are there others waiting outside?"

"Who can say? I saw two men bring you in. And the last time she was here, she didn't come in by herself. She was with a man who was so tall. Practically a giant. But now—"

"Well, that's a problem," said Andrew. "I'm in no shape to deal with someone like that and you—"

He didn't get the opportunity to finish. Germaine Frost spun a quarter turn on her stool and in three large steps moved past the foot of two beds. The girl stopped singing at the commotion, and lifted her hands off the woman's belly as Germaine Frost stepped nimbly as a spider between the beds.

She took hold of the girl by the hair and tugged, but the child didn't cry out: Mrs. Frost had already jammed the wadded-up cloth into her mouth, and with her first and middle finger, pushed the soaking wet cloth into her nostrils. The girl took hold of Germaine's wrist with both hands and tried to pry the hands away. Mrs. Frost set her mouth and held fast. The girl soon gave up on wrist, and tried to claw at Mrs. Frost's eyes. She got close enough to knock Mrs. Frost's glasses from one ear, so they dangled over the bridge of her nose. Mrs. Frost responded by bearing down on the child, and pushing her to the floor between the beds.

Andrew rolled off the bed, and nearly fell as his feet hit the bare wooden floor. He clutched Mrs. Frost's stool like a walking stick and, bent like an old man, moved from that to the foot of the bed beside him, and the bed beside that.

He managed to stay upright as he looked down on Germaine Frost and the child. All he could see of Germaine were her shoulders, wide and round enough to nearly fill the space between the bed. They worked and shifted as though she were kneading dough.

Her skirts were hiked past the knee, her stockings torn to reveal long ovals of pallid flesh. All he could see of the child were her feet. They were pinned beneath Mrs. Frost's crossed ankles, so she couldn't kick or make noise on the wooden floor. She could not make any noise at all by now. She was barely struggling.

Andrew reached down with his good hand and grabbed Mrs. Frost's shoulder. She shifted her weight, and smashed his fingers between her arm and the bed next to it. Andrew gasped. She spared him a glance over her shoulder, catching his eye.

"Don't interfere," she whispered. Andrew tried to lay hold of her again, but it was impossible—the space between the beds allowed him no room to get in and stop it.

Soon—too soon—the feet stopped moving, and Germaine Frost was able to stand, and brush herself off, and turn to Andrew Waggoner and, as though nothing had transpired between them, say: "We have to go now."

§

All Andrew could do was *go*. A small part of him wanted to strike Germaine Frost down, raise an alarm—shout *murderer*! But if he did so . . . what would become of Jason? Germaine Frost was his only thread through this maze.

The girl was dead. Lips blue, no heartbeat, wide eyes staring sightlessly at the ceiling. Germaine bent and rolled her beneath the bed, and took hold of Andrew and led him to the door. It wasn't locked. Beyond was a hallway, and they followed it, and climbed down some steps, and finally came upon a bright room: a small surgery, with a skylight, which was badly cracked. Water rained down in a small torrent onto the bare wooden operating table, in turn dribbling down to the floor. Opposite them was another door, and when they went through this, they stepped outside.

They stood next to a stand of tamarack—not far off was the fallen log where Jason Thistledown had given Andrew Waggoner a pack of meagre supplies and sent him into the wilderness alone.

"What luck!" she exclaimed. "Not a single one! What luck!"

Not a single one. There was one, thought Andrew. "She was a child," he said. He was shaking. "A silly child who they'd let in on her own. You—"

"She would have raised an alarm," said Mrs. Frost.

"Perhaps," said Andrew. "But there might have been another way. There must have been another way. And how did you know she was alone? That her guard wasn't waiting for her outside?"

Mrs. Frost shrugged. "They are degenerates," she said. "Inferior. They have not the wit. Now tell me, Doctor—do you want to meet my nephew or do you want to question good fortune until pneumonia sets in?"

Andrew didn't answer that, but Mrs. Frost evidently took silence as its own response. "Then come along," she said. "Come along."

Andrew followed her around the corner of the building, and the hospital was in sight, rendered grey and deathly through the driving rain—a silhouette, almost, among . . . other shapes.

They both stopped and stared, at one of those shapes. It might have been a tree, but it would not stay still—it bent low and climbed higher than the eaves, as though it were in the clutches of some cyclonic wind. As they watched, it moved past the hospital, and then further along, toward the town. It moaned, a deep, bassoon-like sound, and accompanying it came a song, in clear and high voices. It might be that all of Eliada rose up in song, as the thing—as Mister Juke—roiled and crawled and strode toward the docks, and the town and those many, who had watched and prayed as the Feegers hauled Andrew Waggoner to the quarantine, now awaited their God, as the Feegers led Him to them.

And so it was that unmolested, unnoticed by God or Man, the two of them made their way to the shelter of the hospital's unguarded back entrance and slipped inside.

28

The Old Man

"How do you know where he is?" asked Andrew as they skulked down the corridor that ran the spine of the hospital's basement.

"I cannot be certain," said Mrs. Frost. "But I do know this: against all my advice, the boy took more than a passing fancy to Mr. Harper's daughter Ruth."

Andrew waited for her to continue, then prompted: "What does that have to do with anything?"

"Miss Harper," said Mrs. Frost, "was engaged in a test when Jason left me. If he is half as clever as we both know him to be, he will have joined her."

"A test?"

"The test of her life," she said. They hurried past the dispensary and two of the examination rooms, and rounded a corner. "Hush," she said. "We are almost there."

Andrew had a sick feeling, as it became obvious where they were heading: the autopsy. Mrs. Frost stopped short, and looked at Andrew significantly.

"Here we are," she said, and beckoned him to open the door.

Andrew's skin prickled at the base of his neck, and he shook his head. It was as though . . .

. . . *as though something larger were guiding him, warning him.*

Andrew shook off the feeling. It was a reasonable instinct.

Germaine Frost had murdered a little girl. She might argue the tactic was an effective one—here they were, after all, out of the quarantine that had been overrun with Feegers. The girl was one of them. But Mrs. Frost had murdered a little girl. And they were standing on the doorway of the autopsy, where a week ago, he and Jason Thistledown had examined the cut-up remains of Maryanne Leonard.

This, the place where another girl was undergoing what—a test? The test of her life?

Andrew Waggoner's skin prickled, for good, worldly reason.

"I'm not going in there until you tell me about this test."

"Oh," she said, grinning, "it's nothing you should worry about. If I'm half as right about you as I was about young Jason—I'm certain it won't be even the tiniest problem for you."

"For me?" Andrew stepped back. "What is this?"

Germaine Frost looked down, and smiling, shook her head. She looked up again. Her eyes sparkled in the dark. With madness, with inspiration.

Her hand pressed against the door to the autopsy. Andrew thought he saw a sliver of Nils Bergstrom in her then—he remembered seeing her, coming out of the quarantine with him that morning.

"It is the only way to see," she said. "If you're worthy. If you are a true hero—"

The door swung open then, and pushed her backwards, and a figure in white burst into the hall. Mrs. Frost came up against the far wall, and started to say something, but she couldn't finish. The white-clad figure drove a fist into her face, and with the other hand grabbed her hair.

Then it turned to Andrew, and he recognized it:

"Jason!" he said.

"Dr. Waggoner." The figure took a step forward, hauling Mrs. Frost as he peered at Waggoner. "You're alive. And back. Keep your distance."

His voice was absolutely flat—a tone that did not admit any argument. Waggoner stepped back.

It had been barely a week, but Jason Thistledown seemed like he'd aged a decade. With one hand, he pushed Germaine Frost to her knees. His face was in shadow, but Andrew saw the flat slit of his mouth, the stillness around his eye. It didn't so much as twitch as Mrs. Frost tried to twist her hair from his fist.

"Jason," said Waggoner. "I came to get you out of here—"

"Hush, Doctor," he said. "You should have stayed away. You need to stay clear now. Remember that disease that slew my kin? Good. Well, it's here—in that room. And this one is the one that brought it. In a little jar from Africa. She lied about being my aunt. She murdered all my kin. My town. With a germ in a jar. You understand that?"

Andrew nodded.

"I let her live once today. That was wrong. But things are makin' more sense right now. I was fixing to find her—and that Bergstrom, and do the thing I should have done to both of them. Like Deborah said to her generals: 'Surely the Lord will deliver them this day unto a woman.' Well, the Lord delivered this woman unto me. And I know what to do."

Andrew didn't say anything. Jason did know what to do. The boy—the man—knew very well to do what Andrew hadn't been able to countenance: to kill, when killing was due. He looked away, and Jason obviously took note.

"Now I only know you a little. I know you're a good man. I know you might be thinkin' of getting Sam Green or somebody to stop this. But anyone does that, they'll die. This germ's killed one already, Louise Butler, and I think it's going to . . ."

At this, his cheek finally twitched, and he hesitated an instant before starting up again, quieter:

" . . . I think it's going to take Ruth Harper soon. It's all over the autopsy, and that cellar. It gets out of here, it's going to kill just about everybody. So when you're thinking of goin' to get help from Sam Green and those Pinkertons . . . You think about that. I hope no one will stop me when I go after that Bergstrom, anyhow."

"There's no need," said Andrew. "He was killed this morning. Jason—you've got to let me help her. Not her—" he motioned at Germaine "—but Ruth. It may be possible—"

"You help her, you'll get infected too. Doctor, I'm set on my path. Thank you for tellin' me about Bergstrom. I'll keep away from others, then. But in this room—don't get near."

And with that, he yanked Germaine Frost up—she screamed, and sobbed, and he threaded an arm under hers, and hauled her, feet dragging, through the door in the autopsy.

"Get away!" he hollered, and the door slammed shut.

§

Andrew got away, but he didn't go far.

He made for the dispensary, his mind racing. He felt oddly enervated. Finding Jason Thistledown had been the overriding impetus for Andrew for too long, and it was a thing so large and mysterious, so seductive, that he might lose himself in it, falling off the edge of the world into the madness of the

Juke's false Heaven. Jason's chilling revelation—that Germaine had brought the sickness, that she was using it as an obscene test of fitness, on Jason, on Ruth . . . on Andrew himself—that was something else. It was a cord, tying him to earth. He would grasp it.

There was a sick girl, locked in the autopsy—sick with a disease so terrible it had killed a Montana pig town in three days last winter.

She might well die too—would certainly die without treatment.

Andrew Waggoner would simply not let that happen.

He stumbled to the dispensary, a dark room with a thick wooden door with a lock strong enough to deter a lumber-man with an axe. Less trouble for Andrew, who knew, as did the rest of the hospital's staff, the hiding place for the brass key that opened it, tucked into a space in the door-frame. He was inside in no time, striking a match in the jar next to the wall lamp and setting the wick.

Then he set to work. He brought down a tray, and filled it with what things he might require: a glass thermometer, a bowl and clean washcloths, sterile lancets; after some consideration, a phial of morphine and a clean syringe. He found a cotton mask, and put it there too—although he wasn't confident at all that that would be enough.

What he would have liked to have, was Norma Tavish and her pack of curative herbs with him now; as modern as this hospital was, there wasn't anything that would by itself cure an infection that'd set in here, as well as Norma's miraculous herbs had in the Tavish settlement.

Andrew set against a stool, and shut his eyes, and pushed Norma Tavish out of his mind. Letting regret steal up too close was a bad idea at any time; here, where the machinations of the Juke could make a man believe anything, it could be fatal. It might almost make a fellow think she was coming now, opening and closing the door to the stairwell, and walking down the corridor with efficient purpose.

Of course, Norma Tavish's footwear wouldn't clack on the floor, the way these did.

Andrew opened his eyes and took a breath. It wasn't a Juke imagining. Someone was coming.

It was too late to douse the light or shut the door. Andrew was not in any shape to prepare for a fight, if it were one of the Feegers. He pressed himself against the wall of the dispensary, and prayed the footsteps would continue.

They slowed, and stopped. And then Waggoner heard a familiar voice.

"Hello? Who's there, please?"

He laughed out loud.

"Nurse Rowe!" he exclaimed, and then added: "It's Waggoner."

There was a shuffling in the hall, and then Annie Rowe put her familiar face around the door jamb. Her eyes were wide in the lamplight.

"My Heavens," she breathed as she beheld him. "Look at you. I'd sew you a shroud, I hadn't heard you speak just now."

Waggoner grinned. He was preposterously glad to see her—almost tearfully so. The exhaustion, no doubt, was catching up to him.

"It's been an adventure," he managed. Then he cleared his throat, and drew himself together. "Annie—we've got a medical emergency. Ruth Harper's in the autopsy. She's deathly ill. Whatever it is, it's contagious."

Annie frowned, and looked at the material he'd gathered. She nodded. "You've put together quite a kit, Dr. Waggoner. You were intending to carry it down the hall yourself? I've a better idea."

"Which is?"

"Come with me."

Andrew stood up. It occurred to a small part of him that Annie Rowe had not given him a good reason to follow her—and that part of him thought that he had decided to follow the mad Germaine Frost with scarcely more resistance, and obeyed Jason Thistledown to fly off, with scarcely less.

"I know what will heal your injuries," said Annie, smiling and holding his good arm as they strode down the hall, to the door.

As they stepped outside into the rain, Andrew asked: "What is that?"

And Annie Rowe turned, and pointed to the narrow road that led down to the sawmill, scored now with strange tracks, and said:

"Jesus."

A small part of him tried to bend his arm—send the visions away on a spike of agony—but this time, Annie was there to help.

"Easy, Doctor," she said. "There's no need for any more pain." With great care, she reset the sling. "Jesus Christ will heal all. He told me so, in a dream last night."

And together, they stepped around the hospital, and looked down the road—and Andrew gasped, at the great light that glowed there: warm, and welcoming, and so very melodious. Whether from Jesus Christ or the Dauphin, who rested within—he could not resist it this time. Willingly, he entered into His realm.

§

The autopsy room was not built with windows, but air moved through it all the same, within high vents in one wall that led straight outside. So it wasn't as bad a place to be as the storeroom, where Ruth still rested. The voice from the shadows approved.

As Jason hauled Germaine Frost into it and slammed the door shut, it was only a little humid. Water was splashed here and there, from two large buckets that were foaming with soap. Not long ago, Jason had spent time with those buckets, washing himself as thoroughly as he could—as thoroughly as Germaine Frost had made him wash outside the homestead at Cracked Wheel. After he'd scrubbed himself clean of the Cave Germ as best he could, he searched some cupboards and found a white smock as might be worn by doctors cutting up the dead. He got to thinking that maybe some power had a good sense of humour; that outfit would do fine to cover him up for the work that lay ahead.

He was even more sure that that power had taken a hand in this latest moment of providence: delivering his quarry, the murderess Germaine Frost, right into his hands.

"This is fine that you came," he said. "We can seal this whole matter here, and not put anyone else in harm's way."

"Oh Jason," she said, sobbing, but Jason was having have none of it.

A week ago, he'd have thought when this moment came, when Germaine Frost used tears on him again . . . he would spew anger at her, call her foul names, and laugh when she objected—like a fellow in a book that Ruth Harper might've liked to read over and over again. But as he had held Ruth, comforting her over the death of her friend and sitting there in the dark of the cellar room . . . he got to know his anger a little better. It grew into a purer thing.

So when Germaine sobbed and cried here in the autopsy, he saw it for what it was. She was trying to trick him with tears, the same as when just idly, after she let him be locked up in the quarantine, he suggested he might head down south and pick up some work there. That made him feel badly—and feeling badly thinned that anger, like throwing water in a tub of lye.

You let remorse get in your way, you'll never do the kind of thing you have to do.

"I know, Mama," said Jason over his shoulder.

You let an old drunk's begging turn you around—he'll just get drunk again, and let friends even worse than that Etherton into the house.

"Oh Jason, please—think of your potential! The Harper girl is sick, true, because she's not fit. We'll find you one with whom to breed, and then—"

Shut her up!

Jason swatted Germaine across the ear.

"Don't talk to me," he said. "You talk to me, I'll hit you. That's how it's going to go. Now—" Jason hefted her up by an arm. "Sit on that." He motioned to the drawer.

She won't cooperate. A shadow shook its head beyond Germaine's shoulder. Sure enough, Germaine wasn't having any of it. She might have divined what Jason intended; get her feet up, lie her on the table, and roll it in, and lock it with her inside. That was his ma's wisdom, delivered from the shadows behind the jars: *Show her what she showed me. Take her away.*

So she twisted away from him and planted her feet firm on the ground. One of the lenses was nearly obliterated, and the other hung oddly from her nose.

She stared at Jason steadily. When she spoke, her tone was low and deliberate.

"All right, Jason," said Germaine. "You will have to hit me, because I'm not going to go quietly. What do you mean to do? Take the *germe de grotte* that's in that room, smear it on me, and watch me die of bleeding from the ears?"

"I'm showing you what you showed my ma," said Jason. "What you showed all of Cracked Wheel, with that *germdeegrot*. You murdered Cracked Wheel! The whole damn town!" Behind her, next to the doorway, the shadow nodded its head.

He didn't cooperate. Not even with all the whiskey in him. My, my—but you'd think he would. He certainly did as he was told when Etherton got him drunk, and made him look off while he did his business.

"Are you paying attention to me, Nephew?"

Jason looked back down at her. Her face was beginning to swell where he'd hit her. Only half an eye managed to magnify in the glass.

"You're not," she said. "And you shouldn't have to, because in the scheme of things, I am what? A childless old woman with index cards. One such as you shouldn't grant someone like me the hour of the day. In the end, my contribution to greatness is secondhand. You, on the other hand—you should be fixed upon greater things."

He half-raised his hand, but couldn't manage it. Behind Germaine, the shadow grew agitated. But Jason couldn't hear what it said.

"I'm sorry I brought you here, Jason. When I came—when I brought you—it was only because Bergstrom so grossly misrepresented his discovery here. Remember—I explained to you. Had I known . . ."

Jason found the strength. He hit Germaine again, knocking her glasses clear.

"You use devil words on me, you get this." Then he grabbed her and pulled her up—her back bent on the shelf, so that it creaked on its rails. The shadows in the corners of the room danced, and murmured. A hinge creaked, so Jason could not hear the words. "I should have done this upstairs. First time you started talking. You think I was strong and a hero, but I should have done *this*." He put one hand over her mouth, and the other elbow on her throat. "You can't live, 'cause you'll just kill more. Like you'd have killed Dr. Waggoner. Just to *see*."

"That may be true, son."

The shadows finally coalesced. Jason looked up.

He was tall, and he smelled of fire and heat. His face was half-blackened, the other half swollen in a great sore. His eyes, white and round, stared out at Jason as though from bare sockets. Around him, the lamp-lit walls of the autopsy seemed to melt, and growing from the shadows were the square-cut logs of the cabin in Montana.

"You," breathed Jason.

"Jason," he rasped, and coughed.

Hell had not been kind to old John Thistledown.

§

"What did you do with my ma?"

"I did nothing with your ma. Now this one—you said she murdered Cracked Wheel? She murdered your ma too, didn't she?"

Jason stepped back, as the smells of that cabin—the hint of wood-smoke, the greasy smell of tallow from the candles lighting it, the pervasive scent of his mother—overcame him. His mother's smell was there, but she wasn't. Germaine Frost was crouched on her bed, cowering.

John Thistledown stood in the open door, swirls of snow around his burnt cadaver.

"She murdered everyone," said Jason. He wanted to cower himself, but he put on a brave face. "You back from Hell to see what another murderer looks like?"

The elder Thistledown seemed to think about that, and finally he nodded. "You're fixin' to kill her," he said. "To make her pay for all those other killings?"

"I am."

"You given any thought to what price you'd pay, doing that? Killing a person?"

Jason looked at his father's shade, and unbidden, a memory of him, hard and cold, looking down on the pass with his rifle in his lap, came up. "It was a price you were willing to pay."

"And look what it did to me."

"He's right, Jason," said Germaine. "Killing is not for one such as you—"

She didn't finish. John Thistledown, as tall as a pine, swooped over her. His filthy, Hell-scorched hands took hold of her head. "Look away, boy," said John, but Jason didn't obey, and watched as an instant later, his father's shade twisted his false aunt's head hard to the right, and cracked it. Her hands shook, and then went limp.

Jason kept watching, as his father straightened and walked past him. "You're right, Jason. Sometimes there's got to be a killing. Sometimes it is right. But you're better leaving it to a man with blood under his fingernails already. Keep your own clean for supper."

He stepped around Jason, and through a door that Jason had never recalled in the back of the cabin. That, of course, was because there hadn't been one. He was going into the storeroom, at the back of the autopsy. Where they had been all along.

Jason looked down at Germaine Frost. She had slid to the floor, her neck at an odd angle—her eyes tiny without their glasses.

"Goodbye son," said his father as he came back from the storeroom. There was something in his hand . . . a jar, sealed in wax. "Best you stay put with that girl of yours. She can use the comfort. And what's next—is something you don't need to see, neither of you."

And then John Thistledown stepped out into the hallway, and vanished.

Jason stared at that door for a long time, putting together what he'd seen—where he'd been. There was Germaine Frost, dead on the floor. Had he done that, possessed by the shade of his pa, come up from Hell to guide his hand in killing? What had he done with his ma?

"Jason?"

Jason looked around. Ruth stood trembling, at the door of the storeroom. Her eyes were dark, and she looked thinner in the lamplight. He went to her, deliberately blocking the view of Germaine Frost's body, and took her in his arms.

She looked up at him.

"What was Sam Green doing here?" she asked.

29

The Oracle Frets

The cathedral growled and hummed and came alive, as the Heavens dried up.

Inside its belly, acolytes stoked saw-scrap and wood shavings by the shovelful into the boiler; a plume of white smoke drifted from the high stack and across the town, where others crouched—their faces pressed into the mud of the road, or bent down as they clutched their chickens and pigs and bushels of apples—a proper offering to the God who now dwelt inside.

At the cathedral's gate, the Oracle waited.

She let Lily lead the song; she was uneasy, as she surveyed the crowd of new worshippers as she sniffed at the bundle in her arms and hung back under the shadow of the roof. There were a lot of folk there—more than she'd seen before, and she wasn't sure she liked all of them in such a great number. Were it up to her, she'd send the men-folk out to do a cull—whittle these families down to manageable sizes, feed the carcasses to the Son, like they already were with the false priests—that stinking old man, who'd climbed up a mountain and thought he'd be an Oracle because of it.

A false oracle.

The Oracle stood under an overhang of roof, at the back of a wide platform overlooking the square. Rainwater dribbled off the roof in front of her, like a waterfall. Lily let that water course over her as she sang, and the multitude sang too. They were supplicant, all right. But the Oracle felt a twang of doubt. It was one thing to sing and holler and tell kin—tell Feegers—that they needed to get off their behinds, take up their axes and bows and clubs, and take their Word on a crusade. Another entirely to tell these folk, who only now felt the touch of the Son on them.

Would they follow her? Would it be enough, to speak some words at them and take them along, down the river to the towns of the heathen folk—would they travel with their sticks and axes and bows and guns? Just because the Feeger Oracle said?

She clutched the infant to her breast, let its drying flesh, its needle teeth tease her.

It would be easier, she thought, if she had another—not a false one, but a real Oracle. He might help—keep these folk alive, and strong behind her. Travelling south, with the young. . . .

"Where," she said aloud, "is Missy?"

Lily shrugged, and Lothar—who'd been attending near the gate—got to his feet.

"I go look on her?" he asked, and the Oracle smiled on him. "You go fetch her," she said, and touched her cousin's brow. "Fetch me that nigger too, if Missy think he's right for it."

He bobbed to and fro, and smiled broad, and climbed down into the crowd.

Lily stopped singing and looked at her.

"You think the black man is one?"

"Mayhap." If Missy didn't come with some word—then the Oracle would have to preach it herself. Would it be a fair enough sermon for the Son, who had settled up in the rafters of the cathedral, waiting for His due?

She held the Infant tighter, and watched the crowd—and after a moment, she smiled.

"Mayhap," she said, as she looked to the crowd, and saw the dark, familiar face among so many pale. "Mayhap."

30

Rapture of the Juke

Andrew Waggoner mounted the stone steps of the cathedral. Ahead were great gilded doors, filigreed with sunbeams. Beyond those: the Dauphin waited for him.

Andrew was glad. Dimly, he recalled a time when he'd turned away, and he might have thought the Dauphin would not welcome him . . . that he had spurned Him. This would be enough to cast Andrew down, among the bones of those he'd failed.

If only Andrew had let the Dauphin guide his shaking physician's hand—how much suffering might he have prevented? How much less misery might he have caused?

"Don't cry, Doctor." Annie Rowe stood on the steps to the Cathedral with him, her face glowing in its light. "Christ'll save you."

"I'm already saved, Annie," said Andrew. He didn't know whether he'd say Christ was saving him, exactly. But Andrew had been saved some time ago—on the mountainside he'd wandered alone, full of doubt and anger, befuddled by the hill witch's narcotics. He'd come to him, the Being, the Dauphin—*the Juke*, he thought—and Andrew had turned away, but it hadn't mattered.

Once touched by the Divine, Andrew carried the spark.

If Annie saw that as Christ . . . well, all right. The one thing he'd learned about the Juke—the *Dauphin*—was that he lit that spark differently in every soul.

Now, he bore that spark home. To this great cathedral, swimming with angels, surrounded by a multitude. As he reached the top, one took his hand.

"I'm Lily," said the Angel, and Andrew looked at her again, and sure enough, it was Lily.

"How about that," he said, and walked across the platform—the dais—to the Oracle, who stood waiting for him. She smiled radiantly.

"You," said the Oracle. "You are one. An Oracle too. Yes?"

"I am."

"You stopped asking questions." '

"I have."

"Will you speak?"

"I will."

She unfolded her arms, and indicated where Andrew had been. "Tell them," she said, her arm sweeping over the crowd of the wretched, lost souls of Eliada. "Tell them how to worship right."

§

The last drops of rainfall steamed off Sam Green's bent back. Jason could just see it from the front doors of the hospital: Green had made it a good way down the roadway to Eliada. His shirt was badly singed, and the flesh of his right hand, which clutched the jar, was slick, an awful mix of bright red and black.

"You see," said Ruth, who stood beside him, "it *is* Sam Green. Not your father. Your father's dead."

"I see that now," said Jason. He held Ruth's hand, and looked at her. The flesh of her brow was slick too, even though she hadn't yet stood in the rain. That might be fever, maybe exertion, maybe just all that time kept in that hot, airless room. With Sam Green gone, carrying the Cave Germ, there was less need to keep her there, and when she'd insisted on coming with him to follow, Jason couldn't make an argument otherwise.

Jason squeezed Ruth's hand, and let it drop. "Hush," he whispered, and ran down the steps. It wasn't a long distance, and until he was just a step away, Jason thought he might have gotten the jump on the Pinkerton.

But in that instant, Sam Green spun around, his free hand clenched in a fist.

"Jason!" cried Ruth.

"It ain't your business anymore, boy," said Green.

And then Jason was on his back in the mud. His jaw felt like it might never close properly again.

Green stood over him. In the light of day, it was sure clear that Jason's father hadn't come up from Hell; but Green looked like he hadn't been anywhere too different. Half his face was red and peeling, and bloody meat hung in tatters from his right cheekbone. His hair was patched on his scalp. What flesh was intact was sooty and black. He winced as he reached to his belt and drew his revolver. He aimed it at Jason with a steady hand.

Jason kept steady too—steady as his ma would have, as she had . . .

"You're aiming to let the germ out—ain't you?" asked Jason.

"It's the only way."

"You know what it does, and you're still goin' to do that?"

Green narrowed his eyes. "I know," he said, and gestured over his shoulder with his head. "I know what they do. The Jukes. I've seen it, Jason. You have too. They take men's souls away. Take them away."

"There's a thousand folk yonder. You open that jar, they're all going to die."

"That they are," he said. "But you saw what those things—that Mister Juke—what it can do. Just one of them, not too old . . . drives a fellow to think he's seen God. And then it gets bigger—and what do you think happens then?"

"I expect . . ."

"Everyone thinks they've seen God. *Everyone*," said Green. "They'll do anything for that monster. Their souls—the ones entrusted to the True God. And eventually—they'll run like a plague themselves over the land, mad with that thing." He drew a ragged breath. "The Devil will rule the Earth."

"Mr. Green," said Ruth. She'd come up while they spoke, slowly, teetering in the mud. "What's happened to you?"

Sam Green squinted at her. The gun faltered. "Miss Harper," he said. "There's been a fire . . . and a fight. I'm sorry to tell you—your father, your mother . . . They all died in it."

"And yet you did not." Ruth's voice took a brittle quality. "You survived."

"I fought them off. Best I could. Miss Harper—men from up the hill. Burned the place down—murdered as many as—"

Jason didn't let him finish. He pivoted on his hip, and kicked out and Green shouted out as his knee buckled to one side. The gun flew from his hand, and landed quietly in the mud.

Jason dove at Sam Green's middle. "I'm sorry," he said as he connected, sending the bigger man sprawling under him. The stink of cooked flesh was overpowering, and Green was slippery underneath his shirt, like he'd been skinned. "I know you're hurt."

Jason grabbed for the jar, but Green moved it out of his reach with one hand, grabbed Jason by the hair with the other and yanked him back. Jason cried out, and he felt ashamed: Green hadn't so much as whimpered.

Jason pulled away hard enough that he left a fistful of his hair with Green, and drove his fist crosswise into the other man's gut. Green coughed and bent, and Jason got the upper hand for an instant—just enough to get high and come down hard on Green's shoulders, so he pinned him in the mud. He reached up to where Green's burned-up fist held the jar. He closed his own hand around it and tugged. But Green wouldn't let go.

"You can't kill a thousand folk," said Jason. "I seen less than that killed and it was awful. You can't kill a thousand. Not like that." He yanked again at the jar, but Green's fist tightened.

"Boy, that jar's a gift from God. If what your aunt says's true, it'll be enough to stop this."

"You *can't* kill a thousand."

Jason realized he was crying, his eyes soaking up with tears. His voice was weak, a child's voice. Some damn hero he was being for Ruth Harper and his mama and everyone else.

And Green—that bastard—he saw it too.

"No, Jason. *You* can't kill a thousand. You might've. If you'd killed your aunt . . . you might've been able to. But you can't and you shouldn't. Leave it to one with blood enough on his hands already. You run on and—oh Jesus—look after that girl."

Green glanced over to where Ruth stood, and perhaps trying to distract Jason, shifted in the muck, and pushed up hard. But Jason had the leverage and pushed back harder.

Green glared up at him. "God damn it, boy. She's *got my gun.*"

"It's all right, Ruth," said Jason, not taking his eye off Green. "I got him."

Out of the corner of his eye, he saw Ruth move into view. There was the sound of a hammer drawing back.

"*She wants to make sure,*" she said, in a strange, strangled but supremely confident voice; it seemed to be coming from everywhere at once.

Green struggled and motioned to her. "God damn it, boy. Look at her!"

Jason spared a glance, then looked again. Ruth stood like a lost child, feet close together, eyes darting here and there . . . one arm up over her breast—the other holding up Sam Green's Russian, pointed at them both. Her eyes were wide, and the lids trembled—like there was a scream inside her that couldn't get around that strange talk.

"*She wants to make sure you don't turn on Me too,*" said Ruth, in a voice like a chorus.

"Jason," whispered Sam, "you got to let me up. She's gone like old Bergstrom went."

"Like Bergstrom?"

"Thought the Juke was talkin' through him. Before he died."

Ruth's lips parted—and between them, wasn't there the hint of teeth, sharp and ready to tear at him?

Jason looked back at Green.

"What's happened to her?"

"Juke's in her, I'm guessin'. You two got taken away—didn't you now? Bergstrom said it, before he died. She was in a safe place. Somethin's made her like Maryanne Leonard."

"Raped her, you mean."

"Raped her."

Jason let up on Green.

"And it'll kill her."

"Might just."

Ruth spoke, but this time nothing like words came out—rather a trilling, high song that Jason now understood was not entirely or even mostly coming from her. The trees around the hospital were filled with it—the whistling that he'd heard from the creatures, the Jukes, that filled this town . . . the quarantine.

They were the things that had tried to prick him, and put those eggs inside him, under the skin like a fly lays . . . they were the things whose call Ruth had heard, as they crept around the quarantine last night . . . the things that had drawn her in, to lie with Mister Juke.

The gun moved as though at the end of a tree bough, and settled on them. Jason felt transfixed—like he was when he stepped up to Mister Juke himself, in the quarantine, and only a cut hand broke the spell.

Now, Ruth Harper herself held his gaze, as she aimed the gun at the two of them.

"*She will hide herself,*" said Ruth, "*while I make manifest.*"

And then, the world became brilliant, as the voices—Ruth's included—coalesced, and one solo voice rang out across the Kootenai river valley. Jason swallowed, and felt himself swept in it.

§

"There are not ghosts," said Andrew Waggoner.

He stood on the highest steps of Heaven, and looked down on the multitudes before him. At his side, the Dauphin's woman—black-haired Oracle girl—stood, and whispered to him, in the fast and unmistakable tongue of the Dauphin . . . and she whispered: *Worship nothing but him.*

"There are not ghosts—there are not Devils from Hell," said Andrew, and the people before him nodded, agreeing. "There's no point in trying to impersonate them. You won't fool anybody—any more than you will live well, coming here and sawing up wood for a rich man."

The Oracle whispered to him, and he nodded, and went on:

"You won't live well following those priests—your pastors. Because they talk about God far removed, who promises things later that might not be as fine as you'd heard. Not the one you see, right here in front of you."

As he spoke, Andrew found he could also see farther, and that made a certain kind of sense. This place was high up—a mountain-top. The Oracle whispered at him, and he craned his neck and looked down the great river—all the way down, where men toiled in darkness and made up ways to hate, to elevate themselves above one another. He thought he might be able to see all the way to New York, where his father and his horses toiled too, hauling barrels of beer from a brewer to a tavern—thinking that well, at least he'd sent his son, his boy, to Paris.

"And you'll live as poorly," shouted Andrew to the multitude here, "following your reason. Why, reason misleads us. Same as those false priests, those frightening ghosts. It takes us to places where we can say such is so, and such else is so, and then—without knowing it—this further thing must be so. But it's an error. A fellow could think himself away from—" *from the Juke* "—from this here . . ." *the Dauphin* " . . . this Son."

The Oracle whispered once more: *Get them ready.*

The world swirled about Andrew then, as the golden sands of Heaven flew into the air in a great cyclone, and Andrew drew higher. And he saw this multitude, turning to the south, and in a great line, making their way down the riverbank—some of them crawling on board the steamboat—and bearing on their shoulders a great Ark, that held in it the substance of the Son. Down the river they crawled and floated—until they came upon another Cathedral like this one, filled with folk, but empty of God. With guns and axes, they overtook it. And Andrew—Andrew preached the truth to the ones that lived; and gathered them into their army.

And from there, they swept the world.

Andrew spoke it—but he didn't speak it: with the Oracle at his side and Annie Rowe holding his arm, he sang it. The whole world sang too, sang, and whistled—while in His Cathedral, the Son—the Juke—the Dauphin . . . was pleased.

And if a shadow moved beneath—if it didn't sing as clearly—well, Andrew thought, what's a small speck, in the all-seeing eye of God?

§

She has chosen him.

Lothar Feeger stepped forth from the shadow, his burden thrown over his shoulder. He carried his hatchet in one hand, and looked upon the back of the Oracle. She stood next to the nigger, bent, and held her prize—the prize that he, Lothar, had brought her—she held it between the two of them.

Lothar was not wise—he knew this about himself, and every time he forgot this someone would remind him—but he was wise enough to know that when he lay with Patricia, he had not taken her as a bride and had no claim over her. She was bride to the Old Man if to anyone, now that she had gone Oracular.

Lothar was at peace with that; same as any man, he would stand aside for God. Why, if God chose to murder young Missy, strangle her in the space between beds—leave her there, as the Mothers squirmed and cried out . . .

If that were His choice—Lothar would not object.

But the nigger . . . the pretending nigger—taking up the song, standing here at his Oracle's side . . .

Lothar wouldn't allow it.

Lothar stepped out—he resisted the song, with all the agony in his heart.

He would show her, the sweet girl who would not spill more blood than she needed. He would show her, what the crone and the nigger had done to her sister.

Lothar pushed forward, and knocked the pretender aside. And as the Oracle stared at him, he dropped the still corpse of her sister at her feet. And the nigger . . . he screamed like a pig.

§

The cyclone stilled, and Heaven sloughed away; what had been gates made from gold, turned back to weathered grey timber. Those multitudes, ready a moment ago to do battle for their God, knelt in mud. Andrew Waggoner crouched not at the top of a great stone staircase, but on the loading platform of the sawmill at Eliada.

At his knees—

—a dead girl. Just a child—the child that Germaine Frost had murdered, while Andrew stood helpless.

That's three you didn't save.

Andrew drew a ragged breath. There was no time for remorse; he'd been given a reprieve, the pain that sheared up in his arm gave him a moment away from the sorcery the Juke worked. And that remorse—that guilt—was a fast route back to the lie.

He blinked in the morning light and took stock. The girl was on the deck in front of him; to one side, a black-haired young man dressed in the buckskin uniform of these people, a hatchet in his hand. The Oracle girl knelt now to touch the child's brow; her sister, Lily, stood with her fists bunched, eyes in tears. And just beyond, stood Annie Rowe, her hands clasped in prayer as she looked with eyes that nearly glowed, to the open doors, the dark cavern of the sawmill itself—like she was looking through the Gates of Heaven, toward salvation. Andrew looked there too. It was all dark, but for a square of light at the corner. It could be salvation; that was the riverside loading bay. Past it was a dock, and then the frigid waters of the Kootenai.

Andrew got to his feet, biting down on another scream. His arm was bad now—and he wondered if he would be able to keep it when this was all done. If he survived.

He staggered to Annie, and grabbed her with his good arm.

"Come on, Annie," he said, and when she looked confused, he added: "Let's go see Jesus."

That was all it took to convince her. The two of them dashed into the belly of the sawmill, stepping into shadow even as the buck-skinned man pointed his hatchet at them and bleated into the silence.

§

The angels became quiet, and fell to the earth, the trunks of trees, and a silence fell upon the world. Ruth blinked and looked around, and down at her gun. The angels looked around themselves too, their faces wide, innocent—as Ruth Harper's, only in miniature, in a multitude.

Jason opened his mouth to speak to her, tell her to put the gun down, but no words would come. He looked from one to another—to Ruth Harper, perched in the low crook of a branch, to others on the edge of the road, peering between strands of grass; still more higher in the branches of the tamarack, gazing down at him. Silent.

"They're foolin' you, Jason," said Sam Green.

"I know," he whispered.

"They're the Devil."

Jason looked down at Green. "Ain't so," he said. "They're animals."

Green looked up at him, his eyes ghastly white in their sockets. "They're more than animals. They're liars, Jason. They could . . . they make you think they're God. They could be . . . they could be God."

"You sayin' there's no God?"

"Don't blaspheme," he said. "God's great and true. But these things . . . They act so much like God . . . like Jesus . . . A fellow could be made to wonder, where to place his faith exactly. In God and Jesus, or these things that look just the same? And that's the Devil's work."

"I'm not fooled," said Jason.

"Yeah," said Green. "Not now you aren't. That whistling's stopped. You have to make up your mind. Before it starts."

"*It starts.*"

The voice came from everywhere—all the creatures, in words and whistling. Ruth—the hundred or more of her, that inhabited the trees—they all looked up, and Ruth opened her mouth and the song came up again, and the face of Ruth Harper faded from the world, until it was only Her own, held high.

Jason looked at Sam Green—watched him shift and change again, the features melt, and him grow, until it wasn't Sam Green anymore—but John Thistledown, burned not from a battle at the Harper mansion, but ten years in Hell. Ruth was singing this—making another lie for him, the way the song had before. Filled with the Juke's issue, she was spinning its lie where the other had stopped.

Jason stood up, let go of the jar.

"Go on," he said. "Do the hard thing. Stop the spread."

"Good boy," said the apparition.

And then, as the song she sang grew, Jason stepped up to Ruth Harper.

And she sang, and Jason said, "Yes," and then took hold of the gun in her limp hand. Before she could let go of it, he squeezed her finger on the trigger.

§

Andrew wished he had a notebook, or better, a camera, and the wit and time to use it. Standing before Mister Juke, stripped of illusion, it occurred to him that he might well have been the first man—the first scientist—to properly see this thing. . . .

This God.

Mister Juke hung in the rafters of the great building; stretched out, the creature almost extended its full length, like the branches of some tree. Any resemblance to a man was gone now. The construction that Andrew had made in his own mind, of some great Dauphin, the all-seeing giant who ruled over a Parisian Heaven . . . that was nowhere to be seen in the thing this creature had become. One might be tempted to call it formless, for it was hard to see where a head, arms—even an abdomen—might begin and end.

The only feature Andrew make out clearly was its mouths.

They descended on fleshy stalks, from the rafters over the great saw-blade which now sat still. They were circular too, those mouths, like those of a lamprey eel's. Andrew wasn't close enough to tell if the similarity extended to concentric circles of teeth; the way they dangled and twitched, he decided it best not to check. But small wonder that the attempt to hang this thing had so little effect. Who could say what shape the Juke had possessed, even when Bergstrom took it down from the mountain in its infant state? The creature's seduction of this town, of the fools who would first try to kill it, then attempt worship of it, had drawn its lies from their hearts from the very first. Man or woman or hermaphrodite—the thing was as suggestive as a cloud, and as malleable.

"What—oh Lord," Annie said, and Andrew squeezed her arm hard.

"We have an instant, Annie. And then we're gone." He pointed to the far side of the sawmill, where the bay opened up onto the river itself; he spared a glance over his shoulder, where the north-facing bay filled with shadows of the Feegers.

"Stay!" he shouted at them, and still conditioned to hear his voice as the Juke's, they obeyed.

"Come on," he urged Annie.

She went with him, but as they emerged in the light, she hesitated once more.

"Doctor—are we sure we want to—I mean, how do we know we're not turning our back on God?"

Andrew started down the wooden ramp that led straight into the frigid, fast-moving waters of the Kootanai River, then he looked at Annie.

"All things considered," he said, "we don't."

And then before she could raise another question, he took hold of her, pulled her on down the ramp—and Andrew Waggoner clung to Annie Rowe, and she clung to him, as the freezing waters enfolded them both; and bore them down-river, clear of God and man, and Juke; empty of everything but the clarifying shock of the true world.

31

The Cruelty of Sam Green

Sam Green walked among the living, and they scarcely made a note of his passing.

They were busy with the completion of their own work—work that had begun in the early hours of this day, when one or another had awoken with the idea to go back of the house, take the milk cow by a rope, or to open up the hen house and gather the fattest, or visit the pigsty and take a suckling—take those animals, and bring them down to the Cathedral. They didn't know much when they did that, but now, the Nigger prophet had told them as clear as they could understand: God hungered, there in his Cathedral. He hungered, and He expected something to be done about that.

So the living formed into a column, moving up the ramp to the Cathedral's great doors; past the Oracle, the Madonna weeping over a child, while another sang sweetly, her voice not hitching even as tears streamed down her cheeks. The dead man joined the throng, his filthy, blistering flesh inches from the smooth, near-to-perfect skin of a young blond-haired man with a thin moustache and bright, bright eyes. Sam didn't know his name, but he'd seen him, working the team of horses that had cleared the southern slopes of the hill last fall. The fellow had a pair of chickens—one in each arm, kicking and pecking. He regarded Sam.

"You don't look well," he said.

"I been better."

"Maybe you will be," said the young man, nodding toward the great dark gates of their new cathedral. The song was met with the whine of the saw-blade spinning up. "I bet He's merciful." The dead man huffed, reached into the jar he carried, and dabbed him on the cheek.

"Bless you, son," Sam said when the fellow looked at him oddly.

"Well bless you," he said, touching his cheek and sniffing at his finger.

They drew toward the Oracle—a sickly girl who would have gone by the name of Feeger. Her eyes were hollow and wet, and Sam could see every section of her spine through her soaked-through frock as she bent over the dead girl— another Feeger, surely. Another one—black-maned like all of them, with thick shoulders and an idiot stare—tried to touch the Oracle; but his hand came away, as though burned.

Sam had heard tell of these Feegers often enough, visiting the other folk on the hill who lived in such fear of them. They were certainly terrifying enough, coming into the kitchen of a mansion with big home-made blades and axes, murdering rich men and their wives . . . *setting the beams on fire, as a fellow emptied his iron into their bellies, and more came, stoking the flames and finally leaving that fellow for the dead. . . .*

Here, grieving for their own—they were almost deserving of pity. Weeping, they reminded him of others living on the mountain slopes—poor folk living hard, sickly lives in Heaven's shadow. The people Bergstrom would so methodically butcher.

He paused a moment, dipped his thumb into the jar, and touched the hem of the singing girl's sleeve. The big lad looked up at him, and Sam thought this might be the end of his walk. But he turned back to the Oracle, and tried again to rest his hand on her back. The singer looked at him in such a way that caused him to think: *She knows.*

But she did not spare him by crying out. Sam Green huffed, and continued on through the wide doors of the mill.

"Oh my," said a beautiful young red-haired wife next to him, carrying a pig under her arm, looking up at the dark rafters. Sam looked there too.

"Our Father," he said, "who art in Heaven . . ."

"Hallow'd be Thy name," continued the wife, not sparing Sam a glance as he dabbed her arm.

"Thy Kingdom Come, Thy will be done," said two men a little ways behind him, coaxing their nervous cow into the shadow of the mill, "on Earth, as it is 'n Heaven."

Sam let them finish.

He would like to have prayed now—talked to God, asked Jesus Christ for forgiveness of his sins, because when a man knows the moment of his passing, that's what a man does.

But looking up into the trembling maws of this God—he didn't want to curry favour, be forgiven, granted entry into This One's Heaven. And no amount of supplication before the true one and His Son would do much good. Not held against the thing he was about to do; the thing he'd already done.

As he stood there, he watched as the blond-haired man handed one of chickens to a black-haired Feeger who stood by the whirling saw. The bird squawked and struggled as the Feeger lowered it to the spinning blade. Blood fountained and sprayed high, and a stalk whipped down from the rafters. The Feeger tossed the bird into the air, and the stalk twisted and snatched, and the bird was gone. The Feeger took the man's other chicken.

"Where's your sacrifice?" asked the wife, holding the kicking pig like it was a baby.

Sam smiled as best he could.

"Right here," he said, and held the jar from Cracked Wheel, Montana over his head. He dabbed two fingers in it.

"You sure that'll please Him?" she asked.

Sam Green turned in place, both arms outstretched, and looked up into the face of Mister Juke.

"God forgive me," he said, "if it does."

She gave him a strange look and shrugged, and took her baby pig to the saw.

And Sam Green, fever rising, turned beneath God, like a stumbling, half-drunk dancer—again and again, until his legs gave out and he tumbled to the floor, and the jar rolled from his fingers, and a dry, pale thing no bigger than a thumb fell from it—and as its germ spread among the flock here at Eliada, in the rafters of the sawmill, Mister Juke took what Sam Green prayed would be His last meal.

32

Death and Resurrection

Annie Rowe was a woman of hidden depths.

Andrew concluded this as he sipped the broth from the tin cup she gave him. It was a fish broth, made from a sturgeon she'd managed to catch somehow in the first day. Andrew had no idea how she would have managed such a thing— he was barely conscious when they came out of the Kootenai, and she spotted the ruined cabin and together they hauled towards it, soaking with ice-cold river-water. He might have recalled stumbling over the remains of the door, under the broken roof of the cabin; collapsing against the log wall . . .

But beyond that, all he could tell was that he was alive and dry and warmed by a fire built on bare rock floor under the night sky. Annie was alongside him propped against the wall, her hair drawn back tight and her face smudged with soot.

She'd re-splinted his elbow; bandaged cuts new and old. And there was the broth, which he insisted on holding himself in his good hand, although Annie wasn't pleased.

"I can feed it to you, Doctor. You're still weak. Don't want to spill."

"You've been doing quite a lot," he said. "Saved my life, the things you did."

"Just returning the favour," she said. "Don't know what would've become of me, you hadn't . . ." She trailed off, and Andrew let her. The Juke's call had been strong in her, and she would have been lost to it—were it not for the shock of the river, the distance it carried them. He sipped at the soup, and took a deep swallow. It warmed him fierce, and he made sure Annie saw him appreciate it.

"But you need to get your rest," she said finally. "You've been about the worst patient I've ever had."

He sighed. "How long've I been asleep?"

"Two days," she said. "Nearly."

"And in that time, you found this place, built up a fire, somehow found these—" he pointed to a bandage on his head, another on his shoulder "—and managed to figure out how to catch a fish without tackle or net."

Annie smiled. "Guided by an Unseen hand," she said. Then, catching the expression on his face perhaps, added: "Don't worry, Doctor. I'm not going back to *that*." She crouched down against the log wall.

"How'd all this come about?"

"This place is nothing but an old homestead," she said. "Barely got a roof on it anymore. But you can see it from the river, so spotting it was easy enough, and we had to stop somewhere. You'd have died, Doctor. Me too, likely. Managed to find an old pot and an axe-blade and that cup you're drinking from. Just like home."

"All right," said Andrew. "And you're a secret expert fisher, and you pulled that sturgeon from the river with your bare hands. And where'd these bandages come from?"

"Well, I'm no expert fish-catcher," she said. "The bandages—they came from the same source as the fish."

Andrew handed her the cup of broth. She took a sip herself. "Stop being mysterious," he said. "Where—"

"Outside." She returned the cup to Andrew, and stood. "I shall fetch him."

§

"Jason!"

Jason Thistledown was leaning against what was left of the door frame. He was dressed in a pair of trousers and a smock that Andrew recognized from the hospital, and he looked like he'd just come from there—scrubbed clean, fine hair unencumbered by grease or dirt as it fluttered in the updraft from the fire.

"Evening, Doctor," he said.

Andrew shifted so he sat higher against the wall, and blinked again as a disturbing implication came over him. The Jukes had tried everything on him. They showed him Heaven as Paris. They sent the shades of Maryanne Leonard and Loo Tavish to scold him.

Why not wake him up in this safe place, wounds magically bandaged, warm soup in his belly—set Annie Rowe by his side—and show him the boy, Jason Thistledown, he'd sworn to rescue?

"You can thank Jason Thistledown for the fish," said Annie. "And the bandages too. He appeared here not a couple hours after we found this place. In a canoe. With—"

"Lucky I found you first," said Jason. "You could see the smoke from that fire for miles. Probably as far off as Eliada, if they'd been thinking to look."

"You took a canoe?"

"Found it at a dock not far from the hospital," said Jason. "So I took another doctor's bag, some blankets . . . and we set off down the river. You an' the nurse made it a good way in that river. Surprised you didn't drown before you got here."

Andrew frowned. "You said *we*. Who are you travelling with? Not your aunt—I mean—"

Jason shook his head, and looked into the fire, quiet.

"She was killed," said Annie finally. "After we left. Sam Green did it. No need to make the boy relive it."

Andrew looked at Annie. "Who then?"

"Miss Ruth Harper," said Annie, and Jason nodded.

"She lives," he said. "But she's going to need some help."

"She—" Andrew began piecing things together. "She was infected—with the same thing that killed your town. Germaine told me she'd done that, just before we met. And it's been two days . . . and she lives? So she's immune?" He thought about that—that the daughter of a fine white family, the wealthiest white family in Eliada, was also marked the strongest here by Germaine Frost's diabolical test.

"It's not an immunity," said Annie. "She's showing no signs of that . . . Cave Germ. But we think something else is happening."

"She spent some time with that Mister Juke," said Jason. "Alone. Think he—" Jason finally looked up from the fire, and when he met Andrew's eyes his own were those of a child again, sad and alone. "—think he raped her, like he did Maryanne Leonard."

Andrew sighed. "You've examined her?" he asked Annie, and she nodded. "She's healthy."

"She ain't," said Jason, his voice breaking. "Her foot's bad. . . . She—"

"Hush," said Annie, and Jason jammed his fists into his pockets, did as he was told. "She was shot in the foot. Her right foot. I cleaned it up, and it should be fine, although I'm guessing she'll walk with a limp. But Doctor, there's something else." She leaned close and whispered. "I think she's not just infected. She could well be pregnant. By young Mr. Thistledown."

Andrew nodded slow, and regarded Jason. He held himself as tall and as strong as ever he had, but that hard piece that had glinted from his eye two days ago, when he'd hauled Germaine Frost by the hair into the autopsy—that was gone now. Andrew would have been glad of that, had it been replaced by something other than the aching hurt he'd brought to Eliada, the fearful certainty that more of that hurt was on its way.

"Son," Andrew said. "Don't fear. I owe you a debt, and I came back to repay it. I'll make things right for Ruth Harper."

"Can you even? I mean, look at what happened to Maryanne Leonard."

Maryanne Leonard, and Loo Tavish both. Thanks to your shaking hand.

Andrew felt ashamed; he wanted to look away, nestle himself in his shame and self-pity and doubt. But he didn't. Those things were the Juke's weapons—that was how the beast got inside, and started changing everything about a fellow, succoured him with sweet lies of an easy Heaven, and eventually turned him from man to slave. Andrew kept his eye on Jason.

"You were with her, weren't you? Don't look all puzzled, you know what I mean."

Jason nodded. "I'm sorry."

"Don't be," said Andrew. "I've learned some things since you got me out of Eliada. A woman wise in the lore of these things told me—" *Norma Tavish, who you also let die* "—she *told* me, that when a woman's with child, and infected by a Juke—she's stronger. Because the Juke helps her. Until it's ready to come out. That's why Ruth fought off the Cave Germ. That's why she might stand a better chance now." Andrew drew a breath, forced himself to keep looking at Jason across the fire. "So don't you say you're sorry. The two of you may have saved Ruth's life."

"Just don't hurt her."

"I won't do anything 'til daybreak when the light's right. Not at least. In the meantime, bring me that doctor bag you filched. Then go back and sit with your lady, and I'll see what I've got to work with."

§

Jason made sure they put their fires out prior to dawn, but no one was doing the same in Eliada. The smoke climbed above the shadow of the mountains and caught the rising sun high over treetops, a black-and-gold plume that might've been visible from as far south as Sand Point.

"Do you think they'll come? Have you seen them?" Ruth asked him, from the lean-to he'd made her the first day. She had been awake most of the night, and from the quaver in her voice, she must still have been in a fair amount of pain. Nurse Rowe had offered her some morphine from the doctor's bag, but Ruth had declined, and Nurse Rowe had said she understood. When the pain faded, so did they all.

"I don't think so," said Jason. He'd been watching the river since first light, and not long past that, he'd seen *The Eliada* drift past. The wheels of Garrison Harper's steamboat were still as it turned in the current that drew it downriver; not a wisp of smoke came from its stack. He didn't try to hail it. The river had borne nothing but the dead for two days now, and the steamboat hadn't left town any better off. It was just another corpse.

Jason had only seen two of Eliada's dead up close, as he drew hook and line through the fast-moving river to catch their supper, one coming close after another: a man with a belly either fat or bloated under his white shirt, and what looked a lady, skirts spread like a great dark flower in the churning water. But there were dozens, distant shapes rolling in the fast waters of the Kootenai, bearing north into the wilderness. Jason prayed it was only wilderness . . . not more folk.

He prayed for that, same as he prayed no more boats would come to Eliada, until the Cave Germ had finished its work—starved out that Juke, wiped its many ghosts and devils from the land, and died off itself.

Ruth sniffed. "It's a certainty, then. Mr. Green's mission was a success."

"It was."

"I suppose it was a kind of heroism."

"It was sure a sacrifice," said Jason. He crouched down beside Ruth and took her hand. It trembled for only a moment before it gripped his hand, hard.

She sniffed again, and whispered on scarcely more than a breath:

"*All dead.*"

Jason looked down at Ruth Harper. Her face was smeared with dirt and mud, and leaves and twigs tangled in her hair. The tiny smile that'd bewitched him so on the train, before he knew her name, was gone—perhaps forever. He wanted to speak with her about that. He wanted to tell her: *My ma died too, all my kin are dead—my whole home—just like yours. And I ain't found a place for them in me, but I'm going to. Just like you will.* But as he looked on her face, he saw that wouldn't do. His own trials, as great as they were, marked only half of Ruth Harper's journey. She carried a grief like his own, and another's. . . .

Well, that was not a grief, exactly. More a hunger.

"Do you think they're in Heaven?" asked Ruth.

"'Course they are," he said. "Well, perhaps not all. But Louise? Sure. Your ma—Hell, even your pa. Now, Nils Bergstrom—I don't think so. And Sam Green?"

"I hope Sam Green's in Heaven," said Ruth. "But you answered my question very quickly, Jason. Without thinking."

"Should have asked the question different, then," he said. "Question you wanted to ask is: do I have any reason to think there even is a Heaven for them to go to?"

"I'll try to be more precise next time."

Jason let go of her hand and pushed himself to his feet. He had his own pains—the cut on his leg, a bad rib—scrapes and bruises in a dozen places, taken when he'd tangled with Sam Green—and he relished them as he drew higher, and saw the movement at the cabin's ruin. Annie Rowe came out first, the doctor's bag in one hand, the other helping steady Dr. Waggoner, a branch cut into a crutch under his good shoulder. He was amazed the doctor could even walk that well, the things he'd been through. The two of them made their way forward low along the riverbank, to avoid the ankle-twister rocks higher up. Jason held his hands together in front of him—fingers intertwined as though in prayer, or just clutched against shaking, the line of stitches Waggoner had made in the one palm itching against the other.

"You got to believe in something," said Jason, and Ruth laughed weakly, and agreed; and then, of their own volition it seemed, Jason's fingers spread and his hands came apart, and he hurried off, to help the doctor up the rocky slope.

ACKNOWLEDGEMENTS

Eutopia wouldn't be the terror it is without the sharp eyes of readers and fellow writers Madeline Ashby, Robert Boyczuk, Michael Carr, Laurie Channer, Rebecca Maines, John McDaid, Sally Fogel, Elizabeth Mitchell, Janis O'Connor, Helen Rykens, Steve Samenski, Karl Schroeder, Sara Simmons, Michael Skeet, Douglas Smith, Jill Snider Lum, Dale Sproule, Rob Stauffer, Peter Watts, and Allan Weiss.

Monica Pacheco of Anne McDermid & Associates brought the faith, enthusiasm, and even sharper eye that *Eutopia* needed to find a publisher. And Brett Savory and Sandra Kasturi at ChiZine Publications had the faith and, I like to think, good sense to become that publisher. Special kudos to my dear editor Sandra, who, along with proofreader Chris Edwards, cover designer Erik Mohr and interior designer Corey Beep, put it all in the tidy, lovely package you hold.

And, of course, Karen Fernandez helped in ways that only she could—with love and faith and patience as life transpired during the long haul of the writing.

EVERY
SHALLOW
CUT
TOM
PICCIRILLI

COMING MARCH 15, 2011
FROM CHIZINE PUBLICATIONS

978-1-926851-10-5

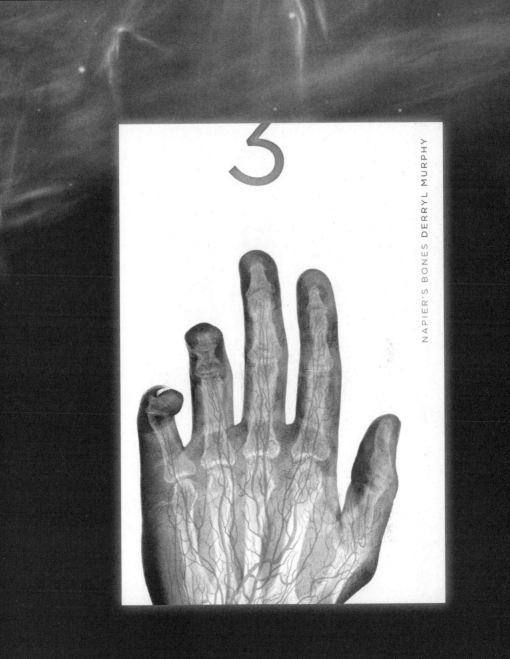

COMING MARCH 15, 2011
FROM CHIZINE PUBLICATIONS

978-1-926851-10-5

THE DOOR TO LOST PAGES

CLAUDE LALUMIÈRE

COMING APRIL 15, 2011
FROM CHIZINE PUBLICATIONS

978-1-926851-12-9

FROM THE AUTHOR OF *FILARIA*

THE FECUND'S MELANCHOLY DAUGHTER

BRENT HAYWARD

COMING MAY 15, 2011
FROM CHIZINE PUBLICATIONS

978-1-926851-13-6

A ROPE OF THORNS

GEMMA FILES

VOLUME TWO OF THE HEXSLINGER SERIES

COMING MAY 15, 2011
FROM CHIZINE PUBLICATIONS

978-1-926851-14-3

978-0-9812978-2-8

CLAUDE LALUMIÈRE

**OBJECTS OF
WORSHIP**

978-0-9809410-9-8

ROBERT J. WIERSEMA

**THE WORLD MORE
FULL OF WEEPING**

978-0-9809410-7-4

DANIEL A. RABUZZI

THE CHOIR BOATS

978-0-9809410-5-0

LAVIE TIDHAR AND NIR YANIV

**THE TEL AVIV
DOSSIER**

978-0-9809410-3-6

ROBERT BOYCZUK

**HORROR STORY
AND OTHER
HORROR STORIES**

978-0-9812978-3-5

DAVID NICKLE

**MONSTROUS
AFFECTIONS**

978-0-9809410-1-2

BRENT HAYWARD

FILARIA

"CHIZINE PUBLICATIONS REPRESENTS SOMETHING WHICH IS COMMON IN THE MUSIC INDUS-
TRY BUT SADLY RARER WITHIN THE PUBLISHING INDUSTRY: THAT A CLEVER INDEPENDENT CAN RUN
RINGS ROUND THE MAJORS IN TERMS OF STYLE AND CONTENT."

—MARTIN LEWIS, *SF SITE*